THE JOURNEY OF SOULS
SERIES
VOLUME ONE

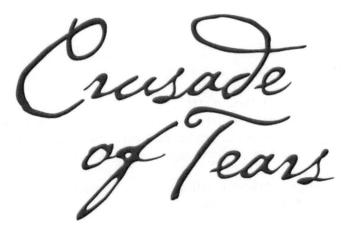

C. D. BAKER

RIVEROAK®
Good News in Fiction

COOK COMMUNICATIONS MINISTRIES
Colorado Springs, Colorado • Paris, Ontario
KINGSWAY COMMUNICATIONS LTD
Eastbourne, England

RiverOak® is an imprint of
Cook Communications Ministries, Colorado Springs, CO 80918
Cook Communications, Paris, Ontario
Kingsway Communications, Eastbourne, England

CRUSADE OF TEARS
© 2004 by C. D. Baker

Cover Design and Photo Illustration: Terry Dugan Design
Map by dlp Studios, Colorado

First Printing, 2004
Printed in United States of America
3 4 5 6 7 8 9 10 Printing/Year 08 07 06 05 04

Library of Congress Cataloging-in-Publication Data

Baker, C. D. (Charles David), 1951-
  Crusade of tears / by C.D. Baker.
      p. cm. -- (The journey of souls ; v. 1)
  ISBN 1-58919-009-2 (pbk.)
  1. Children's Crusade, 1212--Fiction. I. Title. II. Series.
PS3552.A3995C78 2004
813'.54--dc22
                              2004008421

To the shamed, the confused,
and the broken spirits of a troubled world

*Editor's note: please find at the back of this book
powerful discussion questions for group or personal
study (Readers' Guide, p. 491), as well as a helpful
Glossary (p. 503) for clarification of terminology and
historical information.*

ACKNOWLEDGMENTS

I would like to offer my heartfelt gratitude to my most merciful God; my patient wife, Susan; and the wide circle of faithful family and friends whose encouragement and gifts of wisdom gave this story its life. Their devotion to the project and to myself proved to be indispensable. I would like to thank my enterprising uncle, Gordon Loux, and my indefatigable agent, Lee Hough, for their roles in the promotion of this book and the series, of which it is a part. My new friends at RiverOak deserve special mention for their professional support and genuine interest, especially my editor, Craig Bubeck. I also owe a debt of gratitude to Burgermeister Norbert Zabel of Selters, Germany, for his gracious gifts of time and interest. Lastly, I am pleased to acknowledge the generous hospitality of the good citizens of Weyer, Germany, particularly the Roths, Wickers, Lauxes, and Klums, whose selfless accommodation and friendship added great joy to my work.

THE **CRUSADE**

JOURNEY OF
THE CHILDREN

INTRODUCTION
Collision of Worlds

The green fields of France trembled as the horsemen of Islam thundered across the gentle heartland of Christian Europe. Behind their leader, Abd-er-Rahman, two hundred thousand plundering Moors, Persians, Berbers, and Copts had swept into Christendom unchecked, their appetite for the delicious spoils of these bountiful lands luring them ever northward. They swarmed across the Church's domain like the locusts of Egypt, resolved that the Cross would bend to the Crescent.

Ahead of the horde, the simple, native folk scattered like dried leaves in a blast of wind, running to bar both beast and beloved within the darkest corners of their wattled hovels. Unaware that the future of a continent would soon teeter in the balance, these poor wretches could do little more than crouch low in their terror and weep.

The invading army pressed mercilessly toward the Loire River and, by October 732, they were poised to claim the fertile plain between Poiters and Tours. News of their impending assault spread quickly through the manors of upper Aquitaine, and soon the landscape was abandoned to the cool breezes and subtle warmth of the pleasant French sun. Nowhere could be seen the plodding of peasants gathering their lords' last sheaves, nor were straining oxen yoked to heavy-laden wagons. For the dust clouds of a coming storm were rising in the south and the frightened stewards of this good land were hiding.

To the north another tempest was gathering, and its

thunder now rolled ominously toward the nervous plain. In the fore of an opposing army charged Charles the Hammer, King of the Franks, and behind him roared his steely-eyed warriors. These resolute Teutons had vowed to yield not one more green forest, fertile field, sacred church, or golden maiden to the approaching foe. And so, though sweated at the sight of the dark-eyed host rushing toward them, they set their jaws hard, like ice in their own midwinter, and hastened to meet their ruthless adversary with sword, spear, axe, and hammer.

For hour upon hour the trampled fields of Aquitaine wept great puddles of blood as the champions of two worlds collided. The discordant sounds of the cries, the clash, and the crumple of warrior and horse were carried by the wind's weary back to the far, wooded edges of the plain. And behind the silent sun a purposed Providence deliberated each soul's fate. In the end, Abd-er-Rahman lay dead, his vanquished cavalry routed, and the lust of Islam extinguished, if only for a time. The red sod grew quiet, somberly cradling the butchered remains of the sons of Mohammed and the brothers of Christ. And mercifully, the wind now bore only the thankful sigh of a relieved Christendom.

Obedient serfs soon returned to their humble tasks, once again secured and steadied to the yawn and turn of seasons. But for the councils of Europe the great battle would be neither forgotten nor forgiven, and none would ever sheath his sword or turn his back to the strange world that lay beyond. Instead, for centuries to come all would fix a wary eye upon the menacing *infidel*.

And vigilance proved prudent, for by the latter part of the eleventh century desperate reports of Christian pilgrims suffering persecution for their faith in Jerusalem and news of dangerous threats against Europe's easternmost boundaries found their way to the cocked ear of the Roman Pope, Urban II. In response he entreated the kings and lords of his lands to rise, yet again, in defense of the Faith. So, in August of the year of grace 1096, the armies of Christendom rallied to his call and, with crimson crosses draped on their heaving armored chests, the knights of Europe stormed into Palestine in their first Crusade.

For three years the sandy plains and rugged mountains of this ancient land soaked in the blood of crusader and Turk alike until, at long last, in July 1099, Jerusalem was taken for the Church. Sadly, the slaughter that ensued betrayed the virtue of the Cross and endeared none to the One whose blood had been poured out upon these same lands in love. Instead, for generations to follow the soldiers of Islam bitterly resisted their fair-faced conquerors and battled them throughout the Land of Promise until 1187, when they seized the Holy City once more.

Driven from the holy places, the Christian knights continued to engage their enemy for nearly two more decades. But their failed efforts proved costly, and they soon found themselves pressed against Palestine's coast by the massing armies of the Sultan. It seemed that the Cross itself would surely be driven into the sea. Rising to such peril, Pope Innocent III sounded the alarm, calling upon his ever-faithful Franks and Celts, his Saxons and Normans, and those other tribes and races spread across the kingdoms of Christian Europe. But his warriors were weary and hesistant.

Then, in the spring of the year of our Lord 1212, the children of France and Germany heard the pope's plea and began to stir. Inspired by priest and passion alike, they prepared to barter hearth and habit for the hope of God's glory. Near Cloyes, France, a fifteen-year-old shepherd boy named Stephan announced a vision in which he saw the children of Christendom part the Mediterranean Sea and march, unopposed, through the opened gates of Jerusalem. He proclaimed that a congregation of harmless children would acquire the Holy City by the power of their purity and innocence rather than the ruthless force of axe and bow. In response to such remarkable claims, thousands clamored for a new Crusade and heeded Stephan's cry, "We go to God, and seek for the holy cross beyond the sea!"

About the same time, a ten-year-old German boy named Nicholas was heralding a similar message in and around the city of Cologne. He too summoned an army of children to conquer Jerusalem and precipitate the conversion of all Palestine from Islam. He assured his assembled throngs that, where the crusading knights and soldiers of the great kings had failed, they, by their simple dependence on God Himself, would succeed. Nicholas's message spread quickly throughout the Empire's hamlets, towns, and manors—and the children answered.

So, by June, these unsuspecting lambs of Europe began to gather in flocks ranging in size from the twenties to the hundreds for their pilgrimage southward. In an environment where good works were believed to warrant temporal blessing as well as eternal salvation, where self-sacrifice was still a virtue and faith had manifest meaning, legions of children rallied in fealty to the transcendent God in whose hands they gladly placed their trust. Many prepared to march without provisions so that their faith might be proven pure and their utter dependency on an omnipotent God aptly confirmed. Undaunted by the realities of a fallen world, these Innocents departed in guileless enthusiasm and gaily pranced with great expectancy. Considering their inculpable naivete, such extraordinary, steadfast devotion ought to bring a stunned pause to those of feebler faith; it is a rare and noble quality and rightfully honored.

One chronicler would later write that the enthusiasm of the children was so great that no bars could hold them. Presumably, some of the children may have certainly run away from the pleas and restraints of their parents. Not to be forgotten, however, is the disquieting sacrifice of those other parents who willingly released their beloved children with both blessing and tears. The dilemma posed by their offering must have been tortuous, and the excruciating pain can hardly be imagined. But their credence—selfless and devout as it may have truly been—was sadly corrupted by their own indefensible blindness. For faith lacking truth is not faith at all, but merely well-intended folly destined to bear a grievous end.

Of course, not only parents were at fault. Diabolical profiteers from the peasantry, the nobility, and perhaps the Church itself encouraged legions of these young Isaacs toward their sorrows with an eye on their own imagined advantages. In fairness it ought to be noted that Pope Innocent III offered no public endorsement of this Crusade, nor do we have any documentation that demonstrates the Church's overt encouragement. It is of little doubt, however, that the legacy of ecclesiastical support for such movements contributed greatly to the population's willing accommodation. Far from any known attempt to prevent this unnecessary tragedy, the pope is recorded, instead, as having said, "These children put us to shame." In addition, it should be noted that neither this pope nor his successor were willing to release the surviving crusaders of their "vows." Thankfully, others did declare their unabashed opposition to the Crusade, arguing that the Devil himself had deceived the people. Sadly, their words fell on deaf ears.

Amidst these mixed and confusing currents the child-crusaders formed their columns. They were quite different from the seasoned, hard-eyed veterans who had raged before. Instead, this most eager army of Christendom was an assembly of bold youth and adolescents—young adventurers still longing to take a sharp edge to their smooth faces, wide-eyed toddlers, spirited little girls, and young mothers with infants at the breast. Sprinkled among them were the misfits, the unhappy, the abused, and the unwanted. The scent of prey as helpless as these drew wolves, as well, and their foul motives bore particular and added misery upon the Innocents. But a blessed few God-fearing shepherds also joined and these, moved by compassion and concern, offered what they could in guidance and defense. Noticeably less in numbers seemed to be the sons and daughters of the privileged, for they and their parents, it would be supposed, were content to earn blessings by yielding the service of their bound-servants' broods. But some of higher birth did enlist, and many of them likewise suffered and died. Of these the German chroniclers made special note as having been bedecked in gray, Cross-emblemed pilgrims' coats and wide-brimmed hats.

We are told that Stephan's children followed him through the pleasant lands of central France, over the Rhône near Lyons, through Dauphine and the magnificent countryside of Provence until they reached, at long last, the port city of Marseilles. It is recorded that Stephan became known as "The Prophet" and rode in a fine wagon draped in red banners. Along the way he encouraged and enlarged his surging multitude by preaching and prophesying with the apparent authority of heaven itself. After costly delay, a perplexed king of France finally ordered the legions home, but Stephan and his followers refused.

Chronicles and later generations depict the fair-haired army of little Germans as escorted by "butterfly and bird," singing the familiar hymn, "Fairest Lord Jesus," otherwise known as "The Crusaders' Hymn." We believe that Nicholas's vision was to part the Mediterranean Sea at Genoa but we are uncertain of his exact route. The Rev. George Zabriskie Gray in his impressive history, *The Children's Crusade*, originally published circa 1870, argues that Nicholas's column traveled west of the Rhine and crossed over the Alps through the popular pass at Mount Cenis into the Piedmont region of modern Italy. From there he believes it followed the Po valley toward Genoa.

Gray and other researchers generally agree, however, that the German children did not follow Nicholas exclusively. The original army had divided, possibly in Cologne, perhaps in Mainz. A dissident group, as many as twenty thousand, chose to travel the east bank of the Rhine. Their sad path is obscured with even more of history's fog than that of Nicholas's but it is believed they eventually wandered far from the Rhine and into parts of Swabia before arching southward through the treacherous landscape of eastern Switzerland. Gray contends they then escaped the Alps through the St. Gotthard pass before mysteriously turning southeastward toward the Adriatic Sea.

Considering the nature of both epoch and epic, reasonable conjecture also assumes that lost and confused groups of unattached crusaders as well as independent bands may account for the numerous other claims of fair-haired children emerging from unnamed Alpine passes into Lombardy and moving southwestward toward Genoa. It is these obscured and barely noticed shadows which are the object of the story to follow.

Given the meager and sometimes contradictory reserve of data, it seemed both futile and limiting to constrain this tale to the small portion of things proven. The particular route chosen for this work, though admittedly speculative, is offered to express the event in a way that incorporates an amalgamation of the chronicled experiences endured by the crusaders generally. Though every effort has been made to incorporate facts consistent with what historical data exists, it is not the author's intent to represent this story as a documentary. It is hoped, rather, that the reader will turn the last page with a firmer grasp of the nature and spirit of this failed enterprise and the world in which it occurred. It is further hoped that the truths offered on this most difficult journey of souls will reach forward in time to touch the deepest recesses of a new century's heart.

These harmless children of Europe suffered unspeakable hardship in a Creation groaning for deliverance. Whether drought or famine, disease or assault, these stalwart warriors bore the adversities of a world mired in misery. Steadfast in their hope, these nearly forgotten crusaders marched on. No doubt fettered by confusion, they nevertheless persevered to the very end, wanting to believe, wanting to trust, stilled by the perplexing love of the God under whose eyes they patiently suffered.

This author is certain of little, but is confident that those valiant crusaders whose sufferings became a compass to the gates of God's truths would have yearned to be our guides today. For they tasted of a mysterious freedom offered in the very midst of their misery and would surely have longed to share the joy of this sweet liberty with us. Such hope as revealed through their misadventure offers us all the keys to our own freedom in the disappointments, the failures, and tragedies we endure and the courage to face the mysteries we fear. Perhaps their journey is our metaphor for hope in the midst of our own distress.

So come! March toward Palestine alongside these gallant young crusaders. Tramp with them through the feudal manors, the daunting Alps, the timbered towns and towering castles of medieval Christendom and be not faint of heart—for though you shall suffer, you may be set free.

Vincit qui patior!

Book 1

Chapter 1
SHADOWS SHROUD THE MANOR

The timeless Laubusbach coursed quietly toward the Lahn River in the early summer of the year of our blessed Lord 1212. It flowed westward over the soft *Tonschiefer*, ever shaping the wide and gentle valley as it had since long before the primeval Frankish tribesmen hunted deer and fox on the long slopes and broad backs of the forested hills rising easily from its waters. A pleasant day's saunter from the stream's mouth, the valley abruptly cramped into a cupped nook where more stubborn bedrock, the *Diabas,* had narrowed the insistent waters. This deep hollow now served the good folk of the village of Weyer as it had for nearly twenty generations, adequately sheltering them and their squat, steep-thatched huts from cold and storm. And even so, the ancient, dark-stoned church perched atop the hollow's rim offered similar sanctuary from the wiles of the spirits feared to prowl about the surrounding forests and fields.

In this particularly dry and hot month of June the usually cheerful Laubusbach did not bubble and dance over its stony bed, nor did it turn Weyer's mill-wheel with its common vigor. Instead of laughing in the bright light of summer solstice the stream seemed, instead, to weep under the dark nights' stars. And such melancholy did not escape the notice of the simple village *Volk* who paid careful heed to such messages tendered by the forces present in their world. For them the sorrow of the Laubusbach was cause to ponder and perhaps to pray, for it seemed, indeed, a likely foreshadowing of a season of tears.

৵

A brief walk from the water's edge stood the modest hovel of the baker of Weyer. Its sturdy walls soundly bore a well-thatched roof and provided fair shelter for its household. On this dull and languid night the frail light of ashy coals and a single candle dimly lighted its two rooms.

In the corner of the larger room—the common room— sat the baker's younger son, Karl. He squatted by the mound of loose straw that was his bed and stared sadly into the neglected hearth which was placed within a ring of flat stones in the room's center. Karl was usually a happy child, quick to dismiss the distress of life with the wide stretch of a ready smile across his ruddy, round face. Bright and curious, pleasant and cheerful, the thirteen-year-old was a friend to all and enemy of none. Scattered all about him lay the unruly red curls he had cut from his own head in order to pass the time. He had been sternly reminded by a village elder that only noblemen and princes should allow their hair to grow—and Karl wanted to accommodate things as they should be.

In the adjoining bedchamber, the baker's wife, Marta, lay upon her straw mattress, perspired and damp, and failing with fever. On the crude table by her side was a pear-wood bowl half-filled with cool water. Her five-year-old daughter, Maria, stood nearby, faithfully bathing her mother's pale brow with a linen rag she held in her one good hand.

Outside, under the bright stars of a warm night, an angry older son, Wilhelm, retied the loose fence that hemmed the peasant family's vegetable garden. Wil was a thoughtful, sometimes brooding boy of nearly seventeen years with a fair complexion and pleasing features. His light blue eyes were sometimes gentle, but often blazed like two fired-iron swords, readied to defend the hurt and guarded soul within. He rinsed his large hands in the bottom of the rain barrel and dried them through his long, blonde hair. He grumbled to himself that he ought not be burdened with a dying mother, a bothersome brother, a deformed sister, and the duties of an absent father.

The lad walked to the doorsill of his home and grumbled on his way to his mother's side. As he passed the hearth he tossed a small piece of kindling onto its smoldering embers, and he watched a swarm of sparks scramble to escape through the smoke-hole above. He paused, wishing he could fly away with them. In the brief burst of light, he looked at his brother, Karl, and, with some annoyance, rebuked him for his tears. "Stop crying like some woman."

An embarrassed Karl looked at his feet, quickly blotted his tears on a rough sleeve, and offered a gentle defense. "They are for Mother, Father, poor Maria, and you."

Unimpressed, Wil brushed past Karl and entered his mother's room where his sister greeted him.

"Wil," Maria whispered, "could y'fetch us more water? *Mutti* may be some better."

Wil nodded and took the bowl from her hand, glad for a reason to retreat out-of-doors once more. He escaped quickly to the refuge of starlight and paused alongside the rain barrel. He leaned against the wattled siding of his hut and cupped the bowl against his belly. With his fingers drumming lightly on its bottom, he surveyed the silhouetted hilltops enclosing his village and closed his eyes with a weary sigh.

The lad paused to let his mind carry him to the strange lands he had heard of from travelers who told amazing stories of the Holy Wars. He imagined himself a mighty knight upon an armored horse, galloping boldly across the bloodied plains of Palestine. With his red-crossed shield before him, he watched the enemies of Christendom flee the fury of his thunderous charge. A light tap on his shoulder returned Wil to Weyer.

"Could you hurry with the water?"

Wil, startled by the voice, cast a perturbed look at Karl.

"Mother's waiting for the water and, uh, a kind word, methinks." Karl grimaced, waiting for an angry rebuke.

Wil stormed past the redhead to deliver the water to his mother's room. He snatched the moist cloth from Maria's hand and ordered her to the corner as he plunged the linen into the bowl.

Karl followed, brushing close by the tallow candle that cast a yellow light within the room. Its tiny flame danced on a looping wick and bent the shadows, revealing small drops of blood oozing from the corner of Marta's pursed lips.

With sudden concern, Wil wiped his mother's brow and stared at the blood. He summoned his brother to the corner and whispered, "We've need of Brother Lukas."

"Nay, she hates him. She heals more each day and Father Pious says to have faith. If *you* cannot believe, you ought leave Maria and me care for her."

"Believe as you will, I'll fetch the monk." Troubled, Wil left the bedchamber and crossed the common room where he paused for a brief moment to rest his eyes on a clay bowl sitting atop the wooden table. It was his mother's favorite, he recalled, one an uncle had fashioned for her when she was a young girl. He reached for it and ran his long fingers over its smooth brim before setting it into the warped cupboard where it belonged. He stared at the neatly arranged assortment of reed baskets, clay jars, and candles. "And nothing off its proper place," he grumbled. Taking a deep breath, he stepped into the night air where he turned his face north, toward the Abbey of Villmar which ruled his village. There he hoped to find its herbalist and an old friend of his father's, Brother Lukas.

Wil began the two-league jaunt at a trot. He passed by the silhouettes of the sagging, thatched roofs of his quiet village and his melancholy mind began to drift. He thought of his mother lying near death and his legs felt heavy. But he quickly resurrected the haunting sounds of a lifetime of endless demands and he shook his head. *She simply cannot be pleased ... never. And the beatings ... for spilt cider or a forgotten chore.* He spat.

His thoughts then abruptly narrowed to the memory of a distant October morning when the village priest, Father Pious, had urged his restless father to join in service against a far-off peasant rebellion threatening the inter-

ests of the Archbishop of Bremen and the Count of Olden-
burg. The temptation of free rents and the need for a
mighty penance had yielded a reluctant, though willing
assent from the baker, and he accepted a forty-day commission to join as a knight's servant in the alliance against
the obstinate Stedingers. Wil recalled his mother standing
with her hands folded on her apron grumbling a dispassionate "Godspeed."

"Forty days?" the boy groused out loud. *Forty days
indeed; almost six years!* He thought of his father and rage
filled his chest. *Leave us, will you? Well, stay away and
die; Mother says you deserve to. Maybe you already are
dead. I'll do your duty and mine own—and I'll do it very
well.*

૱

Maria held the damp cloth limply in her tired hand and
looked fearfully at her sleeping mother's paled and perspiring face. She bent forward to wipe the woman's neck
but recoiled at finding more droplets of blood beaded in the
corners of her mouth. "Karl," she whispered frantically.
"Look, Karl, there. Please, help poor Mama."

Karl, bravely masking his own fear, took the rag confidently and quickly dabbed the blood away. "See, Maria, 'tis
gone."

Marta's eyes suddenly opened wide and round as if startled. She began to cough violently; her body became tense
and taut. Then, struggling for air, she lurched forward, flailing her arms and stretching her fingers toward her terrified
children. At last, she sucked a wheezing breath, only to
bend forward and spew blood across the patched quilt.

Karl put a trembling arm around his mother's heaving
shoulders and offered what comfort he could. He
glanced nervously at his horrified sister who had
retreated once again into the safety of a shadowed corner. "Mother shall soon be better," he choked. "Just
believe and so it shall be."

Marta's coughing subsided and she eased herself back
into the deep soft of her feathered pillow. She reached
weakly for Karl's hand and squeezed it lightly. She then

turned a hard eye to her quivering daughter. A ribbon of foamed blood drooled through her pursed lips. "Girl, fetch me fresh water at once," she hissed.

As Maria scampered through the outer room, Marta switched her attention to her benevolent son. She stared at him for a moment and then stroked his hair. Her breathing was still difficult and uneven, and she forced a deep breath to exhale hoarsely. "Karl, you have loved me most of all. Whatever I have wanted, you have given. Whatever I have asked, you have done. You have pleased me more than the others ever could. Now reach ..." She struggled for more breath and shook her finger violently at the floor. "Here ... here," she rasped. "Look under this bed and you shall find a box."

She coughed, her face twisting in pain. She then steadied herself, drew a good breath into her chest, and released the precious air carefully. "Karl, open the box and you shall ... find a chain necklace ... *ja*, good ... 'twas given to me by m'father for tending his old age. I should like you to have it ... a keepsake of your dear mother's love for a proper son."

Karl stared wide-eyed at the steel necklace he had lifted out of the box. He held it close to the candle and ran his stubby fingers along its squared links. He was happier at that moment than any other he remembered.

Marta sighed and sank back into her pillow. Her complexion darkened once more. "Now leave me, boy," she growled impatiently. "Can you not see that I am weary ... so very weary? Leave me sleep."

Maria was standing in the doorway with a tin of cool water and looked hopefully at her brother. He smiled softly and tiptoed toward the doorway. "Everything is in order," he whispered. "'Tis time for Mother to sleep. By prime Frau Anka will be tending her."

Maria, content to trust the better judgment of her brother, snuffed the wick of her mother's candle and nestled into her own straw bed where she was pleased to close her eyes with hope as her night's companion.

~

Wil continued on his trot through the small hamlet that had been home to him since the day of his birth. Weyer was an ancient village lying on the edge of an ecclesiastical fief once granted to the diocese of Mainz by the Emperor Friederich Barbarossa. The archbishop then founded an abbey in the village of Villmar and endowed it with numbers of villages to create a modest, but profitable manor.

Weyer's residents were primarily bound men—men who were legally obligated by the oaths of their forefathers to whomever held the land. Whether they owned heritable fields or not, their status was one of servitude—they could not leave the estate, marry, buy or sell, or perform any number of human activities without both permission and taxation by their clerical lords.

Much to the concern of Weyer's folk, succeeding abbots had refused to construct stockades around any of their villages, relying instead on the strong hand of their contracted ally, the Lord of Runkel. Nevertheless, the abbey generally administered Weyer benevolently and with a sternness that rarely offended. Furthermore, in order to sustain the spiritual lives of its flock huddled in the hollow, the various archbishops of Mainz had properly maintained the old stone church, originally built by the great Charlemagne. From here the diocese's priests were to shepherd the humble parish: They were to take the Eucharist on behalf of the folk, grant comfort in death, hope in baptism, and refuge against the wiles of Satan and of men.

So, generations of ploughmen, timbermen, shepherds, and a few tradesmen lived their unpretentious lives in submission to the abbey's authority, content with what few pleasures might befall them. Each endured their station without complaint, willing to submit themselves to the order of their Church and the rule of the manor to which they were born. These good folk were required to toil many hours in the vast fields of the demesne—their lords' land—struggling behind slow oxen with wheeled-ploughs, scything and flailing grain crops, and performing sundry other services. But work for the abbey was not their only work. Some owned livestock or fowl which needed management, and some labored on their own portions of hides—units of land of about one hundred twenty acres. Many of the women carved spoons or spun wool, plaited baskets, or wove fabric to sell. And, were that not enough, each family also needed to tend small, wattle-fenced kitchen gardens where they grew each year's supply of vegetables and herbs.

Wil's father was the village baker. Prior generations had served the monks as shepherds near the village of Villmar, living as humble cottagers sheltered in the shadow of the abbey walls. However, according to family legend, Wil's great-grandfather, Jost, had discovered the abbey's prior in a financial impropriety. The shrewd old man had quickly bartered his discretion for some unusual considerations. Special occupations were granted to both Jost and his sons, but a further promise had been made. Following the line of the eldest males, his great-grandsons would be taught in the abbey school; tutored by the monks in mathematics, astronomy, Latin, and rhetoric. It was a promise kept and one now benefiting young Wil and Karl.

Wil glided through the night, lulled by the rhythm of his padding feet atop a roadway recently dampened by a welcome shower. He had climbed out of Weyer's hollow and was now steadily descending the long, gradual slope toward the Lahn River and the village of Villmar which lay on its banks.

Soon after the bells of matins' prayers, he entered the sleepy village and headed to the walled abbey located at its far end. Wil paused to rest under the clouded full moon and surveyed the edifice looming large and ominous before him. A bit unnerved by a strange, creeping dread that was beginning to crawl over him, he closed his eyes and let his mind bear him to the sanctuary of midsummer days within the abbey walls. He pictured himself under the tutelage of good Brother Lukas, sitting upright on his hard wooden stool in the shade of the linden tree with Karl and a group of oblates. He calmed.

Wil knew the abbey well and could find what he required

at any hour of any day. His mind quickly sketched its design. Its walls encircled large grounds containing, at the center, the abbatial *Kirche*—the single-naved, gray-stone church that served the brothers. Around the church were the monks' graveyard, orchards, and several large gardens. Along the edges were numerous buildings including the abbot's chambers, the priory, the dormitory, refectory, the scriptorium, the granaries, Lukas's fragrant herbarium, the guest house, the garrison, apple press, and sundry sheds and workshops.

The boy strode to the locked gates of the eastern portal, and he viewed the slumped figure of a guard dozing on a stool at his post. Wil approached the sentry carefully and immediately recognized him as none other than the quick-tempered Ansel of the night watch. He muttered to himself, certain of the welcome he was about to receive, but mustered his courage. "You there, Gatekeeper. I've need of your help."

The man jerked in his sleep and grumbled a few indiscernible unpleasantries before repositioning himself against the stone wall that served as his headboard. Wil drew an impatient breath and took a firm hold of the man's large forearm. "Gatekeeper."

This time the disoriented guard awakened indeed. He bounded to his feet and jerked his sword from its scabbard as he stumbled backward against the oak gate. His helmet clanged against the iron hinges. "Halt," he ordered as his eyes flew about the darkness. "Halt or I strike!"

Wil hastily retreated a few steps. "I need the herbalist. Can you call for Brother Lukas?"

"Who ... who speaks?" growled Ansel, still gathering his composure. He narrowed his eyes at Wil. "Whose waif be you to come here by matins? You'd best begone 'fore I scatter yer bones."

"Nay, *mein Herr*," answered Wil defiantly. "I'll not take my leave without the monk. My mother lies sick and may not see morning."

The guard put the point of his sword at the stubborn boy's throat. "You know the brothers don't leave the cloister. Now, peasant dog, turn and scamper home, or by God, I'll strike you dead where you stand."

Wil swallowed hard, uncertain and anxious. The corner of his eye caught a menacing glint from the flat of the long sword just beneath his chin. Wil was suddenly confused; he needed God's help and inside were God's people.

"Well, why do you stand, brat? Go—begone at once."

Wil retired one step, only to set his jaw. "Nay, sire, I'll not leave without Brother Lukas. Wake him or may my mother's death be upon your soul!"

The huge man said nothing but reared back his sword and swung with terrific force at the resolute lad. A startled Wil tried to elude the heavy blade but cried out as its flat side slapped across the back of his broad shoulders. He fell to the ground, writhing in pain, then scrambled on his hands and knees toward the cover of some bramble.

"Go!" yelled the guard as he ran toward Wil. "The next time I turn my sword on edge."

Wil had not yet stood to his feet when the man's thick boot landed hard into his belly. He gasped and rolled onto the dewy grass by the path, desperately gulping for breath.

The sentry, contented for duty done, sheathed his sword and muttered to himself as he returned to his stubby stool. He adjusted his steel cap and belt, tugged at some uncomfortable clothing, folded his arms, and laid his broad head against his dubious headboard for few more hours of sleep.

Wil retreated to just beyond the edge of the village and veered off the path into a small wood to gather his wits. He touched his bruised shoulders lightly and cupped his painful ribs as he bent over to breathe. He lifted his face toward the abbey's steeple, now moon-washed under a broken sky. He was ready for another try

This time he slipped through the night's shadows to the safety of a large chestnut tree a mere ten paces from the snorting guard. He surveyed the wall, the massive wooden gate—and the alarm bell high in the guard tower. He set his eyes on the thick rope of the old bell hanging limply near Ansel's head and he smiled. He positioned his leggings, pulled nervously at the hem of his thigh-long tunic, and began to steal his way toward the gate.

Wil moved across the ground like a half-starved cat stalking its prey, his teeth gritted and fists clenched; every sense was piqued. He was oblivious to the pain in his belly and the aching bruises on his welted back. Instead, he thought of nothing other than wrapping his hands around the stout stretch of rope silhouetted against the stone wall.

Five paces yet, now four, now three. He whispered two quick prayers, one to whatever benevolent angels might be hovering overhead and the other to whatever spirits might be drifting through the woodland. Two paces left. Suddenly the half-conscious Ansel jerked and twisted, wrestling with himself and the old stool. Wil stood paralyzed, one leg lifted in the air. His heart raced and he dared not draw breath. At last, the guard resettled himself and belched.

Then, as if directed by some unseen hand, Wil flung himself forward to seize the rope. He grasped the worn hemp with both of his hands and strained at it with all the power his young arms could muster. But the rusty bell barely gave way. Its wooden supports simply moaned and creaked as if annoyed at such a late-night intrusion. The alarmed lad stood and stared up at the high tower, panic seizing his chest. He squeezed his sweating hands hard around the prickly rope and cast a quick, nervous glance at Ansel, still comfortably asleep.

This time Wil pulled harder, as hard as he thought possible. But again, the stubborn clapper refused to strike its iron, and the obstinate bell yielded no sound other than the rubbing of old rope on smooth wood. Desperate, brave Wil squeezed the stubborn hemp one last time, now lifting his legs off the ground and summoning the spirits of his ancestors to pull with him. This time a deafening clang resounded from the tower above and echoed loudly through the valley!

Poor Ansel rolled off his stool and fell to the ground, howling in confusion as Wil strained on the rope one more time. The sentry clambered to his feet, thrashing his arms like a flustered windmill in a raging storm. He spotted Wil and furiously jerked his long-sword from his belt. Wil, all plans now abandoned, scampered along the abbey wall like a frightened rabbit darting from a mad dog.

The terrified lad raced toward the murky shadows of the distant southwest corner. He paid no mind to the alarm within the awakened abbey, for he could only hear the angry shouts of the pursuing Ansel. He neared the corner of the wall at full speed but suddenly tripped across a fresh-sawed firelog that lay in the darkness of his path. He sprawled into the grass with a gasp.

Oh God, he'll surely kill me now. He heard Ansel's pounding footfalls growing louder and louder. Without another thought, Wil seized the log and stumbled around the corner. There he waited, his back pressed against the cold stone, his chest heaving, and his nostrils flared. Braced in the darkness, Wil clenched his new weapon with both his hands.

The quick-footed soldier dashed around the corner with his sword half raised. His legs took a mere three steps westward when the strong arms of young Wilhelm swung the stout stick across his shins. With a loud cry, Ansel fell facedown into a massive heap of leather and steel, his head striking hard on the earth and his small helmet bouncing impotently forward.

Wil, overtaken more by instinct than reason, bounded over the fallen soldier. His heart, once fluttering in fear, now surged with a strange, pleasing rush of new life. "There, I've the better of you." The boy bolted several paces toward the gate but then stopped, still mysteriously drawn to the pride of conquest. He turned back toward the man lying motionless and silent. He stood over his fallen foe and smiled victoriously. His eyes caught a shimmer of a worthy token tucked securely in the man's belt at the middle of his back. Wil bent forward curiously, and then snatched a dagger from its silver sheath. He stood erect and held his treasure carefully in both hands. He knew at once that he had indeed won a prize befitting the moment. He abruptly stuffed it in his belt and hastily backtracked the wall toward the chaos by the gate.

The peal of the alarm bell had created bedlam within the abbey and without. A small detachment of light-arms was trumpeted to their assigned posts, and nervous monks scurried about in the moonlight slamming and bolting portals and hatches. The whinny of startled horses, the cries of angry sentries, and the distressed complaints of monks mingled poorly. The smoky flames of newly lit torches cast an ill-timed glow over the dark edge of the high wall while young Wil pondered his dilemma.

A column of hooded monks and men-at-arms suddenly burst through the gate and into the darkness in angry pursuit of the mysterious cause of their night's confusion. Wil quickly drew his brown hood over his golden hair and pressed himself hard against the black shadow of the wall as the anxious party snaked past him. Releasing a quivering sigh, the lad moved swiftly toward the open, unguarded gate and slipped, unnoticed, onto the abbey grounds.

I hope him fast asleep ... oh God, let it be so! Wil thought as he flitted deftly through the monks' graveyard and over the short wall by the infirmary. He crouched his way along the refectory and through the shadows of the novices' cloister, scampered quickly by the latrine, and stepped gingerly into a dark corner to allow a group of nervous guards to trot by before slipping quietly into the hollow corridor of the musty dormitory.

By now the garrison was fully engaged and order was taking hold. Mounted soldiers loped across the courtyard in proper form, and the steadier commands of sergeant and churchman alike began to restore calm. Wil listened nervously, fully aware that no matter how merciful Brother Lukas might be, he could expect nothing less than a terrible flogging if he fell into the harsh hands of the monks' lay bailiff.

The determined lad crept carefully through the long dormitory corridor toward the sleep cell Lukas had been exiled to years before. His superiors had mistakenly decided that such nightly banishment from the community might shame the free-thinking brother's rebellious spirit into submission. Wil could hear his heart pounding and felt a cold sweat spread over his body. *Good Brother Lukas,* he thought, *I hope you drank your sleep potion tonight.* A hopeful smile twitched the corners of the lad's mouth as he thought of the monk—his father's friend and once the faithful companion of the beloved old woman by the stream.

In another moment his hand was resting squarely on the iron latch of the narrow door and Wil lifted it. The door gave way with an unsettling creak and the boy stepped lightly inside. He peered anxiously into the darkness at the monk's cot and, to his relief, found Lukas rolled securely in his blanket. The boy carefully picked up the tongs and raised a coal from the small, iron hearth. He touched it to the wick of the candle on the tiny table alongside the monk's rope bed.

"Wake, Brother Lukas," whispered Wil to the monk's back. "Please." The silent monk failed to stir. Wil took a gentle hold of the man's shoulder and shook it lightly. "Wake, please. Wake, please, I need you." The boy, now growing impatient, whispered in more urgent tone. "Brother Lukas, this is Wil of Weyer."

But the man lay motionless. Wil, aware of footsteps in the dormitory, now shook Lukas more violently. "Wake, I say. Wake."

Desperate and nearly frantic, Wil pulled the man on his back and raised the candle just over the monk's face. Straightaway, all speech left the lad and he stood stupefied and numb, too stunned to react. His eyes stretched in horror and he let out his air slowly. He stepped a quick-pace backward. He had seen those eyes before—the dry, vacant eyes of the dead.

The boy's heart fluttered and his legs felt weak. Nausea filled his innards and he collapsed to the straw-covered floor. His mind raced. He closed his eyes and breathed deeply, clenching his jaw and tightening his fists. *What to do ... what to do?*

He jumped to his feet and rummaged savagely through

the monk's tiny cell. On the floor by the far side of the bed Wil spotted three uncorked bottles of herbs, two opened root jars, and a spilled wooden bowl. He grabbed the bowl and quickly sniffed the residue clinging to the inside. "*Ach, what a foul stink. By heaven, Lukas, we told you to stop trying things on yourself.*"

A group of men could be heard rummaging about the dormitory just beyond Lukas's cell. *Now I'm in quite the fix—no help for Mother and none for me.* Wil's legs went weak. *I'll surely be accused of Lukas's murder.* He listened to the guards nearby. They seemed preoccupied with something else.

Then it was as if some unseen presence urged him from task to task. His eyes raced about, suddenly steadying on a small cabinet standing open in the corner, and he quickly held the candle to it. Inside he found dozens and dozens of Brother Lukas's treatments on rows of narrow shelves, and on a peg hung the leather satchel the man had used for so many years to gather wild herbs. The boy hastily collected what cruets, ampoules, tins, and wallets he could grab and stuffed the satchel full. He tied the bag to his rope belt, wisely snuffed the candle, and bade Brother Lukas a sad farewell.

Wil eased open the narrow door and peeked warily into the corridor. The sentries were still rummaging about the main dormitory. The lad tarried in Lukas's shadowed doorway for just a moment, then slipped into the darkness. He ran along the corridor, ducked down a short flight of damp-slickened stone stairs, and stooped into an oft-forgotten tunnel leading to an abandoned root cellar. He crept across the dark, dirt floor, then ran his fingers over the cobwebbed ceiling overhead, feeling for the trap door which led to the courtyard above. *There ... yes, I've found it.*

The hatch gave way stubbornly, its edges bound by the creep of sod from years of neglect. With a good, hearty heave, however, it gave way and the lad pushed his head into the starlight. He peered cautiously into the courtyard and, seeing no one near, slithered up and out the

hole, placing himself flat in the wet grass. He quietly lowered the trap door and crawled on his stomach toward a
small pile of neatly stacked beer barrels stored against
the eastern wall.

Wil was perspiring and his mouth was dry, but he felt a
strange calm as he arrived at the barrels. He glanced
about, eyes sharp, ears cocked, and, seeing no one,
ascended the barrels with ease. After scaling the final barrel, he reached his hands to the top of the wall and pulled
himself upward. His arms strained and he stifled his
grunts as he hauled himself to his forearms, then to his
armpits and finally to his waist. He swung his lanky legs
onto the top and, with a final heave, rolled himself onto the
wide brim.

The panting lad crouched in the shadows, pausing
briefly to recover his breath. He looked to the sky, where a
bank of new clouds drifted slowly toward the setting full
moon. Wanting every advantage, he squatted under his
hood and waited for the clouds to obscure the waning
silver light. At last the moon was darkened and Wil
abruptly swung his body over the outside of the wall. He
hung on his fingertips, then closed his eyes and released
himself into the arms of the angels he hoped would carry
him lightly to the earth below.

As misfortune would have it, however, his body plummeted like an acorn from a high branch and the helpless boy
landed with a heavy thud on the sun-baked clay at the base
of the wall. Wil rolled on the ground, whimpering and grimacing in pain, but quickly composed himself and dashed
through the village to the cover of the nearby wood. He
rubbed his ankles and feet and made a hasty note of his surroundings. Content that he was safe enough for the
moment, Wil took time to consider his predicament and to
listen to the sounds now ebbing within the abbey. While certain he had escaped the first net, he knew the ways of the
abbey's lay bailiff. *Surely he's sent riders along the roads in
every direction.* The lad knew he would need to move warily
and circuitously home, but he also thought it best to wait
just a while longer.

After an hour Wil reckoned his hunters to be spread thinly through the manors. So, with a deep breath he began. Taking no chances, he maneuvered from tree to tree, careful to check over his shoulder from time to time. Leaving the wood he chose a wide route home by way of fallow fields. After struggling through hard furrows for an hour, Wil finally took a brief rest by an enormous beech tree near the road leading to the village of Oberbrechen. He set his tired back against the smooth bark and slid down to calculate his condition.

As he breathed the summer night's clean air, he felt a quiet defiance take root in his young heart—a potent and invigorating sense of self-reliance and independence that was quite pleasing. Like the feeling he had when he dropped Ansel, Wil became aware of an even deeper change, a powerful metamorphosis that was spreading through him. A sense of newfound manhood washed over him and he liked it.

Wil plucked his hard-won trophy from his belt. He held the deer-foot handle in the palm of his hand and lightly caressed the sharp, serrated edges of its finely crafted blade with his fingers. He smiled. But the sound of approaching horsemen startled the boy and he quickly tucked his dagger away. He pressed his back hard against the wide tree, snickering as his would-be captors galloped past. *This quarry you shall not take.* He retied Lukas's leather bag tightly by its cowhide thong and lashed it to his belt as he looked to the nearly moonless sky. The gentle chirps of waking birds reminded him that he must hurry.

Chapter 2
FLIGHT AND FATHER PIOUS

Karl and Maria were awakened by their mother's incessant coughing, and their fears now kept them anxious and alert. Impatiently, Karl stood in the low doorway and stared at the night's sky sometime after matins' bells. He thought he heard the alarm bell from the distant abbey and strained to hear again. He stepped to the fence gate, ears cocked. *Why the alarm?*

Maria came to Karl's side and looked helplessly into his face.

"I tell you she'll be fine," Karl assured his sister, though he wasn't so sure. But, always preferring hope to reality, he nodded confidently and quoted Brother Lukas: "Dawn follows the darkest hour of the night."

The pair went to their mother's room where Marta now lay gasping for breath. Karl dipped the rag into the water bowl and wiped his mother's face and neck. He steeled his heart against the darkness, insisting to himself that he was quite content in his expectations of a miracle. *How good God is … how good God shall surely be*, he mused a little desperately.

Marta rose to an elbow. "Where is Wil?" she cried. "Where is my son? Never, never is he by my side when I am in need of him."

Karl was suddenly not sure how to answer, yet he dare not lie. "Wil has gone for Brother Lukas and …"

"I ordered no help other than Frau Anka, and I do not

want that mad monk near me!" she rasped. At that, her body shuddered and blood spewed out her mouth and nose, spraying the throat of her flaxen robe and the ragged quilt clutched tightly in her hands. Karl, terrified and suddenly unnerved, hastily reached an awkward hand to help her, knocking the bowl of water off its stand and spilling its contents on his mother's bed. "Enough of this," Marta scolded. "You children have failed me again."

Maria's eyes betrayed her hurt and she hid, trembling in the darkness. Karl followed her and leaned close to whisper, "You know how she oft is. She never really means it, and ..."

"I heard that, little man," rumbled Marta. "You think you have loved me well, do you? You and your brother and that ... that sister of yours have borne me sorrow in childbirth and now sorrow in m'death. 'Tis your sins and the sins of your father that I must now bear and 'tis *your* penalties that I must pay." Her acrid charge had barely struck its targets when the bitter woman rolled to the edge of her bed, coughing and vomiting and retching in pain.

Karl's face was flushed and his eyes dammed with tears. He dashed outside with the empty water bowl, desperate to regain his mother's favor. He dipped it into the fresh water and flew back to her side. "Mama, I have clean water for ..."

"Fool," hissed Marta as she struck the bowl from the boy's shaking hand. "Always the fool. You've been little more than a buffoon, a stupid hop-toad jumping about my feet day by cursed day! A clutter follows your every step ... clutter and disorder wherever you go. I'll have no more of it ... least of all at my death." The angry woman trembled as she stole another breath. "Now leave m'room and ... and take that daughter of the Devil with you."

Marta swung her hand at the children. "Begone from me. If I must die, leave me die in peace, away from you both.... Oh, would that you had been the children I raised you to be." The woman groaned and her voice filled with self-pity. "There once were times when I thought, 'Perhaps ... perhaps yet there is hope.' But I've always known otherwise ... always deep in my soul.... Now, let me leave this miserable life the way I have lived it ... alone." Marta closed her yellowed eyes and began to sob. "My life is nothing … nothing as it should have been."

Karl and Maria stared at their mother, stunned and shattered. They backed out of the bedchamber, side-by-side, and huddled before the hearth. "I wish Wil were here," whispered Karl. The boy tucked his knees up tight to his chest and buried his tear-stained face in his folded arms.

"Perhaps we should fetch the priest?" Maria offered with some reservation.

Karl paused for a moment, equally reluctant. "Well, he did say anytime we needed him we should fetch him."

Maria nodded. "Mother hates him so, and Wil, too."

Karl nodded. "But how could fetching a priest ever be a bad thing?" He turned toward the door slowly. Maria, sensing his sudden uncertainty, squeezed Karl's hand and kissed his cheek.

"I … I'll hurry back, Maria." Looking sadly at his little sister, he forced a feeble smile and vanished in the darkness.

෨

Wil stepped away from the broad trunk of the beech, preparing for his final flight home. He adjusted his leggings, retied the rope-belt which girded his woolen tunic, pushed his hood back to his shoulders, and ran his long fingers through his yellow hair. He took a deep breath and began.

The quick-footed lad rapidly passed by Oberbrechen, as the sky brightened before him. Nearly home, he laughed as he recalled the exciting moment of Ansel's collision with the earth. He imagined him lying there with grass and mud stuffed between his teeth, no doubt growling furiously as he fumbled his way upright. But the lad's memory quickly offered the ember-lit face of poor Lukas and at once the reality of his evening's affair gripped him. Sobered by sadness and mindful of risk, he set his thoughts to flight and listened only to his callused feet pounding on the damp earth and the jangle of his leather bag.

Suddenly, his ears filled with the thunder of hooves behind him and he dove to the side of the road. After rolling into a ditch of high weeds he drew his hood tightly over his head and lay flat as three horses bearing bailiff's soldiers bolted past. Wil released the air he was holding and returned warily to the roadway.

೭

Karl hurried southwestward toward the home of Father Pious at the eastern reaches of Oberbrechen. Behind him broke the first golden edge of a new sun; a fresh, light breeze tousled his red curls. Cock and songbird announced the advent of a new day as a cool mist gathered close to the dew-laden fields. The boy, now content in his decision, pressed the roadway with conviction.

Suddenly a group of galloping horsemen rounded a bend and bore hard upon the surprised lad. Startled, Karl lunged to the side of the road to avert certain trampling. The horsemen, equally surprised in the faint light of prime, stood in their saddles to rein their mounts.

"You there, boy," one stone-faced soldier barked. "Stand as you are or die."

Karl stood, trembling as two others dismounted and charged toward him.

A sergeant took a firm hold of poor Karl's tunic and hoisted the speechless boy off his feet. "What mischief be y'bout? Speak. Who has passed you by?"

The befuddled Karl stammered, "I … I have seen only men beginning for the fields. I am seeking Father Pious … m'mother is taken ill … and …"

"Say again … any strangers?"

"None, sire!" cried the boy. "I swear it."

The indignant officer thrust the boy to the ground and mounted his horse. "You had best be speaking truth. I know you … you'd be the baker's son at Weyer, and I'll have you beat if you be lying."

Karl, uninjured and wishing only to please, climbed to his feet cautiously. He called timidly after the man. "M'lord, who should I keep an eye for?"

The soldier turned in his saddle and answered, "An abbey guard was assaulted and lies near death. We're looking for any strangers, any at all."

Karl offered an agreeable nod to the departing horsemen, but his heart felt a sharp pain. *This cannot be Wil's busi-*

ness—*nay, not Wil. What cause would he have?* he wondered. A cold dread swam through the boy's veins and he felt its chill. *Oh dear God, let no guilt be on my brother.*

He pressed on to the double-floored home ahead of him. "Good," he sighed, "there is smoke at the roof ... they are about." As he neared the wood-sided house he saw Father Pious's housekeeper carrying eggs from the fore-yard and he called to her loudly. "Frau, Frau, I needs see the Father."

Startled and not pleased in the least for an unexpected daybreak guest, the indignant woman clutched her egg-laden apron with both hands and scurried through a gaggle of honking geese to the rear of the house.

Karl, slightly annoyed at her reception, strode to the front door and knocked on it boldly. He waited respectfully and took a moment to look about the gray light of early dawn and smell the fresh morning's air. With growing impatience he knocked harder. "Father Pious?" His pleas went unanswered and he raised his eyes to the shuttered window above him. "Father Pious, Father Pious. Please ... it is Karl, Karl of Weyer ... the baker's son."

The shutter flew open and a bleary-eyed priest glared at the early-morning intruder.

"Why be ye about before lauds, boy? ... *Ach* ... never y'mind, I'll attend you forthright."

Karl, relieved for an answer despite its bite, waited for the wide door to open, only to be distracted by what appeared to be a fleeting figure darting near the edges of the winding road. He turned full-face toward the roadway and strained to see what was about when the door flung open behind him. Karl jumped and spun on his heels to face the bulging, red eyes of a most disgruntled and disagreeable Father Pious.

"What on God's blessed earth do you demand of me 'fore lauds, Karl?" bellowed the priest.

"I've urgent need of you, Father." Karl bowed respectfully and knelt to one knee.

"Truly? And has the hour poached thy respect, boy?" whined the churchman as he extended his arm. Karl, astonished at his indiscretion, dropped his other knee and kissed the priest's hand.

"Father, forgive me, please forgive me...." Had not the vexed priest dragged the boy through the doorway there is little doubt that poor Karl would have continued his repentance 'til terce!

"Enough ... I forgive thee."

Pious slammed the heavy door shut and ordered the young boy to stand by the cook-fire that his dour housekeeper was stoking. The priest dragged the woman by the nap of her heavy gown to the far wall and leaned close to her hardened face to instruct her in harsh tones. Karl, uncomfortable and embarrassed, used the delay to study the priest in the light now filtering through the glassed window behind him.

Father Pious was a balded, corpulent sort caught between the vigor of a younger man and the acumen of an older one. Karl thought his face to be as white as sun-bleached flour and as round as a plough-horse rump. His puffed cheeks squeezed his eyes nearly in half, like those of an overweight boar, and his quivering jowls hung over a broad, uncompromising jaw. His manner seemed to be of perpetual annoyance and pending rage, save an occasional wit that brought welcome relief.

Frustrated by his parish status and straining for recognition, Father Pious was regarded by most as ambitious and calculating and clearly void of what virtues a true churchman might reflect. The priest's rash temperament and his inclination toward vengeance silenced those who would be otherwise apt to judge his ways, particularly those aware of his fleshly indiscretions. It would seem his peers and superiors alike were keenly aware of their own secret failings and preferred to avoid risk of their own exposure. So the pitiful man was abandoned to endure his office without the warmth of friendship, the comfort of a colleague's encouragement, or the maturing sting of a mentor's loving rebuke.

Pious finished commanding his housekeeper by thumping a hard fist on her stiffened back and bent in his first attempt to lash shoes to his feet. Karl turned a shy eye toward the man once again, unable to avoid particular notice of the huge legs and the wide bottom that stretched the man's threadbare linen nightshirt. The lad wrinkled his nose. *Man of God or nay ... he is hard to look at.*

Seemingly aware of the boy's eyes on him, Pious hastily wrapped himself in a substantial woolen blanket. Grunting, he dropped himself atop an oaken stool, positioned his thick hands squarely on his bulky knees, and leaned forward over his rotund belly to try the shoes again.

"So, Johann Karl, speak 'fore I box thy ears and chase you home. You're making me defer m'morning's prayers and neither I nor thy Father in heaven is particularly pleased."

Karl fumbled with his hands and nervously placed one set of dusty toes upon the other.

"I ... I ... we've need of you," he stammered. "Mother lies sick by fever and likely near death. Wil has taken leave to the abbey for ..."

The priest furrowed his brow, wrinkling the very top of his crown and wobbled on his stubby stool. "By what hour did Wilhelm leave to the abbey?"

"Evening past, sire, well past compline, perhaps nearer to midnight," answered Karl. "But he sought only aid from the herbalist and ..."

Pious leaned close to the boy. "A detachment of soldiers woke me just before you came and informed me of trouble in the abbey ..."

"Oh, Father, Wil surely had no cause for trouble."

Father Pious slapped his hands on his thighs and struggled to his feet. "Sit fast to this stool, boy, and say not another word. I'll dress and together we'll seek out this brother of thine ... and attend to thy mother."

᷒

Wil dashed and darted from tree to tree. Ahead of him broke the first light of the rising sun against the silhouette of Father Pious's home, and behind him curled the thin ribbons of smoke from the rooftops of Oberbrechen. The boy paused behind a bush and snarled. *How pleased I'd be to plunge this dagger through the fattened*

*hide of that black-hearted pig of a priest. Oh, to feel the drag
of a sharp edge through that baggy throat.*

Wil caught his breath and returned his attention to the
task at hand. He sprang from his bush and raced along the
cover of some wild hedge rimming the roadway. Clearing
Pious's house, he turned northeastward, proceeding from
tree to tree until he found the security of a heavy stand of
trees that stretched the distance to his village.

Nearly in full prime, the manors' valleys had begun to bus-
tle with their summer morning routines. Carts crowded the
narrow road, groaning and heaving, obediently lurching
close behind their sluggish oxen. Timbermen shouldering
their broadaxes and field serfs handily gripping wooden
forks and scythes strode along the roadway, bound for their
day's labors with complacent resolve.

Yet Wil thought this particular morning seemed
strangely different. This day was not bearing itself in its
customary ritual, nor observing its sure rhythm. Instead,
Wil sensed a peculiar nervousness, an unsettling deport-
ment, like the slow, ominous gathering of black clouds on a
summer's afternoon. He slowed, just a bit, and watched
distant shepherds strangely huddled. He looked behind
and noticed yeomen staying their wagons to exchange what
seemed to be important gossip.

Could it be? Wil wondered. *Could all this be 'bout Brother
Lukas? Sad, I know, but all this heed? And why the urgency
of the horsemen? So much for a simple crack on Ansel's
shins?*

The lad reset his quick pace and soon emerged from the
wood, sliding slyly into the hollow of Weyer. Unsure of his
situation, he crouched behind the back of the chandler's
workshop and examined the hamlet for the slightest hint
of risk. Reasonably satisfied, he was about to step into full
light when a troop of angry soldiers burst out of the miller's
door and stormed toward the neighboring hut. Wil stalled,
carefully pressing his back hard against the mud wall of
the workshop. He cocked his head to aim one ear in hopes
of hearing something other than the pounding of his own
heart.

Hearing little other than the honking of geese and the cackle of irritated hens scattering in the dusty wake of the grumbling, armed company, he laid one eye at the corner of the building and considered his predicament. He could see nervous housewives standing stiffly at their gates, waiting on the soldiers' search and the inevitable rough handling of what few treasures they could call their own. Frau Fronica, the broad-girted wife of a yeoman, wrung her hands and stifled tears as she slowly returned to her rummaged dwelling. Frau Erika, the dyer's wife, stood stone-faced and angry outside her doorway, her eyes wincing slightly at the sound of a pot smashed on the hard earthen floor within.

Wil, concerned for what tribute might be required of his own home, sprang from his hiding to the blind of a standing oxcart. Unseen, he then bounded over a low garden fence, danced deftly through a cackling flock of hens, and tumbled lightly into his own yard. Maria, surprised but equally delighted, let her egg pail slip to the ground and ran to her brother, clutching his waist. "Oh, Wil, you're here. Mother is none better ... and men are searching the village ... and ..."

"And where would Karl be?" hushed Wil, angrily.

Maria hesitated and looked at her feet. "He ... he left to fetch Father Pious."

"What! Who told him to do so?" Wil flung his arms in the air and cursed. "By God, I'll beat that dunce for this."

"What should we have done?" Maria began to sob.

Wil bit his lower lip and relaxed his fists. He took his sister firmly but tenderly by the shoulder and knelt down. He placed the edge of his forefinger under her chin and lightly raised her wet eyes to meet his own. "Please, sister, no need to cry. You always cry and it helps nothing."

"I am afraid."

Wil spotted two guards suddenly round the corner of the wheelwright's shed. "Quick, Maria, quick ... inside."

Slamming the door shut behind them, Wil's nimble fingers hurried to loose the bag of Brother Lukas from his belt, and he plunged it and his new dagger deep into the mounded straw of his bed. He ordered his garb, nervously fluffed his hair, and stood erect, waiting in silence for the guards to enter. The soldiers were dreaded mercenaries under short-termed conscriptions to Lord Heribert of Runkel and quartered in the abbey because of concerns for the Empire's civil war. Dry-mouthed and weak-legged, Wil was determined to be bold.

Maria leaned hard against her brother, drawing what strength she could. Though expecting it, they both flinched when the door burst open.

"Move off, waifs. We are about the abbot's business," barked an imposing and foul-breathed soldier.

Wil protested lightly, "Th ... the ... there is nothing out of order here, sire. Perhaps you'd be better served searching elsewhere."

"Off, boy," groused the man, shoving Wil to the ground with a heavy arm.

Maria quickly bent to a single knee, tilted her tiny head upward, and addressed the rough men with submissive discretion. "Please, good sires, have a care. *Mutti* is badly fevered and has need of quiet."

The soldiers grunted and brushed past the girl toward Marta's bedchamber. Wil's sharp mind recalled a story of his father's and he called after them. "M'lords, enter if you wish, but be warned of fever."

The boy's words snagged the two men, and they held their advance. Each looked at the other and then toward the darkened room before them. Fortuitously, Marta groaned. "Humph. I say all's well here," grumbled one. The other cast a haphazard look around the modest quarters, shrugged, and agreed as he pocketed a wooden ladle. "No mischief here ... on to the next."

The soldiers stretched several long strides across the common room and bowed out the low door. Glad to leave fever behind, they pressed their search elsewhere.

Wil set a trembling hand on his sister's head and smiled weakly. "Perhaps the saints are with us this day."

The boy pulled the door almost closed and peered through the available sliver of light. He watched the soldiers complete their search and mount their horses. With a quick command and a cloud of dust, they sped away. Closing the door completely and easing himself against the wall, Wil turned to speak to Maria when a familiar voice bellowed at them from just beyond their gate. Frau Anka, red-faced and flustered, came charging, scolding the abbot's soul and all the saints above with a wagging forefinger and a shrill voice.

"So, *Kinder*," Anka boomed as Maria let her in. "I see Mother Marta has cheated death for a few more hours and is ready to face another day. Good. So, you there, girl, fetch me eggs, water, and millet for a good gruel. And you, Wilhelm, stack more wood. By the Holy Mother! Work, work, all I do is work and you children stand there gawking at me ... now do as you've b'told."

෨

Karl waited mutely while Father Pious struggled into his black-hooded habit and returned to his awkward position on the stool. The boy stifled a grin as he watched the bloated priest re-assault his footwear without an embarrassing plummet to the floor. Pious leaned back, gulped a gaping mouth of air, and forced his thick body forward, straining to accomplish one foot at a time. Upon reaching his mark, Pious furiously lashed the cords, exhaled, and then leaned back to suck more air and repeat the exhausting maneuver.

"The cursed cords are too short," he gasped. "Maid, get longer cords from the abbey storehouse on your next trip there, or by God ... Now, bring that stubborn donkey."

The priest's sullen companion grumbled and glared at her employer, weary of such illregard. She dropped her screaming infant into Karl's arms. "You, boy, hold her ... and hold her right, you idiot ... keep her head up with your hand ... fool."

A very nervous Karl stared helplessly at the crying baby as her mother stormed toward the stable.

"How long has Marta been with fever?" snapped Pious.

"Some days ... 'bout three days."

The priest nodded and rinsed his face and hands in a

bucket of water. He held a polished square of tin close to his face and studied his blurred image. Karl, though shamed by his own thoughts, yielded to them. *He is indeed the ugliest man I have ever seen! His smooth head looks like an egg perched on a black mountain of wool.*

The priest lowered the tin to look up his nose, then, satisfied, turned it to examine the dark mole on his left earlobe, picking lightly at the hairs growing from it.

The maid returned. "You may be 'bout your business ... your donkey is ready enough. This brat had best be bringing all this trouble for good purpose."

Sarcasm traced the man's response. "Well, good wench, the boy's poor mother lies sick with fever and ..."

"Fever! You give my child to the whelp of some plague-rotted peasant woman!" The woman bit off her words and snatched the infant from Karl, setting the babe unceremoniously in its nearby cradle. She grabbed hold of a stout broom handle and raged, "*Mein Gott*, how dare you bring fever to my child." She swung violently at the surprised boy, two hands welded to the broom in a position bearing some evidence of familiarity. "Begone you brat ... and you, too, priest ... out, out!"

Karl, flabbergasted and flustered, ran headlong for the door, dodging and ducking the cornstrand flail. Pious was close to the boy's heels, tripping through the doorsill and doing his best to dodge the broom.

Content for having driven the offenders a safe distance, the furious maid returned her broom to its corner, snapping and snorting a final word at her muttering employer and his young accomplice.

The panting priest adjusted the blanket on his forlorn donkey, cast a nervous glance at his darkened front door, and leaned close to Karl. "Hell on earth, boy, hell on earth. 'Tis barely worth the rewards," he mumbled.

Karl shrugged apprehensively, fearing the Frau might be watching, and waited nervously while the priest collected his wits, adjusted his habit and sandals, and climbed atop the patient beast.

Courage partly restored, Pious wrinkled his nose at his

house and whispered to Karl. "My son, the Good Book reminds us that it is better to sleep on the corner of thy roof than in the house of an angry woman!"

Karl smiled.

The two began their short jaunt to Weyer under a full sun, but before they traveled much distance a bailiff's deputy caught up to them. The man reined his mount gently and called to the priest with respect. "Have you come upon any outsiders, Father Pious?"

"Nay, my son. I am told an abbey guard lies wounded?"

"Nay, Father, not wounded. He's dead. Was Ansel of the night watch. Someone cracked his head on a rock outside the wall."

"Dear God above," said Pious. "I knew Ansel well."

"Take care, Father, and report the whereabouts of any strangers or any behaviors not usual. And I should tell you to keep a watch for groups of children passing near these parts on the new Crusade. Keep a hawk's eye for them; some say they're up to mischief. Some think maybe ..."

"*Ach*, nay, I doubt a child could have killed Ansel. He was a giant, and ..."

"Never you mind, Father. I've seen mere boys do the Devil's business in my day. Now I must be off."

Karl, at first troubled for the coincidence of Wil's absence and Ansel's murder, dismissed such thoughts as preposterous and turned his mind, instead, to the soldier's remark of children on Crusade. He had heard of no such thing, nor was he aware of many children joining men-at-arms on Crusade, save squires and pages.

"Pondering words of Crusade, boy?"

"Yes, Father, I am."

"*Ja, ja*, truth be told, I met with the abbot some Sabbaths past to discuss this very thing. We have considered how God's blessings might fall to our humble manors by its children following the vision of Nicholas of Cologne."

"What are you talking about? Who is Nicholas of Cologne and ... what vision?"

The priest cleared his throat and spat. "Good lad, the villages will be instructed to come to Villmar on the afternoon of Sabbath next. Pious shifted his weight to another hip. "You seem to be a lad of some discretion, so I'll tell you and you alone what the gathering is about. It would seem that our Lord has revealed His present hope for Palestine by favoring a vision on a young boy in Cologne who goes by Nicholas. According to the blessed lad, the children of our Empire shall recapture holy Jerusalem from the heathen Saracens who occupy it."

The flush of excitement in Karl's ruddy cheeks assured the priest of one recruit. The lad restrained his enthusiasm, however, and proposed an observation of some discernment. "But Father, the armies of our kings could not hold the Holy City against the infidels. How shall children win it back?"

Pious laughed. "Ah, yes, yes. It is innocence and purity which God is calling us to tender in this Holy Crusade. As in the days of Abraham and Moses, we offer our spotless lambs in His good service. Nay, He calls us not to bear arms, but to proffer purity.

"Nicholas has seen a vision in which an army of the Innocents of Christendom ford the mighty ocean on dry land ... as did Moses at the Red Sea. When the infidels see such a miracle and witness the devotion and the faith of our children, they shall not only yield Palestine to its rightful people, but they shall also bend their own hearts to the Holy Church and to the one true Savior."

Karl could barely contain his excitement. "How do we go? How do we join? What shall we do? When may we leave?"

"Calm yourself, lad," chortled the bouncing priest. "Nicholas and his host departed from Cologne and have entered Mainz a few days back to gather and put order to the march. But the abbey has learned of other manors to our east, some as distant as Eberbach and Bamberg, yielding their flocks toward the Rhine as we speak. We are certain that God shall show Nicholas the need to tarry for the others. Keep faith, boy. This manor shall not be denied its rightful place in such a pilgrimage as this."

Karl's imagination carried him to Jerusalem, the Holy City, as it was depicted on the tapestries of the abbey and the colored glass windows at the fore of its church. He could easily see its high, white walls and rounded towers; he could see himself marching, shoulder-to-shoulder, midst a huge column of Christian pilgrims bearing their crosses through the arched gates. Thinking only of adventure, the boy's legs lifted into a haphazard trot. He was sharply returned to matters-at-hand, however, by a stern reprimand of the priest who could no longer abide the bounce of the donkey the boy was dragging.

In short order, Karl spotted the roofs of Weyer, and he could hardly endure the eased pace. He wanted to race to his village and spread the news. But his heart suddenly seized when he remembered that his mother lay dying and that his brother's efforts were now shadowed in doubt.

Chapter 3
A BARGAIN STRUCK
AND THE MANOR GATHERS

Wil was relieved to yield the charge of his mother to
Frau Anka and he walked willingly, though somewhat apprehensively, toward the Laubusbach to
draw water for his chickens. Still edgy from the night's affair, he
was wary of conversation. He kept his eyes on the hay fields in
the meadows by the stream.

Surely, 'tis an uncommon season, he reflected. The boy
was well aware that the early drought had stolen the tender green of spring. The dry stubble of scythed hay was
browning, and the rye fields were stunted and stiff. The
leafed trees stood listless and stale alongside the taller
spruce whose dark needles were slightly browned and
hard. He arrived to the bank of the stream and dipped his
large pail into the sluggish water. He recalled pleasant
memories of his father's friend, Emma, who had once lived
at the village edge with her butterflies and gardens of flowers. "The Butterfly Frau!" He laughed aloud. He could still
remember sitting on her ample lap. A voice distracted him.
"Ho there, Wil, have you heard the news?"

Wil turned to see the broad face of the weaver bursting
with excitement.

"'Ave you not heard?"

"Um ... nay."

Frau Gerta, the carpenter's wife, forced her way between
the two, one elbow bent to secure a basket of eggs and the
other wrapped securely around the wings of a fat, orange-

billed goose. "*Ja, ja,*" she offered proudly. "I knows what's happened, I do." The hawk-nosed woman set down her reed basket and stifled her honking goose with a tight squeeze round the neck. "I tell you that a blessed monk was found dead in his bed and a guard is dead of a head bashin'."

Wil's chest tightened and an icy chill shivered through his limbs. His breathing quickened and his mind soon muddled. "*I could not have killed Ansel.*"

A loud, obnoxious belch took Wil's attention. He whirled to see Father Pious rolling off of his exhausted donkey in the center of the village path. With both feet planted securely on the ground, the priest straightened his twisted habit and wiped his hands across his sleeves. He heaved thick phlegm from his lungs and spat it to the ground, cleared his throat, and announced his presence.

"Good morrow, my flock."

The villagers knelt as he had taught them; all, that is, but Wil whose hair rose along his neck like an angry dog's. The lad stormed toward his hovel as the father and a chattering Karl passed through the yard gate.

Karl scampered ahead and politely held open the door. The priest, pleased with the respectful boy, smiled, then filled the narrow entrance, squeezing the morning's sunshine into thin shafts of dusty light.

Frau Anka stepped lightly from Marta's bedchamber, wiping her hands on her ankle-length gown. She promptly knelt to kiss the priest's hand, Maria following in kind. Karl stood proudly behind the priest, confident and hopeful for the blessing Father Pious's presence would surely bring.

But Wil burst through the door and folded his arms with a scowl that was offered with unreserved irreverence. The priest turned to the boy and extended his right hand. Wil stiffened.

"*Junge,*" said Father Pious sternly. "I believe thou hast forgotten thyself." He thrust his hand closer to the boy's face.

Wil sneered. "I should rather pucker my lips to the arse of a pig than that."

The priest threatened. "Bend thy knee and kiss the hand of this servant of God."

"No."

Father Pious slowly lowered his hand and frowned at the defiant boy. "I baptized thee, Johann Wilhelm, as well as thy brother, Karl, and thy sister, Maria. I blessed thy father when he followed duty and have been a protector of this household since that distant day." His voice grew louder. "It is no wonder to me that this family is suffering, with devil spirits like thy father's and thine sleeping under its roof." He spun and faced the others staring dumbstruck and horrified. "Leave me with this incorrigible."

Frau Anka, Maria, and Karl needed no further urging and they rushed out the door, Anka careful to leave it slightly ajar.

Pinked and bulging, Pious seethed at Wil. The nostrils in his bulbous nose flared as he drew a deep breath and stalked the rigid lad. "Johann Wilhelm!" he bellowed, "supposed son of the baker of Weyer. I believe thee to be the bastard child of Lucifer."

Wil opened his mouth to protest, but Pious increased his volume yet more. "Silence. Be silent, wicked son of Satan, or I'll surely summon the angels of glory to snatch thy pathetic, cursed soul and bind it in the Pit where it belongs."

The boy clenched his jaw, determined to hold fast.

Pious raised clenched fists high in the air and roared, "*In nomine Patris, et Filii, et Spiritus Sancti,* I strike thee down." His thick, right fist crashed against the side of Wil's face, splitting flesh by the cheekbone and knocking the boy backward onto the quilt covering his straw bed.

Father Pious charged forward, ready to strike once more when his crazed eye detected the corner of a leather bag now exposed in the straw. He stopped and pointed. "What is this? Hand it to me."

Wil hesitated and muttered an oath.

"I command thee to give that to me."

Wil snatched the bag and clutched it behind his back. "It is nothing of your account, nothing but an ..."

Pious lunged toward the lad and deftly caught him by the throat. He wrenched the bag from the gasping boy's grasp and pushed him hard away. The priest shook the bag's contents onto the table beside him, and, with a look of disbelief, stared at the supply of herbs and medicinal concoctions. He uncorked a small bottle and held the stopper close to his nose. "Humph ... Betony ... a remedy well suited for head fractures and ailments of the skull. One Brother Lukas knew well! Fool. It is thee who the soldiers seek. Ha! I knew this mischief had a devil to it. Murderer ... twice murderer. I'll surely delight in your hanging."

Wil was no longer the defiant intransigent. Instead he sprinted like a frightened child toward the door. But Pious, expecting the lad to run, thrust his left foot forward. The boy tripped through the hearth and crashed, headlong, against the table. The huge man then pounced on him like a hungry bee on a ripe pear. He jerked Wil up by the shoulders and suspended him against the wall, dangling both feet helplessly above the earthen floor.

The priest pushed his face close to Wil's. "Ha, ha! I'll truss you myself and drag you to the abbot."

Wil, rising to the urgency of his peril, gathered his poise with surprising speed and responded to Pious in a calm, though vexing voice. "When you drag me to the abbot, I'll have little choice but to confess my deeds."

Pious, intrigued, maintained his hold on the boy and waited for more.

"I'll offer my confession to the abbey's priest, and then I will share what I have seen of you and the deeds you have done in this house!"

The shocked priest stiffened and his quivering jowls lost their flush. His lips twitched a little and he began to relax his grip. Wil slid lightly to the ground.

"Whatever do you mean?" Pious said in a hoarse whisper. "You have seen nothing ... nothing has been here to see."

It was at that very moment that Wil knew he had turned the trap. The lad now stood erect, almost indignant. He brushed away the straw clinging to his rough clothing, strode confidently toward the table, and began to refill the herb bag. He was steady and well within his wits. "In just a moment I'll be quite ready to take our leave to the abbot."

The priest began to perspire and glanced, for the very first time, into Marta's bedchamber. He turned away and peered through the crack at the doorway into the wide eyes of Karl and Frau Anka. He stormed to the door and slammed it shut, then grabbed Wil by his ear and dragged him toward the far corner of the room.

Wil smirked. *Frau Emma was right*, he thought. *We are ne'er better than our secrets.*

Pious cleared his throat and quickly relaxed. He released the boy's ear and feigned composure. "Now, boy," he stated flatly, "I should like to know what you think you have seen. After all, the Holy Scriptures tell us to bear no false witness against a neighbor." Pious folded his hands, paternally. "Truth be told, lad, I am certain you had no part in Ansel's … misfortune. But, nonetheless, I should like to know what you think of other matters, for it would be most unwise for you to pass through life with some confusion of the facts." He smiled weakly, betrayed by a droplet of perspiration on his upper lip. The priest seated himself on a stool, as if to convey a comfortable familiarity, and set his sweating palms on his knees. "Now, just settle yourself and share thy thoughts and I'll pray for God to heal this day."

Wil, emboldened for having seen fear in his enemy, leaned forward and set his nose a hair's breadth from the man's. "You, priest, since the day you chased my father on his penance, have been favoring my mother with … undo attention."

Pious's face tightened and retreated from the boy's. "Well, of course," he stammered. "I should hardly be expected to abandon the family of such an obedient servant as your father. The bakery is a hard task … and … the apprentice was not sufficient … what with the abbot honoring the ancient vow of thy education. Your poor mother has had much need of attention, and …"

"Enough," snapped Wil. "Enough. My mother needed none of your attentions in her bed."

The priest leapt to his feet. He began pacing and wringing his hands. "That is a lie. That is a vicious lie. You are an ungrateful … lying whelp. Son of Sa—"

"I do not lie. You call yourself priest? Servant of God?" attacked Wil. "You are a servant of yourself. You are nothing but a wild boar on the prowl. You pretended your duty as a priest, but all you ever wanted was our mother's favor. I do wonder if it wasn't you who beguiled m'father into leaving. I have been told things ..."

"Your mother was a tired, lonely woman, hungry for a kind word and a bit of help. The abbot was considering ending your tutelage so you could better support the bakery. It was I who saved you. I. And ... and your mother was grateful for my help. I deny your accusation, boy, I deny it!"

Wil would listen no more and he struck a furious blow squarely on the end of the man's nose, dropping him to the floor with a cry. Wil's flashing eyes were a scalded blue, his lips red with rage, and his fair skin flushed with fury. He darted to his bed and plunged his right hand deep into the straw until his fingers found the haired handle of his dagger.

With blood pouring from both nostrils, Pious desperately tried to pull himself to his feet. But before the clumsy priest could stand, Wil knocked him to the floor again with a vicious strike to the side of the head. The man's eyes rolled slightly and he collapsed to his back. The lad sprang on his fallen adversary and placed both knees on his chest. He set his razor-sharp blade against the rolled fat under Pious's chin and growled, "Blasphemer! Enemy of God. Liar! Admit your crime or make ready to join your fellow demons in the Pit."

The priest lay motionless, his eyes now wide with fear. Too frightened to speak he waited helplessly as the angry boy held his life in the balance. Wil hesitated, then pressed the dagger's edge deeper into Pious's throat, releasing a thin thread of blood. The boy leaned close to the priest's face and hissed. "Tell me, dead man, tell me the truth. I want to hear it in your own words."

Pious trembled and nodded subtly, fearing to move. He whispered hoarsely, "Yes, yes. I did do this." Tears filled the man's eyes and he began to beg for his life.

The boy hesitated, caught between a horrid lust to carve

the man's throat and an unspoken voice urging he leave vengeance in the hands of Another. With a grunt he stood. "To your feet, you pig. I should have you kiss *my* hand for mercy granted."

Pious, white-faced and shaking, stood. "Wilhelm, I assure you that such a thing shall never happen again. Now let us ..."

Wil leaned forward. "Indeed. My mother lies near death behind you!"

The father squinted nervously through the dim-lit doorway and nodded. He dabbed the blood on his neck with his sleeved forearm and crumpled the folds of his robe to hold against his bleeding nose. "Your mother was always a beauty. She was lonely and I wished ..."

The flash in Wil's eyes reminded Pious how tentative his ground was, and so he changed course. He arranged his robe and gathered his wits. "My son, you are aware that should I tell the abbot of your night's visit to the abbey he would no doubt believe me. I have served this parish for nearly twenty years, have collected tithes faithfully and with no hint of impropriety. I am known throughout these valleys as a worthy Christian priest. On the other hand, should you accuse *me*, I should doubt his believing you ... an angry peasant boy caught in a crime."

Wil, prudent for his years, recognized how dangerously he was positioned. Despite the genuine affection of most of the monks, each would surely confess knowledge of the boy's disquieted and perhaps even suspicious nature. No doubt none could, or would, be able to defend his character with persuasive vigor or confidently assure the abbot of the unlikelihood of his deceit. Instead, Wil feared, each would bow to the prospect of his blame. As he considered his predicament, Wil also recognized that Pious must see no weakness at such a crucial moment. "I tell you this, Pious." Wil measured carefully. "We both have much to lose. But I care not one whit if I am flogged and hanged, or deported to the marshes. I would be content to suffer all knowing that, at the very least, you shall spend the rest of your pitiful days under a cloud of doubt."

The priest was wise to the game but unnerved, none-theless, by what kernel of truth might lie within the des-perate boy's words. *Indeed,* he thought, *what does this brat have to lose? His miserable life is worth little. And, though his charge would doubtless be dismissed, he is right to say the abbey would always have doubt ... as would the whole of Mainz. It would be my final undoing.*

"Well said, young fellow," Pious answered in a calculated tone. "Well said, indeed." He sighed dramatically. "Ah, but I do grow weary of this place, and the guilt of my sin weighs heavy. Perhaps this revelation would forever release me from both."

He eyed the boy, then continued slowly. "However, there may be a better way." Pious beckoned Wil to come close. "The Holy Church is sending thousands of her finest sons and daughters to settle new lands in the east, lands in the diocese of Magdeburg. You, Karl, and Maria would do well in such an enterprise. The lords are paying good wages and land is abundant, and—"

"We'll not be spending our lives clearing marshes to make another wealthy. Nay, this is no remedy."

"Ah, I see." Pious set a finger on his chin and narrowed his eyes as if deep in thought. "Then consider this: *Spiritus Sanctus* is stirring a new Crusade in the hearts of the blessed children of our Empire and in France. Perhaps you might consider enlisting in such a noble and righteous enterprise. What better way to do penance for your sins and for those your mother might be suffering? The passing of time shall, most assuredly, blur the unfortunate affair in the abbey. You would be filling thy heavenly coffers with gold. And, perhaps this pilgrimage might yield the time I need to do a just penance for my own sins."

"Or perhaps we'll never return," interrupted Wil. "And what of little Maria?"

"'Tis true enough." Pious nodded sympathetically. "The journey would be difficult and dangerous. I would be happy to look after Maria until thy return."

"Never," snapped Wil.

A long, silent pause followed, each eyeing the other

warily. But no more words were needed; the terms had been decided.

☙

Sabbath dawn bore a brilliant sunrise of red hues and puffed clouds. By late morning the air was summer sweet and fresh and a light breeze fluttered through the trees. Wil chose to remain with his mother while Karl and Maria joined the company of curious neighbors departing for the gathering in Villmar. As the sun climbed higher overhead, groups of Christian faithful began to pass by Weyer's church up the sharp incline leading to the ridge. Rumors of the past week's mysteries and of strangers on the manor traveled with the peasants, flourishing with the addition of new pilgrims from Oberbrechen and Selters. This fair day had a wonderful sense of promise about it, an inkling of surprise. The birds seemed to sense an occasion, and Karl was sure their chirping was louder than usual. He was quite convinced that even the rabbits bursting from bushes and darting through furrows had some extra spring in their quick feet.

As the clusters of folk began their long descent into the Lahn valley and the abbey at its center, Karl and Maria locked arms with the other village children to recite ancient rhymes and sing songs of the woodland. Their mood was contagious and parents and grandparents were soon enlisted in the merry choir. The happy melodies floated gently across the resting fields and drifted behind them to succeeding bands of pilgrims.

As the villagers drew nearer the abbey, they converged with the folk of more distant villages such as Emmerich, Lindenholz, and Niederbrechen, and tarried to behold the splendor of Villmar's valley sprawling before. "Look!" Karl pointed. "I've never seen it so glorious." Indeed, the day had presented the humble abbey in peculiar magnificence. The edifice was draped with handsome pennants of purple, red, and yellow. Standards bearing the Lord of Runkel's crest formed a colorful corridor leading to the opened oak doors of the western gate where trumpeters welcomed approaching knights and noblemen. It was as if the ancient edifice had been suddenly transformed by some miraculous Craftsman into the Holy City of the promised New Jerusalem!

Something good is afoot, thought Karl. *This place has n'er looked so.* He smiled at his fellows, and, despite their deformities, broken teeth, and tattered clothing he was certain he could see the radiance of God's face shining upon each of them this blessed day. Rumors continued to abound, among them one that either a papal legate or His Grace, the Archbishop Siegfried III of Mainz, was preparing to deliver a call of Crusade. Karl nearly burst keeping his secret. And, inside the abbey walls, a great assembly of noblemen and lords had supposedly gathered to pledge their unity in the Empire's civil war. The lords and their archbishop welcomed the prospect of victory and of the new lands it would proffer, and the Sabbath seemed a logical time for them to further bind their mutual ambitions.

The abbey's gate was soon clogged with throngs of folk funneling through and squeezing past each other until they spilled into the filling courtyard. As Karl pressed his way toward the church, excitement chased chills up his spine. He held Maria's right hand tightly and looked desperately for a good vantage. He hoped so very much to be able to see through the church's thick-glassed windows and gaze upon the sacred pedestal from which the message would be delivered.

Welcomed by piercing blasts from trumpeters positioned neatly along the top of the wall, a contingent of knights arrived and charitably maneuvered their steeds through the crowded gateway and into the courtyard. Their swords gleamed at their sides; their high, black boots shined in the summer sun; their gray, mail shirts were graced by flowing capes boldly bearing the colors and insignia of their lord. These men were sworn to support the pope in his claim for young Friederich II (son of the deceased emperor, Heinrich VI) to be Emperor of the Holy Empire, against his rival, Otto of Brunswick. Many proudly boasted bandaged wounds as evidence of their fealty. Others, fresh from the wars near Leipzig, brandished the colors of the vanquished Slavs and brandished their bedecked halberds and maces to the cheers of comrades within.

The long trumpets blew seven short blasts as a silent procession of ecclesiastics humbly entered the church. In the fore were the Archbishop of Mainz and an honorary legate from the Archbishop of Cologne, followed in close order by the entourage of clerks and priests. Behind these shuffled a column of shaved crowns in dark habits, the abbey's own Benedictines, led by the abbot, Udo, and in the rear, the archbishop's four parish priests, including Father Pious.

Karl joined his peasant brothers and sisters in bended knee, reverently and obediently offering due homage. The courtyard was silent and solemn, save the snorting of impatient horses in the grip of groomsmen and the peal of the great bell in the church tower. A brief gust of wind snapped the flags of Runkel and posed a fitting flourish for the column of *cives* and *milites* which then began their grand march.

In the fore strutted Lord Heribert himself, decorated like a peacock in full gloat. His ankle-length cloak was of the finest blue velvet, and silver hooks bound with satin cord laced his proud chest. A puffed, red-otter hat sat atop his shoulder-length waved hair, and sported a silver brooch. At his left strolled his fair wife, Christine. Eager for accolades and most deserving, she was garnished with a superb silk gown and golden clasps set securely in her reddish hair. To the lord's opposite side entered, with noted arrogance, the cupbearer and chamberlain of the Empire, each lifting aquiline noses high above the tiresome occasion to which they were assigned. Close behind streamed an impressive parade of counselors and merchants, burghers from distant free-towns, and an array of lesser lords and vassals. A singular kettle drum beat slowly as Heribert led his vassals across the straw-strewn floor of the church and took his place at the foot of the archbishop with the dignity befitting his title.

Some of the peasants found standing room in the rear of the crowded nave, but most pressed close to the church from positions in the courtyard. Karl wiggled himself to a reasonably good seat atop a beer barrel standing alongside a wide window of the church. With his sister on his lap, he peered through the blurred glass in hopes of watching every detail of the grand spectacle before him. "Oh Maria, 'tis wonderful. I know no other word for it."

Behind him and in contrast to the brightly adorned nobility standing inside, a multitude of shorn-headed peasants covered the abbey grounds like a dingy, tattered carpet. They remained on their knees and hushed, waiting respectfully for permission to stand. These poor souls knew their position in the Creation and yielded in holy submission to the order which had presented itself before them. All, that is, save young Tomas, the apprentice of Weyer's bakery, who defiantly stood by a distant wall whispering into the ear of a snickering woodland witch.

The small, frail abbot commenced the gathering by shouting a customary prayer through the doors opened on three sides. Karl was one of a special few in the courtyard who could understand, having been educated in Latin by the monks. But the others in the massed congregation listened in respectful ignorance, letting their ears be filled with the strange language of heaven.

Karl turned his eyes to the rows of monks' heads bowed grimly along their segregated gradines. He thought of Lukas and a lump filled his throat. The brother had been a humble man. His life had been one of unselfish service and genuine love without regard to estate. Lukas had reflected the grace of God to all and, in the end, what better legacy could any man leave? Karl sighed sadly.

Three sharp blasts of the trumpeters allowed the serfs to rise. The mass of serfs now filling the courtyard stood patiently on dusty, bare feet, most faces grimy and smudged despite the Sabbath scrubbing expected of them. Old men with thin, white hair leaned hard on knotty staffs alongside younger folk, and old women, stooped and crooked with years of hard labor, peered from wrinkled eyes toward the dignity of the sturdy stone church before them. Young and old, they packed together in their belted, gray-brown woolen tunics, blending together like a giant calico. An occasional ribbon or bright sash evidenced gain for some, but these were scattered about and ignored by resentful peers. Little children sat contentedly atop their loving fathers' broad shoulders and infants were clutched close to the breasts of young mothers. Karl believed them to be the noblest assembly he had ever seen.

While waiting, Karl's legs began to numb and he set his little sister's feet atop the barrel as he slid to the ground. He turned a kindly glance to her and studied her as she stood above him. His eyes met hers and she graced him with the gentle smile that seemed to always warm her delicate countenance.

An angel, thought Karl, *an angel on this earth.* He returned an earnest, kindly smile and watched the wind play with her fine, flaxen hair. He noticed her cheeks, pink and chubby, and her ruby-red lips. *Were it not for the tiny brown mole on her left earlobe, her face would be spotless,* he thought. As he looked down her slight form he paused briefly at her withered left arm and he followed its strange shape, suddenly saddened. *Perhaps she suffers from someone's sin. Perhaps mine own. Oh, why should she suffer with such a thing?*

Maria's arm was shortened just past the elbow and in place of her hand were two deformed appendages that served as fingers. And for her imperfection she bore the abuse and mockery of manor child and elder alike, all claiming her to bear the mark of the Devil or the brand of secret sin. Only her brothers and a handful of others ever rose to her defense. It was not uncommon for both Karl and Wil to return home bruised and bleeding for their stubborn devotion, usually to be scolded by their mother for ripped leggings.

Karl lowered his eyes from her arm to her tiny feet, callused and tough from traveling the stony pathways. He drew a deep breath, sighed, and raised his eyes to meet hers once again. Maria was still smiling. "What a good day, Karl," she squealed. "What a good day!"

Chapter 4
THE CALL TO CRUSADE

The church bell echoed loudly throughout the abbey's grounds and Karl tingled with excitement. With sunlight streaming in thick shafts through both colored glass and plain, the entourage of ecclesiastics bowed to positions behind the modest pulpit and the monastery's abbot stood alone. Dressed in humble vestments, the old Benedictine lifted his hands in a protective gesture over his flock and, after a few formal pronouncements, began to speak in native tongue.

"My beloved children, it is our counsel that we have been beset by a mischief from another world. We have buried dear Brother Lukas, our dear friend, who we have discerned was murdered by poison. And, on the evening prior, a good man, Ansel of Limburg, was laid to his eternal rest, also a victim of fiendish ends."

Udo continued. "The Evil One sees all and his reach extends where he will. We are offered our spiritual protection by God and His angels, but not without due homage. Our lords and sovereigns have been mightily blessed with great victories in the east, yet they now fear all shall be lost for the evidence of sin which now abounds in this place. This day was to have been a day of merry, a day of rejoicing for God's bounty in victories granted. Instead, woeful children, thy secrets have invited the legions of the Pit among us.

"Yet, you are our beloved children. So I say to all, this day shall not pass lest we have committed ourselves to join with you in a great penance. We seek God's divine and boundless mercy, we beg the aid of our Virgin Mother, we seek the counsel of others ... for we are all sinful and degenerate sheep."

He raised his hands higher. "I say to you again, my dear children, poor souls, my dear, dear, tender flock, we have sinned against all heaven. We have allowed darkness to loom in our land. You have been entreated for some years to join our Holy Church in settling its new lands in the east and in the north. But few have obeyed. Instead, all stay, selfishly crowding our poor manors. We have paid dearly for thy protection by our worthy neighbor, Lord Heribert. Yet I hear only of grumblings and complaints among you, rebellion and scheming such that Moses never suffered."

The abbot lowered his arms and closed his eyes. "Fairest Lord Jesus, ruler of all Nations, Son of God and Son of Man. Thee will I cherish. Thee will I honor...."

The old man stopped as if overcome by grief for his wicked people. He generously blessed them with the sign of the Cross, bowed his head, and backed away from the pulpit.

The congregation in the courtyard spread his words, then remained absolutely silent, troubled and confused by the reprimand. Karl trembled, overcome with fear and shuddering at the thought of Lucifer's hand around his mother's throat. The powerful Archbishop of Mainz gathered his robes and approached the simple oak pulpit with the legate at his side. Except for the warm breezes that toyed with the pennants and drapes, nothing moved. It was as if an unseen hand had hushed all tongues and turned all faces now fixed on the ambassadors from heaven.

The archbishop stood tall and erect in the ample, silken robes which flowed to the tops of his black shoes. Large, bright red crosses were sewn on each breast of his yellow chasuble and a dark green stole with a white underlining hung neatly across his shoulders. His brass headpiece reflected points of light from the sun-rays beaming through the windows, conferring on him an ethereal authority. The legate, an honorary appointment from the diocese of Cologne, stood by his side in equal splendor. He fixed his hands tightly to his red stole and arched his back forward as he peered into heaven.

His Grace raised his golden crosier over his flock and pronounced a blessing to all gathered, then stood quietly to appraise the congregation. The fix of his steely eyes and the remarkable potency of his silence captivated prince and peasant alike. The souls gathered before him waited anxiously, filled with an anticipation that nearly begged aloud for him to begin.

Then, at last, almost as if it were an act of mercy, the archbishop began to speak. "Come, my children, listen to us, for we'll instruct you in the fear of the Lord. The Evil One is in thy midst and you have suffered most terribly at his filthy hands. For that, you have my heartfelt pity and the merciful sympathy of our Lord. And He shall lead you to His bosom.

"I see in thy faces that you be filled with dread for thine own plight, but what terror do you counsel for the sad course of others? Shame be on thy heads. This selfsame wicked dark Prince of the Air prowls *all* the world. Even as I speak, he leisures in Palestine, the very land of our Lord. You may weep for *thy* troubles, but for six generations the strong hearts of Christendom have yielded life, limb, and fortune to restore the Land of Promise to the People of the Covenant.

"While you rest in thy peaceful valley, our Lord God pleads, 'My land cries out against me and all its furrows are wet with tears. They came up with their livestock and their tents like swarms of locusts, they invaded my land to ravage it.'

"Shame on those who sing songs to God while these locusts, these Saracen infidels, these children of the Wicked One, desecrate the very soil that Christ Himself walked upon." The archbishop looked to the heavens, then backed away to leave the pulpit to the legate, a large man of middling years named Paulus who once hailed from Hohenstaufen— the homeland of the old emperor, Barbarossa.

"If I forget thee, O Jerusalem," Paulus cried, "may my right hand forget, may my tongue cling to the roof of my mouth, if I do not consider Jerusalem my utmost joy. The great fortress of God is abandoned, the noisy city is deserted, citadel and watchtower have become a wasteland forever. Our God's house has become the delight of donkeys, a pasture for flocks."

The legate drew a deep breath and bellowed, "For the Lord says, 'The land I have given to Abraham and Isaac, I also give you, *my children*. They shall neither hunger nor thirst. Nor shall the desert heat or sun beat upon them. You shall be led beside springs of water.'

"Dear children, please come and I'll turn my mountains into roads and my highways shall be raised up. You shall come from afar … from the north."

Paulus softened his tone and turned a kindly, gentle eye out the windows and onto the children scattered throughout the silent courtyard. He motioned them to the bishop's guards. "Bring them to me. Suffer the children to come unto me." He waited patiently, like an indulgent grandfather on a summer Sabbath. The footmen hurried throughout the courtyard and beckoned the wide-eyed children to hurry to the nave where they slowly, almost fearfully, forced themselves between the hips of the astonished adults pressed in around them.

"*Komme, meine Kinder,*" cried the legate. "Come, all my children, and gather before my feet. Sons of shepherds and daughters of ploughmen … come, come you all … all my dear children come."

Karl was as stunned as the others but quickly snatched Maria by her hand and squeezed his way into the sanctuary. Flushed with excitement and nearly trembling with anticipation, the boy and his sister joined their peers near the front of the church.

The legate called twice more for the children to come and, at last, nearly a third of the church was filled with their awestruck faces. The displaced nobility crowded to the margins and viewed the spectacle with notable annoyance, but Paulus smiled kindly. "My precious lambs," he said softly, "thank you, every one, for hearing the Word of thy Lord … for a great task lies before you. It may be that some already know of those Christian youth who have begun a march to carry the good news of our Savior to the heathen occupiers of Palestine."

The children stirred, few having heard any such report.

"'Tis true. An army of children is gathering in the Empire

and in France to rescue Jerusalem. They are marching now and need you, each and every one. Perhaps this sad manor might be rid of its evil presence should such piety be found midst you as well? By faith, I do believe bounteous blessings await this manor should it join its lambs to the flock preparing for Palestine.

"Indeed. God has granted visions of you crossing into Palestine on dry land. *Ja*, as did the Hebrews cross the Red Sea. Oh, dear ones, offer thyselves to the will of thy loving Father in heaven. You depart not with bow or spear or dagger, but rather with gentleness and meekness and simple faith ... weapons against which stands no defense."

The cleric was contented by the immediate enthusiasm evident on the faces of the innocents, but he became alarmed at an uneasiness spreading among their parents now crowding every portal. Sensing reluctance, the man turned his attention to the murmuring elders. He set his face squarely on those eyes narrowing toward him and stretched his open hands over the heads of the little ones at his feet. "He tends His flock like a shepherd; He gathers the lambs in His arms and carries them close to His heart."

The man paused to stand his hooked staff against the pulpit. He clutched his heart and cried to the congregants, "I am convinced that neither life nor death, neither angels nor demons, neither the present nor the future, nor any powers, neither height nor depth, nor anything else in all creation is able to separate these little ones from the love of God that is in Christ, our Lord."

He lifted his chin high and shouted, "I trust not in my bow, my sword does not bring us victory, but thou shalt grant us victory over our enemies, thou shalt surely put our adversaries to shame."

He bent toward the children near his feet and placed his hands on his knees. "You little ones were once in darkness, but now you are in the light. Live as children of the light so that you may be found blameless and pure, children without fault in a crooked and depraved generation. Shine like stars in the universe so that you may boast on the Day of Christ that you did not march in vain."

Karl was speechless. It was as if his heart had been lifted to the heavenly realm. He was convinced that God was speaking to him through this holy man.

Paulus continued as he returned to his pulpit. "Dear children, this is the last hour, a new age is dawning. *Now* is a time for the innocents of Christendom to claim dominion. Our own emperor, Friederich II, is but himself a child, and the visions have been granted to mere boys of ten and twelve. The words of our Lord ring true to me: 'I praise thee, Father, Lord of heaven and earth, because thou hast hidden these things from the wise and revealed them to … *little children.*'"

Paulus paused, then raised his eyes again to the elders. "Thy children shall be mighty in the land, 'tis true, and the generation of the upright shall be blessed. Wealth and riches shall come to you and thy righteousness shall endure forever. Good shall come to you who are generous and lend of thy loved ones freely.

"Oh, dear fathers and good mothers," wailed the churchman, "thy sons and daughters are a heritage from the Lord. Like arrows in the hands of a warrior are sons born in thine youth. Blessed are those whose quiver is full for they shall not be put to shame." The legate's words did not miss their mark. Indeed, apprehensions began lifting like fog past prime.

Paulus turned his face toward the slack-jawed children beneath him and adroitly closed the net. "Children, obey thy parents in all things for this pleases God. Listen carefully to my words: If you be children, then you be heirs of God. Indeed you share in His sufferings in order that you might also share in His glory.

"I send you not to an easy place, but to a hard place, and you shall shoulder the Holy Cross as did our dear Lord. You, my dear, dear children, are sent from God to overcome, for the One who goes with you is greater than the Evil One that is in this world."

The man's constricting eyes swept the congregation. "*If* the Lord is pleased with you, He shall surely lead you into that land ... a land flowing with milk and honey. Go up and take possession of it! Be not afraid and do not be discouraged."

He stared heavenward, now nearly weeping. "And the little ones, dear God, Thy children who know not yet good from evil, they shall enter Thy land. Thou shalt bestow it upon them, and they shall surely take hold of it. Then all mankind shall truly know that Thou art Jehovah, the Redeemer, the Lion of Judah. With windstorm and tempest and flames of a devouring fire, go before this flock of Thy most precious lambs. May Thine many enemies become like fine dust; the ruthless hordes like blown chaff.

"For the wolf shall live with the lamb, the leopard shall lie down with the goat, the calf and the lion and the yearling together ... and the *little child* shall lead them. The *infant* shall play near the hole of the cobra, and the *young child* put its hand into the viper's nest. They shall neither harm nor destroy *any* on Thine holy mountain."

He relaxed a little and secured both hands on the lapels of his robes. "Brave children, the Lord is bringing you into a good land; a land with streams, and pools of water with springs flowing in the valleys and hills. A land with wheat and barley, vines and fig trees, pomegranates, olive oil, and honey. The land you shall take possession of is a land of mountains and valleys that drink rain from heaven."

Paulus closed his eyes. "On a day soon, a song shall be sung in the land of Judah. Open the gates, O Jerusalem, that the righteous *children* may enter in. Keep perfect peace, O my God, for those whose minds are steadfast. Help them trust in Thee forever, O Lord, our Lord, the Rock eternal!"

He opened his eyes and stood quietly for a long moment. Then, with a pleading, inspiring voice he cried, "Children of Christendom ... will you join in Holy Crusade? Will you join with the others and deliver Palestine from her oppressor? Will you serve the Almighty and His Holy Church and enter, victorious, the gates of Jerusalem?"

Unable to restrain himself a moment longer, a young lad jumped in the air and cried, "I'll go, blessed Father! I'll go!"

Then, as if a gust of wind suddenly rushed through the abbey, voices from every corner echoed the boy's cry. "Yes!

Yes! We go ... we go!" Children shouted and cheered, stamped their feet and danced. A wild scramble of child crusaders then poured out the church's doors and spilled into the courtyard. "We go! We go to God!" Many parents, now caught in the moment, laughed and sang, for they would now be heirs, heirs of blessing in a Holy Crusade—a Children's Crusade!

Smiling, the legate backed away from the pulpit. Abbot Udo seemed anxious and he stared forward slack-jawed and speechless. The archbishop stood and nodded to the legate politely, though another's sharp eye might have noticed a hint of restrained objection. His Grace reordered his vestments and slowly quieted his congregation with his raised crosier. After waiting patiently, he finally commanded the bell tower to peal. Then, having gained some measure of control he spoke solemnly. "Know this: that you are sent out like lambs among wolves. Go with God in faith; go with our prayers that He will deliver thee from thine enemies."

The archbishop raised his arms in farewell, grasping his staff with his right hand and extending it over the heads at his feet. He closed his eyes and, with a rising voice, pronounced, "Trust in the Lord and do good. Dwell in the land and enjoy safe pasture. Delight thyselves in the Lord and He shall bestow upon you the desires of thy heart. Commit thy way to the Lord, trust in Him and He shall do this. He shall make thy righteousness shine like the dawn, the justice of thy cause like the noonday sun."

Then he held his place as if numbed by his own words and stood in absolute silence. His audience hushed. He stared at the heights of the ceiling with a look of sudden anguish, arched his back, and stretched his arms wide as if to embrace all heaven and earth. Then he prayed silently, and turned away.

ॐ

Wil had spent this unusual Sabbath nagged by curiosity and he listened with piqued interest to the bells that tolled without good order. He had wrestled with a gnawing guilt over Ansel's death, but now dismissed it as an accidental act of self-defense. To escape his nagging conscience, he minded his ailing mother and passed time studying Lukas's medicinal herbs and roots that he had strewn about his table. He pinched a bit of this and that and held the ground herbs to his nose. Some smelled sweet, others musty, but he recognized few. Several labels had been fortuitously scratched on the pottery vials and the tops of the tins. He shook a handful of dried plants from a wallet and was able to identify thyme and buckthorn. *Ah, there.* The boy brightened. *Yes, thistle and sage, rue and hyssop. These I do know well. And here, sweet mint and camomile. Thanks be to Emma. I should have listened better.*

He recalled Father Pious's suggesting he find *atropa belladonna* for his mother's fever, and though void of affection for the priest, Wil thought the medicinal advice worthy of consideration. Upon close examination of an etching on a narrow tin, he deciphered the faint inscription, "X Atropa Bel." The rest was too worn to read. Content to have found the herb of choice, he proceeded to brew an infusion for his mother.

Marta had shown some surprising improvement during the day and her fever seemed somewhat lessened. "Drink this," Wil offered. He secretly hoped she would notice he had delivered the brew in her favorite clay dish.

Marta cupped the bowl with trembling hands and lifted the hot brew to her lips. She sipped gingerly, then pursed her lips and frowned. "Too hot! And what is it ... some witch's steep, little man?" she scolded.

"No, mother," sighed Wil. "'Tis a potion proposed by the priest ... a remedy for the fever and you'd be well to take it down."

"Father Albert, I hope," snapped Marta hoarsely.

"Nay, Father Pious," answered Wil curtly.

"Pious! I should like nothing more that man has to offer." She set the bowl on her lap and looked away.

Wil nodded. "Aye, but an herb is an herb."

Marta stared at the drink before lifting it again to her lips. "This hardly fills the belly. Get me soup."

Wil dutifully went to the common room and gathered a handful of dried peas, some millet, and a scallion from the row of crocks shelved near the door. He stepped outside to the barrel and ladled some water into his iron kettle when he heard the first sounds of returning villagers. He squinted his eyes in the fading light of mid-evening and strained his ears to the distant groans and creaks of old wagons. *More food ought be thrown in the kettle,* he thought, and as the shuffling feet of beast and peasant filled the hamlet, a thin gruel began to steam over hot coals.

An oxcart paused to unload Karl and Maria and the two charged through the door of the house. "Oh, Wil!" exclaimed the excited boy. "This day is unlike any other. The manor's children are preparing to go to God on the great Crusade Father Pious told us about. The village children are making ready to leave at dawn to march to the great city of Zion with 'neither bow nor sword nor dagger' to reclaim all of Palestine for God!"

Wil answered bluntly, "Good for them, but we've a sick mother to attend. Have Maria feed her, and you eat." He turned and walked out the door.

"But Wil," persisted Karl as he chased after him, "Father Pious says our mother can only be healed by penance. He told me whatever sins our family suffers can be redeemed through our going."

Wil held his tongue for a moment, looking first at Maria and then Karl. He walked slowly back to the hearth and squatted. "What about *her*?" he asked, pointing to their sister. "Would you force Maria to Palestine for a churchman's lie? Why not just make her swim to Cathay and save *all* the world!"

"We are all under God's protection. The Church swears to us that God goes with us. 'We'll be borne by the wings of angels,' the priest from Cologne said, and what of the visions of Stephan and Nicholas? They have been shown the sea opening for us as it did for Moses. God will provide, Wil. Where is your faith?"

Wil stood to his feet and spat. "Where is my faith? Ha! Where are your brains?"

"But Wil," said Maria softly, "see, we each have our cross to carry." She held up three wooden crosses made of apple sticks lashed with hemp twine.

Karl added proudly, "I cut them from the abbey orchard and they were blessed by a priest from Mainz." He clutched one close to his heart with both hands. "I beg you, dear brother, we must Crusade, we must go for God. Frau Anka says she'll stitch red crosses on our shirts."

Wil stared into the *mus* bubbling at his feet for several quiet moments. He struggled with the agreement he and Pious had made. His mind raced. *I must needs leave this place, I want to be gone from here ... I have always wanted away. But dare I abandon that old hag in there ... dare I take poor Maria? What to do?* The tormented lad threw the wooden ladle into the gruel and snapped, "I'll make our decision on the morrow, but we'll not go at dawn ... and that is the end of it."

Karl, disappointed but submissive, filled his plate slowly while Maria scampered away to tend their mother. Wil, sullen and withdrawn, retreated to the refuge of his bed and closed his eyes.

"But you did say you'd decide by prime?" blurted Karl.

"*Ja, ja* ... by terce to be sure. Now be done with your slurping and go to sleep."

Karl was not easily quieted. He was bursting with anticipation, his blue eyes wide and bright, his cheeks red and glowing in the firelight. Unable to sleep, he turned to Wil again. "I learned a new riddle today."

Maria returned and sat crossed-legged on her bed, waiting. Wil covered his ears and groaned. "Nay, Karl, not now. I thought you quit on these fools' riddles."

⮞

Dawn broke early to Wil's mind, though hardly quick enough for the excited Karl. The redhead bounded from his bed and rushed about his chores, paying no attention whatever to the pleasant breezes bending the fields of rye overlooking Weyer. The bakery apprentice, Tomas the Schwarz, stood in the doorway waiting to attend his duties.

Poor Tomas was a foundling; rescued an infant's death from the rear of a shearing shed where an unknown mother had abandoned him to freeze some fourteen years prior. His blazing, black eyes and black hair earned him his surname.

He was a distant, bitter boy, with sinewy muscles stretched tightly over a tall frame. The monks had cared for him in some respects, providing adequate food and shelter, but they failed in offering affection or instruction. Unable to confine the angry lad within the abbey walls, he was released to serve as apprentice to the peasant's bakery two years ago.

Tomas pointed a long finger at the group of children now gathering behind the wheelwright's shed. "Be y'going by this fools' Crusade?" he asked Wil.

Wil shrugged. "Perhaps, though not today."

Tomas nodded. "'Tis a way to escape this miserable place."

Suddenly Frau Anka bustled from a flock of village mothers toward the two boys, waving her arms and calling to them. "Come, m'boys. Come do the will of God. Join the others. We've your red patches ready and ... why do you stand there, Wil? Pious said y'd be leaving!"

Wil and Tomas looked at her and said nothing. Frustrated, the husky woman snarled and grabbed Wil by the hair on the side of his head. "Come with me!"

Wil jerked back, wincing. "Nay, Frau, I'm needed here."

"But y'needs do the penance! The village needs all of you to save us."

"Do your own penance, you old sow," muttered Wil.

Weyer's children were gathering amid the well-wishes of suddenly reluctant elders. A strange uneasiness had begun to stir, a nervous rustling like anxious leaves before a storm. The sun was rising in a blue sky, and Karl and Maria looked wistfully at the growing numbers of familiar faces waiting by the village well for Father Pious's blessing.

At last the priest appeared on his forlorn donkey and he rolled off in his usual manner. The crusaders gathered in a half-circle as Pious approached. He ceremoniously held a large, silver crucifix before his placid face and muttered a prayer.

Karl and Maria stood slightly to the side of the others and listened intently as Father Pious offered his blessing and words of encouragement. Karl looked jealously at his friends. There was Otto, the miller's son, a rather sturdy, blonde boy of thirteen with freckles and bright green eyes. Beside him wobbled Lothar, Otto's youngest brother, a mere four years old and still chubby and soft. And close by the trunk of the linden stood Ingrid, a yeoman's daughter, with her sister, Beatrix, of about eight. Karl thought Ingrid was pretty; he loved how her long red hair was knotted at the base of her craning neck and how she smiled so gently. He always liked Ingrid and, with a sheepish grin, he waved an affectionate good-bye.

Maria whispered to her blushing brother, "Look, Ingrid takes her little brother, too … and he can barely walk. How shall he get to Palestine?"

Karl heaved his chest. "Because God goes with him." He waved to this one and that, and then to three of his second cousins: Georg, sixteen; Wolfhard, fourteen; and Richarda, twelve. They were the children of his father's first cousin, Richard, who had joined the fight against the Stedingers and also never returned.

Over a score of Weyer's children now waited bravely, dressed as they always were in their homespun clothing. The boys, of course, wore leggings—a few wearing them atop shorter linen under-leggings. On their upper bodies they wore hooded, woolen tunics, cut at mid-thigh like field serfs, and bound with rope belts. The girls wore linen under-gowns that were sleeveless and fell to their ankles. Atop this they wore sleeved, woolen over-gowns that also fell to their ankles and were bound by belts. Few had shoes, though some wrapped their feet in strips of cowhide or pigskin. None carried a cloak, though some tied rolled blankets to their backs, and each gripped their handheld wooden crosses proudly. Most had their faces scrubbed before leaving and had their stomachs filled, but few were stocked with provisions.

Pious vowed that they would be fed and sheltered by the angels, for "not a sparrow falls without God knowing." He concluded his blessing, pronounced his benediction, and extended his hand to the company kneeling at his feet. The young crusaders then rose, one by one, to kiss the hand of their priest and the silver crucifix he held to their lips.

To Karl the moment was enchanted, save the impatience it

incited in his heart. He closed his eyes for an instant and pictured his triumphant entrance through the arched gates of the Holy City.

Karl turned to see Maria smiling and waving a final farewell to young Lothar and he suddenly realized that he had no more time to savor the occasion. His good friends were truly on their way. They were standing in a column and beginning to sing.

Pious pointed them southwestward on the Oberbrechen road. "Follow the Laubusbach to Oberbrechen," he told them, "then overland to the mighty Rhine." He instructed them to turn south at the Rhine and find the city of Mainz where they'd reach the main column. From there, he said, they would travel through the great mountains into a strange land, then cross the sea to set their feet on Holy Ground. "Afore St. Michael's Day," Pious cried, "you shall all be fixing your crosses in Jerusalem."

❧

Two days quickly passed and on the final evening of June an impatient Father Pious arrived at the baker's hut with Frau Anka. "You shall soon not catch the others," he warned. "I believe, Wilhelm, that you ought honor thy prior thoughts on this matter ... thoughts that served thee and thine so very well." He raised an eye, then turned to Karl. "And you, you whom God has touched with a special heart, know well what is thy duty. Has thy faith failed thee? Has courage fled away? Or, perhaps you have lost thy love of God. Woe to thy poor mother."

"*Ja*, boy," Anka snapped. "If y've no love for God left, then be out with it. But then say that y've no love for your mama, for she clings to life waiting for your penance. You, Karl, know more than this doltish brother of yours that God only loves those who obey."

Pious nodded and folded his arms atop his rotund belly.

Karl twirled the edges of his tunic and stared at the floor. He cast a quick glance at the steely-eyed Wil, who stormed from the common room and into his mother's bedchamber. Marta had gone from bad to better and to bad again. She was sleeping but breathing quick, short breaths. Wil stood by her side, staring at the wet cloth in his hand.

Suddenly, the priest appeared in the room. He said nothing but leveled his eyes at the boy. Wil stiffened but held his ground like a cornered fox. Each knew the other's mind, however, and there would be no conflict this day, no parry and thrust of words, no threats or insults, no oaths nor blasphemy. Instead, Wil yielded. He gave his mother a half-teared glance and simply said, "We go on the morrow."

So, true to his word, Wil rallied his brother and sister before the next day's lauds and ordered them about their proper duties in candlelight. He gathered what food as could be carried and laid it along the table. He packed the medicines he took from Lukas in the satchel, though he set most of his mother's herb by her kettle. The lad quietly directed Karl and Maria to bind what they could in their thin quilts and make ready for their journey.

Tomas suddenly appeared in the doorway. "I wish to go with you."

"Why?"

"I want to leave this place," said Tomas.

Wil eyed the boy's sack and noticed shoes on his feet.

"How did you come upon those?"

"Uh ... Pious gave them to me if I'd go."

Wil hesitated. Tomas was not trustworthy. Wil quickly reasoned it might be better if the boy was away from the family bakery. "*Ja* ... you may join with us ... but at the first trouble you'll be marching alone."

Tomas shrugged as Wil walked back to his mother's room with Karl and Maria. The three knelt respectfully at her bedside. It was not an easy moment for any of them, Karl least of all, as they each took a turn kissing her hand. He struggled to hold a torrent of tears at bay, his face contorting and swelling with every passing breath. Maria wrapped her tiny arms round her mother's sweated head and wept openly. Wil tightened his jaw and turned from the room as Anka entered the hut.

"I don't know your game, y'old hag," Wil grumbled with a curled lip. "But I am quite sure you've an eye on this house, the bakery, and our half-hide. I warn you and that rotted old husband of yours that we'll return. And when we do, you had best not laid a hand on any what's not yours."

Anka, red-faced, answered, "And who shall pay the death tax for your miserable *Mutti*?"

"Give the bailiff a hog ... and no more. By God I swear, woman, you had best be on your guard for my return. And know this, too. I've the miller watching how m'mother is nursed. I had better have a good report or may God have mercy on you! Now, look here...." Wil directed Anka to the herb. "Pious says we ought give this to her thrice a day. If she lives, you shall have a quarter of our land at my return. I have foresworn it to Father Albert."

Anka grunted. She had been Marta's childhood friend but had spent most of her years envious and coveting. She picked up the tin and nodded.

"Now, leave us."

Anka strutted out the door, leaving the baker's family quite alone. Wil beckoned Karl and Maria to his side, and the three stood quietly at their doorsill for just another moment. They listened to the crowing cockbirds and the early morning rustle of the village. Each seemed to know this would be the last morning of things as they had always been.

Wil adjusted Lukas's worn satchel on his shoulder and secured Ansel's dagger in his belt. Karl clutched his necklace and prayed that the Virgin would spare his mother. Maria smiled and plucked a small wildflower from the ground. They each then whispered their mother "Godspeed," and, without ceremony or song, they and Tomas stepped onto the footpaths of Weyer.

The air was cool and clean; the sun was rising bold and bright. It was then, in the earliest light of the first day of July in the year of grace 1212, that the four began their journey.

Chapter 5
PIETER THE BROKEN

He was baptized Johann Pieter, third son of Otto, Duke of Franconia, on the twenty-seventh day of August in the year of our Lord 1135. A bright and quick-witted student, he had excelled in his studies under the severe tutelage of the school masters at Aachen. His unabashed curiosity and uncommon intelligence eventually earned him entrance into the highly regarded University of Bologna and private study in Salerno and at the prestigious and exacting library at Worms.

Despite his scholastic excellence, Pieter's inclination toward lighthearted mischief had rankled the furrowed brow of more than one of his narrow-eyed examiners. Yet the gentle spirit and soft heart that so clearly underpinned his playfulness inevitably won the affections of the most rigid of his masters.

Pieter married once but suffered a widower's agony shortly thereafter. Brokenhearted but determined, he received his Master of Arts in philosophy from the University of Cologne at the age of twenty on a cool, bright October morning. But no sooner had he gripped the coveted rolled parchment in his steady hand than he announced his intention to abandon the lofty world of the mind. "Instead," he stated flatly, "I'll measure my steel by the bitter business of combat."

And so, despite the pleas and prayers of priest and pedagogue alike, Pieter abandoned further education and bowed his knee to Friederich the Fat of Bremen as a sergeant-in-training for his formidable order of Saxon knights. The spirited young man spent a cold winter of harsh training within the damp and foreboding fortress at Bremen. Friederich's hard-eyed instructors taught their earnest liegeman the macabre arts of warfare, and the youth learned well. Though adequate with a long-sword, he seemed particularly adept with the crossbow, lance, and flail.

Pieter's first encounters with the horror of battle had proven him to be a loyal and courageous soldier, cunning and fierce, but with a ready heart of mercy and compassion. His broad shoulders and sinewy arms bore well his chain mail shirt and leather vest. Long, brown curls draped below the turned edges of his steel helmet, and his large hands gripped the fearsome flail he faithfully carried. Friederich loved him as a son and described him as having "the heart of a lion but the disposition of a court puppy."

His valor in the bloody battle at Tortona was chronicled by Friederich's secretary and read ceremoniously to the court of Barbarossa himself; for it was none other than the stouthearted Pieter who had rallied his troop of footmen to rescue a battered unit of mounted knights from their encircling enemies. The Lombardian *duces* of Milan had all but closed their fist around Friederich and his beleaguered Saxons when the full fury of Pieter's charge crashed against the enemy's flank. A savage butchery released the Germans from the snare, and the day was won, though at a terrible cost.

So, before the assembled host of his knights, a grateful Friederich the Fat intended to knight Pieter and grant him a large tilled and pastured fief in Saxony. But on that glorious morning the young man looked up from bended knee and humbly declined the generous offer. He was heard to whisper, "Forgive me, my lord, but there is no necessity of reward for duty done, nor am I able to pleasure in any such token of slaughter." Pieter had lost his lust for battle—and he was relieved for it.

Young Pieter, ever purposed, returned to a more ordinary life to re-enlist his quest for the understanding of the worlds within himself and without. He had little passion for the material interests of the growing merchant class or the political pursuits of his own titled family. His soul yearned for peace, and he yielded his life to the service of the Church of Rome.

It was behind the arched glass of cathedrals and the high walls of monasteries that he spent the next three decades. Ever the quick learner, he rapidly advanced from a simple parish priest to the clerk of the influential Archbishop Chandeleux. But as the years began to gray his thinning, brown hair and strip his limbs of earlier bulk, his merciless pursuit of understanding drove him deeper into himself and into the mysteries of his faith. Frustrated and searching, Pieter eventually resigned his position to enter a foreboding Carthusian monastery in distant Neumark. *What better way*, he pondered, *to learn of God's ways than to spend my life with feather in hand and eyes on His Word?* So he lived by quill and candle, a copyist, vowed to scratch the Holy Script into yellow parchment on a small, well-worn, wooden table.

During those silent, monotonous years Brother Pieter again learned much. And in his learning he grew restless, for the Word he read seemed contrary to his training. Always wishing to be respectful, yet compelled by conscience, the monk strained to endure the apparent conflict. At last, no longer able to restrain his spirit, he endeavored to engage his fellow brothers, his prior, and finally his abbot. His superiors responded to his appeals with obstinance and rebuke, ultimately spawning a rebellion within Pieter that expressed itself with increasing abrasiveness and a broadening hostility toward the practice, doctrine, and authority of his Church. Even five years of exile to an order laboring within the bleak marshes of Silesia could not silence the persistent man.

In the end, his refusal to repent of his gross insubordination warranted banishment under papal anathema. Though stripped of vocation, title, and inheritance, Pieter's hardy spirit was strangely enlivened, not quenched. He defiantly left his vows behind and wandered the Rhineland and the Alps as a self-declared "beggar priest," serving the spiritual needs of the lowly, the unwanted, and the misfits of Christendom.

He had been blessed with more years than most. His old head was now covered with fine, wispy, white hair which yielded to the slightest brush of even the lightest breeze. His narrow, bearded face was weathered and wrinkled but his deep-set, blue eyes sparkled with a passion and spirit far more vigorous than the apparent state of his poor shell. His torso was bent inward, as if bearing the weight of the world, and dutifully borne by bowed and spindly legs. His long fingers wrapped a well-worn shepherd's crook and at his side hung a scuffed, leather satchel. These were his only accessories other than an olive-wood cross suspended on a braided cord necklace that he sheltered under his tattered, black robe. Pieter treasured his little cross, for it was a gift carved for him a few years prior by an Irish monk whom he had dearly loved. While on a pilgrimage to Palestine the Irishman had discovered the wood at the base of Golgotha and fashioned it into the cross of the Celts—a circle, like the sun, wrapping the intersection of the *T*. Pieter was taken by more than its simple beauty, however, for, unlike the polished silver hanging around most priests' necks, this little cross was a true cross—one complete with rough edges and splinters.

The old priest could be seen from afar stepping the dirt roads of Christendom with his amusing, rolling gait, like a creaking, old wagon with a leaning wheel. More than a decade had now passed since his body had been crushed by the wide wheels of an oxcart that drifted through a ditch in which he had paused to sleep. Cared for by the ample love and adequate good sense of some local peasants, he miraculously survived, his straightaway stride being the only thing lost. From that time forward he was known by the peasants who loved him as Pieter the Broken.

His journeys had taught him well of things common to all men. Pieter had learned to discern the depravation of peasant, prince, and priest alike, and he was not shy about sharing his observations. He grew in wisdom and knowledge and was keen to offer both to ears willing and not.

Not content to be alone always, he was most pleased to travel alongside his dearest companion, Solomon. His trusted friend was a scruffy dog who had found Pieter sleeping in a flax bundle almost six years ago near Limburg-on-the-Lahn. Unlike his master, Solomon was of low breeding, but like his master, was a tenderhearted rascal. His gray hair was usually matted and tangled with briars and brush, and though some would say he lacked an immortal spirit, his trusting eyes revealed an eager soul within.

৵

The sun was hot, hotter than usual for early July, and the summer of 1212 was proving to be a difficult one. The crops stood wilted and stiff in their hard, dry furrows. The grain harvest would begin in several weeks, but the yellowing fields of rye and millet were scant and without promise. Hay had been cut and sheathed but no second growth was expected. Pieter and Solomon sat quietly in the cool shade of a maple tree just beyond the walls of Mainz and watched a discouraged harvester sharpen his scythe.

Pieter, too, was discouraged. For the past two or three weeks he had unsuccessfully attempted to dissuade scores of little crusaders from their holy march. Each gentle effort had been met with an equally gentle refusal as they zealously tread by, clutching their wooden crosses close to their breasts. A band of thirty or so had dismissed his pleading earlier that morning, and Pieter now cast a sad eye toward a distant field.

"Look there, old Solomon," he said as he pointed his curled finger to a flock of sheep dotting the green plain. "Every lamb needs a ewe and every ewe a shepherd. 'Tis how life is ordered. The little lambs marching by us have neither ewe nor shepherd and my heart aches so for them."

Solomon, seeming to understand the old man's melancholy, licked his friend's face and rested his shaggy head on Pieter's lap. Then, with a sigh, the priest pulled himself up by his trusted staff and headed into Mainz, hoping to find a little bread for himself and some scraps for his good fellow.

Mainz was a busy town pressed tightly along the left bank of the Rhine River. Its ancient, stone walls guarded well both Archbishop Siegfried III's huge, red-stone cathedral and the clutter of wattle-and-daub dwellings scattered within its massive shadow. Pieter watched in amazement as clusters of busy workmen clung to towering scaffolding like so many bees on a summer hive. "Indeed," pondered the old man to Solomon, "'tis an awesome sight and most deserving of our sincerest accolade. But I do ponder to whom it confers glory. I propose that God may be easier found by the modest hearths of those timid hovels dwarfed and shamed by such a folly as this." His anger rose and he turned his eyes to the town square.

Mainz's market dated from the days of the Romans and was among the most spirited in all the Empire. It was filled with the noise of commerce, the aroma of flowers, and the foul stench of beast and peddler alike. Brightly clothed Syrian traders pushed and pressed their bolts of colorful linens to passersby, chattering and imploring their would-be buyers with large, pleading brown eyes. Donkeys laden with barrels of wine and beer trotted briskly between tables of stock and baskets. Country serfs prodded sluggish oxen through the crowded market keeping a wary eye on their carts laden lightly with their meager harvests.

Pieter was quite pleased with himself as he had successfully begged some coarse rye bread and a tankard of warm ale for himself and Solomon. He found a vacant corner at a weaver's shop and placed the curve of his old back against the flat of sturdy board. He raised his thin nose high in the air and drew deeply on the summer smells of cut hay and strong fish. "Mid-July is a bit too early for this market's coveted early wine, its *Federweiss*, Solomon," Pieter mused. "Pity, such a blessed, sweet drink ... the white milk of the vine ... ah, but this golden brew shall serve well enough." He sighed and gazed upon the color and motion before him, but no sooner had he wiggled and fidgeted his old bones into a comfortable position than he noticed a small crowd beginning to gather in the square before him. Pieter leaned forward and strained to see the attraction. To his delight, a group of troubadours was assembling on a wooden platform and Pieter, though finally settled in his corner, grew immediately restless. "Up, Solomon, good beast, 'tis time to dance!"

The performers were richly dressed in pleasing satin, velvet, and brocade. In their bright colors of green and yellow and red they laughed and jousted with each other and teased the crowd as they prepared their performance. A particularly robust young fellow stretched his thick arm slowly, almost painfully, into his bulky, homespun sack. At first he seemed to think his sack had no end and his face showed alarm for it. But to the amusement of his audience he quickly withdrew and held his kettledrum high overhead. Another laughed loudly and snatched a flute from the sleeve of his tunic, and the last spun about and deftly caught a lute slung loosely over his narrow shoulder.

"Ah, music, dear Solomon ... listen." Pieter found himself tapping his leather-bound feet and dancing to the rhythms and melodies that he loved so very much. Unfortunately the rickety old man and his unkempt dog became quickly lost in their own delight. The annoyed folk about them withdrew with choice words of advice for the awkward priest and his crowing dog! Neither seemed to mind, however, and they danced about the dusty square, yelping and laughing, unfettered by the mutterings of the townsfolk.

The players soon quieted their audience and presented a rendition of a new, dramatic epic, "The Nibelungenlied." They inspired their audience with brave knights, confounded them with magic, and sang of the hero Siegfried and his beautiful Queen Kriemhild. Pieter's bright eyes sparkled with the joy of it all. He laughed heartily, not the least bit embarrassed by the single yellow tooth that occupied the front of his gaping mouth. He watched with the eyes of a child as the stage teased his mind with illusion and touched his heart with song.

When the troubadours took their final bow, those blessed with some measure of prosperity tossed pennies into the baskets offered them. Pieter, never wishing to take without giving, approached the unsuspecting troupe and offered a blessing. The players smiled and winked at each other as the old priest raised his feeble arms in benediction. *"In nomine Patris, et Filii, et Spiritus Sancti ..."*

Returning to the wall of the weaver's shop, Pieter sat down in the dust and patted his panting dog. "Ah, such a glorious afternoon, Solomon. I should have hoped, however, they would have sung the Song of Hildebrand ... but beggars cannot choose, can we?" He laughed.

Pieter settled against his wall and looked wistfully at the crowd of serfs and merchants, men-at-arms and nobles mulling through the square before him. He was about to close his eyes and nap when he caught a glimpse of some children emerging from the market in his direction. "Ah, Solomon," Pieter sighed, "behold the look of Crusade. Surely, this must be the end of the column?"

He raised himself on his staff and walked toward four young pilgrims striding through the crowd. "Hello there, crusaders. Might I have a word with you?"

The tired children stopped and eyed him warily.

"Yes, my children," continued Pieter, smiling but anticipating their reserve. "Yes, I am told that I look a bit odd, but I am surely safe enough."

Pieter ambled toward them slowly, Solomon trotting slightly ahead. "I wonder if I might be of some service?"

The dusty children stared back uneasily, somewhat overtaken by the sight before them. There were three boys and a very young girl. The little girl giggled and reached over to rub one of the dog's ears as Pieter continued. "It is plain to me that you are all of fine stock, though a bit worn." Pieter's eyes twinkled. "Oh, your pardon. I ought introduce myself. I am Pieter; some have called me Pieter the Broken." He leaned heavily on his staff and bowed deeply. "And this fine beast is my one true friend, Solomon."

He commanded the dog to sit and raise his paw, bringing a squeal of delight from the little girl and a happy smile from one of the boys. The two older boys looked at Pieter carefully and a blonde-haired lad stepped forward. "Your pardon, but we needs be off. We've lost nearly a fortnight for a three-day march!"

"Ah, yes," answered Pieter, "journeys are fraught with the unexpected."

The lad shook his head. "We ought make four leagues a day at the least. The caravans do six or better. We couldn't find the blasted Rhine, then crossed by ferry in search of Nicholas's column, only to wander too far west. Then we were held by some dolt reeve for three days under charge of thievery! Stupid man."

"Ah, I believe you must be joining the others in the great Crusade ... you'd be a bit behind them, you know. Ah, never you mind. 'Tis a fine Crusade, I might say, a noble and sincere gesture of obedience, I am quite certain of it. But ... forgive my wondering if you were prayed for or did you, yourselves, invest much time in prayer before departing? But of course you did, otherwise ..."

"Move off, old man," growled a black-haired youth. "We've better things to do than speak at some old dolt with an ugly dog."

"Well, truly," answered Pieter, "it is evident to me that you have much more weighty things to do than humor an old fool ... remarkable things actually ... godly things at that. I simply thought it prudent to pose such a question. After all, if a journey begins on the wrong foot, it is bound to end at the wrong place ... would you not agree?" He grinned and noticed that his words had reached one mark for certain.

The redhead furrowed his brow. "I think you to be right, old sir. And no, no one prayed for us and we've not prayed for ourselves."

"Ah, yes," said Pieter with a tone of patient sympathy. "That does happen. That does happen indeed. I am an old man and I do know very little sometimes, I am certain of it. But you might consider returning home to receive your blessing."

The black-haired lad stepped forward and stared into Pieter's twinkling eyes. "You'd be right when you say you know little, you old beggar. Now be out of our way."

Pieter put his hand lightly on the boy's hard shoulder. "Now that is something I do know much about ... that I know little, that is."

The boy was confused and Pieter seized the silence. "You all look as though I have baffled you with some riddle. Actually ..."

The redhead interrupted, his interest pricked. "Do you like riddles, old sir ... uh, your pardon, I mean, Herr Pieter? May I call you Herr Pieter?"

"Ah, yes, of course, but 'Pieter' will do just fine." His face glowed with hope.

"Well, I do love riddles so and I have one ..."

The blonde boy interrupted him. "Tie your tongue, brother. We needs be 'bout our way. Your pardon, Herr Pieter, but we must beg your leave."

"*Ja, ja,* to be sure, my son, I believe that to be a sound idea indeed. You must be a proper leader. I ... I presume you mean you shall be on your way to your homes for prayer and blessing?"

The boy had done his utmost to maintain his patience and his manners. After all, the monks had insisted he respect all elders, but the old man now irritated him and he found it hard to restrain his tone. "What are you, a banished priest or ... outcast monk? And no, that would not at all be what I mean. We are on our way to Palestine ... now Godspeed and good-day."

Pieter ignored the boy's annoyance and studied the children carefully. "Well, children," he said quietly, "might I ask your names before you depart? I should like very much to pray for you ... very much, indeed."

The blonde sighed. "Yes, yes. But then we are on our way. I am Johann Wilhelm of Weyer. This is my brother, Johann Karl, and that is my sister, Maria. And he is Tomas the Schwarz, also of Weyer. Now, off we go."

Pieter winked at Maria as she passed close by him. She giggled and returned a clumsy wink of her own as she waved the four fingers of her good hand at him. Pieter's eyes grew moist and he raised his arm slowly. But before they were out of earshot he quickly called after them. "Children, forgive me for my intrusion, but I have just one more simple request."

"What now?" asked Wil, sharply.

The old man hobbled toward them. "I wonder if I might accompany you so I could behold the glory of the Holy Land before I am taken from this wretched earth?"

"Surely you are mad!" snapped Tomas. "You are nothing but a pathetic, old beggar with one tooth and a bent-over back and wrinkled fingers and toes. And look at those legs of yours. We have no use for you."

Karl looked gently into Pieter's steady eyes. "Old man, this is a journey for young soldiers like us. You ought be resting in the shade of a good linden, not marching to Palestine."

"Well, now that is a very kind thing to say, good lad, but I should very much enjoy journeying with you. We might share riddles as we march."

Pieter turned to Wil and offered in a respectful, almost submissive tone: "And you, young fellow, you truly do have the look of a courageous and wise leader, one who is under the protection of God Himself. I should like very much to learn from you along the way. I should feel safe, as must these others. As I think of it, this would be most comforting, for I would be under the care of ... God's Wil." Pieter raised his eyebrows and chortled, pleased with his wit.

Wil paused for a moment, looked at the dust covering the leather binding his feet and walked a few paces away. Pieter shuffled to Maria and dropped down to his knees in order to look directly into her angelic face. "My dear child, what a precious lamb you are. You are like a tender, springtime flower. An old man like me needs to be near a new life like you."

Maria smiled at him. "Father Pieter, you have a lot of deep wrinkles in your face, and why is your back bent over? You look like the old men of my village."

Pieter laughed and reached to hug the little girl. "Well, well, my dear little lamb, not all in this world is pretty like you."

Maria's pink face blushed and her red lips began to quiver. She was about to burst into tears when she stepped back and held up her withered arm. "My mama says I am ugly, Father Pieter. See my arm."

Pieter looked tenderly at her deformed arm and stroked her fine blonde hair. "Well, nay, nay, little one, I think you are most pretty. And perhaps you could be rather thankful for that very different arm. Just think how much happier you are for your good arm because of it!"

Maria brightened and looked first at her deformed arm and then at her good one. She smiled. "Yes, I think so, Father Pieter. I *do* love my good arm better because of this one."

Pieter hugged his new friend and patted her gently on the head. He took a deep breath and walked toward Tomas. "And you, my young friend ..."

"I am not your friend and never shall be, you foul-breathed old pauper. I don't know what yer game is, but stay out of m'way. I've little time for priests ... you *are* some kind of priest, methinks."

"Well, yes, young Tomas," said Pieter softly. "I suppose I am. And I am something of a wretched creature as you so aptly describe. I would not argue the point with you. Another old man once wrote, 'Whoever corrects a mocker invites insult.' But I do believe, whether wretched or priestly, I could be of some service to you. I have seen the world; I have seen the great mountains that lie in wait for you. My humble request is to be allowed to follow."

Wil opened his mouth to respond but hesitated as Karl and Maria urged him to accept the old man's offer.

"Please, Wil, let him come," whispered Karl. "He's a priest. You must let him come."

Wil examined the old man carefully but, though he sensed something unusual, bluntly rejected Pieter's request. It would not be prudent, he imagined, to slow his Crusade with a white-haired man who had little more to offer other than his seasoning. "Nay, methinks not."

Pieter nodded. "I accept your decision, lad. Just answer me this: Who do you follow?"

A division had occurred in Mainz some days before when the main column of crusaders arrived from Cologne under the control of the young visionary, Nicholas. A dissenting group had formed, most arguing for a different route to the sea. Nicholas wanted to follow the left bank of the Rhine south, then swing southwestward to enter the Alps from the French passes. The others disagreed and chose a leader to take them on the right bank with an eye for the passes more to the east.

Wil answered firmly. "We've decided to follow our own noses. Some merchants suggested we go straight south along the east bank, then through the smaller passes that lead more directly to the city of Genoa where all are to meet."

Pieter nodded. He knew the world of Christendom like no other and agreed. "Godspeed, then," he offered softly, "until we meet again."

~

Though it seemed longer to the four crusaders, two days passed since they left the walled city of Mainz and entered the flat, ever-widening *Oberrheingraben*—the valley of the Rhine. On this particular sunny morning, Wil distributed the last of their bread. Tomas wrinkled his nose at the hard, moldy crust of rye he was handed. "Now what, Master?" he asserted sarcastically.

Karl and Maria watched anxiously as Wil stood to his feet. "We'll surely find some manor to welcome us, or a church on the way, and I am quite certain they'll yield a bit of bread or a turnip or two."

A determined Karl quickly added, "Yes, 'tis sure, by faith. We are on God's journey and His people shall provide!"

Tomas grunted and reluctantly followed the others along the dirt roadway of the Rhine riverbank. The sun was hot and climbed high above the hungry, thirsty crusaders. "So, Karl," he grumbled, "where'd be the butterflies and birds that you boasted would follow us?"

Karl blushed a little, beginning to feel ashamed of his earlier expectations. "I only repeated what I heard at Mainz."

Tomas curled his lip and sneered, "Karl, there ne'er was nor ever shall be butterflies and birds … in the name of God, when are you going to see the world as it is?"

Wil, too hot to hear more of this, clenched his fists. "Tomas, leave him be."

"For all those hours in the school, you'd be no less a fool than him!"

Wil had had just about all he could endure of Tomas and ground his teeth. "Bind your mouth; say no other word."

The band tramped silently as the sweltering sun beat on them, and many hours passed until they finally felt relief from the evening breezes blowing gently up the wide river valley. The air was cool and smelled fresh, and they paused to feel it swirl about themselves. Karl looked to the sky and said he imagined their sweated bodies being fanned by a "legion of angels fluttering their golden wings."

The crusaders stalled in the evening caress and they were blessed again, for the angels now carried the sounds of a distant song to their tired ears. The children raced to the top of the next hill and listened carefully. To their great joy they heard a familiar melody, *"Schönster Herr Jesu,"* a song to be known for centuries after as the "Crusader's Hymn." Karl beamed and joined his awkward voice to the faraway chorus:

> Fairest Lord Jesus,
> Ruler of all nature,
> Son of God and Son of Man.
> Thee will I cherish,
> Thee will I honor,
> Thou, my soul's glory, joy, and crown.
>
> Fair are the meadows,
> Fair are the woodlands,
> Robed in the blooming garb of spring:
> Jesus is fairer, Jesus is purer,
> Who makes the woeful heart to sing.
>
> Fair is the sunshine,
> Fair is the moonlight,
> And all the twinkling, starry host:
> Jesus shines brighter,
> Jesus shines purer
> Than all the angels heav'n can boast.

Beautiful Savior.

Lord of the nations.

Son of God and Son of Man.

Glory and honor,

Praise, adoration,

Now and forevermore be Thine.

Little Maria hugged her brother. "You sing nice, Karl. Sing it again."

But before Karl could begin, Tomas laughed, his black eyes shining with an unsettling rage. "By faith you are surely a dunce, aren't you, *kleiner bube*? You do not sing 'nice' … and 'tis a fool's song anyway. Ha! 'Fool' is the right word for you, indeed. Fool!"

Karl was hurt and embarrassed but did not respond. He ran his fingers along the necklace his mother had given him. *She never thought me a fool. She loved me,* he thought. *She must have, else she would not have given this.*

Wil cast a disdainful look at Tomas. "Shut your mouth or I'll be jamming a stopper in it. Now, all of you, get started again. I want to catch the heels of the group ahead. They might have food to spare."

"But I *am* very hungry, Wil," said Maria gently. Her blue eyes looked yellowed to her brother. "My belly hurts and I feel so tired."

Wil nodded. "I know. Just walk a bit farther and I'll find someone to help."

The crusaders ahead of them were still out of sight and after an exhausting attempt to reach them, Wil's company found themselves collapsed along a quiet cove by the darkening Rhine. "We have fish at our feet," complained Tomas, "and no net, no hook, no trap. We've boar in the woods all 'bout us and no arrow or spear. Where is this loving God of yours, fool?"

Karl shrugged and lay on his side as Wil stood to his feet, tired of the quarreling and very much aware of his own unadmitted doubts. With forced confidence he announced, "I'll find some kindhearted yeoman and be back with food as soon as I can."

Wil left his companions and crossed a dry field in search of some morsel of mercy hidden within the looming darkness. The others waited quietly in the deepening night, staring blankly at the stars appearing above. It seemed forever to Maria when Wil finally returned.

"Each of you put a block in your mouth. Not a word from a single one of you. I … I was chased from two yeomans' huts and one horrible village. This onion is all I could find so … just be glad for it and say nothing."

"And where did you find such a thing? 'Tis half rotted," observed Tomas.

"If you don't want your share, give it back."

"I wager you scrumped it from some swine trough. And we've no fire … or even a coal bucket and you lost our flint. I think it a good thing y'found no rabbit or venison!"

Maria, frightened by Tomas's tone and feeling all the more famished, began to cry. Wil took her in his arms. "There, there, little sister, all shall be well." He glared at Tomas, no word needed.

Karl blushed slightly and bent to his knees. "I … I know no Latin prayer for food. Do you, Wil?"

"No."

"Well, does God understand German?"

Wil shrugged, confused by his brother's novel idea, but Tomas laughed out loud. "Did you ever hear a single prayer in German? You dunce … German is not God's tongue."

Wil leaned close to Karl and said sternly, "For the sake of the saints, just pray if it comforts you. Perchance some angel shall translate."

Karl tilted back his red head and stared quietly for a moment. Then he began to whisper words he knew well. "*In nomine Patris, et Filii, et Spiritus Sancti.*" Each word grew a little louder. "We are hungry and we are about your business. Please feed us, your soldiers. Amen."

Tomas snickered and shook his head. "Oh, how very much like a little monk you are. Be prepared to be hungrier on the morrow than you were this day."

Chapter 6
NEW COMRADES

awn broke faithfully but its red sky brought no promise of mercy from the sun now rising overhead. The four stood and looked hopelessly about. Wil broke the silence. "This day we'll reach the band ahead. I am certain they'll have some food to share." So Wil set his doubts aside and prodded his companions southward on the dusty road.

But by sext the draw of the river had proven too powerful a temptation, and the young commander consented to a quick splash in the slow-moving water. Maria squealed and Karl laughed. The water felt so clean and cool as it pressed over their hot bodies. The smooth, round river stones tickled their bare feet and the gentle lapping of the waves against the muddy shore was soothing. Even Tomas smiled.

The respite was brief, however, for the ever-present pangs of hunger drew the crusaders back to their roadway where they spent the whole day begging food from passersby. Night fell and the only treasures of this day would be the dimming memory of the river and a sturdy coal bucket Wil found fallen in some tall weeds by the way.

Darkness brought little relief from the day's heat. Wil collected some chunks of hardwood and dropped them into his tin bucket as he stared wistfully at the stars. The weary boy fashioned a lash for his new prize from a discarded length of rope tossed off some passing cart. He sighed, suddenly uncertain of his Crusade, and paused to stare at his sister in the bright moonlight. He thought she looked yet more drawn, and he noticed the dark circles under her bagging eyes. Wil wiped his hand through his hair and turned to find some soft grass to lie in.

Tomas was about the business of sweeping his grassy bed for sharp stones and sticks and turned to growl at Karl. "As I said, either your God is not there or He cares not one whit. Which do you claim?"

Wil overheard the remark and prepared to defend his brother, but his spirit faltered. He, too, was confused and could find no words.

Karl was taken by surprise and looked to Wil for help. Finding none, he fumbled. "I ... I don't know how to answer you just now."

Tomas grinned, quite content with himself and the awkward corner in which he had placed Karl. He drew a quick breath and was about to speak when Karl blurted defiantly, "But, no matter, I'll pray again. And if He fails me I ... I'll pray again!"

Tomas's black eyes danced and he laughed. "Then prepare to pray for all time."

Morning came as an unwelcome intruder into the sleepy campsite. The four sat up reluctantly, dreading another new day. Each yawned and stretched, complained of the early morning's fog, and rubbed their eyes.

Suddenly, Maria blurted, "What is *that*?"

"What is what?" grumbled Tomas, still half asleep.

"That."

Maria pointed her finger and, with ever-rounding eyes, jumped to her feet. "Look, look," she cried.

By now all four were standing, confounded to find four small loaves of bread positioned neatly at the center of their campsite.

"There, too!" shouted Karl as he pointed to two sharp pieces of flint setting atop a flat rock. "Praise to God!" Karl cried. "Praise to God, Tomas! He is there and He does care, after all, and ... and you were wrong." The happy boy gleefully snatched a loaf and shoved half into his mouth.

The rest he lifted to the morning sky and with his ruddy cheeks stuffed with bread, cried, "Many thanks!"

Tomas looked dazed and sullen, like an arrogant general whose armies were just outflanked by unforeseen misfortune. He chewed slowly on his portion and said nothing.

Each crusader knew that something special had happened. But they knew not that they were being offered something greater than bread and something more lasting than the little loaves they consumed so quickly. But Tomas had no sooner swallowed his bread when he groused, "It was only one little chip of rye, Karl, one small piece of bread in two days and a bit of flint." He paused and leaned toward the redhead. "If it came from God," he sneered, "He could have given us more. And if He gave this to us this day He could have given us some on days past." Suddenly confident he had once again gained the high ground, he pressed his attack. "But I think it's not from God at all. I think Wil was hiding it all the while."

Wil, surprised at the unexpected accusation, snapped, "Liar." He pressed his nose against the other boy's. "Stop your mouth before I stop it for you."

Maria climbed between the two pleading, "Please, please don't fight."

Wil and Tomas glared at each other and backed apart slowly. Wil relaxed his clenched fists but the edge in his voice had sent fair warning. "I don't know where this came from. Perhaps it *is* from heaven, or perhaps we missed it when we came in the dark. All I know is that I've eaten and am ready to move forward." Confused, he bent to take the flints and stuff them into the satchel slung on his shoulder.

In the days that followed, small loaves of crusty bread again were found placed neatly in the center of the camp. One day spelt, another rye—and always welcome. Judging by the faint peals of distant church bells, it was about terce when the crusaders rounded a bend in the roadway and saw ahead what appeared to be the elusive group of fellow pilgrims they had been struggling to reach.

At last, thought Wil. His heart lifted. *At last.*

Wil urged his tired comrades to hurry as he lifted his weary legs into a steady trot. Filling with excitement, all pressed forward, but as they drew closer they slowed, suddenly wary of the scene before them. Wil had a peculiar stirring in his chest. He halted his band and strained to focus on what had at first appeared to be a large group of children sprawled beneath a draping oak. Yet the tree looked oddly shaped and the children beneath it were lying down or squatting or walking aimlessly without any visible purpose.

Wil waved his hand forward and led his fellows judiciously, eyeing the picture with marked suspicion. Suddenly he stopped and stood stiffly. Crowding close behind, Karl gasped. It was now evident why the ancient tree looked so curious. From its thick boughs were suspended four or five bodies, their feet dangling undisturbed above the heads of a dozen or so dazed fellows.

Wil cast a nervous glance at his shocked comrades. Even Tomas looked shaken, his eyes wide with surprise. The young leader set his jaw squarely and feigned a confident stride toward the mysterious gathering.

As Wil and his group neared, one of the children spotted them and jumped to her feet. "Oh please, please, please help us!" Others rushed to cling to the new arrivals, their confused eyes reflecting both terror and hope.

Wil whisked past the children and stood under the feet of the five hanging limply above him. It was not that he had never seen a hanging before. His mind quickly sped to a memory etched deep in his mind: the hanging of six-year-old Stephan, the poor foundling caught thieving a peck of flour from the abbey's garrison. But this seemed somehow different to the troubled lad. Here were no priests, no men-at-arms, drums, nor bailiffs and their cursed parchment proclamations. Instead were only lonely children, an old tree, and a quiet river.

Above him dangled the tiny, bare feet of two little boys, each bearing the cuts and calluses of miles and miles of dutiful service. Their eyes gazed heavenward, fixed in what Wil sadly mused as eternal bewilderment. On another limb hung a girl, her face obscured by the shadow of thick leaves. Wil judged her young, but by her tender curves, not so very young. He looked to her side where two older boys hung, each bearing an innocence that defied their end. One looked almost angelic, thought Wil, his golden curls and chubby, freckled face revealing no hint of any wickedness that could have earned such an end as this. Wil turned stiffly to the oldest of those crowding close to him and choked, "What has happened here?"

A frightened, black-haired boy wiped his eyes with a dirty sleeve. "These were chased by an old man through a village just by there not three days past." He pointed eastward. "He thought them to be scrumping his bread.... Then he tripped over a wheel and knocked his head against a timber corner and died at once."

"Aye," blurted another. "The villagers bound us all but charged these. The lord's provost came by next day and held trial."

"'Guilty,' he says," another voice choked. "'Pay the man's widow two shillings *wergeld* or meet the noose.' We'd not a single penny between us ... so here they hang."

Karl slowly advanced toward the bodies and looked sadly into their placid faces. He reached a shaking hand and gingerly nudged the girl's feet to turn her face to the light. He fell backward. "Wil! Wil! See ... oh, God, no ... 'tis Ingrid."

Wil spun about, pain cutting through him. The boy trembled and gazed at her now familiar, braided red hair hanging tangled and unseemly by her bloated face. He remembered how confidently she smiled at him as she marched out of the village. He looked away. "Someone take these bodies down," he commanded hoarsely. But the children did not move. They simply stood and stared at one another. Wil opened his mouth to command them again but closed it slowly and sprang onto the lowest limb himself. He climbed into the leafy gallows and stretched out on the heavy branches. He withdrew his dagger and sawed angrily at the thick rope above each tilted head.

As one body after another dropped to the ground Karl

winced. Each thud sickened the poor boy and he soon found himself vomiting into the dry weeds. Even Tomas was mute. Unable to watch, he stared at his feet, but the corner of his eye caught Ingrid crumpling on the ground and he quickly wiped a tear off his stiff cheek.

A boy's voice suddenly startled everyone. "What if some of us did steal some food? And ... so some priest did warn us ... but we are so hungry. And none pushed the old man or tripped him or nothing of the like. Some of ours had died a few days back and look, some are so sick that they cannot stand." He began to cry.

Wil looked carefully over the group. *They all seem so helpless*, he thought. A chill ran up his back. *Am I to care for all these?* He swallowed hard. "Give me your names," he said slowly.

"I am Jon," answered one. "This be m'brother, Jon. And this be my youngest brother, Jon."

"Well," muttered Wil, "that shall never do. You are the oldest, so you shall be Jon I; the next, Jon II; and the last, Jon III. And what about the little girl by my sister?"

"She is called Maria," said Jon I.

Wil paused for a moment. "She shall be called Maria the Younger since she is younger than my sister Maria."

Jon I nodded. "And the others, I know not many of the others ... they joined us 'bout three days back. The little boy there seems most weak. I think he be called Lothar."

Karl's heart stopped and he spun about, looking hard for Lothar. He immediately recognized the little one as his friend from Weyer and ran to him. "Oh Lothar, Lothar, 'tis me, Karl! And look, here is Wil and Maria and look there, there is Tomas."

"Karl, Karl!" Lothar chirped. "'Tis good to see you. Look, over there is Otto ... he'll be surely happy to see you, too! Most of the others are with another group. We got mixed up in Mainz and went separate ways. Methinks the main group is on the other side of the river with your cousins."

"Well, you are with us now, Lothar, and we'll take good care of you ... you can be sure of ..." Before he finished talking, Otto wrapped his arms around him.

Karl laughed and begged his sturdier friend to release him. "Enough! Enough! I can't breathe!"

Wil saluted Otto and Lothar and looked carefully at the others. "All of you ... give me your names," he commanded.

"I am Conrad," said a dark-haired boy straightaway. He was about fifteen, lanky and strong-featured.

"Friederich," said a quivering voice. "And we are sorry we scrumped food." The boy was a skinny lad of about seven.

Wil nodded.

"Anna," a very soft voice added. She was a gangly, white-haired girl just a year or so older than Maria.

Wil circled the group and tried his best to learn the names of all the rest. His mind whirled. *I'll not remember them,* he thought. *I want none of these following me; I can barely feed the four of us.* He then looked into their sad faces. "What is right is to be done," he sighed.

Wil abruptly ordered Tomas and Karl to carry the bodies to the riverbank and arrange them in a row. "And you others, fetch some rocks ... we'll cover them and then we move on."

Maria the Younger and Conrad gently removed the wooden crosses from the belts of the dead and secured them at the head of each mounded grave. Karl, disquieted by the moment, fumbled a small, though poignant prayer to the angels and the Virgin Mother.

Wil stood solemn and erect, staring thoughtfully at the group assembling silently before him. "How far is the village you scrumped?" he said slowly.

"'Bout a half-day," answered Jon II.

Wil paused and pursed his lips as if sucking a bitter herb. He dreaded hearing his own words and measured them carefully. "Those who wish to resume may march with me. Otherwise you'll needs take leave to the village and plead mercy of the reeve."

Tomas laughed. "The same reeve that just stretched these five?"

That thought had not escaped Wil's own fair logic and he responded in swift order. "If he had wished more hanged he'd have done so."

Despite the reasonableness of his answer, the blank faces staring at Wil betrayed reluctance. The lad continued, almost harshly: "The sick shall be delivered to the village for certain. Have faith that pity shall be shown. Some good fellow's wife shall nurse them to health in time for harvest." Wil turned away to hide his own doubts, wondering if he had sentenced any to certain misery, or worse.

The uneasy children murmured in hushed tones, frightened of both this young master and the villagers. After a few moments of stifled whines and yielding grunts, the group broke into clusters. Some resolved at once to press on, willing to adventure the perils waiting for them. Most, however, chose to risk themselves to the dubious mercy of the village.

Jon I circled the groups and approached Wil. He pointed a steady finger at his two brothers, Maria the Younger, Anna, Conrad, Otto, Friederich, and Lothar. "These here wish to go on. The others choose to stay."

Wil swallowed hard. He had hoped they would have all chosen the village. "So it is then," he clipped. "At dawn we'll go our separate ways."

࿇

The rising sun lit upon a sad huddle of children embracing one another on the dewy riverbank. Too sick or too fearful to continue the journey, the largest portion bade their farewells to the lesser and formed a reluctant column. Notwithstanding Wil's logic, they nestled close, one tightly pressed upon the next, and shuffled ever so timidly toward the dreaded village. They cast a final glance over their shoulders at their fellows, forever preserved from the knowledge of the ill-fortune awaiting them.

As his new line assembled on the dry roadway Wil surveyed each new recruit, and, once satisfied, ordered them forward. Karl was delighted to have more fellows by his side and chattered so incessantly that after several hours of hearing his persistent voice the group cried out in near unison, "Stop, Karl. Enough." Karl, startled at first, soon joined in the laughter offered so generously at his expense. It had not taken long for strangers to become comrades.

Hunger quickly took the soldiers captive once again, and Wil ordered his exhausted friends to rest. But no sooner had they collapsed atop shriveled weeds when four new voices were heard at the edge of the camp. "*Gut'tag....* Hello.... We, too, are crusaders and beg leave to join your company."

Wil bounded to his feet, startled by the intrusion and in no mood for more responsibility. "Nay. Nay. Find your own way. I have no means to feed you." He growled and cursed and flailed his arms at the gaunt faces staring at him.

The disillusioned newcomers stood respectfully still. They were pale and drawn, tattered and fragile. Judging them as well as the waning light would allow, Wil thought them to be unable to fend for themselves for many more days. Compassion, so oft kept at bay by the boy, crept over Wil and his heart groaned.

"Not such the grand master after all? Not so able, are we?" taunted Tomas.

His words landed on Wil like a stick on an angry dog. He gave Tomas a furious eye and started toward him. His better sense took hold, however, and he abruptly turned toward the four hopefuls and forced a kind word. "*Ja ... ja.* You are granted my leave into our company ... and we ... welcome you."

Wil turned another savage look at Tomas and with one eye on his foil and the other on the newcomers, continued. "The more hands, the lighter the load." He paused for a moment and looked thoughtfully at his silent company. "Listen, all of you." He folded his arms. "On the morrow and each day thereafter you shall go by twos and threes to beg at each village we pass by." He switched his gaze and fixed his eyes hard on Karl. "We'll soon learn if this God brother Karl is so certain of shall help us or not."

The next morning was heavy-dewed and misty, and Karl woke to wipe the wet from his eyes. He stretched and yawned and was startled to find something quite strange at his feet. "Wake, everyone!" Karl jumped up, nearly bursting with joy. "Quickly! Look ... look ... a fish!"

Indeed, a large, big-eyed cod, still shiny and wet, was

flat on a rock in the middle of the campsite. Wil squinted his sleepy eyes and shrugged in surrender to the mystery. He reached for kindling and soon an early-morning fire was snapping amid the baffled band. In short order, the fish was impaled on a stout, green stick and held by impatient hands over the flames, only to be ravenously reduced to bones before the sun reached half orb over the horizon.

By early afternoon the company descended a slight decline into a leafy glen where the road was lined on either side by a thick wood. The dark shadows which edged the path were a welcome refuge from the day's heat but formed an eerie corridor leading toward a narrowing view of the roadway. Wil cast a quick glance over his shoulder at his tired, shuffling band, secretly hoping for some assurance. Instead, he shook his head. *How did I come to master such a brood of weaklings and misfits as this?*

The steadfast company followed their leader into the shadows without a whimper and greeted the unknown with hearty courage. A few more children dressed in tattered, red-crossed homespun seeped into the column from the woodland shadows. Each arrival weighted Wil, for the column now numbered more than twenty, and each new pilgrim was yet another mouth to feed and another soul to shepherd. *If but I could worry only of m'self.* Wil's heart felt as heavy as his weary feet and he imagined slipping away into the night's shadows, abandoning his burden. His thoughts drifted to his days inside the cool walls of the abbey—drinking a cup of cold water from the monks' deep well, splashing in the root cellar's icy spring with the novices. Suddenly, three large, filthy men bounded from the dark wood not three paces from the startled boy.

"Halt where y'be, waifs," bellowed one huge, bearded man. He set his dark eyes close to Wil's wide ones.

"Such a look on such a pretty face."

Wil stammered, "Out ... out of our way." The lad quickly studied the man. The intruder wore a coarse tunic slit far up the sides like a field serf's. Wil would have taken him for a common ruffian, but the tall black boots of a nobleman rose up his leggings and the man wore a wide, leather belt which suspended a large, sheathed saber. Wil knew this to be a highwayman.

The man laughed again and elbowed his nearest companion. This one tipped his wide-brimmed, leather hat. "Well, we've found ourselves a tender brood." He sneered and stuck his thick thumbs into the bright red sash which girded his round belly. He immediately seized command. "Push them together," he barked.

The other two jumped to the task and encircled the frightened children. With the sharp points of their swords they herded the trembling crusaders into a tight cluster in the middle of the path. Wil began to protest but was slapped on the head by the bearded rogue. "Bite that tongue, my bold friend, else we might add it to our stew past vespers."

"Now then, m'little poachers," chuckled the fat one. "We should like you to share with us those things what you've scrumped during this most holy of all crusades." He plucked a well-worn knife from his belt and scratched his dirty face while he waited for a response.

Karl first looked to Wil, then nervously answered, "But m'lords, we've stolen nothing. We are on a pilgrimage for God."

"You ought sew your mouth shut, little man," ordered the third villain. "Now, do as he says and strip your tunics and empty your satchels. Now, I say. Do it at once else we strip y'bare where y'be."

Wil and Tomas looked at the ugly little man standing wide-legged before them, and they both defiantly folded their arms across their chests. The furious man yanked a plumed, woolen cap off his head and threw it violently at Tomas. He jerked a short-sword from its scabbard and held it against Tomas's throat. "Do it now or I vow you shall surely die where y'stand."

The fury in the man's voice chilled the children. Wil, perspiring and suddenly straining for courage, opened his mouth to speak. "Good sirs ..."

But before he could continue a voice bellowed from the

roadway. *"Tutena? Atque cuius exercitus? Tutena? Atque cuius exercitus?"*

The surprised highwaymen swung their eyes toward the strange voice. A black-hooded, badly bent man on rolling legs stormed toward them and surged past the baffled children. His eyes burned hot from within the dark shadows of his black hood. His bony hand drove his crook deeper into the dust, twisting it harder with each advancing step. Again the voice barked, *"Tutena? Atque cuius exercitus?"*

Karl looked at Wil, wide-eyed. He and Wil had studied Latin in the abbey and he was almost certain of the stranger's words. The three men, now angry and primed for a confrontation, swaggered toward the newcomer.

Karl studied the stranger and his eyes suddenly brightened. He leaned close to Wil and whispered, "Look! 'Tis Pieter ... the old priest from Mainz."

"Aye," answered Wil quickly. "Listen ... I think he said, 'You and whose army?'" Karl agreed and shuffled cautiously toward the encounter building before them.

"Shut y'er mouth, old man," snapped the stout one. "I can better do without such foul air in m'face. And you'd better use a tongue I understand or, by God, I'll cut it off."

Pieter now was standing directly in front of the three and, choosing to ignore rather than respond, began to dust his robe starting atop his shoulders and following his slight frame until he finished by patting the dust from his shins. He lifted a wooden cross from within his robe and kissed it before finally raising his eyes to meet the dumbfounded trio. The cunning old man then cleared his throat, stood as erect as his old back would permit, and held his cross close to each angry face. Standing before the round-bellied rogue he asked, *"Nonne aliquantulum pinguescis?"* But before the befuddled man could respond he turned toward the one with the plumed cap. *"Ubi possun potiri petasi similis isti?"*

The confounded rogues retreated a half-step and stared at each other. Tomas moved slowly to Wil's side. "What's this about?"

Wil was gawking in disbelief at old Pieter and answered with a mischievous grin, "He told the first that he is fat and he asked the second one where he might find such a hat."

Tomas nearly laughed out loud. Pieter stepped to the bearded man and, in similar fashion, placed the edge of his nose upward by the man's chin. The man was clearly intimidated and nervously offered Pieter something of a pathetic smile. Pieter lifted his sparkling eyes to the heavens and extended the cross to his last victim. *"Caput vacans, in dentibus anticis frustum magnum brassicae habes."* This last pronouncement was offered with such authority that the ruffian immediately bowed forward and backed two steps away.

Karl and Wil squirmed, stifling an almost irresistible urge to burst into laughter. Tomas, frustrated for his ignorance, tugged on Wil's tunic and demanded a translation. Wil leaned close to his impatient ear and whispered, "He said, 'Your head is full of air and you have a huge piece of cabbage in your teeth.'"

The men were bewildered and suddenly seemed to be like little children themselves, dazzled and dumbstruck. Pieter, knowing full well he held the clear advantage, walked to the three directly and shook his staff sternly at each of them. "I am a priest in the service of the Lord and I demand an immediate accounting of thy intentions toward these fair children."

The flustered ruffians pulled nervously at their tunics and mumbled some indiscernible jumble of words and grunts.

"I say to ye foul three again," bellowed Pieter, "kneel before me now and confess thy transgressions, otherwise I am obliged to pronounce judgment against thy cursed souls."

The three hesitated until Pieter lifted his hands to the heavens. Sensing an invocation of divine wrath they fell straightaway to their knees and begged pardon. Pieter delayed for a painful moment, like a schoolmaster pondering mercy, and then walked abruptly to the black-bearded one. He placed a bony hand upon the rogue's trembling, uncovered head and held his cross toward the man's face as he pronounced, *"Stercorem pro cerebro habes."*

Wil giggled in disbelief and whispered to Tomas, "He told him he has dung for brains!"

Pieter reached toward the next repentant and placed his hand likewise. *"Podex perfectus es."*

Karl could not bear to let his brother lay hold of this one. "He told him he is a perfect arse."

Pieter concluded his dubious benediction by slapping both his hands atop the third head. *"Modo vincis, modo vinceris."*

Karl giggled and smiled at Wil. He leaned to Tomas. "'Some you win, some you lose.'"

The three men, oblivious to the degradation they had just endured, each kissed Pieter's outstretched hand in reverent submission and boundless gratitude. Then, duty done, they disappeared into the woodland grateful for the preservation of their souls.

The old man took a deep breath and walked toward the crusaders, feeling rather good about himself. He smiled, sucked a small splinter from his thumb, and placed his cross within his robe. His kindly, wrinkled face radiated warmth and love, and his eyes shined. He extended his arms.

One little child ran to Pieter, uncertain as to what magic had just transpired, but indebted just the same. He wrapped his chubby arms around one of Pieter's legs and squeezed with all his might. "Thank you, Father ... thank you!"

The priest stooped to kiss the top of the boy's dusty, white hair. "Such a pleasure for me, good lad. I am most happy to serve you."

The other children crowded about the grinning priest, cheering and clapping and grabbing at his arms and legs. Wil, Karl, and Tomas jostled their way toward Pieter, Karl gladly translating for the rest of the group the humiliation that had just occurred. Wil, happy and relieved for it all, extended his hand of welcome.

Pieter's eyes met the lad's and he clasped his hand firmly, surprising Wil with more strength than he had expected from such a time-worn grip. "'Tis most satisfying," offered Pieter gently, "to stumble upon you again. And you, boy," he said as he reached his hand toward Karl. "It is a joy to find you as well. Remind me to share a small riddle I have for you."

Pieter turned his attention to Tomas. "And you, young master. Tomas, I believe is your name. It bears me well to come twice upon a proud young fellow as yourself." Tomas hesitated, sensing a bite in the old man's words. The two clasped hands briefly.

Pieter smiled and turned toward a tender voice squealing impatiently for some attention. To his soul's delight he beheld Maria, and the old man fell to his knees, stretching forth both his arms to receive her.

"'Tis very good to see you, Father Pieter!"

"Ah my blessed, blessed little one. It gives my heart life to see you!" He closed his eyes and embraced the happy child. "However, my dear Maria, you have my leave to simply call me, Pieter, or even Papa Pieter if you like. 'Tis a bit odd, perhaps, but it is some easier to recognize one sound rather than the many titles which do fall upon my old ears."

Pieter stood to his feet, radiant and beaming, happy as a schoolboy released to a spring day. It was the children, the blessed Innocents that encircled him who lifted his spirit to high places. He held his arms wide and spoke kindly. "I am known as Pieter and I am your friend. If you should be so kind as to allow, I should like very much to travel in your good company."

Wil thought hard for a moment, drawn by a growing inclination toward the enticing old man and his good wits. He surveyed the hopeful faces staring back at him and the eyes begging his consent. At last he answered with surety, "Yes, Pieter, you may join with us for now. You brought us an easy end to that bad business and we are in your debt."

Pieter bowed respectfully and winked at Maria. He stood, but startled those about him by abruptly shouting, "Solomon, Solomon!" To the delight of all, the gray dog came bounding from the wood, jumping gleefully through the happy band.

࿊

The crusaders pressed southward, engaging each other in playful banter until they could not help but consider their hunger more weightily than their fellowship. The troop came to rest, collapsing by the side of the road. Pieter fell to the hard ground and propped the arc of his back against the smooth bark of a huge maple. Quite content to skirt the conventional position, he simply folded his hands and began whispering a prayer.

Karl, Wil, and even Tomas waited respectfully, though a bit impatiently, for what seemed an eternity. At last, the priest opened his eyes and smiled. Karl blurted, "So, by faith, you'd be a priest truly, Pieter?"

"Ah," Pieter answered. "The truth is that some would say 'aye' and others 'nay.'" Pieter pulled himself up on his staff.

Tomas cast a suspicious eye at the man. "Oh, more tricks with yer tongue, eh? What is it to be, old man? Either you be a priest or you be not."

Pieter lingered for a moment, adding to Tomas's frustration. "Some believe that to be a way to see life. I, however, have learned that on occasions most things are not so plain. Sometimes we are a grasp of this and a pinch of that.... I calculate me to be a pinch of priest and a grasp of not." He smiled.

Wil shook his head stubbornly. "Tomas's is a plain question and deserving a plain answer. That is how I see it."

"'Tis a remarkable thing to see a man of such determined opinion," answered Pieter. "Remarkable indeed. And I should be remiss if I withhold other truth on that matter. You see, strong faith and strong opinions rarely share the same heart. Ah, but your pardon!" The old man bowed, satisfied for the planting of the seed. He pointed his forefinger into the centre of his chin and measured his words. "That was not our discussion. So, let me plainly say that, as children of God, we are all priests of a sort. I am trained in the holy traditions and you are not, but without the charge of a parish, that would be the only difference."

Wil was unwilling to yield the point. "I say we are *not* priests and I find it unfit to pretend you to be so. I have yet to meet a priest who behaves as you."

"Yes, yes," smiled Pieter, "for such a compliment I do offer my hearty thanks."

Wil scratched his head and looked at Karl.

Pieter leaned on his staff and rubbed Solomon's ears. "You do know, ah yes, what a fool I am. You *must* know," he said firmly, "that the Good Book says, 'Do not be over-righteous, neither be over-wise. Why destroy yourself?'"

The perplexed children stared at him.

"Well, 'tis the truth." A huge smile stretched his wrinkles and nearly squeezed his eyes shut. He turned again to Tomas. "And what say you about such of Scripture?"

Tomas grumbled and looked sideways for rescue.

Wil stepped forward. "And I still say you do not look like a proper priest!" He set his fists firmly on his hips and rocked up on his feet, confident of his assessment. "What sort of churchman do you pretend to be? Your robe is black and looks to be more a Benedictine habit than other-wise. But your hair is wild, the crown of your head is not shaved ... so you'd be no monk. And you don't speak like a churchman ... and ... and I say you laugh more than any priest ought."

Pieter's eyebrows arched high and he threw his head back with a howl that brought grins to the whole circle. "Oh, now, lad, you have just shared more truth than you know. Ha!" Pieter, still chuckling, wiped the tears from his eyes and sighed. "As for my robe, it was stitched by a peas-ant wife for the priest of a humble parish. I had baptized a child in his village soon after the poor priest's death and was given it as my payment. I thought it rather becoming and just uncommon enough to raise a brow here and there.

"As for my hair ... ah, what can be said? I was a monk once, but felt the cold too much upon my crown. And, for my speech ... ah, yes, so I have learned to speak both the language of the haughty and the language of the true. Dost thou believeth me, or dost thee linger in thy doubt?"

Karl was confused. "Pieter," he fumbled, "the Church is mighty and wealthy and even those sworn to poverty have at least something more than you. I confess I have never seen such a priest as you."

Pieter grew quiet for a moment and answered, "'Better to be lowly in spirit and among the oppressed than to share plunder with the crowd.'"

Karl wrinkled his nose and scratched his head. He glanced about the blank faces encircling him.

Wil broke the silence with a sneer. "Well, if you are a priest, why not call us some bread from heaven?"

Pieter paused and patiently answered, "Now that is a fair request ... and shrewd to be sure. You and your brother are bright fellows, educated in a church school, I would surmise. *Ja, ja,* I am certain of it. It is good for you to understand that all bread is from heaven.

"As to my powers to summon loaves from the air, I am in some doubt. But it is heaven that has given each of us the strength of our hands and the keenness of our minds to provide such nourishment."

Wil shrugged, not surprised at the old man's answer.

Pieter moved close by the lad and set his hand confidently on his broad shoulder. "Let me say, young sire, that I am new to your company but it is clear to me, just for the looking, that heaven has blessed you with keenness of mind. I am certain that you have employed it in the setting of a fine plan for this Crusade."

Embarrassed, Wil surveyed the anxious faces now staring expectantly at him. He stammered, "I ... I ... did bring some provisions from home, but all has been used. We tried begging bread from the villagers but they failed us."

Karl interrupted. "And for several mornings we woke to bread or fish and you have yet to claim from where they came."

Wil answered sarcastically, "So very well said, little holy man. What of it?"

"What of it?" snipped Tomas. "What of it? I'd say you to have no keen mind, I'd say ..."

Pieter cleared his throat and caught the boys' attention. He stretched his long fingers into the sack hanging from his shoulder. "Wil, I have something to show you." Wil watched curiously as the old man pulled a tangle of cord from within his leather satchel and held it out as a large ball in his opened palm. "I beg your command," grinned Pieter.

The boy plucked the knot from the priest's hand and held it by a single strand to shake it apart, violently. He then nodded approvingly. "Ah, a fish net."

"Indeed," answered Pieter. "Might I humbly suggest your sending some of your charge to the water for a good night's supper?"

Wil's mood changed and he quickly agreed. He sent Jons I and II and two girls scampering to the river.

Pieter pointed his crook toward the crest of a nearby hill. "If you so order I'll go to a hamlet I have knowledge of just beyond. I suspect I might return with some begged loaves or a turnip or two. I have learned that folk will allow a child to starve but will rarely risk losing the blessing of a hungry priest ... unseemly or not."

Wil nodded, relieved for the fresh ideas.

"Fair Wil," the old man offered as he prepared to leave. "'Tis my thought that even our old emperor, Barbarossa, would have been daunted by your task and most uneasy for the weight of it. You must take heart. This dry summer is going badly for the manors. The harvest of yesteryear is gone and the fields are sparse. We are close to new harvest—the Feast of Lammas is less than a fortnight away— yet look about you at the wilted rye, small fruits, stilted oats and barley. And now have I heard words of plague. 'Tis no wonder few are willing to help a stranger."

Pieter motioned Karl to his side. "Now you, lad, if you should be so kind as to gather some small vines or long roots and some small sticks, I'll show you how to build a fine trap before I leave."

In less than a winter's hour, fishermen and trappers were busy at their appointed tasks and Pieter was sauntering out of sight and into the woodland. Wil ordered others to build a fire and instructed Jon III to select some hardwood to be charcoaled for later use in the coal bucket. "Some good wood, boy. Else we'll be striking flint all the days to Palestine!"

By nightfall the crusaders had begun to filter toward the

cook-fire from all directions. Jon I raced from the riverbank shouting gleefully. "See, see here!" He had an unwilling, gasping river trout held high by the gill. Lothar grunted close behind, dragging a stiffened cod through the grass by its tail. The other boys had built a fair rabbit trap but failed at finding suitable bait. They entered the campsite reluctantly amidst the jeers of their disappointed comrades.

Wil looked hopefully toward the dark forest with an eye for Pieter. He had become quickly dependant on this strange, old man. But he had no sooner surrendered to the prospect of the priest's disappearance when he heard the friendly bark of Solomon and a few discordant melodies drifting toward him from the darkness. He released a sigh.

Pieter emerged into the pungent, welcoming smells of burning wood and roasting fish. He emptied his sack carefully, spilling a few black crusts, half an onion, two leeks, a handful of barley, some old oats, and a sound, though badly dented, tin pot. The children were reasonably impressed, and, before long, a meager, though delicious vegetable pottage was boiling over a crackling fire.

After enjoying their good meal, the children snuggled peacefully together atop their grassy beds oblivious to the perils poised before them. And soon each brave crusader was fast asleep, each stomach adequately filled with the pleasure of a satisfying portion, and each heart wrapped tightly in the secure love of Pieter the Broken.

Chapter 7
PESTILENCE AND DEATH

The next morning's sun beamed hope into the campsite as the faithful cheerfully roused themselves to their given tasks. Pieter welcomed daybreak on his knees and stretched his arms over his flock, "*Gratia, gratia Dei tibi....*" Contented by his lauds the old man pulled himself to his feet to join the assembling children.

Wil preferred to place Pieter just behind himself, keeping the wise counselor within a whisper or a glance. Karl was always close to the old man's heels and was trailed by Maria. The others gathered in a various order that was determined each new day by the feuds or friendships developed around the prior night's camp. Wil thought it wise to use Solomon as a shepherd's dog and suggested Pieter send him periodically to circle the pilgrims in order to keep the strays tight to the group. The priest found the idea agreeable and set the dog to the rear of the column as Wil counted heads. Content that all was in proper order, the young commander then ordered his fresh-faced soldiers southward.

The band tramped along in a complacent quiet and grumbled little of the hunger beginning to gnaw at them once again. Each eye, however, scoured the roadway for any scrap of fallen food that may have escaped the truant eye of a passing wagoner. Pieter, growing a bit bored and wanting to distract his own mind from his hollow belly, called over his shoulder to Karl. "So, lad, you fancy a proper riddle, do you?"

Karl's face lit and his lips parted into an impish grin.

"Ah, then, venture this: A magpie fluttered into a noble-man's manor house to sip of some wine from the very bottom of a fine cup. The nobleman's cup, however, was rather tall, the sort that Frenchmen boast, and the poor magpie failed to reach the wine. Yet, after reasonable contemplation, the clever bird was delighting in it. How would the magpie have accomplished such a thing?"

Karl's certain grin turned immediately to a confounded pucker. He scratched his head. "I ... I must think on this some, Pieter. But I vow to answer it in short!"

The lad was soon riveted in thought and paid scant attention to anything other than its answer until the column rounded a corner and came upon two sobbing children hobbling toward them from behind a thick shrubbery.

Wil halted his queue. "Yes, and who comes?"

"We're lost," a boy answered nervously as he approached the stern commander. He wrung his hands and his pleading eyes cast about the faces now encircling him. "And m'sister turned on her ankle and cannot walk very fast."

Wil grunted and stepped past the boy. "You, girl, let me see this leg of yours." He took the trembling girl's ankle gently in his hands and ran his nimble fingers over the swelling. Satisfied that no bones were broken, he turned toward her brother.

Pieter's blue eyes twinkled and he moved toward the newcomers with a smile and a tender tone. "Ah, what have we here? More lambs for our flock, I presume?"

Before the man could utter another word, Wil grasped him by the sleeve. "How can we feed more?" he groused. "We must stop increasing. No more of this." He tipped his head toward the two and pressed the old man. "Look there, her ankle is badly swelled and she cannot walk without help. He looks to have fever. Nay, we'll add no more."

Pieter answered gently, "To you, my brave friend, these little ones are something of a curse, another burden to be stacked upon your crowded shoulders. Yet, to them you are an answer to a prayer, a gift from the angels. Which is correct?"

Wil's lips worked to form an answer but none would come, and he cast his tired eyes to the ground. Pieter placed both his steady hands on the boy's shoulders and squeezed confidence into the lad's frame. He turned to the two. "Ah, dear children," Pieter said, "by what names are you known?"

The tense, though hopeful young boy stepped forward and choked, "I am Johann Lukas and this be my sister, Maria Marta."

"Yes, good names indeed. With Wil's permission, however, we'll call you by Lukas and Marta for it seems we've an abundance of Johanns and Marias as it is." Pieter put his arm around Lukas. "Are we agreed?"

"Oh, *ja ... ja*," answered the relieved boy as he pulled his fingers through his brown curls. "And we'll vex none ... and I think m'sister's ankle to be a bit better ... and ..."

"*Wilkum, ja*," interrupted Karl. "So Pieter, I've the answer to your riddle...."

"Hold, Karl," laughed Pieter. "Hold for a moment. Y'must make known to our new comrades, Lukas and Marta."

Karl gave the pair a quick nod. "But I've your answer: The magpie dropped gravel in the cup to raise the wine."

Pieter clapped his hands and rubbed the boy's red head. "Well done, well done indeed."

"And now I have one for you, Pieter."

Pieter smiled and sat down by Marta's side. He placed his palms flat behind him on the dirt and tilted his old head back to soak in every word the boy was about to offer.

"The forest spirits cast a woman with a spell. She could meet her husband only under cover of night, but by lauds she changed to a rose planted with three other roses in a pot by the bedroom window. If her husband could pluck her bloom she'd be free, but should he fail, she'd die.

"By each day's prime the husband came to the pot and looked carefully at the beautiful roses. Each was so very much alike he bedded each night uncertain which could possibly be his wife. At last, one dawn he bounded from his bed and ran to the pot and plucked a bloom and freed his wife of the spell. How knew he which to choose?"

Pieter set a bony forefinger to his pursed lips. "My, my, Karl, 'tis a good one. It shall take some time to unravel it."

                          ❧

The children marched on under the hot July sun eating bits and portions of sundry castoffs from passing travelers or of the good fortunes of the net in Pieter's pocket. The river served them well as their daily source of water for boiling gruel or bathing, and God was praised for the healing of Marta's ankle, Lukas's fever, and the varied maladies plaguing little Lothar. The group seemed to be constantly singing and whistling, shrieking and giggling, which often embarrassed their commander who thought such behavior most unnatural for warriors of the faith!

The fields of rye and barley bordering the roadway were wilted but stubbornly maturing as the coming harvest drew closer. The hay had long since been cut and sheaved, and white sheep now dotted the sickled meadows. Early fruits were beginning to appear within walled orchards, enticing the bolder boys to pluck an occasional young apple or pear to soften in the gruel.

The increasing fatigue of the journey had limited conversation, but a bond of earnest comradeship had begun to bind the children fast to one another. Pieter and Karl seemed to grow closer with every step along the way, each teasing the other with a short riddle or quick-spun sally. But it was Maria who had captured the old man's heart more than all the rest. This dear *Mädel* loved Pieter so very much and he, her. She shared the old man's lap with Solomon as evenings' fires lulled them both to deep sleep. It was about those same campfires that Pieter spun the tales of his youth to the speechless children circling the embers on hard-pressed elbows.

"*Ach, ja.* The furious battle of Tortona," he blustered one starry night. "Yes, 'tis true, m'lads and ladies, I did war there as a footman." Pieter's eyes widened and burned like the fire that roared at his feet. He stood wide-legged, his hands clutching his old crook which he now wielded over the heads of his audience like a mighty mace. "The good knights of Friederich the Fat were harried and bloodied, driven into a tight knot of leather and steel at the center of the Lombardian snare.

"Then, from within our retreating ranks, roared a giant of a man. A simple footman but unlike any I had ever met. To this very day I know not whence he came, nor whether his breast bore the heart of a lion ... or a devil. He stood two heads above every man among us and when he turned his mace upon the foe ..."

The children sat still as rabbits in the eye of a fox as Pieter wove them a rich tapestry for their dreams. He loomed them images of heavy-armored cavalry thundering o'er blood-stained fields and brave knights crashing in thunderous collisions of horseflesh and steel. Then, breathless and flushed, he proclaimed the glorious victory and whispered in hushed tones of the valiant footman who saved his lord's mighty army. The cheering crusaders stood to their feet and clapped.

But Pieter had merely paused to swallow a hearty gulp of begged mead and soon was at the easy task of drawing giggles and guffaws from the farthest stretch of firelight. He squatted by the snapping logs and told of Lord Friederich's huge, jiggling belly which "chilled the resolve of many a sturdy horse in waiting." He laughed and laughed and further revealed the agitations and tempers of Sir Balder the Bold whose nose always offered a good dripping "till his helmet was clasped fast. And then, good children, the oaths which bellowed from behind that bound face blushed even the rugged faces of the crudest knights in earshot!"

The girls soon begged for fancied tales of life in the court of Pieter's father, the Duke Otto, who, it was told, bellowed and barked so as to "weaken the knees of a hardened Templar" while nimbly picking pennyroyal and primrose for his beloved wife. They smiled dreamy smiles as the old priest spoke of the brocade silk dress his gentle mother wore, of her fine headdress of red satin and yellow silk from Syria, and of her silver necklaces from Greece and Persia.

Pieter's eyes closed and he wet his dry lips as he recalled the bounty of feasts past—of pheasant and venison, of fine roasted boar and duck buried in honey-sauced cherries. *Ah*, he thought, *even yet do I smell the crackling spit and the sweet glaze.* The children stirred politely and their entranced elder was called to his present company. "Ah, quite ... aye, aye, to other matters."

Pieter spoke freely and with passion of his days as a manorial priest and the years as a monk cloistered deep within the dark, damp walls of his Carthusian abbey. The children listened intently of his final exile to a harsh Cistercian order in Silesia, where his superiors believed depravation and hard work would quench the yearnings of his spirit. "It was there," Pieter reflected soberly, "while clearing timber from endless forests and trenching those miserable marshes that I learned to know the God of creation. 'Twas there my ears first cocked to the soft steps of a wolf in a winter's snow, and my nostrils twitched to the smell of the coming of rain on a summer's night. It was there that I began to grasp the very essence of the *kosmos*, for in that wilderness my eyes opened to our world's depravity, its dignity, and the ever-present hand that bears it firmly in its flux.

"My little ones, listen to my words: I beg you to understand so that you can believe. God has blessed you each with a sound mind, and the clues to understanding Him lie all about. It is for you to gather them to yourselves, arrange their proper order, and someday you shall surely seize the mystery of the mind of Almighty God."

Pieter's words gained force as he spoke with grave resolution. "If only we could fairly reason what lies all about us. We must needs conquer the confusion that blinds the eye and disturbs the mind. If we understand we can believe. I so swear."

Karl was inspired and rose to speak. "It is like a great riddle, is it not, Pieter? 'Tis like to a riddle where the answer is just beyond the knowing. But when we keep our mind to it, we do find the answer ... and are the better for it."

Pieter sat still for a moment and stared across the campfire into Karl's eager face. "You have said more, my young son, than some of the great philosophers. Indeed, there once lived an old Frenchman, St. Anselm was his name, who has darkened the world with his infamous blasphemy, *'Credo ut intelligam,'* which is to say, 'I believe in order to understand.' Can you see, m'children, how he has the forward to the rear? With such perilous reasoning, if it be 'reasoning' at all, 'tis no mystery to me why our world is as it is. Nay, nay ... we must understand *first* ... so that we are thereby enabled to believe ... I am certain of it. Learn to love your minds, little ones, and trust what you learn, so when you understand your God, you shall surely trust Him."

But Karl was suddenly puzzled. He held his tongue for a moment, reluctant to challenge his elder, but finally blurted, "Pieter, you did say *Saint* Anselm?"

Pieter nodded thoughtfully, uncertain where his young study was taking him.

"If he is a saint I think he must be right and true ... and ... and perhaps not you." His voice sagged at the end of his words and he looked at his feet.

Pieter's nose twitched ever so slightly and his face tightened just a little, but he managed a steady, kindly gaze at the earnest boy. "Well ... yes, my boy," he answered slowly. "Yes, well ..."

Before Pieter could fully compose his response, Tomas suddenly attacked. "Old man," he sneered, "I know nothing of this world and even less of God, but I'm true to m'self and confess no belief. By my oath, you don't know enough to truly believe in anything ... nor shall you ever. Hypocrite, y'be no different than me, only y'fear to say it."

Pieter lost his tongue as the boy's pointed darts stuck fast and deep. He turned away from Tomas and fixed his blue eyes into the dying, red embers of the night's fire. He slowly pulled his black hood over his tired, white head and wondered.

≈

By prime Pieter awoke without revealing the slightest hint of inner turmoil Tomas's unexpected discernment had caused. As the day's journey began, Karl walked close by his side and coaxed the old man to speak of new things. The distracted priest forced a patient smile. "This fine day I'll instruct you and all interested persons on the thoughts of Aristotle as taught in his most treasured books of logic."

Before Pieter could continue, a whining voice from the rear of the column suddenly pleaded, "Nay, nay, can y'not speak of else for us?"

"And might I inquire who is addressing me?"

Only the chirp of a passing bird broke the silence as Pieter glared over his shoulder, feigning anger. He turned to Karl and winked before clearing his throat. "I believe I'll teach something else, after all. Aristotle does not suit me this morning." So, instead, he marched until nearly noon reciting the works of Boethius and St. Augustine and all the while quite unaware of the disinterest of his captives. Most of his audience had done their best to avoid listening, Lothar being the first to stuff his ears with grass. A few managed to kick Karl in the rump as a warning against any such future requests! Finally, Pieter turned around, grinned at the weary column, and prepared for more.

Maria, not the least impressed with the old man's eloquence, stooped by the wayside and plucked some wildflowers. She tugged Pieter's hem with enough authority to convey mild displeasure. "Papa Pieter, 'tis time to stop talking and eat."

"Aye," an anonymous voice complained. "Why not fill your mouth with food instead of words?"

"When I was a young priest," chuckled Pieter, "I begged a rather ancient and exceptionally dull pastor to shorten his homily. 'Brevity is a fine substitute for ability,' I counseled. Perhaps I ought listen to my own words!"

His comment drew a few cheers as the exhausted pilgrims dropped onto a grassy clearing by the roadway. In short order, Wil distributed small portions of salt pork and tripe that Karl had been given by a kind dame and carefully rationed a wheat loaf begged by Jon I. After all had eaten and rested a while, Pieter reached carefully into a secret pocket he had sewn deep inside his robe and retrieved a well-worn pigskin wallet. He slowly, almost reverently, opened it and gently withdrew three stiff, partially blackened parchments stored carefully within. The children closed tightly around him as he laid each mysterious piece gently on his lap.

"I show only my dearest friends these treasures. As you have learned, I spent many years as a monk, vowed to the duties of copyist, and as such, I worked for years bent over a small table scratching God's Word onto parchments such as these.

"Ah, but sadly, one cold winter's night, a novice in our order was careless with his coals and caught his bed aflame. Unable to extinguish it, his dormitory was soon a roaring furnace and then, in turn, the whole of the cloister. Unfortunate for us brothers, the novices were bedded by the scriptorium and soon the work of a century was but smoke and brittle ash. It was most awful. I had set aside my worthless water pail to rescue these pages of the Holy Scripture from a burning Bible and this charred paragon from one of Aristotle's books."

Pieter held a parchment between the thumb and forefinger of each hand. "Behold my most esteemed possessions: a portion of the Psalms in my right hand and nearly an entire page from First Corinthians in my left. Poor Aristotle is so very damaged I fear it best to leave it lay on my lap. Someday I vow to learn a way to return it to whole."

Pieter affectionately returned Aristotle's page to the wallet and then cradled the Scripture on his lap. The inquisitive children drew even closer, straining over and under each other like a litter of curious kittens watching a butterfly bend a blade of grass. Most had never seen a written word of any kind and the sight of such a marvel hushed them. Finally, one little boy stretched his dirty finger to touch the parchment.

"Ah, my son," said Pieter kindly, "it would be better for that pointer of yours to be washed."

The boy plunged his forefinger into his mouth and offered it again to the chuckling priest. The boy moved his finger toward the strange shapes slowly, almost fearfully. When he touched the paper he recoiled for a moment, wondering if some power would be unleashed on him. He looked at Pieter for reassurance before leaning toward the page again. This time his finger eased along the lines of the letter *A.* He grinned and proceeded to follow the rest of the letters as Pieter read them aloud. "A-M-O-R, which is to say, 'love.'"

"Why not just 'love'?" asked a confused little girl.

"Because these words are written in Latin," answered Pieter.

Karl blurted, "Yes. Latin is the language of the pope and the Holy Church; it is the language of heaven itself, and of Jesus and the Holy Virgin."

Pieter answered with measured words. "It is truly the language of the Holy Roman Church, but I do not accept it to be the language of heaven nor of Jesus or Mother Mary."

Karl was shocked. "What?" he exclaimed. "Every priest, every monk, the abbot, and even the archbishop speak to God and listen to God ... in Latin."

"Ah, dear boy, you are aware, I am certain, that the Romans who crucified our Lord spoke Latin, and the Caesars who slayed our brothers and sisters in antiquity also spoke this ... this language of heaven. Have you ever considered that perhaps God wishes to speak to His children so they might understand? Could you believe that God could speak German to Germans, French to Frenchmen, and even Arabic to the Saracens?"

Karl was speechless.

Not wishing to pursue the matter, Pieter returned his attention to the parchments and selected one of them. "This page is from the one-hundred fourth Psalm. I am sorry I've but portions." Pieter knew this to be a powerful moment for his children. "Ah, my lambs, grant your loving Father in heaven leave to speak through His Holy Word, and tell me, I pray, whether you hear Him." Pieter held his parchment at arm's length and slowly translated.

Bless the Lord, O my soul, O Lord my God, thou art very great; thou art clothed with honor and majesty ...

He watereth the hills from his chambers: the earth is satisfied with the fruit of thy works.

He causeth the grass to grow for the cattle, and herb for the service of man: that he may bring forth food out of the earth;

And wine that maketh glad the heart of man, and oil to make his face to shine, and bread which strengtheneth man's heart ...

O Lord, how manifold are thy works! In wisdom hast thou made them all: the earth is full of thy riches ...

Pieter stopped and closed his eyes. He held the singed page lightly to his heart and sighed before gingerly folding it and securing it in its proper place. The children said nothing as he spread the next passage on his lap, gently straightening each fragile corner and smoothing it with the clean side of his bony hand.

"These verses are found in a book called First Corinthians and you shall find them most pleasing: 'If I speak in the tongues of men and of angels but have not love, I am but a resounding gong or a clanging cymbal. If I have a faith that can move mountains but have not love, I have nothing. If I give all I possess to the poor and yield my body to the flames but have not love, I gain nothing. Love is patient, love is kind. It does not envy, it does not boast, it is not proud. It is not rude, it is not self-seeking, it is not easily angered. It holds no record of wrongs. Love does not delight in evil but rejoices with the truth. It always protects, always trusts, always hopes, always perseveres. Love never fails.'"

The children sat hushed, unable to grasp the full measure of either the message or the occasion, but awed nonetheless. Maria broke the silence. "Papa Pieter, it seems God must love us much."

Pieter's eyes watered. A large tear tumbled across his

weathered face and disappeared in his beard. He reached for the girl and laid his hand tenderly atop her golden head. "And my dear, precious lamb, only He could love you more than I."

ॐ

The next morning Wil was awakened by a distraught Karl and Jon I. They reported that three or four of the smallest children, including Maria the Younger and Marta, the sister of Lukas, were stricken with fever and were desperately ill. Wil roused Pieter from his grassy bed and both dashed straightaway to the groaning girls.

The girls were sweating profusely and lurching about the ground in delirium. Maria the Younger was breathing quickly and trembling, her yellowed eyes slightly rolled backward in their sockets, and Marta fared no better. Pieter knelt to hold Maria the Younger in his arms. He plucked a poppy still dewy from the night and placed it on her chest as he prayed.

Wil quickly retrieved the satchel of herbs from Brother Lukas and offered them to Pieter. "Here, I've some medicines."

Pieter brightened and gently laid Maria on a small blanket. His eyes narrowed and his fingers scrambled through the vials and ampoules. "Karl, fetch some water, quickly. We have need of an infusion ... aye ... we'll use this basil, thyme, and sage ... yes, yes, this should be most helpful, most helpful indeed."

"And here," urged Wil, "here is a little *belladonna atropa*. The priest at the village ordered its use for my fevered mother, and ..."

"Nay, you have misunderstood him, boy. This is no remedy, 'less murder is the ambition." Pieter heaved the contents of the tin, scattering the deadly herb across the wet grass. "We've no need of that Devil's herb."

Dumbstruck, Wil stared at Pieter angrily. His mouth was suddenly dry. "What say you, old man ... old madman? Poison? 'Tis not so!"

"Yes, 'tis poison. I believe I spoke plain enough. What ails you now, lad?"

Wil's face paled in the early day's light and perspiration beaded on his brow. "B-but, the ... the priest ordered it be given to Mother ... and ..."

"Hear me, lad," Pieter offered gently, concerned for the boy's sudden terror. "I am certain your memory is a bit confused. For all their wicked ways, I've yet to know a priest to give such to a living soul, and ..."

"But he did, he did! He said it would end m'mother's fever." Wil wrung his hands and looked fearfully about the circle of blank faces staring at him. "He did ... I swear it." The boy slowly backed away from the camp before fleeing into the shadowed woodland.

Karl returned with some water and the troubled priest began to prepare the brew. "Young fellow," Pieter said, "would you recall any instructions for the remedy your village priest offered for your mother?"

Karl thought for a moment and then answered casually. "Methinks something of an infusion from an herb called *Bella ... Bella Atrop* ... I do not actually remember for certain.... Why do you ask?"

Pieter nearly dropped his pail and his face darkened with rage. He pursed his lips and breathed through pinched nostrils, but held his tongue. With a sad look to the forest he answered mercifully, "'Tis no matter."

Early in the evening of that same day the cold hand of death plucked a soul from the faithful band. Maria the Younger had drawn her last breath and now lay lifeless and stark-white on the dry grass. Poor Marta was failing and the sight of Maria's drawn face gave her fair cause to cry out in fear. Two others had shown symptoms of the same distress and Pieter suggested the three be taken by first light to a small village he had noticed in the distance.

But before the stars could find their place, poor Marta had passed to her rest as well. Both girls' bodies were washed by loving hands in the dark Rhine and tenderly and tearfully laid in shallow night-dug graves. The weeping children stood respectfully on the moonlit riverbank and stared at the stony mounds as a heavy-hearted Pieter addressed the Almighty.

"*Pater, Filius, Spiritus Sanctus* ... Oh, Lord of all Creation, we know not why You chose to withhold Your awesome might from these helpless ones. We know not why the Great Physician heals not on most occasions. We understand little of You, but You are our God. Help us understand so we might be empowered to love You more deeply. Now we beseech You to spare these departed souls the horrors of the Pit and receive them into Your heavenly realm, forever. Amen."

Wil stood at a distance, still reeling from Pious's betrayal, and observed his weeping band with some disdain. His grief and frustration had turned inward and an unrequited wrath seethed in his bones. The haunting awareness of his own ignorance and his misplaced confidence fed his fury. He yearned for vengeance and vowed to never trust again.

Maria cuddled with Solomon between the two graves and sobbed quietly to sleep. Others slowly drifted to their grassy beds at the roadside and stared sadly into the late July night's sky. Only Pieter's restless groaning broke the silence of that sorrowful night and soon all were fast asleep.

The rustle of birds at prime stirred the travelers and set them to their morning's tasks. After bidding a sad farewell, the fevered children were escorted to the nearby hamlet while others prepared for first-meal. Before long a few eels were roasting over a snapping fire and three good, round turnips were boiling in the pot. Pieter had finished his morning prayers and returned to the camp quietly.

"So, Father Pieter," smirked Tomas, "resolve this riddle: Say how you use these deaths to understand your God."

Wil stared hard at the troubled priest and stepped to Tomas's side. Pieter looked first at his feet and then at his beloved Maria who was holding his bony hand in a firm grip. He stroked Solomon's head and sighed. "I ... I am without a reply, my son. I simply do not know."

Pleased with his perceived victory, Tomas sneered and walked to the far side of the camp. The other children soon finished their small portions and reassembled, the escorts having returned. All tucked their crosse securely into their rope belts and now waited patiently for Wil's command to march. Pieter dragged himself to his position but his mind was plagued by the vision of the pale cheeks and purple lips of the two girls he had interred the night before. He turned one final look at their graves and shook his head.

The crusaders marched silently southward that day with little to distract them from their exhaustion other than an occasional peddler or passing pilgrim. Pieter, determined to leave the past in its place, leaned hard on his staff and bent low to scratch Solomon's ears. "Ah, Karl … I've a bit of bad news for you."

Karl stepped quickly to his side. "Bad news?"

"I've the answer to thy riddle." He smiled weakly.

Disappointment shrouded the boy's round face and he kicked at a stone in the dust.

"'Twas a fine riddle, though, one I'll endeavor to remember in m'old age." Pieter chuckled. "By the look of you I should have been better to fail at it."

"Just end m'misery, Pieter."

"The husband plucked the bloom that had no dew upon it."

Karl shrugged and reluctantly affirmed the grinning priest's answer. "I'll confound you yet … priest."

The weary column finally arrived at the top of a long, upward grade and the crusaders threw themselves on the hard ground. They had barely closed their eyes, however, when a light breeze filled their nostrils with a terrible, odious stench. Pieter groaned and begged God's mercy, for the air bore him a dreadful familiarity, an unwelcome and horrible memory that awakened every unpleasant emotion in his anxious soul.

Wil ordered his complaining soldiers to their feet and drove them over the crest of the hill, hoping all the while to escape the noxious odor. But as they descended, the air became more rank until each whining pilgrim had pulled his tunic over his nose. Wishing to get past whatever ghastly rot was near, Wil led them at a quick pace and the column was soon charging down the roadway. They rounded a sharp bend where their advance was suddenly arrested. With a single gasp the band halted, most turning their faces away, for they had come upon a spectacle which so sickened and dismayed them, so wholly overwhelmed them, that they could barely endure the sight.

Piled at the side of the roadway was a tangled, putrefied heap of fellow crusaders. Their tiny corpses were bloated and bursting in the heat, their flesh torn and ripped by dispassionate vultures now crowing high overhead. Their trickled blood had dried in a ghoulish, dark cascades which spidered over them and puddled in blackened, grassy pools beneath. Those eyes not yet gouged from little faces stared helplessly toward heaven itself, as if begging for some explanation. But none was offered.

Pieter stiffened and, submerging all emotion, advanced solemnly with Solomon by his side. He stood silently a few paces from the pile and considered each body singularly, wishing to grace each child with at least a moment's dignity. He then dropped slowly to his knees, raised his hands in blessing, and moaned a benediction for their departed souls. When he finished he kissed his cross and pulled himself upright to trembling legs.

Pieter leaned hard on his staff, lost in thought and entranced by the buzzing of the swarms of flies shrouding the corpses. He finally furrowed his brow and leaned over the mound to discern any sign of wound or injury. All his trained eyes could detect, however, were tiny lesions on a few faces. The old man was still curious, though fairly certain of a diagnosis, and reached out his nimble fingers to probe the children's thin limbs and protruding ribs. Having concluded that these crusaders' ends were wrought by starvation and fever, the priest turned to his flock.

"My soul cries within me." Pieter's face twisted in a building rage and he roared to his crusaders. "I yearn for judgment against those wicked, heartless demons who have stacked these poor little ones like so much tinder! Had they no heart at all for such as these? We'll not simply pass them by."

He quieted. "There are too many for us to bury and some were beset with fever, so, dear lambs, we must ... burn them." His voice choked on his command but his fellows understood.

Pieter was not pleased, however, with his children's response, for though they dutifully set upon the task at hand they did so with steely resolve and not so much as a whimper. The man's heart ached for them. *Gott im Himmel,* he moaned to himself. *Can they have been so hardened in so short a time?*

Tomas intruded. "All's ready for the torch."

Pieter looked speechlessly at the boy and the circle of children staring at the wood-ringed bier waiting before him. And, without a word, he set a thin branch ablaze from an ember in the coal-pot and slowly touched it to the bramble piled at his feet. He dropped it from a quivering hand and retreated to the side of his fellow pilgrims. With eyes reddened by sorrow and glowing with anger, he watched as the fire crept over the unsuspecting kindling and rose to pounce from one darkening corpse to another.

The heat and stench soon drove the poor company backward as the flames flared like the torches flanking the gates of hell. For Pieter it was as if Lucifer and his demons were laughing at him from the fire, dancing and frolicking, taunting and hissing in a gleeful celebration of death and damnation.

Chapter 8
GOOD GEORG

Quietly, Wil continued to lead his crusaders south through the Rhine valley. Each haunted face now belied a young soul in turmoil, save the dark-hearted Tomas who found it amusing to share his morbid satisfactions regularly. And who could dare refute his endless commentary on the spectacle they had left behind? Karl, bewildered and utterly undone, spent the hours choking on tears and dodging the apparent logic of his black-haired foil. He had nothing to say, no answer for the doubts swirling about his own mind let alone the outrageous blasphemies of Tomas. The abiding agony for poor Karl was the insufferable vision of tiny red crosses curling in the flames of the burning crusaders. His ears filled with the echoes of the past, those joyous cries in the abbey: "We go to God, we go to God." *Indeed they did*, he thought as he clutched his necklace, though not the way he had imagined.

Wil's hard eyes gazed steadily at the horizon before him. Anger raged within and he felt little else. He was neither willing to reject nor embrace his faith but the sights and smells of the day prior had seared his soul. He had become a young man with a crumbled foundation, filled with confusion yet secretly desperate to retain some remnant of the hope now fleeting away. He withdrew deep into other memories, at which point he marched more contented for having found some rest within. But such respites were short-lived at best, for no sooner would he submerge his mind to far places when the ghost of his poisoned mother burst from the shadows to accuse him. It was at those moments he was glad he had taken his apple-wood cross and thrown it into those dreadful flames. *Better to trust in this dagger than in that cross,* he thought.

The day passed to night and the next morning brought its routine of duties for the crusaders. Wil sent several of the boys to fetch water, others to break kindling, and still others to beg provisions with Pieter at a forester's cottage by the road. The girls were set about the chores of ferreting through the blankets and bags for what few provisions might be discovered for a morning's mush when Jon I suddenly burst from the trees. "Wil! Wil! M'brother's in a well! Come help afore he drowns!"

Wil, followed by the others, raced behind Jon I to an abandoned stone-lined well the boys had discovered deep in the wood. He could hear the trapped boy's cries echoing eerily through the forest and soon was peering into the dark hole. Wil could barely see Jon III but knew the boy could not hold fast to the slippery walls much longer.

Jon III could see only dark silhouettes ringing the bright opening above him. "Help!" he pleaded. "I think m'leg to be broken ... it hurts and I cannot climb ... I cannot hold ... I fear to drown ... hurry, I beg you!"

"We need rope to pull him up or branches for him to climb," Wil ordered. "Hurry! Find me a stout branch ... or ..."

Pieter burst through the wood. "Aye, but we've no rope, no ax."

Suddenly Karl cried out, "I have it. I have it!" He turned to Wil and Pieter, his face flushed and his eyes wide. "Pieter, remember m'riddle? The riddle ... do you remember my riddle?"

The old man stared blankly.

"We needs dump all we can lift to the well and rise the bottom 'til we float Jon up."

Wil and Pieter's eyes met as Karl's novel idea settled. "*Ja!* By the saints, boy, you've settled it!" exclaimed Pieter.

The words had barely left the old man's lips when the

crusaders began heaving rocks, brush, logs, and whatever other rubble they could handle over the well's wall.
Poor Jon III was ignorant of the fine scheme and
protested loudly as he dodged the falling debris. But
soon, to the delight of all, the boy began to float up a little
... then a little farther.

"More!" squealed Karl. "More! He's coming up."

The gleeful children charged back and forth, dropping
whatever they could manage past the bruised and bleeding face of a very hopeful boy. At last, the lad stretched
his fingers to the top edge of the well and was plucked to
safety by the strong arms of Wil and Tomas. He collapsed to the ground exhausted but quite content to
spend a few moments basking in the love of his cheering
comrades.

Though the boy's leg was badly broken, Pieter was able
to make a sturdy splint of stout sticks and knotted vines.

"Good fellow," comforted Pieter. "I'll find you a worthy
household for healing and you shall dance the ringdance
by Christmas feasts."

Karl, pleased with his own good sense and relieved for
good news, boasted to the others, "God is still with us. We
have been worthy crusaders and God *does* care for us."

Tomas shrugged indifferently. "If God cared I should
think Jon would not have dropped into the well at all."

Karl dismissed Tomas's remark with a sweep of his hand
and a wrinkle of his nose, for his mood had changed. In
fact, the whole company was now encouraged, happy for a
bit of light on a darkening journey. The black fog that had
enshrouded them all was once again pierced by a merciful
glint of hope.

࿄

By prime of the following morning Pieter set out to make
good his pledge to Jon III and climbed beyond the crest of
an eastern knoll in search of a good home for the lad. Some
might say it was rare fortune, indeed, that led him to a
nearby cluster of tidy cottages placed neatly in the shadow
of an orderly manorhouse where Pieter soon found himself
in the company of a kindhearted lord. And somewhere

between the courtesy of a good cheese and the bond of a hearty laugh, the priest and the gentle lord agreed on a fitting household for Jon III. The lord promptly ordered his servants to fetch the lad, and they returned quickly with the splinted boy and a column of curious crusaders.

In the meantime, the manor's fuller, his wife, and three children had been summoned from the wash-house so that their duties as Jon III's caretakers might be firmly imposed. To Pieter's cautious eye, the fuller seemed to be a decent man, young and soft-spoken, sturdy of build and quick to laugh. His wife, he thought, was gracious for a peasant woman, ample and ruddy.

Jon III was introduced and seemed pleased to imagine life with these good folk. He smiled shyly as the woman embraced her new charge, and he yielded to the teasing of his former fellows with a deep-hued blush.

The lord's wife beckoned the crusaders to enter the great hall of her gracious home and commanded her servants bring a generous assortment of foods and beverages to the wide table at its center. The odd time of day notwithstanding, the children spared no reserve and soon filled themselves with early fruits, wheat bread, mead, cider, honey cakes, and pork.

When all had finished, Pieter stood and bowed respectfully to the lord and his lady and blessed them for their kindness. "You shall be remembered in all eternity for your selfless kindness this day, my good lord and lady."

The pleased man bowed and took Pieter by the shoulder. "It is but a pittance, Father, a modest token of the bounty of blessing which this household has enjoyed."

"And would that we could repay such …"

"Ah, yes. Truth be told, you may indeed offer something in return." The lord's face broadened. A timid boy emerged from behind a tapestry, red-faced and nervous. The lord beamed with pride. "Father … crusaders … permit me to introduce my son, Georg."

The boy stepped to his father's side and stared at the floor. The lord wrapped an arm around the boy's sloped shoulders and continued. "Indulge me, I beg. Would you follow me to my courtyard?" The man's amiable, bearded face lighted with joy and his eyes twinkled. He led the assembly out of the hall and into the sunny gardens just beyond the manorhouse gates. He chuckled to himself, excited for the moment, and clapped his hands. Then, from the corner of the orchard wall came a peasant leading a donkey laden heavily with sacks of provisions.

The lord ran to the beast and helped his servant unload the stock. He spread baskets and satchels at the feet of the wide-eyed children, uncovering a storehouse of smoked fish, smoked venison, salted pork, onions and leeks, turnips, millet, oats, and fresh beans.

Pieter was astounded. "May God bless you, m'lord," he offered quietly.

"Think nothing of it, nothing of it at all. The pleasure is surely mine to savor as I humbly share my bounty with such a noble company." The man summoned his son close to his side once again. "Ah, but I should fail you lest I not confess my own selfish ends in this."

Pieter's ears cocked.

He gripped the edges of his purple cape. "I do so wish to bless your pilgrimage, but I find it doubly comforting to be certain that my own crusader, my sole son, Georg, has ample provisions as well."

Pieter and Wil winced at his words, though the wise priest was the more careful in revealing his mind. Wil blurted, "My lord, I think n—"

Pieter hushed the boy with a raised finger and stern eye. He smiled politely at the lord and turned to study the blushing candidate. Pieter thought the lad to be about fourteen years and considered "plump" to be the kindest word of choice. *Nearly as round as tall, and not the sort that has the look of adventure.* Unlike the peasant children, this youth had doubtless never missed a meal. *A dandy with kindly eyes,* mused Pieter. *Though 'tis hard to discern them 'midst the puffed cheeks that squeeze them so.*

Georg's broad head was covered by a fashionable, wide-brimmed hat which was pressed snugly over his long, straight, brown hair. But, fancy as was the *hut,* the peasant children paid more attention to his linen breeches. His were the new-fashioned leggings some had heard of: belted at the waist, worn to the knees, and suspending long hose which stretched over the feet. Most thought them to be unnecessary. After all, their own simple, one-piece leggings had served folk since the dawn of time.

Instead of a tunic, the boy wore a white linen shirt with cuffs and a collar, and over that he sported a green waistcoat embroidered with a newly stitched, bright-red crusader's cross. He shuffled slightly in his thick-soled shoes.

"Good and gracious sire," said Pieter finally, "my fellows are surely enlivened by the noble tender of your valiant son. We'll march on, all the more secured by the knowledge that such as he is hoping for us, yea, perhaps yet praying for us from within the sanctuary of this home so blessed by God. It is more comfort than my humble words might express for us to know that Georg is serving the cause of Christendom, ah, even our cause, from within the sound walls of this blessed manor."

The lord's mood changed and he spoke deliberately from behind fixed eyes. "It is my behest as well as Georg's firm resolution that he join with you." Softening his tone, he added, "He ... he would have joined another company had he not suffered a great pain in his belly a fortnight past."

Georg's face paled at the snickers born of that remark.

"And now it is my wish and the wish of my Frau that you receive him as one of yours."

Pieter raised a brow to Wil, shrugged his shoulders, and embraced the trembling boy. "Welcome, Georg, welcome. And may God go with us all."

The old priest stepped aside as the lord and his wife hugged their son. "Go, Georg, go with God and return to us soon."

Georg closed his eyes and received a final stroke of his mother's hand across his face. He met his father's moistening eyes with an anxious, though determined gaze and walked cautiously toward his new comrades.

The peasant-warriors eyed him suspiciously. Serfs and nobility rarely shared a word, let alone a pilgrimage, but they were grateful for the lord's kindness and yielded dutifully to Pieter's threatening stare. They lined up behind Wil and bowed respectfully to their hosts before bundling their new supplies in their blankets. Then, with a few tears for Jon III and a chorus of thanksgivings and gratitudes, the crusaders filed out of the courtyard and disappeared over the hill.

The children were now cheerful and well fed, high spirited and ambitious. No longer did the Rhine road daunt them, but rather it invited them to press ever southward on their holy march. The day passed more quickly than others, and, having made good distance through the wide Oberrheingraben, Wil ordered a brief rest in the shade of the forest now bordering the roadway.

Though pleased with improving morale and ample provision, Wil nevertheless abided a growing resentment toward Georg's recruitment. Unable to restrain his feelings he dragged the new recruit behind a large tree. "Listen well, fat boy. You shall do as I speak and when I speak it. You'd be one of us now … none better. You are not our master. You shall march at the rear and had best keep those flabbed legs striding. You'll have no greater portion than I allow and we care not one whit 'bout your belly pains. And should one grouse, a single complaint of any sort fall on my ear I'll drive you away. Do you understand?"

Georg's gentle face quivered and flushed. He offered a weak smile and nodded respectfully.

୭

The next day passed with Pieter walking cheerfully at his customary position just behind Wil and with faithful Solomon by his side. He raised his chin and baked his wrinkled face in the brilliance of the bright sunlight, contemplating for a brief moment the darkness of his future grave. His beard bent in the soft breezes and he sighed before turning to wink at Karl. "Now Karl, dear boy, this would be a fine opportunity for me to offer you yet another riddle."

Karl smiled in eager anticipation.

"This particular riddle shall be presented in a number of parts and we'll see if you might answer it before the last clue is offered. Ah, I truly must confess, lad, that I am only now beginning to grasp its meaning and *that* dubious success comes only after years of reflection. So it is. Are you ready?"

Karl nodded.

"Good. The first is this: 'To what sun-washed haven must the dying daisy flee and in what wonderland abides the snow-lade' holly tree?'"

Karl's nose wrinkled.

Pieter chuckled. "So, *when* you are in need of another clue, you shall ask and I'll give!"

Wil turned his head toward his brother and the priest but his eyes fell upon his sister. He slowed his pace even more and took careful note of her thinning frame and the awkward way her legs now seemed to bow. *She looks so very tired*, he thought, but she had scarcely ever passed an hour without offering him a ready smile and gentle wave. *Would that the others complain as little as she*, he thought. Always seeking to offer encouragement, the little girl often strayed from the pathway to pick bunches of wildflowers.

A pain pierced Wil's heart as his mind suddenly envisioned her tossed atop that cursed pile of corpses with flames stretching and leaping to blacken her lifeless body. An icy chill clung to his skin and he pressed back tears. His guarded spirit, toughened from years of hurt as a child, was not wholly lost and its tenderest remnants warred earnestly against a creeping hardness born of a deepening cynicism. *Maria shall surely die on this journey*, he thought as he tightened his fists. *I know that God will kill her. Nothing lovely lasts. Not the flowers in spring, not the colors of dawn ... nothing. And if she is spared, life shall change her into the monster our ... mother became.*

To Wil, Karl had the look of an exhausted but ever-faithful dog; always present, always working, rarely complaining and ever eager. His round, ruddy face seemed ever flushed by sincere effort, but his frame was thinning and his once, cheerful eyes sparkled less as the frequency of heartache had worked to extinguish them.

At the rear of the column trailed Tomas, usually alone and at some distance from the others. His darkening disposition created unease, and his secretive and ever-sullen mood had cost him the camaraderie and fellowship of his companions. He missed few opportunities to complain and was quick to nourish Wil's doubts. His black eyes stalked the faltering and he would be seen pouncing on such prey with whispered words of discouragement. Lately he had begun to wander away, sometimes for a day at a time, always to return with some fantastic tale of woodland spirits or fairies, or a fearful yarn of witchcraft or sorcery in the dark forests to the east.

Pieter, however, faithfully pressed forward with his beloved flock, deftly hiding from their view the grave concerns that so disquieted his soul. In its hidden chambers his mind reeled and he wrestled to put order to the confusion all about him. *What can be said of this God of mine? He saves one from a well ... yet why not all from fever? He saves these from starvation ... yet why not those?*

Pieter's thoughts whirled within his whitened head as his beloved flock followed obediently. They complained on occasion but not so often as they would surely have been entitled, choosing instead to search for strengths within and without themselves. The ever-giving Georg was always willing to squeeze a quick smile between desperate wheezes and he pressed his heavy legs forward without as much as a murmur. Gentle Lothar, though weakened and frequently carried on Wil's shoulders, calmed many with a soft song. The others, like little Anna and the always-true Jons, marched ever onward with an earnestness that would have heartened the most war-worn Christian knights.

❧

The day following, the crusaders rounded a bend in the dusty road and paused to survey the scene spread before them. Their faithful companion, the Rhine River, was now dotted with flat-bottom barges and the single masts of sailing ships. On the near shore women pulled reeds for weaving, while along the farther shore fishermen worked their cod nets, deftly throwing them toward the river's bottom with well-trained arms.

"Look there." Lothar pointed. "Must be a city at some distance. See the busy roadway."

The children peered across the river toward the faraway walls of Strasbourg. A parade of carts and horsemen could be seen as tiny figures along the road leading from the ferries. "Aye," answered Pieter. "'Tis a city out there, indeed … and a good one. Ah, if you could only enjoy its innards … the markets and fairs, the foods, the fine homes and cathedrals." Pieter put his arms around Jon I and Karl and recounted his times wandering the place. He spoke of its grand marketplace filled with wares from the East—silk and perfumes, spices and fine silver. "Beautiful tapestries hang within the courtyards of the wealthy and women adorn themselves with the finest of gold. And the wine, ah, the wine! I am told the markets now sell a new accessory for the *cives* called 'buttons.'"

The children waited for an explanation.

"Buttons, as they are described to me, are round or squared bits of carved wood or brass used to bind tunics fast by the chest. Seems clever enough. They are stitched to one side and pushed through a hole cut in the other."

The children laughed. "Buttons," chuckled one. "Why not a few for Georg's breeches!"

"*Ja, ja*, let us be kindly toward our friend Georg." The old man smiled and proceeded to speak of the city's minstrels and jugglers, of fools and jesters who could make both peasant and nobleman laugh to tears. "My children … know this, that merriment belongs as surely to prince as pauper. When people laugh we laugh without station, for our chortles are not those of lord or serf, high-birth or low, but of all who are made in the image of a God … who also laughs. 'Tis a joyous wonder to see the silked sleeve of a burgher wipe the same salted tear as the homespun of a peasant."

The crusaders soon turned their eyes away from visions of Strasbourg and rejoined their attention to days of hard marching. Late one sultry evening a turn in the road delivered them to a view of the trading town of Dunkeldorf set some distance ahead. The sun was setting and Wil suggested the group make camp. In short order a small fire was snapping amidst a circle of forlorn and dirty faces.

For the past fortnight many such occasions were a pleasant, if not happy, respite, but this night's fire nurtured a brooding melancholy. Pieter offered his usual blessing and a few strips of eel, a grasp of dried apples, and a final hard piece of spelt bread. But the pilgrims were painfully aware that they were about to swallow the last of the provisions Georg's father had provided, and they knew hard times were upon them again.

Sensing the depressed spirits of his children, Pieter stood close by the quiet flames and, with a large, one-toothed grin began to tell tales of the ancient Germanic *volk*. The children's distress dissolved into the darkness as the old man immersed his flock in the adventures of their Teutonic forebears.

Pieter thrust and parried his staff at the shadows as his voice bellowed the legends of the soldiers of the Mayfields, of battles against dragons, of the rescue of maidens, and of the guardian spirits of the valleys beyond their sight. "And soon, my children"—he pointed his staff into the darkness—"we shall come upon the edges of the endless Schwarzwald ... a forest said to teem with elves and fairies ... a place filled with mystery; a place where stars sprinkle magic dust and the trees are keepers of secrets. Ah, my dears, such a place of wonder."

The children were still. Pieter walked slowly to the rim of the campfire and placed his hands solemnly atop his crook. "Close your eyes, my children, and see with your mind the sights of your world. Everything that can be seen has purpose."

Pieter's voice hushed to a whisper and he drew his black hood over his head. "The falling leaf in autumn, each summer's dewdrop, every cry of the owl, each breath of the wind ... all have purpose."

A voice chirped from the shadows. "Even so the fairies?"

"Ah, yes, child, even the visions of our … imaginations."

A rumble of protest circled the ring of earnest faces. "Nay so, Pieter!" cried one. "Nay so. M'*Vater's* been about the wood and seen such with his own eyes."

"Aye, and for me too," stated another. "M'village is circled by elves near to every Midsummer's feast.… 'Tis not in our heads."

Pieter had no wish to challenge such things, and the sparkle in Maria's hopeful eyes was enough for him to yield his own thoughts of the subject. He remembered his own days of longing for a glimpse of the pointed leather cap of a happy troll, or the fleeting wings of a woodland fairy. "Ah, perhaps true enough," he answered. "I confess no certainty on these matters. Perhaps the spirits dwell in both our minds and the forest."

Contented for having their dreams spared, the crusaders returned to the comfort of the fire and the warmth of the old man's words. And soon enough their eyes weighed heavy and yielded to a good night's sleep.

Dawn came too soon for most, save Wil who was eager to search for treasures in the town just ahead. So, with little food to prepare, the column formed quickly and followed their leader to the gates of Dunkeldorf.

"Have y'been at this town, Pieter?" asked Karl.

Pieter nodded slowly. "*Ja*, my son. I have been here and I doubt it wise to return."

Wil was in no mood for reservation. "Pieter," he snapped, "we've no choice but to enter and seek provisions. Lammas feast is soon and methinks the town must have a bounty to share."

Pieter sighed and ignored the boy's bite. Instead he cast a loving gaze at the weary faces of his flock. He looked sadly at their tattered clothing and swollen feet. All were hungry and some were sick, yet there remained a glint of stubborn faith and an abiding glimmer of hope in each eye his met. The sight of such resolve stirred Pieter's heart and he whispered a silent prayer for his wisdom and for their protection.

The old man turned to Wil. "I do yield to your command, m'young lord, yet heed my words: this is a place to fear. Be wary, stay close, and confer all respects upon the folk within."

Suddenly Georg squeezed through the column, a tentative expression spreading over his face. "Might I have leave to speak?"

Wil nodded.

"I have not journeyed here, nor, to my knowledge, has my good father. But I have heard our huntsmen speak of it as a dangerous place for all. They report it to be corrupted by an evil burgher and magistrate. 'Tis said to be a sanctuary for the lawbreakers of the realm and of the kingdom of France."

Tomas sneered and strutted toward Georg. "If y'be afraid, fat boy, you may stay and tend a fire for our return. I would surely not want y'to suffer another belly pain from your fears."

Georg blushed.

"His words might be true, Tomas," offered Karl.

"Aye, so they may be. But the fat one'd be a coward by any count."

Pieter set a comforting hand on Georg's shoulder and addressed the group. "It is proper for Georg to share what he knows and we thank him. I, too, am aware of the dark words spoken of this place ... but our provisions are nearly exhausted. We'll follow Wil forward ... with the greatest care."

With little more than a few grunts and gestures, Wil directed his soldiers toward the walled town. Pieter set his mind to prayer but had barely offered his first petition when Karl interrupted.

"I'd be ready for the next clue."

"Clue for what, boy?" Pieter wondered.

"Your riddle."

The old man smiled. "Now? Ah, very well, here is the next: 'The songs of thrush and nightingale are born upon the breeze, but toward what Country do they drift while passing o'er the trees?'"

Karl's face grimaced and twisted as he wrestled with the words. "*Ach*, y've given a hard clue, Pieter, and I've still no answer."

"Rather difficult 'tis sure, but there is little joy in simple riddles. Have you another one for me?"

Karl paused for a moment, while Maria, who was listening to the two of them, skipped to Karl's side and whispered in his ear. "Well, 'tis an old one," answered Karl. He looked to the rear of the line and beckoned Georg and some others to move forward. When a few had huddled close by he continued. "Maria has a riddle for you: A young priest was sent to observe a feast in hell. Upon his arrival he noticed that the damned had been given sharpened staves as long as a man is tall to eat with. The famished souls tried as hard as they might, but they could not reach their mouths with the meat they impaled. This, in turn, led to fighting and cursing.

"The sad priest was then escorted to heaven where the angels invited the guests to play the same game. The heavenly residents were handed the same staves to eat with, yet in heaven each was able to enjoy the good meat and there was great joy and fellowship. Why was this so?"

Georg squeezed his eyes into his sweating cheeks as he strained to think. *It would be so very good*, he imagined, *to win Karl's friendship by being good at these cursed riddles.* His mind spun but before he had an answer, he found himself at the imposing gates of Dunkeldorf.

Chapter 9
DUNKELDORF

The free town of Dunkeldorf was a trading center set squarely on the east bank of the Rhine some two days excursion from the French city of Colmar and within a comfortable journey of Basel to the south. Because of its location, the town bustled with the trade of two realms and served as a convenient market for merchants transversing the Rhine valley. Its independent status was recently declared and its borders were defended by a stockade wall and a garrison of mercenary soldiers.

The townsfolk resided in timber-framed homes set in random order along narrow, uncobbled streets. Some of their houses were built with wide, rough-planed planks and plaster, some handsomely appointed with fine glass and shutters, but most were simply crude cottages of wattle and straw.

The log chapel near the market square provided a temporary location from which the spiritual needs of the people were served, though on the hill at the south end of town construction of a proper stone church had begun. The diocese at Mainz had bestowed absolute authority on one Father Silvester for all such matters. The town had been organized under a burgher and council and had received its independence from the clerk of Emperor Heinrich VI. Its laws were enforced in unabashed deference to the interests of the influential, and mercy for others was rare.

Missing the feast of Lammas, the children huddled

closely as Wil and Pieter led them into the confusion of the busy town. Wealthy and poor, thieves and priests, rogue soldiers and wayfarers of every stripe were soon pressed around the crusaders who stared in awe of the tapestry of humanity now enveloping them. The loud shouts of merchants huckstering linens, tanned hides, fruit stuffs, and weapons; the brays and whinnies of livestock and the occasional clang of church bells made for a noisy but intriguing blend of sounds. Yet the pilgrims felt a mood of darkness which subdued what might otherwise have attracted their eager curiosity.

Pieter mothered his children like a nervous hen with her chicks and admonished them repeatedly to be vigilant and evoke no annoyance. "By the saints, you be angels in this place ... and do exactly what I say."

Usually confident in the abilities of his own wit and worldly wisdom, Pieter seemed uncharacteristically apprehensive as he led his Innocents through the streets. Still willing to believe the Church to be of some potential benevolence, the old man humbly asked for direction from a simple beggar and was pointed to the timber chapel. He knocked loudly on its heavy oak door. "Greetings ... I say greetings to thee."

No answer was forthcoming so Pieter pounded harder and cried loudly, *"G'tag?"*

The door cracked a bit and a beaklike nose protruded from the shadow.

"Yes, what is it?" hissed a voice from within.

Pieter, confused by such an odd reception, shrugged and proceeded to introduce himself and his congregation. The door opened enough for Father Silvester's leather-capped head to emerge. Silvester said nothing but glared from beady, dark eyes at the dusty, tired children. He sucked a long breath through his nose, nearly collapsing his nostrils and then whined, "Get hence and begone, thou dirty herd of brats. Go ... go at once. We have no need of more of thy kind."

Pieter clenched his jaw. "I implore thee in the name of our Lord to have mercy on these little ones. Might ye find a place in thy Christian heart to share a bit of food and refreshment? Surely thou would'st earn bounty for thy parish for so blessing our Holy Crusade."

The priest snarled and flung the door wide open. "Holy Crusade? A *Holy* Crusade methinks not. It seems they've turned good to evil. We are told of these would-be pilgrims as no more than poachers and common thieves ... stealing and murdering passage through our Empire and France."

His volume increased and he hurled open the door to set his finger by Pieter's nose. "A just God shall not tolerate such hypocrisy and neither shall His Holy Church. In the name of all that is sacred, more of these impostors need be flogged proper for such wickedness, and methinks some ought be hanged. I am told that our offended Lord even now strikes legions dead with fever and starvation as a fitting reward to such blasphemy. Such is evidence enough of the heresy and evil of this abominable masquerade! If they were honoring God, such misery would not be their bedfellow."

"Would'st thou neglect the compassion of our Holy Mother for even the most imperfect of his little ..."

"Speak not to me of the Virgin and keep thy tongue from the discourse of the cleric. How dare thee. Filthy beggar ... impostor. How dare thee wear the robes of the Holy Church! Perhaps thou ought be bound by the magistrate and sent to a fate fitting of thine own deception." Silvester piously clutched his robes at the chest, then steadied his voice. "However, I am a man of God and as such I do offer the mercy of which you speak. I'll not summon thy destruction, though consider this a final warning. You'd best enjoy my forbearance and take thy litter of broken misfits far away from this good town." The priest then slammed the door, leaving the stunned crusaders open-mouthed and empty-handed.

Pieter closed his eyes in prayer, asking God to forgive the hatred now raging in his bosom. He then stared to the heavens for some explanation. "Is it I, Father? Is it I? Am I mad ... or am I one of but a few sane creatures assigned to roam this asylum?"

He turned to the confused and frightened faces gathered around him and tried to speak, but his tongue was bound by the anger frothing in his throat.

The trembling voice of Lothar broke into the moment. "Shall he not help us, Father Pieter?"

Jon I clutched the old man's robe and desperately implored, "If God's people shan't help us, who shall?"

Pieter's response was sharp and razor-edged. "God's people are not always people of God. Guard yourself, children ... you need the mind of a fox never more than when the pious prowl about!"

A loud, commanding bark from Solomon suddenly beckoned the crusaders to a tight alleyway squeezed between two guild-houses just behind the chapel. The band hurried to the entrance of the passage and Pieter and Wil followed the excited dog warily into its shadows. There, huddled in the darkness, were three frightened children squatting against the wall, legs drawn tightly to their trembling chests and each clenching a crusader's cross. They stared at Pieter and Wil with wide eyes and cringed as Solomon leaned his pointy nose toward them.

"Be still, my children," said Pieter softly. "We are friends ... here to help you."

The three hesitated but one finally stood. "I ... I am called Frieda," said a long-legged, blonde-haired girl of about fifteen years. She squeezed her hood tight at the throat. "I come from the kingdom of Westphalia, and ... I ..." Unable to contain herself any longer, the poor girl choked on her words and her brown eyes swelled with tears. Pieter laid his hand upon her shoulder and she collapsed into his embrace.

"Yes, yes, my child."

As her weeping gave way to calm she backed away and dried her face on her sleeve. She took a deep, quivering breath and introduced her younger brother, Manfred and her younger sister, Gertrude. She then proceeded to relate their tale of suffering. "Most of us were dead by fever and hunger in the woodlands north of here. What few lived found this evil place. We asked but thrice for food from three merchants when a magistrate's soldier ordered us be beaten. Then ..."

Manfred, nervous but clearheaded for a boy of eleven, quickly chimed in. "Aye, so 'twas, but we ran quick-step and hid whilst they shouted to drown the yellow-haired witch."

Gertrude, about ten, then stood and, in a weak and shaking voice added, "My lord, we've been hoping God would help us ... might you be His answer?"

Pieter nearly wept and his throat thickened as he reached a hand toward the little girl. "*Ja*, fair *Mädel*, your hopes were prayers of the best sort and God has answered them this day. I suspect His answer to be a bit later than your preference but that oft seems to be His way." He winked.

Wil took the priest by his sleeve and whispered, "We cannot care for a single more."

The priest nodded sympathetically and drew the boy aside. "Brave and patient Wil, like our Lord you have been given charge to care for the misfits, the destitute, and the unwanted. Consider each a blessing and your burden shall lessen."

Wil sighed, resigned to yield to the priest's gentle insistence, and joined the others as Pieter led the three relieved additions out of the alleyway. After a brief introduction, Frieda and her siblings merged with their new comrades and waited calmly for direction.

Pieter stood by Wil's side and gazed warily across the courtyard at the hurried townsfolk rushing about the market. He was reminded of the famous squares at Champagne and Troyes and Basel, but here he sensed darkness, a pall of evil, that seemed to weigh heavy in the air itself. He deliberated on the mélange of faces pressed in the crowd and grew ever more concerned. Field serfs with straw hats pulled suspiciously over their eyes seemed to walk stiffly behind their reluctant oxen, prodding them with uncommon impatience. Merchants from the East cried their wares loudly but with an uneven canter, most untypical for their kind. Peasant women rushed about with no interest in chatter, instead pushing from table to table with their long gowns bound short by one hand and their heads burdened by baskets of bread or turnips. Pieter noticed the occasional nobleman strutting through the throng, though these, he noticed, bore a familiar demeanor—a cast of condescension for the crush of rabble all about. Of greatest worry to the old man were the excessive numbers of drunken and rancorous men-at-arms, most bearing the colors of Brunswick and a comportment of anger, arrogance, and acrimony.

Yet to Pieter the town seemed prosperous and without cause for such gravity. Long, wooden peddlers' tables were scattered along the streets, and throughout the square were booths packed with fish, leathercrafts, tapestries, bakers' breads, silks from the East, brass and tin wares, and bolts of beautiful cloth. Wagons and carts were piled high with carded wool and bundles of flax newly arrived from nearby manors. Sheaves of hay were bundled and stacked neatly against storehouse walls. But despite the apparent bounty, beggars sat at nearly every corner as a reminder of the drought of compassion the town's citizens endured.

Pieter decided to whisper a few cautions to Wil before the boy led his company into the marketplace. The children were keenly aware of Pieter's reserve and walked slowly past a long table bending in its center with the weight of honey, salt, butter, early fruits, and preserves. Their eyes widened at the casks of ale, spits of ducks, baskets of biscuits and of salted pork stacked neatly by barrels of eel and sturgeon. They drooled over wheels of cheese, and mounds of peas and onions, and baskets of almonds.

Considering the hunger gnawing at their innards, the display of such plenty fast became a temptation to sorely endure. Wil's coveting mind was distracted by a tug of a tiny hand on his belt. He turned to see Lothar staring at him from eyes now yellowed and runny. "Master Wil, might I rest a bit?"

Wil hesitated but agreed. "We'll take a short rest but we've work to do."

Lothar smiled and followed the troop to a quiet corner where most collapsed in the dust. Tomas took a place near Wil, embarrassed by the immediate scoffs of passersby. Pieter stared at the town thoughtfully, then looked at his forlorn comrades. "I've an idea. This wretched place has a dreadful lack of music. Has a single one of you seen a minstrel or troubadour? Nay. So, methinks a good song might earn us a bit of food."

Before the dumbfounded crusaders could object they found themselves rushed to the middle of the market square and positioned in a tight semicircle. In moments they were led by Pieter through a rather feeble rendition of the song they had sung in such earnest just weeks before. "Fairest Lord Jesus," they began, "Ruler of all nature...." But as they choked their way nervously through the lyrics their voices grew fainter, costing them the initial curiosity of a few townsfolk. Pieter aspired to rally their pluck by joining his voice loudly to theirs. Unfortunately, his shrill pitch and discordant notes drew laughs, not alms, and the crusaders' glorious chorus faded beneath a volley of jeers!

Wil, shamefaced and embarrassed, turned his back on his comrades and melted into the roaring crowd with a disgusted Tomas at his side. But good Karl stood by his duty, straining to sing despite the tears of humiliation over his reddened cheeks. Close to his side crooned Georg, eyes pinched shut and fists tight.

At last Pieter mercifully silenced the choir, assuring his children that even if no mortal esteemed their fine singing, the angels in heaven had certainly noticed. The cackling townsfolk returned to their duties as the old man gathered his flock about him again. "Now, children, 'tis time for a new plan." The priest chuckled at the few grumbles sent his way. "With Wil's consent I suggest we go in pairs to beg from each and every merchant and from each opened door."

Frieda, nervous and ill-at-ease, interrupted. "Father Pieter, m'brother'n'sister were nearly flogged for such a deed a few days prior and—"

"*Ja, ja*, this I know, my dear. But we've little choice and with so many opened hands the deputies may not know which to snatch!"

Frieda was not comforted.

"Ah, and I'll be watching my flock, little one," Pieter added. "I'll damn any who might lay harm to you! Now, all of you, listen well. Be humble; show proper respect. Bow your heads and look none in the eye. Now, off and be quick to it and return to me."

With little complaint the faithful children yielded to Pieter and divided into pairs to scatter through the marketplace. Pieter watched them like an old hen spying her chicks now straying from her wings, and prayed for God's safekeeping. He was particularly anxious for Wil and Tomas and was not the least bit encouraged to see them set out together. He watched them carefully for the next half-hour, and his heart began to race as the two boys approached a nobleman and his wife.

The wealthy couple strutted toward the lads with a confident stride, and the boys, in turn, approached them in a similar manner. The lady was adorned in a fine silk dress which lightly brushed the top of her black, leather shoes. She wore an embroidered vest and a smooth, red satin cape which was draped over her braided, blonde hair and clasped at her throat by a beautiful gold brooch. A silver necklace lay lightly against her milky white throat and the cuffs of her sleeves were fastened with large pearls.

The gentleman wore a proud pair of satin leggings with polished boots rising halfway to the knee. A long, embroidered satin cloak was fastened with new brass buttons, and his long, black hair was covered by a rich velvet hat, accented neatly with a purple peacock feather.

The flash of the man's buttons enlivened Wil's curiosity. He cleared his throat and hailed the couple, bowing in reluctant submission to their status. "M'lady and m'lord," he said awkwardly. "I beg your grace for this poor servant of yours. Might you spare a few pennies for him to buy a bit of bread for his gentle sister?"

The lady's face belied a hint of compassion and a glance toward her husband seemed to convey sympathy. But the lord set his fists squarely on his hips, threw his head back, and laughed as he elbowed his way between Wil and Tomas. "Out of my way, whelps."

Pieter had hastily moved toward the boys and arrived as the couple were leaving. But before he could reach the pair, Wil suddenly barked after the couple, *"Caput tuum in ano est."*

He winked at the startled Pieter when the nobleman suddenly spun on his heels and charged toward the three with his fists in the air. The trio wisely chose retreat and vanished into the throng until the sputtering lord returned to his perplexed wife.

Wil sheepishly turned to a perspired Pieter and was quickly instructed in the finer points of verbal warfare. "Choose your targets more carefully!" scolded the old priest. "The Latin tactic works best when it is not understood! Now, we ought collect the others."

The grumbling crusaders slowly reassembled around Pieter. None had been successful in obtaining even the slightest morsel from a single soul. Pieter sighed, though relieved to have escaped the ill will of the authorities. Wil, now frustrated and angry at their predicament, insisted his company try again in the market area farther from the gates.

The children obediently followed their leader around the corner where they beheld another remarkable bounty of wares. Pieter studied the new market and suggested his children repeat their pairs' begging. But his senses quickened as Solomon whined, and he felt greater danger than before. He turned to Wil. "Lad," he offered, "pardon my continued interference but I should ask your permission to stand in the center of this market ... there ... atop that barrel. From there I'll keep a sharp eye. Should any feel frightened they ought call for Solomon and I'll be close behind."

Wil nodded his approval.

The old man furrowed his brow, deep in thought. "And this also. All of you, listen well ... look to me on m'barrel often. If you see me do this"—he spread his arms and spun round and round—"if you see me do this, just come to me. Do not hesitate and do not wonder why, just come … just trust me and come. You *must* believe me. Do you understand?"

The children nodded.

"Do you *truly* understand?" added Wil. "Yes? Good! Then off with you."

With a nervous sigh, Pieter ambled toward his barrel and climbed carefully atop it. From this, his wobbly watchtower, Pieter kept vigil like the Lord Protector of Christendom, praying all the while for a legion of angels to swoop from the clouds and hedge his Innocents within the safety of their mighty wings.

For two hours the children begged fruitlessly. The day was aging and the sun was beginning to stretch shadows over the marketplace. A good number of the merchants had packed their wares, and it was becoming evident that the night would bring only hunger and disappointment to the crusaders. It was not easy for the children to resist the temptation to steal a loose turnip or dropped pear, but they held true.

Poor Pieter was weary and his legs ached as he stood his faithful watch. He was about to relieve his pain by squatting for a few moments when he suddenly spotted some soldiers entering the market square with that certain swagger he recognized from his own youth. He was shamefully familiar with the concocted power of stout ale, hot sun, and boredom. The old man's veins filled with fresh vigor and his eyes flew across the thinning streets in search of any of his lambs now in harm's way. He spotted the fair Frieda and her sister, Gertrude, not more than fifty paces from the soldiers. His heart stopped.

Without hesitating, Pieter quickly stood as erect as his bent body would allow, stretched his arms wide, and began to spin on the barrel. Thrice he lost his balance and crashed to the ground, but thrice he scrambled back to his place to spin around and around and around. True to his command, his children had kept a sharp eye for him and immediately began to race from the far corners of the marketplace as Solomon barked loudly for them to hurry.

Frieda turned to see Pieter just as she was noticed by the drunken soldiers. She grabbed her sister and obediently scampered away from the taunts and calls of the stumbling men and then ran to the priest as fast as they could go. And so, two by two, the pilgrims reassembled alongside a most relieved and joyful Pieter.

"Well done, my children!" cried the old man as he dropped to the ground. "God be praised. Well done. Wil, count their heads and let's be off from this cursed place." Pieter lifted a prayer of thanksgiving and cast a final worried glance over his shoulder at the soldiers who now stalked different prey.

"We must try one more time afore we yield," announced Wil stubbornly.

Karl protested. "There'd be no place here to sleep and we've need to seek cover in the forest by dark."

Before Wil could respond, a magistrate's deputy and two guards suddenly appeared. "Stand fast or you'll each swing."

"M'lords," said Pieter sharply, "we are simple Christians traveling in a Holy Crusade and I expect thy indulgence as we offer thy good townsfolk the occasion for a special blessing."

"I've not patience left for the likes of these," growled the deputy. "This filthy litter fouls my sight and, by God, I've a mind to stretch every one of the thievin' rats. And as for you, old man, Father Silvester charges you as an impostor. Perhaps we needs pull yer lyin' tongue from its roots. Now begone!"

Frightened, little Lothar crowded against Pieter's legs and offered the soldiers a gentle smile, hoping a gift of tenderness might soothe the moment.

"What would y'be laughing at, devil imp?" snarled one.

Lothar strained a whisper, his hands now clutching Pieter's robe.

"So, more of yer mockery? I'll show you what be done here with cocky whelps." Before Pieter could react, the soldier snapped the heel of his boot toward the boy, striking

Lothar's turning head just above the ear and tumbling the lad away from Pieter's legs and into the dust.

Pieter cried out and swung his oak staff furiously into the face of the soldier. The surprised guard fell backward, grabbing at his bloodied nose and covering his face from the raging priest who now pummeled him with the wrath of heaven.

Bellowing, the deputy knocked the old man into the dirt with two heavy blows to his face. But he did not do so without paying a price of his own, for no sooner had the old man fallen than the faithful army joined the fray!

Otto of Weyer, sturdy and square-framed, burst from his fallen brother's side with a deafening cry and rallied his comrades against the three surprised officers, kicking and flailing and assaulting any bit of flesh within grasp. Jon I came tripping his way close behind and immediately fell into a large, well-muscled thigh. He wrapped it with his arms and gnawed as large a bite as his grinding jaws could fare, yielding a most satisfying scream! The howling soldier pounded on his determined diner until Georg rammed his own thick head into the unfortunate man's unguarded crotch.

Meanwhile Solomon supported Karl's charge, snarling and snapping wildly at their common foe, ravenously tearing away large shreds of fabric and flesh. Wil and Tomas leapt upon the backs of two of the outraged soldiers and delivered blow after blow as a mob of their fellows punched and bit and scratched at the staggering threesome.

But the furious guards soon recovered themselves and began striking the children mercilessly about the shoulders and heads with their truncheons, pounding the crusaders hard and sending them sputtering and tumbling to the ground. At last, the beaten crusaders begged for quarter.

The bloodied soldiers stood wide-legged and poised as poor Pieter raised a trembling hand toward them. "Enough," he whispered. "Enough." The old man pulled himself slowly to his feet, his swollen face bloodied and bruised but a fire still kindling in his eyes.

The guards grunted and threatened the priest and his defeated army. "Quarter? Quarter indeed! You shall surely swing for this, y' ..."

"We'll not surely swing!" answered Pieter defiantly. The old man spat a wad of blood to the feet of one. "Indeed, ye have needs to fear for thy miserable souls for having struck a priest ... ye—"

Pieter's words were abruptly halted. "Come, Papa Pieter, come quick!" Maria suddenly cried. All eyes followed the weeping girl as she ran to Otto now holding Lothar's little head gently on his lap. Pieter brushed past the guards and fell to his knees by the child. Lothar lay still and motionless, his tiny, brown tunic stained with the dark blood which had now ceased flowing from his ear. The old man gently held the poor boy's peaceful, whitened face in his hands and groaned to the heavens.

The guards stormed toward Pieter and threw him into the street, pushing his face into a pile of fresh horse manure. The deputy growled to the huddled crusaders. "You'd best take heed for yer souls. Y'be hanged on the morrow and this impostor shall drop first."

The muffled sounds of Pieter's contempt rose from the street as he jerked his face free from the droppings. "Woe to ye three. Woe I say!" He turned, eyes blazing with the righteous rage of the archangel of heaven. "Thy mortal souls are in peril of damnation. *In nomine Patris, et Filii, et Spiritus Sancti* ... I am near to banishing thy wicked souls to the eternal hell! Release us at once!"

The deputy scoffed. "What sort of madness be this? Y'be no priest ... look at you. Your words are horse *scheisse!*" He and his fellows roared. "Horse dung indeed," added another. "And there'd still be some hangin' on yer lips, old fool!"

The deputy grabbed the priest's robe with his two large hands, but Pieter fixed an unnerving gaze into the man's eyes. The old man stood erect and dignified and held his Irish cross toward the three. "With this cross of the true Church," he began sternly, "I shall shortly pronounce eternal damnation upon each of thy souls ... but before doing so, I should remind you of thy temporal consequence as well."

The soldiers grew uneasy, now less certain of his masquerade. One whispered to another, "And what if he be a priest ... y'know, one of those wandering sort we've heard some about?" The other shrugged. The deputy yielded to his own curiosity. "What consequence, old man?"

"Humph. Look at thyselves. I pity the soldier who'd report such a beating at the hands of little boys and girls ... and an old man."

The soldier looked at his bloodied fellows. He grumbled a few oaths and jammed his knee into Pieter's belly sending the priest to the ground once more. "Now get you and your filthy whelps out of m'sight and out of m'town at once ... or by God, m'men and me shall cut y'to pieces in yon alleyway."

As the soldiers stormed away, Pieter closed his eyes and sighed a brief prayer of thanksgiving before crawling to Lothar's side where Wil and Karl sat staring at their fallen friend from home. Pieter said nothing as he watched Otto gently fold the little boy's body into his arms. Wil and Karl helped the old man climb to his feet where he stood for a moment and surveyed his quiet companions.

Pieter laid a hand on his lambs, one by one, and offered a comforting smile to his flock. Sobbing, he put his arm around poor Otto, and led his bloodied crusaders in a quiet procession toward the gates of Dunkeldorf.

The children stared forward, paying no attention to the townsfolk mocking them or to the occasional stone or chunk of clay thrown their way. But a unity born only of suffering now bonded them more tightly than any word of scorn or ridicule could divide. Mercifully, they soon emerged from that dreadful place and were returned to the river roadway where they found a suitable night's encampment. It was here, under a gnarled oak tree and in the pink light of the setting sun that they laid little Lothar in his shallow grave. A weeping Otto clutched Lothar's wooden cross to his heart, then placed it in his own belt, setting his own gently above Lothar's head. "I shall carry your cross, my brother."

The children quietly withdrew into the lengthening shadows of twilight and drifted in pairs toward the river to bathe and bind each other's wounds. And in the healing starlight they began to whisper among themselves of the drama and tragedy of the day past. But Pieter sat blank-faced before the small, snapping campfire as the flames in his own heart began to rise again. He ordered limping Solomon aside and wandered restlessly into a clearing where he lay amidst the dewy weeds and faced the canopy of stars above him. His aimless stare soon changed to a fixed gaze and he stood up with fists raised to heaven.

"Why, my God, why? You ought hide in shame! Why have You such little regard for these innocent ones? Look upon them at Your leisure and You shall find they love You … and yet You keep Your tongue and hold still Your hand. With a mere thought You might rescue them, but You pay no heed! Would that You were but a poor figment of my mind … such would be a lighter burden than You.

"I know not what to do with a God I do not understand. And yet, in such confusion You expect my gratitude in all things. Ha! Hard as I do try, I only know of one paltry thing to so give thanks for … the tear in Tomas's eye when Lothar was laid to his rest. More than that, I'll not grant."

Pieter thrashed about the darkness swinging his staff at heaven and earth and fell to his knees in frustration. "You said, 'Suffer the little children to come unto Me and I'll give them rest.' Liar! Deceiver! These suffering children *have* come to You; they have begged Your mercy and there is *no* rest for them … only misery and death.

"'The earth is the Lord's and the fullness thereof'? You refused to have them spared a single morsel this day. What sort of God are you? What nature of monster do I serve?"

Pieter climbed back to his feet and paced in a hurried circle. 'Round and 'round he stormed, driving his crook hard into the sod. He began to shout. "For seventy-seven years I have walked this woeful earth, and I still do not understand You. I have studied Your Word faithfully. I have dutifully endured the piety of Your pathetic Church and have faithfully befriended the outcasts of Your miserable creation. I have spent painful hours on my knees in prayer ... *despite* Your eternal silence! I have trained my mind on things here and above, and yet I have less understanding of You now than ever before. Why do You hide Your truth from me? Are You not there? Do You not care?"

Unbeknown to Pieter, Karl was hiding wide-eyed and shocked behind a small tree, carefully watching and listening to the old man wrestle with his Maker. The priest's words cut deeply into the boy, and Karl began to tremble in his own confusion. The lad had never suffered such chaos of the spirit, and such doubts as had come over him in these last weeks had never so shadowed his mind. Pieter's struggle frightened him.

The war for Pieter continued until the man was too exhausted to fight on. At last he fell to the ground and cried out the words of the psalmist, "'Awake, O Lord. Why do You sleep? Arouse Yourself! Do not reject us forever. Why do You hide Your face and forget our misery and depression? We are brought down to the dust. Our bodies cling to the ground.'"

Then he lay silently, as if waiting for an answer. But the night was mute and he eventually stood to his feet, wiped his face on his rough sleeve and reluctantly returned to the children. As he entered the yellow light of the campfire the crusaders were hushed, for they now gazed upon a different Pieter. His gentle smile and kindly eyes were gone; in their place was a hard-set jaw and odd stare.

Glaring at the crackling sticks, he broke the uneasy silence. "Woe to he who builds a city with bloodshed and founds a town with violence. Woe to you, you who are treacherous while others did not deal treacherously with you. As soon as you shall finish destroying, you shall be destroyed."

Then he motioned for Wil and Tomas to come to his side and whispered to them. In a moment, the three hurried off into the darkness.

෨

Night had settled upon Dunkeldorf, and its vacant streets were now shadowed by smoky, pine torches. The town had become a macabre menagerie of loud, brawling taverns and murky, threatening alleyways; its folk slumbering behind the safety of clasped shutters and well-barred doors. Pieter and his two comrades slipped past a drunken guard at an open gate and crept cautiously from one dark corner to another as they sought the market square.

The priest found some blankets strewn across a fruit cart and snatched one for Wil and one for Tomas. The three peered through the shadows for any sign of guards, moving like stalking cats from alley to table to barrel to crate, gathering salt pork, salted herring, vegetables, fruits, and breads. They packed their blankets quietly and quickly. Before long the three were heavy with provisions, including a clay jar of sweet honeycomb Pieter picked off a window sill. Then, as deftly as they had entered, the thieves slipped out the gate and hurried toward the safety of the forest.

Once they passed a reasonable distance, Pieter asked the boys to stop. "Go forward without me and feed the others," he said. "I've a bit more business to settle and shall be along shortly."

"But where are you going?" asked Wil.

Pieter refused to answer. Instead, he pulled his hood slowly over his head and vanished into the night where he found himself at the gates of Dunkeldorf once more. Again, he slipped past the sleeping guard and proceeded straightaway toward the timber chapel. Without the slightest regard for his own jeopardy he boldly grabbed a curl-flamed torch propped on a nearby post and carried it high overhead toward his mark. "There is a season for all things," he muttered to himself. "A time to love and a time to hate. Silvester, thou hast earned thy wicked *burg* a proper judgment this night." With not so much as a moment's hesitation, Pieter hurled the flambeau on the dry, thatched roof of the chapel. He stood perfectly still and listened with perverse pleasure to the firstborn crackles of the fresh fire. Then, as a soft breeze wafted through the square, the flames suddenly rose higher and roared into an inferno, immediately pouncing onto the thatch of neighboring shops.

Pieter's face illuminated in the yellow light; the hard edges of his nose and jaw cast deep shadows, his blazing eyes bearing the reflection of the fires within and without. Suddenly, however, a twinge of nausea stirred his inward parts and unsettled him. He closed his hood tightly under his chin and turned away, quickly retreating through the marketplace past the rush of soldiers and folk now scurrying toward the fire. He jostled and pushed until he slinked through the gate one last time.

The old man stumbled hastily through the wood toward his flock, though less joyful with each passing step and ever more mindful of the evil just exposed in his own heart. He looked over his shoulder but once, and the sight served only to worsen his vexation.

Wil and Tomas startled poor Pieter as they dropped from a treetop where they had kept vigil for their mysterious companion. The boys had watched the flames lick the night's sky over Dunkeldorf and were suspicious of the priest. Tomas stepped forward and challenged him. "Pieter … you've set the place afire, did y'not?"

The old man said nothing but looked to the ground.

"I say it again. Did you set the town afire?"

Pieter locked his lips tightly. He gripped his staff and drove it deep into the earth, pushing past the two lads toward the camp.

"Ha! I knew so," laughed Tomas. "Well done, Father! Well done, indeed."

When the three entered the camp, Pieter walked to the darkest edge of the circle and sat quietly against a tree. Wil and Tomas had not yet shown the booty of their night's scrumping and proudly carried their blankets to the firelight. But before either could speak, Georg bubbled, "Look. Look at that!"

The boys turned to see a rabbit roasting on a spit and heads of cabbage boiling in the pot. Jons I and II ran to Pieter. "Pieter, Father Pieter!" Jon I shouted. "While you were gone, Karl said we ought pray for God's mercy. And ... and just when Karl was praying, Frieda hollered 'bout an owl with a rabbit."

"Yes!" exclaimed an excited Frieda. "I heard wings flappin' hard above and looked up and—"

"And then she screamed at it and threw a rock hard."

"She spooked the owl and it dropped its rabbit ... we heard the thing thud and found it!"

Karl beamed. "And then Maria and two others went to fetch more water from the river and found some cabbages that must've rolled off a cart! God is good, just as you've said."

Gertrude charged toward the dismayed priest with a fistful of cooked cabbage. "Taste! And the rabbit's near to done."

Pieter was staggered and withdrew, confounded and unwilling to share the slightest hint of his vendetta. He turned into the shadows and became ill. In the meantime, Tomas and Wil displayed their quarry to the complimentary assembly. Though the children were impressed with the storehouse of ill-gotten treasure, Tomas and Wil were keenly aware that their own success paled in comparison to the odd events at the campsite. Nevertheless, the hungry crusaders were delighted to add some fruit and bread to their feast of roasted rabbit and boiled cabbage and were soon happily filled to satisfaction.

Some time after all had eaten, a few of the children noticed poor Pieter still sitting in shamed silence just beyond the ring of firelight. Karl, perplexed as were the others, motioned for all to gather 'round their forlorn friend and offer their kindness. After several had taken a turn, the priest spoke. "My dear, dear children, you have instructed this old fool in faithfulness and my heart is blessed. My spirit had stopped believing, and the evil within me rose up. May God have mercy on me and may you each forgive this wicked man."

Solomon rested his head on the old man's lap and looked up at him with sad eyes. Pieter stroked his friend's head and thought quietly for a few moments. He turned to the children with watery, tired eyes and sighed. He leaned to Solomon and whispered softly, "'Food gained by fraud tastes good to a man, but his end is a mouth full of gravel.'" Pieter returned to the campfire with his young fellows and put his back against a smooth-barked tree. He closed his eyes to listen to the chatter of his children and was comforted by their gentle banter. He was touched by the ongoing compassion of those comforting Otto and how the whole circle paused to shed new tears for their lost little comrade. But then the biting tone of Tomas rose above the rest as he relived the other events of the night. "And why did Pieter leave you and Wil in the wood?" asked a voice.

The old man's heart sank as he waited for Tomas's sneering reply. "Ha. 'Tis the best part yet! Our good, godly priest had a fair night's play. After he had us scrump the town, he went back to put the torch to it!"

Pieter wept.

Chapter 10
GLORY LOST

Friederich woke with a start. He sat up in the pre-dawn darkness with his brown eyes stretched wide with fear and looked nervously at the dark silhouettes of his sleeping comrades. "Wake, Karl," he whispered as he yanked insistently on the sleeping lad's tunic. "Please, wake up."

Karl responded slowly to the persistent tugs and pleas of the anxious boy. He rubbed his eyes and sat up, peering in the moonlight at the dirty face of his friend. "What is it?"

"The trees are talking to me again."

Karl sat quietly for a moment and pondered the little boy's unusual comment before answering with a yawn. "Yes, Friederich, no doubt, but speak to me of it at prime."

"Nay," begged Friederich. "Hear me. Danger is afoot and we must waken the others."

The lad's rising voice stirred Lukas and Frieda. "Please, Karl, believe me. Tell them we must move!"

But there was no need to wake the others, for a perturbed group of grumbling crusaders had begun to huddle around their nervous comrade. Pieter, exhausted and bleary-eyed, stumbled into the circle and sat quietly between the others to hear Friederich's fears.

"M'*Vati* taught me when I was little," began the eight-year-old, "that the trees speak to each other by rustling their leaves in the wind. He says he knows not if it were the spirits of the woodland or the trees themselves what done the speaking. He says the leaves were their tongues and in their season they send their news from north to south and east to west … whatever is the way of the wind."

Pieter raised his eyebrows a bit, but Tomas scoffed. "You'd be a madman to believe a sally as that. And then to wake the rest of us with such a tale! Aye, yer either a madman to believe it, else a fool. And yer papa is mad as well."

"Listen all, and hear m'words. You've surely seen and heard how the trees act in a coming storm, then how they rest when it passes."

Many nodded.

"Ah, yes," observed Pieter. "And we've seen them flutter happy in a gentle summer breeze and we've seen them fall silent in autumn."

Wil had listened quietly. He remembered old Emma of Weyer spinning similar tales. "Friederich truly believes he has heard a warning in the trees and, whether it be by trees or spirits I say we give him heed … so prepare to march … now!"

The dutiful crusaders held their tongues and prepared a hasty gruel of soaked oats and millet. And, before long, they found themselves rushing away from the reach of Dunkeldorf.

The sky began to lighten but an uneasy dread crept over the soldiers as they hurried on their way. They looked warily to either side of the roadway as if the very shadows of the misty forest were stalking them. Perhaps it was the sincere passion of Friederich that had affected their imaginations or the rush of the morning's meal, or perhaps the trees had, indeed, given a fair warning. Whatever the cause, the fear was now shared by all, and the column began to run along the roadway until, at long last, the welcome edge of the sun broke the horizon on their left.

Pieter was equally relieved by the light of a new day. The night before his dreams had returned him to his failures in Dunkeldorf—the stealing and the arson, his wish to murder Lothar's assailants, the hatred. But in the dark hours of that black night he had humbly confessed his humanity and resigned himself to rest in the mercy of his perplexing

God. For Pieter, this was a day to leave the past far behind.

As the sun presented itself fully in the fresh morning sky, the priest looked at Karl and kindled a weak twinkle in his blue eyes. "My dear boy, I failed to answer your riddle of the other day."

Karl brightened.

"Yet, I must say with some sorrow, my son," said Pieter, "that you have failed to present me with a riddle worthy of your skill ... this was the easiest of all, one quickly recalled from times past."

"Well, go on then, Pieter, since you know so very much. Say the answer."

"Very well, the answer is this: The souls of the damned are, by their very nature, selfish and self-centered and think only of how the world affects them. They took their long staves and tried to feed themselves. In so doing they paid the price of all such selfishness ... they were left empty and hungry and angry.

"On the other hand, my dear boy," Pieter continued, "the souls of the saints departed had learned the futility of serving the self and had experienced the joy of sharing and serving others. They used their staves to feed each other and each received the blessings of a life given to service and a life given to loving one's neighbor."

Karl nodded grudgingly.

The crusaders pushed hard until noon and came to the top of a slight rise where they stopped to take their rest. "Children," Pieter announced, "look, we are at the edge of a magnificent forest."

The children stood quietly as Pieter pointed to the tall trees pressing close to them. "This needled wood spreads for as far as one might see, and under its scented canopy is a wonderland of deer and fox and hare and squirrel. And here and there you may find woodsmen with arms like oak trees who cut and saw the timber for use all over the Empire.

"But here also dwell witches and sorcerers and the demons of the shadowlands. At night, even the moon cannot press its silver beams to the ground, and in the day the sun strains to pierce the green with even the thinnest shafts of its golden beams. In the east it is called the Black Forest."

Pieter raised his eyebrows at his spellbound crusaders. "This woodland is refuge for saint and sinner alike and we may find it either a safe harbor or the fearful den of Satan." Pieter had somehow managed to frighten himself with his own words and he now stood stiffly, eyes darting across the landscape. He had been worrying all morning about the magistrate of Dunkeldorf and the troops that might be pursuing them on the road. Now he was equally anxious of the huge woodland before him. Unable to decide which was the safer risk—the open road or the ominous forest— he sat by a large tree while the children boiled some cabbage for a midday meal.

While the others were attending their duties, Wil wandered down the road and then into the forest where he came upon an unusual clearing. He walked quietly through knee-high wildflowers and stopped to feel the heat of the full, yellow sun on his face. With his blonde hair shimmering in its light, he turned slowly north and thought again of old Emma, the wise Butterfly Frau. *She and her flowers!* he mused. He picked a bloom and put it in his satchel. He thought of Brother Lukas sneaking away from the cloister to laugh under the summer sun with him and Karl, and their father. His teeth clenched and he considered his father. He imagined a far-off bloody field in which his dead body was surely buried. Wil envisioned meeting him at the Judgment and he laughed to himself. *How pleasant it shall surely be to seize him by the throat and throw him down on heated cobblestones*, he thought. *How dare he leave me behind!*

The boy thought of his mother, Marta. He wondered on which day she had died and who had buried her. He angrily suppressed the lump swelling in his throat. *She'll demand no more of me now*, he thought. He remembered Father Pious and spat. He shivered as he thought of his horrid great-uncle Arnold and he shook his head with memories of the busybody Anka. He wondered who had been given his family's tiny hovel, their land, and who had stolen their bakery. Other faces came to mind until another shiver crept along his spine. It was as if he could see the ghost of Ansel and a wave of guilt came over him. *Enough of this.*

The boy ambled back to the road and tossed a few pebbles aimlessly when a sound like rolling thunder startled him. He spun about and fixed his eyes on a cloud of dust now billowing some distance away. As the road beneath his thin-soled shoes shook, the boy squinted to discern three mounted knights rushing toward him at full combat gallop, clustered tightly, as if a single mass of steel, leather, and horseflesh.

Wil was so taken by the moment that he stood paralyzed, his heart captured by the pounding of iron hooves and the clatter of armor. Then, as if commanded by a single voice, the horsemen reared their mounts in unison, spreading their cloud of dust over the entranced boy.

Three golden-haired knights on three black, snorting stallions bore their steely blue eyes into Wil's. Not a single word was spoken but instead there seemed to be a mystical commingling of spirits as if the knights were somehow merging their war-weary souls with the young spirit of a new warrior. The heaving horses pawed and whinnied and threw their heads impatiently, eager to charge on. But the knights sat steady in their saddles, steeled for what horrors were ahead. One's mailed fist clutched a morgenstern, the "morning star" mace; the second, a short-handle battle-ax, and the third a menacing flail. Against their muscular thighs hung sheathed long-swords and each colored robe bore the sign of the Cross. Their pot helmets sported thick, black plumes and their shields the crest akin to the Order of Teutonic Knights, the proud warriors from the strange lands of the terrible marshy north. Their yellow beards were coated with a long journey's dust and their weather-worn faces looked weary.

Mesmerized, Wil drew a deep, chest-swelling breath, snatched his dagger from his belt, and raised it in high salute. The three horsemen held their mounts a moment longer and returned Wil's tribute with silent nods. Then, as quickly as they had appeared, they charged past the boy and vanished around a turn in the road.

Wil stood silently and gazed as their dust cloud drifted into the trees and he knew he had been somehow changed. His thoughts were interrupted, however, as his fellows came running forward, chattering wildly. He looked at them with sudden contempt and he replaced his dagger firmly into his belt. "Enough. Stay to this road. Now move on."

Old Pieter walked silently behind Wil, troubled by the strange look in the boy's face. "Those were mighty warriors, to be sure."

"Aye, old man, indeed they were and I'll be as one of them in time. When I come to Palestine I'll be wearing a knight's armor and I'll strike fear into the hearts of the Turks."

"Well, yes, 'tis sure so, my brave lad," answered Pieter carefully. "I am certain of it ... if God goes before you."

Wil looked sharply at Pieter.

The priest continued. "Many years past I read something written by a man far wiser than I who was a soldier far greater than those you have just seen. He wrote, 'I do not trust in my bow. My sword does not bring me victory. But *You* give us victory over our enemies. You put our adversaries to shame.' Of course he was speaking to G—"

"Will you never stop talking of God? Your tongue wags of little else, yet you robbed a town and burned it!"

Pieter's face tightened and the color left his eyes. "Aye, my son, I know myself to be oft a hypocrite ... I am only echoing the wisdom of another."

"Then take such wisdom, old man," snapped Wil, "and offer it to Karl. He cares for it more than I."

❧

The road began to darken under twilight, and Wil commanded his followers to stop and make camp. Pieter walked into the forest for vesper prayers, but could not shake a vague sense of ill-ease. *Perhaps the column should have left the road in favor of the wooded range a mere half-day's march east.*

At the campsite, Friederich also felt something to be amiss and tugged on Karl's arm. "There is danger here, Karl," he whispered. "Say nought to the others else they'll laugh, but the trees ... listen to the trees again."

Karl listened to a gust rush through a nearby towering spruce and nodded. "Tell Pieter."

Friederich readily agreed and scampered into the darkness to fetch the old man. Then, with Pieter in tow, he and Karl approached Wil and the others.

"I must confess my own sense of peril on this roadway as well," said the priest.

Tomas pressed his way into the discussion. "So, would y'be taken by the talking trees of Friederich and the dreams of this old man?" He turned to Pieter. "Would y'have us walk into that black forest filled with witches and spirits?"

The youngest children became anxious. They peered into the daunting forest on either side and feared such a venture. None relished the thoughts of trespassing the realm of haunts, but they also feared what awful fate might snag them along the open road. Wil was confused and Tomas seized the moment.

"So, Wil, methinks we've all a problem. You've got neither a plan nor the mind to make one ... and you'd be listening to trees for answers. Your crusaders show little trust in y'now. Methinks y'be no longer fit to lead."

Wil was surprised by the ambush. Tomas pressed further. "I think it time, Wil, that I lead. After all, it wasn't I who let Lothar die, nor I who abandoned John III to strangers, nor I who set fire to a city. 'Tis no wonder Pieter feels danger. Thanks to him we may all get hanged yet. It isn't me who has us half starved ... but it was me who got all this food and it was me who—"

"Shut your mouth, y'snake," Wil retaliated. "I am in command and you'll either follow me or find your own way."

Tomas stood firmly, almost amused by Wil's cross tone. He folded his arms and leaned into Wil's face. "Look at them. You've given them no choice, have you? They now fear the wood *and* the road, and they certainly cannot go back to Dunkeldorf, and they cannot swim the river."

Wil looked about the group of faces encircling them. He could not fail to notice their eyes dropping one-by-one to the ground.

"So, Wil," pursued Tomas, "I take command. You are free to dream of soldiering in Palestine, but I'll see that these children are properly cared for."

Tomas turned to Karl. "You there. Take the fat boy and start moving camp over the bank of the river, out of sight of the roadway."

Karl looked confused and waited anxiously for the befuddled Wil to respond. Pieter immediately recognized the danger of the moment and stepped quickly toward Tomas. "My wise and skillful young friend, I am most impressed with your great wisdom and equal charity. It is most noble of you to offer yourself in the service of others. I thank a loving God above for bending your heart toward us."

Tomas wrinkled his nose. "I thank Him for nought and I've no heart for the likes of you. I be weary of trailing behind this golden idiot. These sheep can now do my bidding."

Pieter paused to let Tomas's words cut deeply into the others. Then he eyed the boy and whispered, "Oh, dear boy, how useless it is to spread your net in full view of all the birds."

Tomas knew the words were not intended kindly. "Stop with the riddles, you old, worthless beggar, and do what I say before I box yer head."

"Forgive me, lad," Pieter answered slowly. "But allow me to humbly remind you that a man who controls his temper is better than one who takes a city."

Tomas felt the sting of that last comment and took a menacing step forward. Solomon's hair stood along his back and he curled his lips with a deep growl. Unable to restrain himself, Wil jumped between the two and grabbed Tomas by the tunic, pulling the boy's sneering face close to his own. "I tell you once and only once, Tomas," he said.

"You shut your mouth. Our camp is here tonight and on the morrow it shall be where I say."

Tomas's black eyes flashed and he swung a hard blow into Wil's cheek, staggering the boy but failing to drop him. Instead, Wil struck back furiously with one punch, then another and another, as he pounded Tomas in the stomach, chest, and face. Wil finally struck a ferocious blow on the end of his rival's nose, sending him yelping into a heap on the ground.

Tomas was not finished, however, and lunged at Wil, clawing and biting and kicking in a furious, shrieking assault. The two battered each other within a widening circle of their yelling comrades. Blood flowed from each grimacing face and oaths flew until, at last, Tomas fell to the ground, bloodied and bruised and gasping for air. There in the darkness he lay listening to his fellow travelers cheering his defeat. Tears came to his eyes as he wiped his tattered woolen sleeve across his bleeding nose. He struggled to his feet, feigning a backward step, then surprised Wil with a hard kick to his side and a quick punch to his jaw. In a flash he snatched the dagger from Wil's belt and thrust it toward the heart.

Wil stumbled backward to safety, now facing an opponent with murderous intent. The ring of children was silent and terrified as the gladiators faced one another. Tomas's eyes were swollen and red as he gave way to the years of rage that had burned deep within. With snarling lips raised like that of a wild wolf smelling the pending slaughter of his prey, he slowly circled Wil.

Pieter was stunned by the abrupt change of fortune and felt helpless. He cast a despairing look at his own rickety legs and arms. In frustration he pounded the ground with his staff and raised his eyes in desperate prayer.

Suddenly Tomas lunged again, but Wil stepped deftly to one side and snapped his right leg into the stomach of his attacker as he slammed his fist to the back of Tomas's head. Tomas sprawled face forward into the weeds and Wil pounced instantly on his back. Before Tomas could gather his thoughts, Wil snatched the dagger from his grip, pulled his head up by the hair, and placed the sharp edge of the blade on Tomas's quivering throat.

Wil's eyes were wild and his hands trembled as he snarled, "Give me one reason to spare you!"

Tomas could not respond.

"Well done," intruded Pieter, who nervously approached the combatants. "Well done, brave Wil. It is now time to extend a hand of mercy to your fallen friend."

"Friend?" answered Wil. "This treasonous snake is no friend of mine and his blood ought be spilled now rather than later."

Pieter laid a gentle hand on Wil's arm. "My son, please look to me."

Wil turned his flushed face reluctantly toward Pieter's firm but loving eyes.

"Please, lad. For the sake of the little ones watching, spare this boy," he asked quietly.

Wil grumbled an oath beneath his breath and pressed Tomas's face into the dirt as he stood.

Tomas climbed awkwardly to his feet, brushed the dirt from his clothing, and stared at Pieter with the fire of hell in his thankless eyes. "You shall pay dearly, old man ... and so shall all." He stared defiantly at Wil and Pieter, and then heated a final glare at Karl and Georg before vanishing into the dark forest.

Karl made a step toward him. "Tomas!" he called. "Come back! We forgive you. Tomas ..."

Pieter stopped him. "Let him go, son. A hot-tempered man must pay the penalty. If you rescue him, you shall needs do it again."

❧

By next prime Maria and Frieda tended a bruised and swollen Wil by skillfully bathing his cuts and bruises with rags dampened in the cool water of the nearby river. Frieda's touch felt especially comforting to the lad. "Tomas is utterly black-hearted, Pieter," mumbled Wil. "There is nary a good bone in his body."

The old man paused before answering. "Well, my son, we may all be wicked, but we are not all wicked."

Karl smiled.

"Young master, if you are to lead men, know this: Though each unredeemed heart shall someday stand unworthy at the throne of a blameless Creator, each yet walks the earth with some mark of the image of his Maker. 'Tis a telling of His goodness. It would go better for you to find that elusive stamp in both friend and foe."

"Aye, Pieter," Karl blurted. "We'd all be good at our roots. We'd be like flowers in bloom—some in good soil, others bad, some with rain and sun and some without—but all good just the same."

The boys waited for Pieter's answer.

The old priest smiled. "Ah, so I wish it to be, my son, but I fear this garden to have but fouled roots. I have known men of honorable repute, men of upright and honorable station to be sure, who oft—to their own astonishment—do at last wilt in their own evil. Aye, and I've seen to my wonder the vilest of scoundrel bloom in kindness or mercy, if but for a brief moment—like a flower on the deserts of Palestine. I fear, lad, all our roots have rot, but God in His mercy, blooms through those He wills, and when He wills."

Karl was confused and strangely angered by Pieter's rebuttal. His round face reddened. "I ... I do not believe I've rotted roots, Pieter, and I'm oft blessed."

Wil stood to his feet and secured his dagger at his waist. "Pieter, you've missed the mark with me as well. I've fine roots, clean and strong. Save such sermons for the Dunkeldorfers or the Tomases or the Piouses of this world. I am well served by m'self, and that'd be the only one who's yet to fail me." He smirked and stormed defiantly past the priest as he barked his marching orders. "Make your line quick to the foot. We are marching east to the wooded range, then south toward Basel!"

෴

With a stiff breeze to their backs the children followed their confident commander obediently eastward until they reached the dubious safety of a forested mountain range. Yet, despite the uncertainties of their new surroundings, the cool shade of the endless spruce was welcome, and the crusaders were quite cheered to leave the parched roadway behind. They smiled as they set their weary feet on the heavy carpet of soft needles and filled their nostrils with the clean and refreshing scent of the forest air. Squirrels and forest mice bounded at the children's feet and the sappy boughs above gave rest to birds whose happy songs echoed gently between the barked columns standing proud and straight as far as their young eyes could see.

The children soon turned southward and, to their delight, followed a deer trail over clear, cold streams. The pilgrims journeyed through the dark forest, relying on occasional glimpses of the shaded sun to guide them. Their spirits were higher now than ever and the journey made easier by the singing of cheerful folk songs and the sharing of engrossing stories of myths and legends from generations past.

By now Karl had dismissed Pieter's admonition and cheerfully approached the old man. "I need a bit of help with that blasted riddle of yours."

"Then I'll offer another clue," said Pieter. "'To what merry hearthstone speeds the twinkle of an eye and where in solemn duty waits the grayness of the sky?'"

"Yes ... go on."

"Nay, 'tis the next clue as you've asked. You need add that to the mix and find your answer."

Karl groaned. "Let me recite what I know:

To what sun-washed Haven must the dying daisy flee
    and in what Wonderland abides the snow-laden holly
    tree?
The songs of thrush and nightingale are borne upon the
    breeze,
But toward what Country do they drift while passing o'er
    the trees?
To what merry hearthstone speeds the twinkle of an eye
    And where ..."

Karl froze.

"Ah yes, lad ... 'And where in solemn duty waits the grayness of the sky?'"

Karl shrugged. "It seems you are speaking of a place, a very special place, I venture ... a place that receives the soul of a flower, the music of songbirds, the power of the wind ... and the hopes of a man."

"Well done!" cried Pieter. "Well done, indeed. You have a keen mind, lad."

Pieter motioned to Wil to slow down. "My old feet are a bit weary."

Wil raised his hand and stopped the column. He looked at the priest with unmistakable chagrin. "I told you when you joined us your welcome was no better than your ability to keep step."

"Aye, 'tis a certain recollection, indeed," Pieter answered humbly. "And I do resolve to keep with your ... new pace." But surveying the children who were also showing signs of exhaustion, he added, "It would seem to these old eyes, young Master, that your young soldiers might be near their own limits as well. I might respectfully ..."

"You would do well to keep your thoughts in that white head of yours," snapped Wil. "I decide the pace; your duty is to obey."

Pieter chose not to respond but leveled a stern eye at the haughty lad while nodding in strategic submission. His heart was heavy for the boy, for he knew all too well the dangers of pride. He scratched Solomon's ears and remembered the words of an old French vase-maker who reminded him many years past that clay cannot be molded until it is properly crushed and its imperfections borne to the surface. "And so, Solomon, we wait, we watch, we pray, and we hope."

Several exhausting hours passed until Wil finally allowed for a brief rest. The group collapsed onto the soft forest floor and stared at the green canopy above. Pieter whispered to Karl, "Young fellow, if my thinking is correct, we might pass through Basel in proper time to arrive by Burgdorf for the Feast of the Assumption at midmonth."

Karl's eyes widened and Georg, always walking in Karl's shadow, beamed with anticipation. "I traveled to the Assumption Feast in Mannheim some three years prior," he blurted. "'Twas *wunderbar*. I remember so very well the troubadours and minstrels and ... plays by Englishmen. And the food ... so much food!" He stopped and laughed. "Papa drank too much ale and m'mother a bit more wine than proper, and we found them both sick behind the walls of Lord Conrad's orchard!"

"Indeed, Georg," remarked Pieter, "I have paid that price myself."

Frieda and Friederich overheard the conversation and clapped with excitement. "Might it be true? Might we see the feast, Pieter?" asked Frieda.

"Well, I think perhaps so, m'lady. I reckon this to be about the first week of August, and methinks us to be no more than two days north from Basel, and that would mean about a week to Burgdorf. By the saints, we may make it!"

☙

A shift in the winds wafted a putrid odor through the evergreen forest bringing a chorus of complaints from the waking children. Pieter groaned and climbed to his feet slowly. He knew the odor well and feared its source was in their path. The company broke camp and pressed forward, but the stench had become like an invisible gauntlet the crusaders had to make their way through, retching with pinched noses and covered mouths. Friederich vomited. "I warned of something. I warned you and you would not have it."

Suddenly Solomon froze and lifted his long ears slightly. He pawed the earth by Pieter's foot, then dashed wildly away through the trees ahead. His barks could be heard echoing through the woodland until they faded in the distance. The unsettled crusaders looked blankly at Wil and Pieter, waiting for some explanation of the unusual display. The quiet was abruptly pierced by a long, whining, distant howl. It was a howl of soul agony, of a deep sadness that Pieter understood at once and he trembled.

The old man cleared his throat and put both hands firmly on his staff. He inhaled deeply and cried loudly, "Solomon, Solomon, come here!" The wails of the dog stopped instantly and in short order Solomon came crashing through the trees toward his master. He stopped, however, about twenty paces from the band. He pawed insistently at the ground and spun in a circle ... like Pieter had in Dunkeldorf. Karl immediately remembered the signal.

"He wants us to come to him, Pieter."

Pieter nodded. "Aye, lad."

In a moment the curious children and the old man were racing behind a panting Solomon up and down needled ravines toward the borders of a wide clearing now seen breaking in the distance. At last they burst into the clearing, only to halt abruptly at its edge to gape at the likes of which none had ever seen before. None, that is, save Pieter, who stared sullenly at the picture oft seen in his own past. The view stirred the demons within him and tears began to stream down his tightened cheeks.

The crusaders were shaken to their souls. Some quickly retreated into the still refuge of the wood, but most were instantly prisoners of the appalling portrait of death and destruction spread before them. Those stood wide-eyed and speechless, entranced by a scene which wreaked havoc in their young hearts, pillaging and violating them, murdering whatever innocence yet remained.

Before them was strewn the residue of a recent two-day battle—the ruined remnants of once-splendid columns of valiant warriors. Nearly one hundred corpses of opposing soldiers and their mounts lay tangled in an unholy collage of rumpled armor, butchered flesh, and broken banners—nearly a hundred souls had been released from their brutally violated bodies.

Friederich broke the silence. "Pieter," he whispered hoarsely, "they choose to do this to each other?"

The old man held his tongue but nodded. He knew why the boy would ask such a question. *What a horror it must seem*, he thought, *for men to yield such devilish consent for their own mutilation. It is as if those butchered do willingly proffer themselves to such an obscene degradation, believing in their pride that they shall be spared.*

Pieter turned his eyes on the dumbfounded faces of his children and sternly ordered them back to the wood. But Wil interrupted. "Pieter, there may be wounded in this field. Does not your God call us to some compassion?"

Pieter was surprised at Wil's sudden interest in the call of God. He looked at the shaken boy carefully and nodded. "Aye ... 'tis worthy of a look, lad. Methinks the younger ought not climb through this, but perhaps Georg and Karl and a few of the other older ones ... such as Conrad and Otto shall do."

So in short order Pieter, Wil, and some fellows slowly picked their way through the battlefield in search of any poor wretch still drawing breath. Wil was stone silent, drifting far into his own thoughts while his brother's confusion mounted with every step. *Where is God?* wondered Karl. *I wish my eyes would fail me now. But if He sees all, He sees this as plainly as do I.... Oh, why does He allow such a thing?*

Suddenly Georg waved frantically from the far side of the field where a young man of about twenty lay near death. An arrow was lodged deep in his shoulder and a slash wound had split his belly. By his colors Pieter knew him to be a footman in the service of Pope Innocent, a defender of the crown reserved for Friederich II.

Pieter lifted the lad's head gently and set a flask of water to his lips. The soldier coughed and sputtered but took a feeble sip. Then the priest cradled the lad against his breast and laid a hand softly on his forehead. As Pieter offered a prayer, the boy managed a quivering smile before the comfort of the old man's words mercifully escorted him through his final breaths.

The boys looked at the footman's face, for it was easy to see he was but a few years older than they. Wil swallowed hard and resolved to be courageous, but as he turned away he stumbled over the edge of a broken shield and fell squarely atop the battered body of a knight bearing the crest of the rebel king. He shrieked and scrambled to his feet but not before his eyes locked onto the vacuous eyes staring back at him, and a cold chill braced his spine. There, at his feet lay the mangled corpse of one of the golden-haired knights he had so recently met on the roadway. Wil stared at the soldier numbly. He had been so very certain that this knight was invincible.

Wil tore his eyes away, only to have them fall upon another of his knights, this one crushed beneath his slaughtered stallion. Wil clutched his dagger and backed away only to stumble over another dead soldier, then another. Being able to endure no more, he turned and leapt over the mounds of bodies now seeming to imprison him and raced far into the forest.

Pieter ordered the boys to gather some necessaries off the dead, such as flints and flasks, foodstuffs, satchels, small boots, and the like. Then he directed all away from the clearing. He stood at the forest's edge to perform a final prayer for the legion strewn before him. When he finished, Maria ran to him and clutched his robe and pressed her tearful face against his legs. "Ah, dear one," comforted Pieter, "we should find your brothers and be off to a better place."

Wil was sitting alone in the forest, pressed tightly against the sure trunk of a wide spruce. He had been so certain of the power he thought he had drawn from his golden-haired knights, and now the vision of two of them beginning to rot in that awful place gnawed at him. Little else mattered to the boy than his quest to rise above the pull and push of his world, but the haunting futility of such ambition now stared back at him from the impotent eyes of the dead. He cocked his head around the rough bark and watched his pathetic old friend calling for him in his tattered, black robe, weak and helpless. Wil saw no power there either, and he sighed as he climbed to his feet.

As Pieter waited for the young commander, he whispered a prayer that God in His mercy would cleanse the children's minds from all memory of this horror. He begged the angels to fill their nostrils with the sweet smells of wildflowers and brighten their eyes with the golden light of a new day.

Chapter 11
HOPE RESTORED AND A FRIEND
IN BASEL

J ust before prime, the crusaders were awakened by the
barks of a startled Solomon. Despite Pieter's sincere
prayer, the angels had not come at all but, instead, two
large men burst past the dying embers of the night's fire and
were rousting the confused children from their blankets. "On
yer feet, brave crusaders!" mocked one. "On yer pitiful feet,
you peasant whelps."

"Who's there?" Wil shouted.

The men laughed. "We'd be the demons of the woodland
y'mamas spoke of and we've come to take yer miserable
souls."

Pieter pulled himself up on his staff. "By my leave, let
these children in peace!" His rebuke brought a rousing
guffaw and a few oaths from the intruders.

"Now what've we here?" The figure stepped into the red
glow of the campfire and suddenly looked very much like a
giant troll. "Look," he shouted to his fellow, "look at this
breathing skeleton."

The other laughed and kicked the deep bed of embers
with his large, black boot, sending a flurry of sparks into
the night sky. The sudden burst of light illuminated the
faces of villain and victim alike. "Well, my, my," the first
one scoffed. "Aren't we the fearful little army of Jesus.
And, y've good cause to fear, for it may be m'pleasure to
stuff this old man and his noisy dog with all the rest of y'in
a shallow grave." He paused to stroke his beard. "*Ach*, but

it seems m'manners have taken leave; dawn is fast upon us and by prime we'll take a reckoning of what treasures y've scrumped in this not-so-holy Crusade. Until then, little lambs, m'good fellow and I must needs bind y'fast with this rope." With a snicker he handed his partner the end of a thick, bristly hemp, and the two corralled the children and poor Pieter against the trunk of a wide beech tree. They laughed and snorted and wound the rope around and around the helpless crusaders until they were secured tightly against each other and the old tree.

"By faith, you'd be a clever bunch. Had y'struggled, m'comrade would just as soon slit yer skinny throats and pick through y'sacks by light. Y'needs thank yer angels that I've come, too."

As the light of dawn brightened the camp, the terrified children got a better look at their captors. Each was huge and hairy and covered with filth. They had broad, bulky shoulders; wide faces; stout, heavy legs; and full, rounded arms encircled with wide leather bands. On their feet they wore black leather shoes and mail ankle-guards particular to the horsemen of the pope's armies. They were wrapped in heavy leather vests and mail shirts. Pieter was certain their reddened eyes revealed the raging self-contempt born of cowardice and disgrace.

"What think you, Leopold, of our little captives?"

"Well, Alfred, methinks them a worthless lot in need of quick dispatch ... like the footmen of Otto!"

Alfred pressed against a frightened and embarrassed Frieda. "Now this is a pretty prize. Perhaps each ought *not* die? Eh, Leopold ... what thinks y'on that?"

Wil suddenly spouted, "If you touch her I'll send you to the gates of hell m'self!"

Pieter closed his eyes in disbelief and Karl stared dumb-founded at his impetuous brother.

"By the spirits, Leopold. Seems we've a champion."

"Ha! And champions would be hard to come by Methinks we ought unbundle this bunch and see what stuff this brave lad is made of."

The two soldiers untied the large rope and yanked Wil

from the center by his hair. They toyed with him, like well-fed cats with a freshly caught mouse, shoving him back and forth and slapping him about his face and head. "So, peasant boy, I'd wager you fancy yourself as a great warrior in this Crusade of yours. *Ach*. But hold fast. You've no little cross in yer belt? I see only this very nice, deer-foot dagger."

Alfred plucked Wil's treasure from his belt and admired it before placing it squarely into his own leather sash. Wil remained silent. "So, you've no objection to sharing this little bit of thievery with another thief?" The soldier laughed.

Pieter stepped forward slowly. "My brave warriors, we have seen the great—"

"Shut yer mouth, old man," barked Leopold. "I've no interest in your words and if you speak again, I'll"—he paused and smiled at Frieda—"I'll introduce that fair, yellow-haired *Mädel* to the ways of a man." Frieda winced and looked away in terror, unable to bear the sight of his gaping mouth of rotted teeth. Pieter bowed respectfully.

The thieves began to wander among the children, staring at each until Leopold's menacing eye rested on poor Georg. "Now here'd be a fine fattened hog," he said to Alfred as he grabbed the frightened boy. "Look at this little lord, complete with his linen cloth and his stitched leather shoes. I should think, belly-boy, these peasants to be fortunate to share your good company. Methinks such clothing to bring a high price in Basel."

His companion smiled.

Georg began to stammer. "Beg ... begging your pardon ... I ... I ... am the son of—"

"We've no care who's the sire of such a sight as you," growled Alfred. "Take off yer clothes!"

Georg looked desperately for help from his trembling companions, but nothing could be done. Gertrude, Maria, Frieda, and the other girls mercifully turned away while Alfred squeezed Georg's cheeks hard and bellowed, "Be y'deaf? I said take off those clothes at once!"

Georg's beet-red face dripped with sweat, and tears

began to stream down his quivering, chubby cheeks. His shaking fingers slowly untied the strings of his waistcoat and he carefully loosed the fine, tailored shirt beneath. He reluctantly removed his breeches and then painfully stepped out of the soft under-leggings his mother had made for him to stand shamefaced and naked in front of the laughing men.

"Now there'd be a body to make a father beam!" cackled Alfred. "All those bulges and rolls of sloppy fat would make me proud! 'Meet m'strong, strappin' lad,' I should say to all my friends. Methinks Otto could dub him, 'Warrior of the Realm'!"

Georg bore his humiliation silently while Pieter slowly moved toward him, shielding his nakedness from the soldiers.

Alfred picked through the boy's clothing and suddenly held up a leather pouch that jingled with coins. "Ha, ha!" roared the soldier. "It would seem, children, that your round comrade has been carrying a treasure ... and I'd wager you knew nothing of it! It feels to me like you've got a nice stack of pennies to share ... how 'bout we count these, fat boy?"

Alfred began thumbing the silver coins onto the ground as Leopold picked and tossed his way through the provisions of the others.

"Ah, here'd be some fine salt pork and some nice salmon and, by the saints, an unspoiled onion. Some millet and oats and two crusts of bread ... ah, and a soldier's flask ... *ach*.... flints and good boots and ... by God, y've picked the pockets of the dead. Y'needs have yer throats cut for such a—"

Alfred interrupted. "The toad's been bearing 'bout twenty shillings worth. Aye, a little more than a full pound. Well done, good lad. You've our many thanks."

Pieter watched carefully as Alfred dumped the pennies into the leather pouch tied tightly on his belt. "This makes three pounds in m'sack, Leopold, plus the one in your own ... I'd say a good week's labor."

Leopold eyed him suspiciously. "Methinks now to be a good time to reckon the counting and even the load."

After muttering a grudging oath, Alfred conceded the point and once again counted each penny to the ground: twelve pennies to the shilling, twenty shillings to the pound, and the extras divided meticulously. The plunder was then apportioned into each man's pouch and the two locked eyes. "We've no further need of this brood. I say we put the sword to them—all, that is, save the yellow-haired wench."

The children drew close to Pieter like frightened pups. Suddenly, Karl blurted, "You'd be true to one point!"

The surprised soldiers stared blankly at the boy.

"Uh ... um ... m'lords, you believe us to be able poachers so, rather than kill us, perhaps you ought give us leave to scrump about these villages for treasures. By faith, methinks us to be quite able, mostly because this priest helps us fool many."

Pieter swallowed hard.

The two soldiers looked at each other and considered the offer. "Humph!" growled Leopold. "A good thought but we've no use for these little ones." He plucked one of the small children out of the group and rested the edge of his blade on the child's throat.

Karl continued dispassionately. "Aye, you may do that, sire, but we have found the littlest ones to be the best at creeping about small places ... and their tears open the baskets of the wives."

Alfred threw his head back and laughed. He grabbed Karl by the ears and bellowed, "By God, you've a good thinker. We'll set you little demons to your task tonight, in Kandern."

Without further delay the frightened flock was herded out of the forest and returned to the river road where they were driven south toward Kandern. By nightfall the soldiers were grumbling and weary and ordered the children to camp within earshot of the fenced hamlet.

"I know for certain of a miller, a baker, a wheelwright, and a brewer in this village. I fear there to be little else, but I'll leave that as part of your test." Leopold wiped his rough sleeve across his mouth. "Ten shall go and fetch us whatever's to be had. If a single one fails to return, I vow the edge of our blades on the rest, and, if the booty be light, this shall be the last night on earth for any of you."

The men studied the group and picked Wil and Karl, Friederich, Conrad, and six others for the venture. Poor Georg hid by the trunk of a tree, thankful for having been spared the pick and quite content to remain wrapped in his woolen blanket. Alfred laughed and instructed Wil to be sure to bring new clothes for his fat friend.

"Good sirs," offered Pieter, "might I beg thy forbearance and accompany these good lads?"

Leopold squinted. "Are you a priest or a madman? I've yet the company of a priest who gave aid to scrumping!"

Alfred chortled, "Then you are blind as a mole. I've yet to meet one that don't."

"Ah, now, my friend, Alfred," said Pieter, "thou hast spoken more truth than you know! I met a thief once who was a priest and I have met priests who are thieves, all one and the same it seems to me ..."

"Enough of your riddles!" barked Leopold. "But I know those robes of yours to be the best trick I've e'r seen to wile the unsuspecting ... so get on with you."

Pieter cast one final glance at the woeful faces of the children left behind and stole into the darkness. He and his accomplices proceeded quietly a short distance until they arrived by the wattled fence of the sleeping village.

Wil whispered to Pieter, "We must make a plan. I surely don't intend to be their slave and neither do the rest of us."

Pieter answered, "I've a plan, my son, and a sad part of it is that we return with a bounty from this poor village." He motioned the children to circle tightly around him and he whispered softly. "Now listen very, very carefully...."

As Pieter finished his instruction, nausea squeezed about his belly, for he remembered Dunkeldorf and felt uncomfortably qualified as a common thief. He sighed. Soon the eleven slipped through some loose stakes of the wall and crept from the night shadows of the slumbering village. The group skulked noiselessly through the hamlet, darting between the smoky columns of the past day's fires and crawling deftly by dark doorways. Friederich's nimble fingers snatched an assortment of foods and sundries from windows left unshuttered in the still, summer night, while Karl stole in and out the thatched huts harvesting a bundle of breads and honeycomb. All through the village tiny silhouettes slid along fences, under windows, and between the tiny hovels of the unsuspecting folk. Only the sounds of snoring peasants and the occasional low growl of a suspicious, sleepy dog broke the silence.

Before long, the anxious group reassembled beyond the village fence and collapsed in the safety of the wood. After a few heavy sighs and nervous titters each offered their loot for the approval of the rest. One lad proudly held a pair of mutton-fat candles to the moonlight; another, some hemp rope and a clutch of pennies; still another, a clay jug of cider and a basket of early apples. Friederich offered a handful of smoked pork strips and entrails and Wil displayed a large cheese, a fine lead buckle, and a small pail of honey.

"Well done, lads," Pieter congratulated as he studied the plunder. "Well done indeed." He himself had pilfered a sloshing barrel of ale that he rolled toward the astonished boys. "And see what else's been found. This ale shall be our weapon," he chuckled. "Watch how it hits its mark!"

The band returned to their impatient captors and emerged into the firelight to present their spoils. Leopold and Alfred laughed loudly when they saw the ample bounty of varied items. "Well, by God," laughed Alfred, "not so much of treasures but ample necessaries. Methinks we've a good partnership, after all! Pity you forgot a homespun for the little hog, though. *Ach.* No matter—you've brought us ale."

Ignoring the children, the two soldiers plunged their thick hands into their packs and jerked out two large wooden tankards which fell immediately to duty under the tapped keg. Pieter winked at Wil, for he knew what fruit the froth would soon yield! And, true to form, the intruders were soon laughing and lurching about the darkness, singing one moment, then threatening each other with their swords the next.

Pieter slowly moved the children to the edges of the campsite where they watched the two fools swig tankard after tankard. When some hours had passed, Leopold staggered toward Pieter with malice in his glazed eyes. "If you think, priest, to beat us with ale, you … you … uh … Me mind fails me…."

"I assure thee, my good friend, I have no such intent."

"Indeed," mumbled the soldier as he returned to his brew.

The two men drank until the eastern sky showed its first signs of light and Pieter was now concerned that the village people would soon be about and notice their loss. *Aye,* he thought, *they'll be on us and'll not be believing our story.* He looked at his red-eyed captors who were still conscious despite the herbal concoction he had secretly added to their ale. *Ach, too little henbane,* he grumbled to himself. *Oh, if only I had kept the belladonna!* But this was not the time for regrets and Pieter knew he must devise a new plan—and quickly. He stared at Solomon for a moment, then carefully whispered an idea to Wil.

Wil smiled and motioned for Friederich to come close. He confided Pieter's plan in Friederich's ear and the three cautiously moved toward the groggy men.

Pieter cleared his throat and stared squarely at Leopold. "And a fine morning to thee, my son. I am waiting to learn of our day's duty."

Leopold rubbed his grimy cheeks and mumbled, "*Ja, ja,* old man, by God …" He yawned. "By God, we'll do this again. We s—" Leopold's heavy eyes drooped, but Pieter leaned close to him and presented a low, numbing discourse on the purpose of man, the complexities of God, of philosophy and rhetoric, astronomy and the like, all of which assured sleep of the deepest kind!

Meanwhile, Alfred had lowered himself against the trunk of a sturdy spruce and was fading into a deep sleep. Wil squatted in front of him to test the man's wit, and, alas, the ruffian was only able to rally one final grouse. "Move off

... brat or you'll ... pay a dear pri ... ce." His head fell forward. Wil motioned for Friederich to hurry and in an instant the nimble fingers of the little tyke raced to untangle the man's pouch strings and seize some coins from deep inside. The lad grasped a handful of pennies and set them softly on his lap. He reached inside for yet another and then deftly retied the cords. He winked at Wil, then scampered between the trees to Pieter's side.

Pieter's drone had served its purpose as Leopold was now slumped in near unconsciousness. The old man warily watched the snoring dimwit as Friederich then carefully added Alfred's coins to Leopold's pouch.

Alfred suddenly lurched in his half-sleep, startling Wil backward off his haunches and so startling Gertrude that she chirped a panicked shriek and bolted into the dawn-grayed forest. Her rash fleet loosed the constrained fear in others, and the whole campsite was immediately filled with the cries of stampeding children.

The commotion drew the soldiers from their sleep and they clambered to their feet. Leopold swirled and thrashed about, barking at Alfred and grabbing at the fleeing children. He chased Maria into the wood and snatched her by the hair. She squealed as he yanked his sword from its scabbard. "Halt, I say, or by the spirits I'll lift off her head."

"Aye, and if he don't, I surely shall. Now hold fast, each one of you," bellowed Alfred.

Most of the children stopped in their steps, and those too frightened to hold soon yielded to the imploring cries of their comrades.

"Good Leopold." Pieter's voice seemed strangely calm and soothing. "None sought escape, oh dear Lord no, I so swear it. These frightened children simply thought it wiser to be out of harm's way when Alfred learned of thy ... theft."

The befuddled soldier cast a perplexed glance at Alfred. Alfred, quick to heed such a comment, tore open his pouch and dug for his coins. Leopold twisted Maria's hair nervously. "What ... what sort of seeds are y'sowing, old—"

"Well, methinks silence the wiser path. Yes, yes, I am certain I—"

"Answer me, priest, or the girl's tongue's out!" boomed Leopold.

"Ah, 'tis certainly no need of that," said Pieter. He looked impatiently at Alfred awkwardly counting his coins. *What a dolt! What a laboring brain!* he mused. "My lord, my only wish is to be a peacemaker," he offered with a smile.

Finally Alfred's face began twisting and bulging. "Where'd be m'other coins?" he demanded.

Leopold shrugged and stared speechlessly at his raging companion. He turned hastily to Pieter. "Y've made some mischief, priest ..."

"Beggin' thy leave, sire, I am under vow to speak only truth and—"

"Speak man! Tell me where my money is!" Alfred bellowed.

Pieter bowed. "I must confess, Alfred, that I saw Leopold take thy pfennigs as you slept and secure them in his own purse."

"A lie, old man! A lie!" shouted Leopold. He ripped his pouch off his belt and bounced it in his hand. But his eyes suddenly widened for he felt the added weight in his bulging bag and he began to stammer. But before a discernible word could fall from his lips, Alfred unsheathed his sword and rushed him.

The trap sprung, Pieter instantly ordered his smallest children to run toward the safety of the forest. "Run! Run! Quickly, lambs! Wil, Karl ... Georg, you, Jon ... you, Frieda, grab what y'can carry ... quick. Quickly!" The older children ducked and dashed between the combatants and gathered all the blankets and stores they could carry before vanishing into the morning mist behind the others.

Leaving behind the sounds of clanging steel and the grunts and oaths of the fighting soldiers, the band raced through the wood, tumbling over logs, rolling down one side of deep ravines and clambering wildly up the other. Poor Pieter was quite the spectacle as he hobbled and lurched on his spindly legs through the early light and looked quite like an old wagon on bent axles, tilting first this way and then that! At long last, the group came to a fern patch where the panting crusaders collapsed into the cool, soft plants. But Pieter was not content to allow much rest and urged his flock to press on. "Your pardon, children," he wheezed, "but we must flee farther and we must make haste!"

After many more minutes, Pieter finally felt secure and he allowed the exhausted children a brief respite. The company fell onto the thick, needled floor of the forest and groaned. Wil wiped the sweat off his face and seized the moment to remind the gasping priest of his authority.

"Yes, yes, good heavens, lad," panted Pieter. "You are our commander." He coughed and sucked huge gulps of air and shook his head.

Wil grunted and shrugged and ordered the others to prepare a quick meal. When all had finished, he gathered his band around himself. "Well done. We've escaped with a fair portion of our stores and, look, I took my dagger off Leopold's belt!" The boy laughed and slid his thumb lightly over the sharp blade.

"And here, Wil," boasted Karl. "I took m'necklace from Alfred's bedroll!" A devilish smirk crossed his red face.

Pieter called for Solomon and slowly walked away from his flock toward a large rock rising between two huge pines. He knelt and raised his hands to the heavens. "'Oh Lord, our Lord, how majestic is Your name in all the earth. From the lips of children and infants You have ordained praise because of Your enemies. I will praise You, oh Lord, with all my heart. I will tell of all Your wonders. My enemies turn back, they stumble and perish before You.'" The old man wept for joy.

❧

The crusaders marched as quickly as they could to add distance between themselves, their former captors, and the village of Kandern, and were soon walking on the river road once again. By mid-morning they rounded a bend and could see the timber-and-stone walls of Basel edging the far banks of the bending Rhine River. It was a marvelous sight for the peasant children and they hurried toward the city until held by Wil. "Halt. All of you, move off the road and rest there." He pointed to a low-fenced sheep meadow where the children obediently settled in lush, green grass overlooking a haphazard collection of poorly kept hovels on the north side of the Rhine.

Pieter leaned on his staff and scratched Solomon's head as he surveyed the small fleet of flat-bottomed river cogs ferrying loads of nervous passengers across the hard-flowing river. The boats listed with the weight of horses, pack-mules, men-at-arms and peasants, merchants and priests, all crowded uncomfortably together. Most were crying every foul oath and sacrilege the priest had ever heard. Pieter shook his head in sorrow.

After a short rest, Wil and Pieter walked apart from the others. "I say it holds good fortune for us," insisted Wil.

Pieter answered gently. "I am yours to command, of course, but as your ... advisor, I must heartily implore your allowing my singular reconnoiter. The city is most unfamiliar to you, and I have been here before. She nearly burned to the ground just twenty-some years ago so I doubt she'll be in any mood for mischief. I tell you, this city is more like a woman than any other I've tarried; she may be warm and welcoming at first glance, then mean-spirited and moody the second."

"Methinks me able to manage a woman," retorted Wil.

Pieter stroked his beard and sucked hard on his lips to bridle the smile straining to escape. Uncertain how to respond, he simply answered, "Ah, *ja*. Your faculty in issues of the heart may be something I have yet to appreciate, but I surely heed your skill in the command of this column. I should think it plain to you to see the merit in my scouting this fair city.... But wait. By faith, I fear I have stepped ahead of your own command again! Of course you would have so ordered ... I am certain of it. Ah, a thousand pardons."

Wil thought for a moment, then stiffened his back and pronounced loudly, "I'll stay with the others and I order you to spy the city ... and report to me the conditions of it."

Pieter bowed in acquiescence; then, putting Solomon under Maria's care, he bade the children farewell. "I'll return some past compline and you may pray for my safety." He smiled and waved and pulled Wil to his side. He pointed toward the muddy river. "Notice, lad, the high waters of the Rhine. The summer's uncommon heat has melted more snow than is usual in the high mountains, and I warn you now that this means danger in the passes ahead. Listen, if I fail to return, do not enter the city. And if you *must* continue, when you enter the great mountains, take special care in the passes."

Wil nodded.

The crusaders watched their friend amble toward the ferries and, as he disappeared into a throng of travelers, they settled around a small campfire to do an accounting of their provisions. "*Ach*, brother," whispered Karl to Wil. "It would have been charitable for you to have grabbed Georg's clothing instead of your dagger!"

Wil looked over at poor Georg who sat wrapped in his scratchy, woolen blanket rubbing his bleeding, bare feet. "Aye, and it would have been charitable for you as well. Y'took that cursed necklace instead."

"*Ja.* But I'd not be the leader here. You'd be the one to care for the others," snapped Karl.

"Georg," hollered Wil, "you ought have rescued your breeches." Some of the children giggled but the blushing Georg could only stare back helplessly and offer a feeble smile.

Wil offered a friendly laugh. "Well, I'm about to send Karl and Lukas to find you something fit to wear. Has someone anything to barter with … or any coins?"

Friederich perked up and bounded toward Wil with a wide grin spread over the whole of his bony face. He reached his fingers into his satchel and giggled. "Well, sir, I kept me a fair portion of pennies."

"Ha! Friederich, well done!" cheered Wil.

The boy proudly dropped his coins into Karl's open palm. "Find Georg a good homespun."

෴

Basel was home to the legions of Rome nearly eight centuries before Pieter's arrival, and the old man marveled at the impressive sight spread before him from the bow of his squat vessel. As he rested his eyes on the twin spires of the cathedral just beyond the dock gate, he began recollecting his memories of the city and the plan of its streets. *Would be good to stretch the mind and shorten the walk,* he thought. He could picture the long rows of thatched roofs running up narrow streets to the hilltops of the wealthy. He remembered the wretches who lived at the bottom and how their homes were so apt to flood.

Basel's streets were cramped but inviting nonetheless. Pieter recalled the peddlers and minstrels, jugglers and fortune hunters; the multitude of inns offering tables of breads, wines, cheese, and ales from much of the world. This was a gateway of the Alps and here converged the dark-eyed traders from the eastern duchies of Moravia and Carinthia, the colorful dancers of Burgundy, and the elaborate emissaries of the pope. The city's comforts were a welcome sight for those exhausted northbound travelers who had transversed treacherous mountain passes and rugged terrain in their journey toward the Teutonic north. And it was a restful hospice and ample storehouse for those about to negotiate those same trails southward.

A stiff, warm breeze coaxed Pieter's single-masted ferry forward and, with a few mighty heaves of the oarsmen, the weathered boat banged harmlessly into a warped dock. After gently reprimanding several impatient fellow passengers, the old man climbed safely atop the stretch of planks leading to the bank. But nearly to the shoreline, his faithful staff suddenly wedged firmly in a gap in a badly split plank. The loud oaths which promptly flew from his curling lips were conspicuously inconsistent for a man of the cloth and caught the curious attention of a dusty traveler.

"Good day, old fellow. It would seem as if you've a small problem."

Pieter wrinkled his brow, visibly annoyed. "Aye. And it seems that you've a good eye for what's plain to see."

The stranger grasped the staff with his one arm, jerked the old crook loose, and handed it to the frustrated priest.

Pieter sighed. "Well ... bless you, my son. I suppose I am in your debt."

The stranger smiled and nodded and set his hand on Pieter's bony shoulder. "It would seem so. And I might add, sire, that by your look y'be, or at least once were, a priest?" Pieter blushed.

"Aye. And so I knew. Now, forgive my boldness, but y'd be the better for your cause if y'd be a bit more mindful of your tongue."

The old man's eyes sparkled and he laughed heartily. "I am undone by such a gentle rebuke, stranger, and am in your debt again. I should like very much to repay both your kindnesses with a tall tankard of ale."

"Ah, Father, thank you, but it seems we be traveling in opposing directions."

Pieter grasped him by the shoulder. "Of little import, good man. Your simple kindness must needs be honored. I beg you to join me over bread and a quick ale."

The traveler hesitated. "I ought press on; perhaps some other time in some other place?"

"Should you take a moment to study me, you'd be sure to see I've but a few more times and places left to my account," noted Pieter. His twinkling eyes snagged their prey.

"*Ach* ... so. Very well, old man," sighed the stranger. "I yield to your magic."

The stranger was of moderate height. His curly hair hued red-brown under the full sun and was long and rather unkempt. A close-cropped beard edged his broad and kindly face and his right eye was covered by a black leather patch tied behind his head by a thin cord of wound hemp. He wore a rough-spun, long, brown tunic over a well-worn pair of leather leggings, each covered by the dust of many months or even years of traveling. His feet were bound by shin-high leather boots and at his left side hung a short, stout blade on a wide belt. His left arm was missing and his sleeve was tied neatly under his stump. He bore the countenance of a sad though gentle man whose humility of spirit one might easily measure in the tone of his speech and the ease of his carriage.

Pieter and the stranger mixed well, like honey in hot tea. They laughed and joked of easy things as they passed through the city gate and under the menacing eyes of Basel's terrifying griffen. The stranger pointed to the end of a row of shops running awkwardly up a steep hill where he spotted a welcoming inn, complete with a collection of long tables bordered by badly warped, wooden benches.

"So, stranger," said Pieter as they settled at their table, "by God, in all my many years I have n'er drank with someone whose name I did not know."

The stranger looked away sheepishly.

Pieter pressed. "Your pardon, sir, did y'speak your name?"

The man answered slowly, "You ought be content to call me Stranger."

"Nay," answered the priest. "'Stranger' is no name ... ah, you've yet to learn of mine own. I am known as Pieter ... and y'may be content to call me Pieter."

The stranger smiled. "I'd rather forget m'name," he said quietly. "And I've fair cause."

Pieter looked on with sympathy and gently asked, "Might I at the very least call you Friend?"

The stranger's eyes moistened a little and he nodded.

"There you have it then," said Pieter. "I am Pieter and you are Friend, and I am most content with that."

He turned to a stout maid rushing past and, with as much bravado as he could muster, blustered, "You there! Ale-maid! A tankard for Friend and Pieter." He giggled like a schoolboy, remembering the riotous days of his youth. Unfortunately, Pieter had given more thought to his lively memory than to his empty purse and when the ale was presented, his merriment abruptly ceased. He now found himself staring squarely into the angry face of the buxom wench standing over him.

Friend thought Pieter's hair looked all the whiter against his fresh-reddened cheeks. The old man cleared his throat and timidly tendered his one-tooth smile in defense.

The growling ale-maid folded her arms over her ample bust and glared down her flared hook nose at the perspired priest. "Stop smiling, y'crusty old man and pay me. And be quick about it ... I've others, y'know."

Pieter grimaced. His inventive mind had failed him and he could think of nothing other than the swollen face of the miserable maid drawing closer and closer to his. He began to fumble for words. The amused stranger chuckled and tossed a penny on the table. Pieter bowed his head. "I am in your debt again, my friend. Please believe I'd no plan for such a thing. I ... I'll pray a special blessing upon you ... you ought know these robes do give my prayers some weight."

Friend looked hard at Pieter and responded sternly. "Pieter, accept my kindness for what it is and do not try to buy it."

The man's words were straight and true, and the surprised Pieter was even more ashamed. "Again I am in your debt. You do well to rebuke me for my own sake ... 'Faithful are the wounds of a friend.' Forgive me."

Friend patted the old priest affectionately on the shoulder and ordered another ale and before long the two had hoisted not one tankard but many, many more than prudence would have hoped! After drooling a gulp, a melancholy Pieter leaned in closer. "So, Friend, forgive m'intrusion, but yer eye b-betrays the look of a man under a heavy p-penalty. What offense has cost y'yer good name?"

Friend looked down at the table and began to speak slowly. "I could not bear m'wife and was in need of a penance, so I joined with the armies of the lords as a servant in their war against rebellious serfs in the north. I ... I worked to hide my hatred for her in such good deeds ..." His voice began to rise. "*Ach.* I am but a liar, a pretender, and a weak man. I fear my soldiering had but little to do with serving the Church." He paused and chased the lump in his throat with a long draught. "And yet worst, in so doing, I forsake m'two fair sons."

Pieter listened intently. The spirits of the ale had not

clouded his compassion. He studied the heavyhearted stranger and gently touched his arm. "I, too, know something of pain, my good man," he said.

Friend simply stared at the brown brew in his tankard.

"Nay, nay, I do know something of it," Pieter insisted. "I have told few of this, but when I was a youth at university I wed the beautiful daughter of the Duke of Rheinfeld. Her name was Anna Maria and I thought her the most precious flower of the Empire." Pieter wiped his eyes. "She had long hair and deep, green eyes. Her skin was pure, without pockmark or blemish, like the finest wheeled pottery. When she laughed, her eyes lit like candles and her cheeks blushed with the color of a deep-summer red rose. Her body was shaped in gentle curves and was full and firm. She was warm and tender and quick of wit. We spent hours laughing in the gardens, picking flowers together and dreaming."

The old priest's voice began to quiver and he paused. His expression suddenly changed. "But I soon learned of what poor clay my heart was formed. I was sent to Salerno to study medicine and apothecary and she came to my side for that warm, wonderful, Italian summer. But in September, the first day of it, as I recall, a Benedictine told me of a plague in Lombardy and, as I was oft wont to do, I seized opportunity and departed to observe what manner of healing might be of most profit. I spent nearly two months apart from my Anna Maria and spent my days and nights among the dying. My mind was filled with learning, but I soon longed for her touch and returned to her side without a thought of what demons might accompany me. So, a few brief days after All-Saints, she fell sick with fever and within a fortnight, at the very bells of terce, her spirit departed from me.

"I was required to burn her body myself and live in quarantine for two months. Those two months, my good man, were the times where I saw the selfishness of mine own heart in ways that few could possibly imagine."

Pieter's voice faded and his eyes filled with tears. An uncomfortable silence seized both men as well as a small group of rough patrons who had been drawn into the priest's sad story.

But those listening were suddenly embarrassed by the tenderness creeping into their hearts and they worked quickly to break the mood. One toothless man abruptly raised his drink. "To ... to Anna Maria," he bellowed. Another cleared his throat and described in some detail how his wife was so unlike Pieter's Anna Maria. "Aye. M'hag is like a rose as well—the thorny stem!"

A bald-headed peddler hastily wiped his eyes and roared that his wife had more the shape of an ox than a woman. "Much like yon ale-maid," he roared. Another howled that his wife's curves were most appealing, but it was her face that brought him terror by night!

Pieter and his new friend smiled, then chuckled, and soon joined the uproarious cackle of wild tales and loud guffaws. Pieter set his melancholy aside and grinned from ear to ear. Not to be outdone by tales of courtship and marriage, he climbed atop his table and commanded silence. A fellow held Pieter's scrawny arm high as another splashed more ale into his tipping tankard and the tavern grew quiet. The dizzy priest cleared his throat and pronounced, "'A quarrelsome wife is like a constant dripping on a rainy day'!"

His companions cheered and clapped and called for more. Pieter was now quite carried away by his ale and stepped down to a wobbly stool, laughing and gasping for air. "'Better to live in a desert than with a quarrelsome and ill-tempered wife'!" he wheezed.

"Aye! No more a truth has e'er been spoke!" roared a voice from the crowd.

The ale-maid huffed and squeezed between the tables with pitchers of new ale, slapping the giddy, grasping men. Her face was flushed and she made no effort to disguise her disgust.

Pieter was struggling to recall more Scripture. He scratched his head and then spread his arms wide over his dubious congregation. He hushed his friends and choked back a giggle. He made a halfhearted effort to recapture a sanctified composure before slurring, "'Like gold in a pig's snout is a beautiful w-woman who shows no discretion.'" He barely finished the verse before he toppled off his stool into the arms of his cheering companions.

But the ale-maid had reached her end and she stormed over to Pieter. "Old fool," she bellowed over the din. "Your poor Anna Maria showed little discretion in choosing you."

Pieter shrugged his shoulders and, wounded by her words, slinked back to his bench. The party was over.

Chapter 12
THE EDGE OF THE PIT

arl and Friederich foraged the nearby villages and returned to the others happy to present Georg with a full set of clothing. "We found a miller who'd part with this all for but eight pennies!" boasted Friederich.

Georg offered a halfhearted smile and politely restrained comment on the selection. Wil, however, was all too eager to offer his. "You spent nearly a shilling for these moth-eaten tatters? You ought know better than trust a miller."

"No tatters here!" snapped Karl. "The tunic's a good wool and the leggings are heavy linen. We've even a flaxen undersuit and, look here, we've leather shoes with but one hole at the heel."

"Karl," sighed Wil, "this 'good wool' is threadbare at the shoulders, the side splits run beyond their seam, the leggings are badly worn in the seat, and both knees have holes. The shoes are dry and cracked. What's wrong with you, y'dolt? You'll not be a merchant, 'tis plain to see."

"But, Wil," said Georg, "these are far better than the blanket I'd be wearing now!"

Karl interrupted. "And look. I squeezed the miller to give these shears as well. We needs present ourselves proper to Basel and we've all need of a head shearing."

"You're mad, Karl!" laughed Wil. "And stay clear of me with those clippers of yours!"

"I'll be as Mother says is right to be. She says that others fail to offer trust when we're off our proper way, and—"

Wil spun on his heels. "Speak not of Mother's endless instruction! I've no regard for such and I've less regard for others' trust."

Karl was unprepared for the rebuke. "I only thought it good for us to appear properly shorn for the city and for the Feast of Assumption.... You do hope we'll get there?"

Wil did not answer but a bright-eyed Lukas added that he thought a feast was "a fit remedy for our troubles." Others echoed his remark and soon a lively discussion ensued in which each dirty-faced crusader described his particular idea of a good and proper festival. They chattered of tables heaped high with early fruits and steaming venison, of minstrels and jugglers, of bright colors and laughter. Oh, what dreams they shared, what joyous visions revelled in their sparkling eyes!

While the others chattered and gibbered, Georg addressed a more immediate concern and shuffled off behind a clump of small bushes to change into his new wardrobe. And, after a succession of long, strained grunts, he emerged from his cover to return to his comrades with what modicum of dignity his new attire might stubbornly yield. The shocked children fell abruptly silent and looked carefully at their red-faced companion as Wil studied the poor boy from head to toe. "Karl and Friederich, 'tis clear y'gave no thought to the boy's size, y'ignorant fools."

Karl glanced at Friederich and struggled to decide whether to beg for pardon or release a hearty laugh! Georg's linen breeches gripped his thighs like wet silk, exposing every bulge and crease to eager critics. They stretched to a place just below his knees, far from his ankles which they ought to cover. His shoes were far too big and Wil thought them to be like giant buckets planted at the end of his stout legs. His poor tunic was strained over his belly, the side seams gaping and the edges curling just above his hips. His sleeves clasped his forearms not halfway from his elbow, and his armpits suffered with every chafing swing of his arms. Each step brought the sound of ripping and popping as he waddled uncomfortably toward his rollicking friends.

"Perhaps if I bend a little, this shall yield to follow my figure some better, say, Karl?" Georg asked sheepishly.

"Well, methinks you unfamiliar with the clothing of a peasant, but—"

"The clothing of a peasant?" Wil interrupted. "This is more the clothing of a madman!"

That remark sent the wheezing children into another chorus of belly laughs while Maria plucked a small wildflower and tucked it in the poor lad's belt. "Perhaps this shall help?" she tittered kindly.

Georg looked down at the little flower squashed indelicately between his belt and his paunch and his face suddenly brightened. "Look at me," he roared. "Just look at me!" The cheerful boy laughed and laughed a good, hearty laugh, an honest laugh—a belly-shaker and a tearmaker—the kind of laugh that good friends share.

When the crusaders finally quieted, Karl offered a sincere apology to Georg and the two clasped hands. He then commanded all the boys to assemble so that he could shear their hair and make them the kind of "proper Christian soldier" that they ought to be. Reluctant, but submissive to such a familiar charge, they formed a row, each nervously waiting his turn as Karl went to work quickly, clipping and chopping and pulling at their stubborn locks. It seemed that he was finished before any could react and the boys soon stood grimacing at each other in disbelief. The little warriors looked like poorlyshorn sheep waiting for some sympathetic shepherd to herd them from view! But the proud barber was oblivious to all grievances and cut his own red curls before stuffing his rusty shears in his blanket.

Karl flopped down on the grass next to his brother, who simply shook his head at such a pitiful spectacle. The two sat quietly as the day slowly passed, each lost in thought. Below them was the faithful Rhine dotted with struggling ferries and a few passing sailing ships. Beyond the river were the city's walls and merchantmen's homes which overlooked them from within. Beyond that waited a beautiful world of rising, green mountains against a rich, blue sky. "Oh, how beautiful, Wil. How truly beautiful. If only I might be an angel and fly high above. It is such a wonder."

Wil hesitated for a moment before answering. "I would've wagered you to see it that way. Nay, poor, unsuspecting brother, what I see is a world to be conquered; a giant fortress of opposing walls which we'll scale."

"*Ach*, Wil, can y'not see the beauty in it? Are you blind to those deep shadows growing in yon valleys ... and oh, how beautiful the green. I have ne'er seen such green before.... And the look of the city, and the banners and flags, and ..."

"Y've seen green before, and y've seen shadows ... humph ... more shadows than you'd ever dare admit. Aye, and y've seen a blue sky and y've seen pretty colors—so what's new in it?"

Karl shrugged his shoulders. "I've ... I've ... no answer, but when I look there, m'eyes do prove the world to be a better place than what you and others charge. The world is a place of beauty and hope and ... and good things to come!"

"So 'tis true? Ha. Speak to Lothar about hope, Karl, and tell Maria how very comely is her arm. What of the good news for those hanged from that accursed tree? By God, Karl! You are blind to the world as it truly is. You needs open your eyes and see how to overcome it or you'll be lying 'neath a stony grave before you scrape a whisker off that angel face."

Karl was woefully unprepared to counter. "You ... you have always thought yourself to be the better of us all."

Wil smirked. "Now you see the world as it is ... at last. By the saints, you've stumbled upon truth. Aye, I am not wont to err like most, nor shall y'find me a servant to any man. Nay, all I need are these good arms of mine. And you'll ne'er find me cowering in battle, never! I see the evil in wait all around and I am its better." Wil jumped to his feet and smiled a haughty smile, a self-serving, offending smile—a hate-maker and a heartbreaker—the kind of smile that wounds.

Karl stubbornly rose and stared at the unyielding face of Wil. "We cannot both be right. Perhaps in time *you* shall learn."

Wil dismissed the remark and abruptly planted his hands on his hips. He looked beyond his brother and barked to his company, "Set the column. It shall be dark soon enough and we need to find the old man. I fear he's fallen into more trouble with that splendid wit of his."

The children promptly gathered and obediently followed Wil toward the bank of the Rhine and the busy path leading to the docks. "We'll need some silver to cross." Wil reached into his satchel and retrieved the fare. He handed his pennies to a grizzled ferryman and soon the crusaders were packed tightly aboard a wide-bottomed boat. As the grunting oarsmen pulled them closer to the south shore, they could begin to hear the snapping of the city flags. To these young children of the German heartland it seemed as if they were about to enter the portals of the City of Zion, and they were suddenly nervous.

"Methinks we ought sing!" cried Karl.

With a roll of Wil's eyes, the company disembarked and gathered on the crowded dock to sing a chorus of hope.

&

A snicker wound its way through the alehouse as a sheepish Pieter succumbed to the ale-maid's rebuke. He shrugged and sought sympathy from the smiling stranger when his heart seized. *"Mein Gott,"* he exclaimed. "My children!" Pieter abruptly stood to his wobbly feet and begged his new friend to come with him.

"I'll escort y'to the bridge but then I've needs be on m'way."

The pair hurried through the crowded streets as Pieter grew insistent. "I am excited for you to meet my little lambs, good friend. You heard it said, 'A look into the eye of youth adds a year of good life'!"

Friend slowed his pace. "No," he said slowly, "I find children an unbearable reminder of m'own dear lads, and I fear such pain."

Pieter stopped to catch his breath. "Poor stranger, your sadness weighs on me, but I am most certain you shall find my brave little band a blessing. They are oft so eager, so determined, and so very stouthearted. I vow they shall touch your heart and bring hope to your weary soul."

The two soon passed through the wide gate and hurried to the docks when Pieter suddenly recognized the familiar melody of his beloved children. A huge smile spread across his weathered face and he grabbed Friend by his tunic and pulled him through a surging crowd toward his flock now climbing up the bank. "Ho, ho, my children!" Pieter bellowed as he stumbled toward them. "'Tis so very, very good to see you. I humbly beg your pardon for my delay."

Wil's scolding eyes would have said enough but the lad felt compelled to press his complaint. "You've been spending time with a tankard of poor hops," he said sharply. "I can smell your breath from here and I can see you need this fellow to steady you."

Solomon jumped playfully on the priest and the old man rubbed his scruffy ears. *No judgment from this one*, grumbled Pieter to himself. "Ah yes, indeed, lad … you ne'er fail to go straight to the mark. My prayer is that you shall learn from my counsel and not my example."

Wil surrendered. "By heaven, Pieter, you do frustrate me. I'd be a liar to say 'tis not a relief to find you … though, be sure, we'd be certain to press on without you. Now, I trust you've found us some food and a lodging for tonight?"

"Ah," fumbled Pieter. He directed his eyes to Karl. "Ah, boy, 'tis good to welcome you to Basel and I trust—" Pieter stopped and stared. "Dear lads, what has happened to your poor heads?"

The girls began to giggle but the remark bore sudden indignity among the boys who abruptly stuffed their crosses back into their belts and growled at Karl. "Ah, so I see," continued Pieter. "Methinks you to now have the look of fine, disciplined soldiers, quite unlike this scoundrel here," he said with a wink, pointing to Wil.

Having stood in the way of others passing by, the company followed Pieter and his odd companion through the city gate and to a quiet corner of the fish market. "You've not yet answered my question," pressed Wil.

"Yes, yes. And a very fair question I might add. Ah, but first I should like to introduce all to a friend of mine." Pieter gestured toward the embarrassed stranger. "He has chosen to free himself of a name and so we have the privilege of calling him what we wish. I believe we should call him Friend, for that is what he has been to me this day."

Seemingly troubled, the blushing man smiled faintly and nodded shyly to the wary children. Maria pointed to him, shyly. "Where is your arm?"

Friend was surprised but strangely warmed, nevertheless, by the engaging child. He knelt in front of her and looked at her gently. Her skin was weathered some, he thought, but bore a pleasant pink from the summer's sun. Her golden hair was tied in uneven braids which framed a face he considered angelic. His eye fell to see her withered arm and he understood. "Well, my dear little *Mädel*," he said softly, "I am one who really needs but one arm."

"And why so?" she asked.

"I do quite nicely with one arm; I've but one nose to pick … er, to wipe, one mouth to feed, one head to scratch. You understand?"

Before Maria could respond, Lukas interrupted. "Are you a soldier?"

"I once was a soldier, aye."

Wil studied him carefully and said, "And where do you come from?"

"I come from the north."

"Where?"

"It matters not where, lad. I come from the north and the north is where I return to."

"Aye, and we, too, come from the north," Karl added.

"Yes, 'tis good to be sure, lad."

Friend was perspiring when Wil pressed him. "And why do you not tell us of what prince y'serve?"

The stranger looked for help from Pieter, but the old man simply shrugged. Before Friend answered, Friederich called out, "And what about the eye and yer arm? Were you a crusader in Palestine?"

The stranger, slightly irritated with more questions, answered curtly, "No, I was a soldier but not in Palestine. I lost my eye to the mace of a different foe and lost—"

"And who was your foe?" asked Karl.

Friend stared at Karl for a long moment. "I should like to think no one, ever again."

Friederich pursued. "Was the man who took yer eye a brave man? And did y'kill him?"

The uncomfortable stranger turned once more to Pieter. The old man shrugged again. "These would be soldiers as well, Friend, comrades of sorts and eager to learn of you."

Friend turned back to Friederich. "I'll say this and no more: The man who took m'eye was, indeed, a brave soldier, and he fought with heart. But at the moment his mace struck me I thrust my glaive beneath his jerkin. By faith, I know not if the fellow lived or perished."

Karl and Wil had carefully studied the strange man all the while he was talking, and they had caught his eye on them as well. But before either could ask another question, a deputy and a dozen men-at-arms suddenly charged through the fishmarket and confronted them. The deputy grabbed Friederich by the collar. "Ha. More brats for the rats!" His soldiers laughed. "'Tis my sworn duty to inform you that you are hereby under arrest by the authority of the magistrate of Basel on cause of theft."

Pieter protested, "Thou hast no just grounds. None at—"

"Silence, old fool," snarled the deputy as he tossed Friederich to the ground.

Perhaps he was encouraged by the ale, perhaps some other demon whispered in his ear, or perhaps the instincts of a guardian lion seized command of his tongue, but, for whatever cause, Pieter promptly set his long nose squarely into the face of the black-eyed officer and lashed him with a string of expletives that would have reddened the face of the foulest fiend!

The surprised deputy recovered quickly and unloaded his own cache of ill-tempered oaths as he pulled the furious Pieter even closer to his own whiskered face. The loud exchange occupied the attention of the soldiers, and Friend wisely spotted an opportunity.

"Lad, have the children drop whatever they can into my sack. Now! Otherwise the guards shall steal all."

Wil looked warily at the stranger but then whispered his command to the others. Pieter's crescendo of profanity scalded the tender ears of some temperate souls now retreating from the marketplace, but it served to incense the officer and his troop all the more. The crusaders used the diversion efficiently and they slipped deftly around Friend's sack one by one, dropping in their onions, a few turnips, strips of salted pork, bits of crust, and sundry other treasured provisions. Wil reluctantly surrendered his dagger and Karl his necklace into the dark bag and watched anxiously as the stranger hastily secured it. Then, in a moment both the sack and the stranger faded into the shadows with Solomon tethered to his elbow.

At last the furious deputy ordered his guards to shackle the howling priest and to bind the children one after the other with a heavy rope. The column of prisoners was then herded like sheep to the slaughter, prodded and poked by the sharp points of the guards' long lances. The terrified flock tramped obediently through the narrow streets and bravely bore the taunts of the folk pressing in all about them. All spirit fled them, however, when they turned a corner and faced the foreboding dungeon gate yawning wide and terrible before them.

Friend maintained a prudent distance from the crusaders but followed them faithfully. He peeked his eye from a nearby alleyway and groaned. A beggar jostled past him and turned. "Ha. Y'see those imps, d'y'not? Aye, they've worn out their welcome, they have. I've seen them come here by scores and, by God, I thought to 'ave seen the last of 'em. I say let them rot in the dungeon."

"*Ja,*" cackled a wretched old hag passing by. "Now we've some justice, methinks. These misfits be from parts north and've scrumped and murdered their way to our good city. I say hang 'em all."

Another voice in the growing crowd added, "Aye. Indeed so it is. I have heard that they poach manor and town alike and be doing the same in France. And I've heard them to be carrying plague."

Friend did not comment, but shoved his way through the jeering crowd and moved closer to the iron-barred entrance of the dungeon. He strained to see the children, and when his eye fell upon them, his jaw clenched and his fist whitened with rage. But he could do nothing other than stand mute and helpless as the priest and his Innocents suffered the slaps and punches of the unmerciful troop. Though he desperately struggled to concoct a rescue, all such hope faded as he beheld the defenseless crusaders and their guardian disappear into the cavernous mouth of the prison.

అ

A badly bruised Pieter was pushed roughly into the dark dungeon's chambers, and if any could have seen him they would have seen his lips murmuring a desperate prayer. The children followed close after, most quaking in abject terror. Wil's fear fueled his cynical inclinations, and everything within him now raged against what good he secretly hoped existed in the worlds around and above him. He turned toward his frightened brother. "Your goodness fails you."

Karl could not answer. His round face was yellowed and drawn in the torchlight, and beads of perspiration trickled from his temples to his jaw. He trailed close behind Maria, who clutched Wil's tunic and hid her face in the small of his back. All obediently followed the stone-faced guards through dank passages lit only by smoky pine-torches scattered randomly along the slick, rock walls. The crusaders shuffled and stumbled their way through the musty halls, past rows of iron-hinged doors, until they finally were commanded to halt before the one destined as their own.

A guard snapped orders for those inside to stand back as he fumbled through a tangled ring of keys. The children stood in numbed silence as he finally rattled a long key into its rusty hole. The stubborn lock yielded with a groan and a snap, and the door creaked open. Two guards advanced through the entry with their halberds lowered and corralled the other prisoners to the center of the large chamber.

The children gaped fearfully into the reeking cell now awaiting its new quarry. A choking torch cast a dull light from its high mount on a far wall, scattering a ghoulish glow over the horde of inmates below. Its fire did not chase the darkness but rather seemed to mystically fuse with it as a hellish collusion of flame and shadow. Beneath it, a murky mass of bodies crowded tightly together like a ball of writhing worms, coiled and tangled, contorting and twisting, reaching and stretching at the little lambs who were now herded toward its lurid grasp.

With a frightful thud, the cell door suddenly slammed shut behind them. Pieter and his flock stood motionless, gagging on the stench of human filth and diseased flesh heavy in the air. A few of the children plucked enough courage to cast a look at the shadowy center but failed to discern more than a few glimpses of the ghostlike faces glaring at them from under drawn hoods. To Pieter, it felt as if he and his charges had been abandoned to the horrid pit of hell itself.

The menacing prisoners began to creep toward the children, some laughing, some shrieking, others sputtering indiscernible threats and profanities. "Come 'ere, m'pretty, pretty."

"Over here, little one, over here to be with me."

"I'll hold you, little *Mädel* ... come to me. 'Tis Papa."

The prisoners pressed closer and closer, pawing and clutching and threatening, but it was their devilish laughter that unnerved Wil the most. He set his trembling jaw bravely and held his sister close to his side. Poor Karl quivered nearby.

Pieter, ever acute and quick-minded, inspired a sudden calm as he spread his arms over his flock and pronounced a blessing upon them. *"In nomine Patris, et Filii, et Spiritus Sancti...."* His priestly words suspended the prisoners' advance for a fleeting moment. Such words had not echoed in that chamber for decades and their long-forgotten sound gave pause to evil desire. In the brief interlude Pieter hastily whispered to Wil to move the girls and the littlest boys to the middle and the stronger boys to the outside. Then he softly instructed the children to walk close together toward a corner where two walls would buffer them.

The children obeyed instantly and began to pick their way carefully past the stalled inmates. But no sooner had the crusaders begun their move when the prisoners began inching forward once again. Pieter squeezed his eyes closed in desperate prayer but his pleadings had barely left his lips when, as much to his own surprise as to others', he began singing. There was no known reason for such a thing, no known purpose whatever, but his raspy voice had become suddenly clear and miraculously resonant, and he crooned the children's favorite hymn with the vigor of a man half his age. Then, as if summoned by an unspoken command, the little voices of the tender lambs suddenly joined their shepherd and together they sang to the glory of their Savior:

> Fairest Lord Jesus,
> Ruler of all nature,
> Son of God and Son of Man
> Thee will I cherish....

In their terror they sang and they sang, louder and louder. And oh, if only their eyes would have been opened at that moment! For in that horrid place they would have seen a chorus of angels singing with them; a legion of light from the heavenly realm defending them from the dread and gloom of Hades. For the first time in unnumbered years, the brilliance of heaven was pouring into that black dungeon and nothing could dull it. Their Savior had placed a shield about them—and it would not be moved!

The surprised inmates retreated in confusion from the choir and gathered themselves at the center of the chamber once again. The crusaders kept singing until they reached the distant corner where they assembled in a tight cluster. Here they began another stanza which they sang with equally determined passion.

When the song ended, Pieter placed himself at the point nearest to the other inmates and raised his arms. The priest closed his eyes and dismissed all sense of the offense he and his beloved were suffering and, instead, imagined himself to be standing in a sturdy, hand-carved pulpit high above a group of well-scrubbed parishioners in a fine, sun-swept cathedral in the south of France. He stretched his arms wide and began to preach a homily of love.

At first the astonished prisoners reacted with rumbling oaths, but the undeniable familiarity of the chant and rhythm of Pieter's voice and the power of his words soon stilled them. Before long their empty, haunted eyes began to close and they gave their yearning souls leave to be carried to a hundred different altars in a hundred different towns and manors spread throughout all Christendom. Each was mysteriously drawn to the calm and order of a previous life and it felt so very good. For most, this unexpected encounter with the love of Almighty God in such an insufferable place was overwhelming. The picture of the Savior and His angels filling their dungeon with a heavenly presence was more than could be conceived. And those who were so touched fell to their knees in tearful worship.

છ

Outside the prison, Friend paced through the dark streets, pausing only to offer Solomon a distracted scratch on the head. The man was keenly aware of what ravages would surely be unleashed against the crusaders and he swore an oath to rescue them. He would never again abandon children to peril, he thought. Never.

Solomon suddenly darted to the other side of the street and retrieved Pieter's staff which had fallen on the cobblestone walkway. He presented it to Friend, who held it to his breast hopefully. "I've need of a plan, Solomon, a sound and worthy scheme. *Ach*, m'head must needs stretch itself." Friend thrashed about the moonlight until, at last, a confident smile wrinkled his weathered face. He charged toward the dungeon's gate.

"You there, guard," he yelled. "You there. Answer me at once!"

"Who speaks?" grumbled the guard as he pulled his torch from the wall. "Who speaks?"

"I speak."

Unimpressed, the guard groused, "*Ja, ja.* And what's this about?"

"'Tis said you've dragged a band of children through these very streets and they'd be bound inside."

"Aye. And what business is it of yours? Had I a say, they'd all be drowned in the river."

"What's m'business? Ha! Y'd be a dolt if ever one lived. I tell you what m'business is!" said Friend. "My business is your business ... you've brought plague through these streets and you've set it just behind you. We've both business here and, aye, the mortuary shall soon have business as well!"

The soldier stiffened. "Y've no proof of such a thing."

"Nay? I've seen the yellow sweat on 'em up close and I've seen the marks on their faces. Y'think me to have nought else to do but bother with a pack of little brats as they? By God, man, use that dung-filled head of yours."

"None else has spoke of it and—"

"Listen, fool! I can swear to what I've seen. Call your magistrate ... wake him from his bed and have him stand close to look with his own eyes. Aye, and you'll be needing a new magistrate in a fortnight!"

The guard hesitated, then shook his head. "If your words be true, then the worst of it is for that bunch inside ... no loss to me."

"Walls can't contain plague, y'dolt!" boomed Friend. "Plague is plague—have y'forgotten Bern during the Whitsun Feast just two years prior? Any brushed by a single breath of the sick were cold and stiff in a winter's hour."

The uneasy guard was familiar with the stories of Bern, and imagining Basel filled with smoking biers was enough for him to beckon his sergeant and whisper a few hushed words. The sergeant abruptly ordered him to summon the captain of the jail who emerged from his quarters in an impatient rage.

"What say you?" the captain barked at Friend.

Friend narrowed his eye and growled, "Your dimwitted deputy paraded plague through these streets but a few hours past. Have y'ne'er seen plague? I have. And I'm here to warn y'that y've brought death and misery upon us all. Y've time to expel them yet ... while the streets are empty ... and I swear by the Virgin Mother and the Holy Church, if you simpletons don't, I'll stand in the square on the morrow and tell all of your murderous deed this night!"

The captain began to perspire. Friend leaned closer. "Have you ever seen plague?"

The captain shook his head.

"Well, I have and I've seen what it does. It seizes a stout and sturdy man like your very self and rots you from the innards out. From your toes to your scalp, your skin shall blacken and bleed and you'll soon cry out in pain as you suck for breath. You'll be set in a row by others who share your plight until your miserable soul is snatched to the Pit and your putrefied body piled in a wagon and hauled to the fires. And, were that not enough, your pathetic name shall be stricken from the memories of all but Lucifer, who shall bind you in his furnace forever!" Friend was surprised at his own eloquence, but yielded no hint of charade. He bored his eyes into the captain's.

"And ... and which prisoners bear this ... plague?" queried the captain, suddenly anxious.

"Aye, the children ... I saw the marks on most and 'tis certain y've heard how they've carried such a curse over all the Empire."

The captain stared blankly at the prison gate. "*Ja*," he answered slowly. "Perhaps I ought inform the magistrate."

"*Ach*. I knew y'to have more wit than the louts following you about. 'Tis a good man who spares his *volk* such an end. If y'fail to exile those whelps, your city will be filled with the litter of a thousand black corpses by Assumption ... and y'dare not hang 'em, nor put them to the torch and risk the wrath of the Church.... But why call the magistrate? I'd wager he'd put a foot to your arse for trussing him to such a blunder!"

The captain's lips twitched and he wiped his sweating hands on his leggings. "I've the authority to arrest and dismiss at my will and ... methinks it best to rid this city of any risk of plague. You, sergeant, drag them beyond the walls and be quiet about it. Let 'em die in the mountains." He turned a sly eye to Friend.

"And I suppose we are in your debt, stranger? You ought be rewarded for such a warning and for your ... er ... discretion ... *ja*? Take this silver and begone."

The stranger was but a peasant, a commoner and a foot soldier of sorts, but he was keen to a fair bargain. He promptly placed the coins in his pouch and slipped into the darkness.

æ

Four angry soldiers jerked open the cell door and stormed through the murky shadows toward the huddled children. The startled crusaders cowered as the huge men then flailed them out of their cell and into the dingy corridor. With vile oaths and curses, the guards chased them from the belly of the dungeon toward its opened gate and, to the children's amazement, rushed them through the silent streets and beyond the city walls. After lashing them with a severe warning and a few licks of a strap, the guards turned their backs and left the pilgrims to stare at each other in the cool, quiet night air.

Pieter was too dumbfounded to utter a single sound. And the children seemed equally dazed, fearing to embrace their good fortune lest it be snatched away as suddenly as it had been granted. Then, before any spoke, Solomon charged them from the darkness and jumped into Pieter's arms. As the happy dog licked the salt from his laughing master's face, a hearty voice called toward them from the darkness. "Ha! You're free!" exclaimed an emerging figure. "Pieter, have you all the children ... each and every one?"

"Oh, dear God in heaven!" cried Pieter. "Good Friend. *Ja, ja.* We've need to count ... children, form your column."

Wil ordered his excited company to their positions and Pieter counted twenty-six. "So? It seems we've grown."

A few nervous children stepped forward. "Father, we were put in that place some days ago," a timid boy offered. "We are crusaders, as are you, and would be grateful to join you."

Pieter embraced the lad. "My name is Pieter and your new commander stands before you ... his name is Wil. On the morrow we'll have a look at you in sunlight, but for now, be at peace. God has spared you."

Friend paced along the line of children and studied them anxiously through the night's dim, silvery light. "Were any left behind ... any at all?"

"I think not, stranger," Wil answered.

"Aye ... is the redheaded one here?"

"*Ja*, I am here," said Karl.

The man was silent for a moment. "Ah, 'tis good. I ... I wish you all God's mercy. I must be on m'way."

He emptied the sack full of the children's effects and handed Pieter his staff. The tearful old man embraced Friend warmly and thanked him. "I have no idea why or how our Lord has delivered us, but I believe Him to have used you somehow. My beloved Friend, He has revealed His loving care this very night, and I shall never forget such mercy, nor shall I ever forget His faithful instrument."

Pieter and the children pleaded with the stranger to join them in their journey but the man stubbornly refused. At last, Friend reached his arm toward the old man and they embraced one more time. Then he stretched his hand slowly toward Wil's tall frame, stopping just short of touching him. "I ... I wish you all God-speed," he choked. "'Tis past time for me to take your leave." And with that the stranger turned and disappeared in the darkness.

Some of the crusaders called to him, others stared sadly after him, and Pieter quietly whispered a blessing on the man before turning to his children. "Well now," Pieter sighed. "Wil, you are in command and we await your orders."

Wil cleared his throat, surveying his young soldiers with a slightly upturned nose. He began to smile. "I believe us all to stink!" He pointed his laughing friends to the dark bank of the Rhine. "My orders are ... that we wash."

The shrieking children raced toward the cold water of the mighty river. With shouts of joy they splashed and frolicked under the stars; and all the while, smiling angels circled all around.

Chapter 13
BENEVOLENCE

The children finished washing in the cold river and raced through the moonlight around the walls of Basel, south toward the safety of the mountains rising silently before them. They were determined to set a wide gap between themselves and the torch-blushed sky above the city, and their rush into refuge provoked no complaint.

The stars twinkled kindly far above the straining column but they could not ease the horrid memories which drove them through the night and far into the next day. It was afternoon, some past nones, before Wil ordered his anxious soldiers to halt in the hollow of a sharp ravine. "Enough," he panted. "We've made a good distance and 'tis a good place to rest. I think there to be water near. Conrad … take … Friederich and find us a good stream. You others, open your sacks and make ready a fire."

The children gleaned what provisions were secured by the quick-witted stranger while Pieter raised yet again a tearful prayer of gratitude for the salvation of his precious children.

"Ho, Wil!" called Conrad as he and Friederich emerged from the wood. "We've a good bucket of cold water."

"Then stew it is!"

The children were famished but so savored their freedom that the meager soup of mixed grains, broken crusts, and half-rotted leeks seemed to them a royal feast and their ragged ravine a banquet hall fit for kings. Two of the newcomers, Albert and Jost, crouched apart from the others and stared at their fellow travelers from eyes rolling nervously deep within darkened sockets. But hunger proved a worthy prompter and, setting aside all reserve, they abruptly lunged toward the pot and cupped a handful of lukewarm stew before retreating to the safety of a large, gray boulder. A weary Pieter hobbled stiffly toward the two and leaned against their warm rock.

"My dear lads," he said, "forgive me for not greeting you with a proper welcome."

The boys knelt to kiss his hand.

"'Tis no need," chuckled Pieter kindly. "Stand up ... rise ... allow me to embrace you and welcome you to our family."

Albert was about nine years with curly brown hair and large, round brown eyes. He eagerly received Pieter's comforting arms, but Jost, perhaps a bit older, fixed his hazel eyes warily on the old man. By their sallow complexions and bony frames it was obvious to Pieter that neither had eaten in a very long time.

In the daylight Wil now numbered his band and, upon completing his regular administrative task and eaten his portion of stew, found a soft bed of grass to stretch in. He laid his head back and closed his eyes to the sounds of Solomon playfully pawing and frolicking with his relieved comrades. The comfort of laughter and the warmth of sunshine soon drew the lad to a well-deserved sleep.

Karl and Georg, however, preferred dreams to sleep and chattered wildly about the Feast of the Assumption they hoped to enjoy in Burgdorf. Such infectious enthusiasm was a healing balm for the circle of excited faces gathered roundabout, and soon all revelled in visions of troubadours and plenty until the silver moon slipped over the craggy edges of the mountains. Then, at last, the most spirited of imaginations could not hinder the weight of heavy eyes and all settled in for a good night's sleep.

Morning came quickly with its predictable specter of hunger, but now, for the first time in their Holy Crusade, the children were no longer near the faithful Rhine. No eels would be trapped, no fish netted. Instead, the pilgrims scanned the rugged countryside in search of a manor-house or smoky village where a gracious lord or peasant might be baking bread or stirring a good stew. Sadly, these mountain valleys offered no such mercy and the children had no option but to eat the last of their salt pork and crusts. They spared only what little grain was found in a few small satchels and reluctantly marched forward in hopes of finding help over the next ridge—or the next.

Though still many days' journey away from the heart of the mighty Alps, the path up this range grew more difficult. The thin-soled shoes and badly worn wraps of those fortunate to be shod ripped and tore on the sharp rocks and knotty roots of the sheep trail Pieter had chosen. The old man leaned hard on his staff and set his bleeding feet carefully against the tentative earth beneath, slipping and falling against the gravel path and working hard at binding his tongue.

Wil and Karl led the column up the hard grade, a sense of expectancy pulling them to the crest. And they were not disappointed, for the panorama that awaited their arrival filled their eyes with sights unfamiliar to these youth of a more gentle terrain. The joy of discovery lured the company toward each next ascent like discoverers in a new land, and they were thrilled again and again by each such landscape that sprawled before them.

"Look all, come see," urged Karl as he crested one such summit. The boy's round face beamed with enthusiasm and his wide, blue eyes strained to absorb the splendor that lay hushed and still below him. Stretching as far as he could see were wide valleys lush and green, dappled with pockets of dark shadows and patches of yellowing spelt. Clumps of hornbeam and oak spotted portions of valley and hillside alike, and many-colored wildflowers fluttered gaily in the gentle breezes. Flocks of sheep dotted the green carpet like sprinkles of pure-white salt, and here and there ribbons of smoke curled from the roofs of the *Mittertennhäuser,* the timber farmsteads of the mountain peasants.

Pieter was last to reach the top of the ridge, and his mouth opened wide to draw deeply of the clean air. He set one hand on Solomon's shaggy head and the other on gentle Maria's. He gave no thought to either hunger or fatigue, but instead turned his moist eyes toward the brilliant blue sky above. "Shout for joy, oh heavens, for the Lord has done it! Break forth into a shout of joy, you mountains. Oh forest and every tree in it, for the Lord has redeemed us." He swallowed hard on the lump in his throat. "'O Lord, our Lord, how majestic is Your name in all the earth. When I consider Your heavens, the work of Your fingers, the moon and the stars which You have set in place, what is man that You are mindful of him?'"

The children were moved by Pieter's passionate prayer which revealed yet more of the deep love the old man had for his Creator. Pieter turned to them. "Oh, my children, 'tis a beautiful sight that touches m'heart, but what a marvel yet awaits you. Beyond these splendid valleys stand the grandest of all wonders ... the great mountains called the Alps. God has molded them as the white-haired elders of His creation, the silent overlords of His imperial workmanship!"

"Pieter," interrupted an impatient Wil, "we needs move on."

The shadows were long when the crusaders finally reached the valley floor and the exhausted children hesitated at the foot of the next ascent. Georg suddenly pointed to some smoke from a farmhouse partially obscured by heavy pines.

"Look, Wil ... there, food, perhaps a bit of food?"

Wil called for Pieter and they huddled for a few moments to discuss a plan. Wil thought it best that his cheerful brother accompany the persuasive priest to present their needs to the peasants. "You must win the Frau with your smile and red curls, Karl, while Pieter wiles a bit of charity from the husband. You others ... make a camp for the night and know this: With or without food, we march by lauds."

Karl and the priest ambled obediently toward the unsuspecting farmhouse nestled quietly in the green forest. "I certainly hope these folk to be kindly, Pieter. I am very hungry and can hardly walk another step."

"Humph. Y'think yourself to be hungry and tired, boy? You ought spend a few moments in this old shell!"

"You *are* old, aren't you ... I think I've never known another as old as you. How is it to be so old?"

Pieter stopped walking to catch his breath against the trunk of a large oak. "Well, I may not be so very, very old. Y'might ask this tree or that smooth boulder instead. By truth, boy, I've not seen m'self as you see me, so perhaps I think not of myself as I should! My body fails in parts, 'tis true ... more aches and stiffness, you know ... but the test is my bowels and they serve me well ... far too well at times, methinks!" Pieter grinned. "But m'mind is richer and my heart feels more deeply. I've more memories than I once had and that's mostly a good thing."

Karl interrupted, "Aye ... but you'd be closer to death than any of us."

Pieter smiled weakly. "Oh, that ... yes. It seems none think of aging but as dying. Well, as a priest I am called to not fear death—but I confess I do some—at least the dying part. The truth is, I am not so much afeard of death as I am disgraced by it. It seems to be a final act of helplessness, the final failure; it is shame itself." Pieter closed his eyes and sighed.

"I think I am very afraid to die," offered Karl slowly. A tone of confession mellowed his words and he looked at his feet.

Pieter looked gently at the worried boy. "Ah, good lad, even so do I. But sometimes I yearn to sleep and then I think it to be a good thing. As far as the dying, I know that our heavenly Father would no more leave us alone in that dark valley than He would in any other. We'll be escorted into His glorious kingdom by the same angels that walked with us out the dungeon gate!"

Karl smiled, comforted in part, and the two turned their thoughts to the duties at hand. After scrambling over some rough rocks and stepping through a thick grove of spruce, they finally arrived at the timber longhouse set securely against the breast of the steep hill.

Pieter and Karl paused behind a wide trunk and surveyed the house before making their approach. Though he had been told of such, Karl had never seen a building as this before and was intrigued by it. It was a long, rectangular structure, similar to the houses of the far northland described to him once by an elder of Weyer. It was built of logs, mostly hardwoods, he thought, and had an unusual rock chimney on one end. It was enclosed by a wattle fence and beyond the far end was a larger fenced farmyard in which could be seen an ox, several sheep, two milking cows, and numerous chickens, geese, and ducks. Smoke poured from the chimney and the sounds of hard work could be heard coming from the threshing floor within. The woodland behind the house was partitioned by movable fences and contained a small herd of swine busy foraging for roots, early nuts, berries, and other mast.

Karl marveled at the thought of these folk as freedmen, not bound to a manor and laboring for none but themselves. Pieter and the boy stepped from their tree and approached the farmhouse slowly. Strangers were either welcomed or slain, well-fed or beaten, but they were always a surprise.

Pieter whispered a quick prayer and called softly, "Hello? Is anyone about?"

The sounds of threshing were loud and over them boomed the occasional oaths of the yeoman. Pieter motioned for Karl to follow. They cautiously entered the corridor separating the threshing floor on their left from the living quarters on their right. Pieter again called, *"Mein Herr, meine Frau ..."*

Still no answer. Now somewhat annoyed, Pieter extended his hand toward the wooden latch on the threshing-room door. But before his fingers grasped the handle, the door was flung open.

"By the saints!" screamed the startled housewife. "Dieder, Dieder, come quickly." The plump woman dropped her basket of threshed spelt and rushed away.

The grain had barely hit the floor when her broad-shouldered, bearded husband came crashing to the doorway, eyes flashing and fists clenched tightly around the hinged flail he now held as a weapon. He glared at the trembling strangers, his sweated face covered with dust and chaff. It was quite clear that his surly mood was now further fouled by his unexpected guests.

Pieter raised his cross timidly toward the farmer. "B-blessings on this good house?" he stammered.

Karl dutifully offered a half-smile. But Dieder had no mind for courtesy. The day was nearly spent; he was tired, hungry, and had not finished his work. His face furrowed. "Aye? Begone afore I smash y'both." It was an efficient command.

Pieter gulped but did not yield. *A black heart would've struck by now,* he reasoned. The priest displayed his tooth with a winsome smile. "Ah, yes. And I say again, blessings on this good house in the name of our Savior. May your harvest be bountiful and your health sustain all herein."

The farmer's wife peeked out from behind her husband's wide back and a little white-haired child toddled behind his knees. Dieder said nothing for a moment, looking first into Pieter's twinkling eyes, then into Karl's.

The man's face relaxed a little. "You'd be crusaders, say not?"

"Aye," answered Pieter.

The farmer paused again before speaking. "And I should think you to be more than two … are y'not?"

Pieter nodded.

"And I should think you to be in search of food and a roof for the night?"

Pieter bobbed his head respectfully.

"And what gives you to think I've either?"

Pieter answered simply, "We presume nothing, my lord. May the Lord bless you whether you offer charity or nay."

The eyes of the farmer softened and he looked at his wife. Yielding to the old man he set his flail aside and bent down to pick up his little child. "God has been merciful to this family and 'tis right for us to offer charity. Come, enter my house."

Pieter's heart lifted as he followed Karl and the family into their living chamber. The house smelled of field and forest, of manure and wool and lard and cheese and baked bread. The odors took Karl to his own home and he swallowed hard on the lump filling his throat. *Oh,* he thought, *if only I could lie down on mine own bed.* He so very much wanted to smell the good smells of his bakery and to see his mother fuss and hurry about his little hovel so very far away.

Pieter and Karl were led across the dirt-floored kitchen lined with baskets of fresh-cut dock, sorrel, madder, and woad. They followed their hosts into a small parlor at the front of the house where their eyes widened at seeing something very new. Dieder spotted their interest and proudly stepped alongside his new heat-oven. His wife, now comfortable with her guests, smiled proudly and chattered about her warm, smokeless parlor.

"No more smoke," she exclaimed. "We've a room to gather without the reek of green wood! I swear to you we passed the winter last with no smoke in the house. And I can cook atop the oven and dry wet leggings on it and ..."

"Enough, woman. Be silent. *Ach,* Father, they can go on so. But 'tis true enough. We sit together along our table most content to sit by our stove as the snow piles heavy. Ah, a stout table, a sound roof, a warm room, a plump wife, quiet children, and a tankard of mead! What more might a man want?"

Pieter smiled.

"Now look here," pointed the yeoman. "Gerta stokes the oven from outside ... not inside. Ha. Then, now look here, the smoke follows this stone chimney and out the house. No more smoke-hole."

Dieder beamed with pride and pulled his blushing wife hard against him. "We've never been warmer, aye, wife? Save the winter we first wed!" The man roared as poor Gerta reddened. "Ah, *ja,* and our little beauty, Beatrix, is not sick so much anymore."

"My husband is the first of all parts by Liestal to have one," boasted Gerta. Her blue eyes pinched and twinkled from within her beaming cheeks. "Aye. He was the first to produce two hundred cheeses to the count and ..."

"Nay, nay, my Gerta, my little round gourd, you speak too much again." The farmer seemed truly embarrassed by such public veneration, but the joyful smile straining to escape the constraints of his humility was evidence enough of his delight! "I … I was blessed with good sheep and good cows and God gave us the cheeses as were needed. I worked no harder than any other man, but m'Gerta worked harder than all. She churned from prime to compline. And she carded wool for others to buy extra milk for yet more churning. Nay, 'twas not these hands that won the prize … 'twas m'little mutton chop."

Gerta turned purple. She, too, was not accustomed to such a display and, by Pieter's amused eye, she loved it. Karl was intrigued with the new contraption and interrupted the two. "So, sire, where does this come from?"

"Basel," answered Dieder.

"And you say you've no smoke in the house, no embers flying through the roof?"

"*Ja.*"

"'Tis a wondrous thing. I think you must be an obedient servant of the Holy Church to be so blessed!"

The farmer leveled a hard gaze at the boy. "What mean y'boy? I'd be no more obedient than my fellows."

Pieter sat by the table and grimaced as Karl explained. "Well, my lord, clearly God's blessings are for those who obey His Church and His curses are for those who fail. You are much blessed, so methinks y'to be a good Christian."

Pieter groaned inwardly as Dieder's mood darkened. The yeoman crossed his thick arms and wrinkled his weathered brow. "Three years past m'two sons died of fever. Would y'be claiming them to be unworthy Christians? Was this house beset with sin then but not now? Perhaps we'd be better for their passing. Four years ago, our baby Maria was torn apart by a wild boar just out that very door…. Tell me, boy, tell me about her sin."

Pieter remained silent as Karl's eyes begged for help. The objection was unexpected and the boy's mind whirled. "Uh, well …"

Dieder set his fists hard on his hips and leaned his broad face close to Karl's. "Listen, and listen well, y'cocked whelp. You'd be no judge of good and evil under this roof."

Again, Karl looked desperately for help from Pieter. But the old man wisely allowed the lad to spend a few painful moments wiggling in his own snare. The boy stared blankly at the angry farmer and his hushed wife and then finally at his own shoes.

At last Pieter mercifully broke the silence. "Indeed, Herr Dieder and Frau Gerta, indeed. Our God prospers and plagues those whom He will and for what He will, according to His own purposes. 'I have seen everything during my lifetime ... there is a righteous man who perishes in his righteousness and there is a wicked man who prolongs his life in his wickedness.' I confess to you that I, in all my years, am not so certain in these matters as my young friend ... I hope you shall forgive him of his ... youth."

Gerta cast a longing look at her husband who reluctantly assented.

"You speak good words, priest. Now, how can I serve you?"

Pieter answered with neither hesitation nor constraint. "We are in desperate want of food, blankets, a hunting bow, some herbs, and a good night's rest under a roof such as this."

Dieder's demeanor changed slightly and he cast an awkward glance at his quiet wife. "You seem to be a kind and gracious old man, *Vater*," he said slowly. "But I tell you that children have been crossing these ways for nearly a moon. They've come in bunches and in scores. Many by Liestal have sent their own in this Holy Crusade ... we've sent our own stout-heart, Rudolf."

Gerta began to tear. "We have been told that many have died and many are sick and we are not sure if we'll ever see our Rudi again." Her voice trembled and Dieder held her close.

"We'll help you as we can for the cause of our boy." The farmer took his wife's hand. "But hear me, Father, some of these children have poached manorlands and some have brought fever. The miller and all his brood were stricken a fortnight past and some in the count's household are now near death."

Pieter nodded but remained silent.

Dieder picked some chaff from his long, brown beard. "You and your children shall not be welcomed by many. Those who have gone before have brought much misery. We have been spared the drought which we hear of in the north but it has not rained since the children began to come. There are some who believe these crusaders to bring such troubles with them."

The man patted his wife who was now sobbing in her apron. "How many are with you?"

Pieter answered, "Just a few more than a score."

"And how many sick?"

"None that I have seen, though some are very weak."

The farmer looked carefully at Gerta and then at his daughter, Beatrix. He thought for a moment, then said firmly, "You'll not bring any here, but I am happy to send you away with some food. You must be gone from my hectares by prime. And I ask this in return: Should God mercifully lead you to our Rudolf, tell him we love him, and his mother and I miss him very much."

Gerta choked and scurried out of the parlor, weeping all the more. Pieter stood with tears welling in his eyes and grasped Dieder's callused hands in his own. "*Gratias tibi*, my son. I'll not forget to pray for your Rudolf and for his safe return."

Quickly brushing a tear from his own eye, Dieder went to the kitchen where he reached into the barrels and baskets stacked neatly along the walls. His large hands then piled generous gifts onto Pieter's and Karl's opened blankets. He gave them cheeses and some fatty pork, a few leeks, several loaves of spelt bread, a wooden pail of millet and oats for gruel, and his own favorite flask of mead. Pieter smelled the fermented honey-water and winked. "You are too kind, my lord!"

After loading Pieter's blanket, Dieder turned to Karl. "Beware your expectations, boy. They'll surely confound you and burden others."

Karl nodded.

"Now, wife, hand me those woolens ... no, not those, the ones on the short peg."

Gerta scurried to the parlor wall and retrieved two blankets, each a bit worn, though a welcome sight nonetheless to the two crusaders. "These belonged to my sons," said Gerta softly. "You'll have need of them in the cold nights ahead." She stroked Karl's red curls and cradled his cheeks in her hands. "God protect you from the spirits of the forest."

Night was falling and the cool mountain air chilled Karl and Pieter as they bade a thank-filled farewell and struck a path toward camp. The sky had become dark and the stars sparkled like fine jewels on rich, black velvet by the time the pair spotted the familiar fire-glow in a wide clearing just ahead. They entered the campsite and the children cheered gleefully as the yeoman's gifts were spread before them. Pieter looked carefully at the circle of faces and measured the need as prudence would incline. He handed a blanket to Jost. "Share this with Albert," he ordered firmly, "and you shall thank God above for sending it to you."

He studied the yearning eyes of the others huddled close to a snapping fire. All were cold and others shivering; many had no blankets and those who did were doing their best to wrap two or three others with them. Pieter held the remaining woolen and looked closely at each longing face. At last he walked to Gertrude, Frieda's long-suffering sister, and draped it over her quivering shoulders. "Here, little one, share this with another."

☙

Morning brought its usual routine of grunting and burping, yawning and complaints. Frieda, Gertrude, Anna, and Maria were stirring a watery gruel of millet. "I never said so," snapped Anna. Her pale skin suddenly flushed a bright pink.

"Gertrude swore an oath you did," quipped Frieda.

"Well, 'tis not so, I have never thought so, and I do not say what I'm not wont to think."

"Nay. Methinks you to think it, else you'd not have so said."

"No! I do not think you to be fairer than Gertrude, so I would not have said such. There."

"Then why did Gertrude say it?"

"Gertrude, did you say I said so?"

Gertrude blushed. "Well, I remember little about it and ..."

"What? Liar. You said you were angry at Anna for hurting your feelings. You said she ought not be your friend anymore."

"What? Gertrude? You don't want to be m'friend? Just evening past you spoke of liking me better than Frieda!"

Jon II had covered his ears but now reached his end. "Girls, girls! Shut yer mouths. Every morning, 'tis more of the same. I hear, 'She said so and she said not'; 'I like Wil'; or 'Ain't Conrad a delight?'"

"Who said me that?"

The girls froze.

"Uh ... methinks ... oh, never y'mind. Wil's hollering for us to hurry."

And then, like so many mornings gone by, the crusaders lined up in their customary order, received Pieter's blessing, and dutifully tramped behind Wil toward the next mountain.

This morning's rising sun brought warmth and hope, and Karl and Georg chattered endlessly of Burgdorf and the Feast of the Assumption about one week hence. "'Tis surely to be better than any we've ever seen, Georg. The drought hasn't hurt these folk; their harvest is good and food shall be plenty and ..."

"Do you truly believe the food to be plenty?" interrupted Georg with a grin. "I should be most happy to see tables full of food again!"

Karl laughed and poked Georg in his belly. Before long, their enthusiasm spread and the whole company began jabbering about feast days and minstrels, jugglers and dancing. It was good medicine for their hearts, a better remedy than an apothecary's cupboard could ever offer.

Pieter had fallen behind a bit and he labored to catch up to Wil. After wheezing his way past the others, he found himself matching the boy step for step as they crested another ridge. "I am convinced," he panted, "that struggling through these hills is much like struggling through life."

Wil rolled his eyes.

"Would you agree, my boy?"

Wil bit his tongue, weary of Pieter's ceaseless commentary on the nature of life, of God, and the condition of the world.

Pieter nodded, agreeing with himself. "Yes, we think only of rushing out of the valley to find the glory of the next peak. Yet, when we think only of the summits we miss what can be learned in the valleys. The beauty of the valley, even its shadows, is lost to us. And this, too: On each peak we see only another, one higher and more beautiful. Nay, I prefer to think we are called to find our peace in the journey itself. Some of us shall find our end in shadows to be sure; others, perhaps near the heavens. But methinks it to matter not one whit. What matters is that we delight in whatever journey we are granted."

"By the Virgin! Save your sermons, old man," grumbled Wil. "I intend to be a mighty warrior in m'youth and a nobleman as an elder. I'll ne'er be left in a lowly place—not ever—I swear it. I am like neither you nor this company. I shall make this life what I will. You may find your end in some pitiful valley, but I shall stay to the summits; I'll spend m'life atop the hills, like the rich men of Basel!"

Wil's arrogance quieted Pieter. His heart sank. He had hoped to plant seeds of wisdom in soft soil but it was not to be.

The sun was settling toward the western sky as the quiet soldiers pressed faithfully southward. Wil kept a steady pace until finally offering a brief respite by a shimmering stream in the midst of a broad valley. Karl and Georg collapsed on the bank by Pieter and watched some distant sheep nibble the green grass on the breast of the next slope. Karl tapped the tired priest on the shoulder. "Pieter, if you were yet a boy and were free, what labor would you choose?"

Pieter pulled at his beard and quietly considered the question for some time. He ambled to the water's edge and cupped some cold water to his parched lips and returned. Still pondering, he scratched Solomon's ears. A ring of curious crusaders gathered around and waited impatiently for his counsel. "Aye," he finally answered. "'Tis a matter of some interest to me and its answer is not certain. Methinks perhaps a mason: to set strong fingers against the rough of a good rock; to take such simple splendor from the bosom of the earth and set it to the wall of a good man's home would be a good thing.

"But, so would be the joy of healing the sick or training the minds of youth. But, by truth, hmm … of all the labors under the sun … I should prefer to be a farmer."

The company stared open-mouthed and speechless. The disappointment of his selection removed all shyness from Jost. "What? My papa is a farmer and he hates each day!"

"Mine too!" cried Friederich. "The whole world is filled with such and I've ne'er thought a single one to like it."

"Well, yes," answered Pieter. "We make of life as we will, but consider this: The farmer wanders over a fallow field and says, 'I have hope.' When he plunges his plough into the earth he is saying, 'I believe.' He spreads his seed and says, 'I trust.' When the warm sun and the gentle rain nudge tender blades through the hard ground, he smiles and he says, 'I knew.' And when the harvest is yielded and his storehouse is full, he knows he's been blessed."

"Well, my father is a miller and says farmers to be dolts!" cried a voice.

Pieter closed his eyes.

"Eh? I'll pound yer face."

"My papa says millers to 'ave heavy thumbs!"

And, as the old man expected, soon Wil was pulling apart a tangle of wrestling boys and tossing them into the stream.

"Now, children," continued Pieter, "as I was about to say, farmers may be simple, but they are hardly dolts. Most simply lack enough words to think with." He paused. "You are aware, I do hope, that we've need of words to think."

The children looked confused.

"Ah, another matter. For now 'tis enough to know that farmers may not understand, but they are wise enough to rest in the mysteries of the Good Gardner above; something schoolmen are apt to forget."

The band thought for a moment. Some shook their heads in stubborn disagreement while Pieter smiled to himself. He thought it a rather fine presentation. But before the old man became too contented with himself, Karl blurted, "Ah, Pieter, you could ne'er have been a farmer!"

Pieter waited.

A smirk broadened Karl's face. "A farmer trusts without understanding!" The boy laughed.

Pieter had no answer. He nodded his white head and smiled faintly. He knew Karl had exposed that abiding haunt, the thorn in his soul that kept him from delighting in the simplicity of faith that he had just so eloquently honored. Oh, if only he could believe, simply accept the mysteries of God with the plain and untangled trust of the littlest of these children! How insistent was his need to comprehend the incomprehensible. Indeed, it was a relentless predator that stalked his mind and emotions, ever menacing what joy that set upon his troubled heart.

Book 2

Chapter 14
HEALING HANDS AND THE STORM

The company roused before dawn and by prime arrived at the small, timber-walled town of Olten. Pieter suggested they enter in search of provisions, but the crusaders protested. An angry Jon I barked, "Nay! We must needs press to Burgdorf. There'll be more food at the feast than ever here in this stinking town. I say we pass by."

The gathered band applauded and cheered until the priest quieted them. "All shall do better if stronger. See there, Maria is nearly spent; she collapses against me every night and shivers in the cold. And there, look to Albert, and over there, even Jon II and Frieda stand pale and tired. We've need of more food, Wil; more blankets. Please, let us spend a brief time here to test for charity … and then we'll all press on."

Wil stood stiffly and pondered his dilemma as the disquieted company waited for his orders. At last he set his fists on his hips and announced, "Heed my words. We'll hold here and get what we may but shall advance by terce. Now bite your tongues and follow me."

Wil led the grumbling children to the opened gates of Olten where the gatekeeper bade them a gruff welcome. But they had barely stepped through the gate when the town's magistrate suddenly charged toward them with a small troop of guards. "Begone, you fever-laden whelps," he commanded. "We've no need of you or the sickness you bring."

Pieter was too tired to be either angered or intimidated by the brash order and lumbered toward the man with Solomon close by his side. "None here is sick," he sighed. "And I do expect thee to offer Christian benevolence to each of these helpless lambs."

"Christian benevolence?" scoffed one of the guards. "You'll 'ave the points o'these lances if you fail to turn away … now!"

Ignoring the remark, Pieter looked beyond the blustering magistrate at the quiet town within. To his wise eye something seemed amiss, for it was far too still, certainly far too hushed for prime. Only a few folk were about and they seemed to move awkwardly as if laboring to avoid making the slightest sound. Pieter thought them to be like frightened mice tiptoeing by a sleeping cat. "Is there some trouble? Sickness perhaps?" asked Pieter.

"Nothing you need bother with," advised the magistrate. "Now begone." His tone was harsh, but restrained.

"I am skilled in medicine," persisted Pieter. "I have been trained at the university in Salerno and would be most pleased to exchange my services for some food and perhaps some cloaks for these poor children of mine."

The magistrate's temples tightened. "We've no need of yer services. Now for the last time, be off."

"Ah, my good friend," he began rather loudly, "I fear that you've missed my words. I say, again, that I am here as thy willing servant and seek only modest provision for these children." Pieter hoped his raised voice might reach a ready ear inside and indeed his hopes were satisfied. A young lady approached the magistrate and, with a slight brush of her milk-white hand, dismissed the officer and his men. By her dress and demeanor it was clear to Pieter that she was of some noble standing, and he thought her to be among the most beautiful ladies in all Christendom.

She stood quietly, studying Pieter and his flock with a wary, though kindly eye. She wore a long, blue, silk dress draped with a beautiful red cape tied securely to her neck. Her blonde hair hung in long braids at the sides of her creamy face and her head was adorned with a rose wreath.

"My name is Dorothea and I am the daughter of Bernard, the burgher of this town and lord of the manor lands at large."

Pieter bowed. "My lady, I am in thy service."

"My father lies inside these walls suffering from the agony of a fouled tooth that has defied all his physicians and his apothecary, and, ah, the witch as well. The slightest sound adds to his misery, and so he has ordered silence in the marketplace. I suggest you hush your tone or you shall surely bear his wrath.

"The hoofs of all beasts are ordered bound with heavy cloth and it seems that even the birds do sit quiet and fearful on our rooftops. Now I should think, *Pater,* if you could work some sorcery and end his agony, you would find him a most grateful and generous benefactor for your little band." She smiled.

Pieter's eyes twinkled and he bowed more deeply. "Indeed, I am so skilled, my fair lady."

Solomon knew his cue and promptly raised a friendly paw. Dorothea smiled briefly at the shaggy dog and beckoned Pieter to follow her. "We shall see. But I ought warn you, it might not go well with you should you fail."

Pieter smiled politely, then hastily ordered Wil to grab the satchel of remaining herbs and join him. "Aye," whispered the boy. "And y'others wait beyond the wall and keep your tongues tied."

The walls protecting Olten were constructed of a combination of tall, unstripped timbers, sawed planks, and sections of mortared stone. The streets were somewhat rutted and surprisingly soiled with unshoveled manure. Apparently none thought it wise to engage in labors other than those most necessary. Pieter and Wil quietly followed Dorothea past long rows of narrow, two-story homes with steep, thatched roofs where nervous residents watched the three from partly shuttered windows. Wil strode through the town boldly, his long, golden hair flowing proudly over his hood, but Pieter was stumbling along, desperately working to remember the treatment for toothache. His distraction cost him the pleasures of the beautiful flowers that adorned many of the street's windows and the bounty of the town garden surrounding the fishpond.

The trio turned a final corner and approached a shuttered, three-storied timber-and-mortar home. A tall linden amply shaded nearly all of one side and the other was bordered by a delightful garden of flowers and sundry vegetables. Several soldiers fidgeted at the front door. Suddenly the howls and the angry shouts of a man in pain pierced the silence. Dorothea proceeded, unflustered by the outburst, though her companions paused briefly at the doorway. Upon entering the parlor, Pieter and Wil dodged several attendants scurrying past them with trays laden with roots and herbs, steaming compresses, and a menacing assortment of dental instruments.

As the priest and his young friend entered Bernard's room, an exasperated physician and apothecary were arguing with the angry lord. "Sire," the physician pleaded, "this misery can be ended with a simple extraction." He clicked his crude pliers near the face of the raging Lord Bernard whose brown, baggy eyes widened in terror at the very thought of such a remedy. The lord snagged the physician's ear with one grasping hand and with his other clutched the poor man's throat.

"You shall relieve this pain and I'll surely keep my tooth!" he bellowed. "Or, by God, I'll have your brainless, Lombardian head in a basket." The physician jerked himself out of Bernard's grasp and fell away.

"There is nought else for cure, *mein Herr*. I fear you must needs heed my colleague," offered the apothecary timidly.

Bernard slammed a fist onto the table by his side and roared, "I'll not allow some Italian dimwit to grab about my mouth with that contraption."

"But sire, begging your leave, 'tis no con—"

Dorothea's gentle voice interrupted the physician. "*Vati*," she said, "I have found a more delicate healer who comes to us from the lands of the north and swears an oath to help you."

Bernard's physician and apothecary stood aghast, quite

offended at such a contemptible incursion as the likes of Pieter! "Nay," blurted the apothecary. "Na—"

"Silence, fool!" thundered Bernard. "I'd be the one to say 'nay' or 'aye.'" He studied the newcomers, curling his lips as if to bark again. A pain twisted his hardened face into a schoolboy's grimace. "By the saints," he moaned, "'tis a fine predicament I'd be in. I've a choice of being butchered by a lunatic from Lombardy or a Teuton with only one tooth of his own."

He turned to Pieter. "Your empty gums are a tribute to your skill."

Pieter grinned sheepishly.

"And you, whelp," Bernard blustered at Wil. "What brings you here?"

Wil was not the least bit ruffled by the raging nobleman and answered calmly, "I'd be here to help this good priest mend your foul mouth."

Bernard mumbled and held his jaw for a few moments. He stared at Pieter again. "Priest indeed. *Ach.* Well, by faith, I should rather put myself in the care of someone of your many years than these other idiots.... So, be about your trade. On with it."

Pieter turned to Dorothea. "Ah, my dear lady, I'll need a few things. I have need of vinegar, oil, and ... sulphur. I should also like a candle of mutton fat. And ..." He dug into his satchel, praying to recall what else his remedy required. "I have seed of sea holly, but I should like a tub of water." He suddenly brightened. "Oh, yes, I'll also need a mixing bowl and a piece of linen."

Bernard groaned loudly and begged Pieter to hurry. Pieter had him lie on the bed and peered into the man's opened mouth. "Ah, good fellow. You needs say when I've found the culprit." Pieter winked at Wil before bouncing his wooden poker atop a red-gummed molar.

"Aaah!" roared Bernard as he leapt to his feet. "Y'dung-brained dolts! I'll flog the skin off both yer cursed backs, I'll p—"

"Ah, 'tis good, m'lord, aye, we've the proper tooth. You would've been displeased had I served the wrong one, eh?"

"What? Aye, you've the proper tooth, 'tis sure, y'son-of-satan. Now you had better heal it, or I swear on m'dear Margot's grave y'shall hang from a rope by next prime."

Pieter folded his arms. "You'll not be threatening me or the lad, and I've no intention of helping until we've settled our terms. After all, I'm a steward of a company of young crusaders and must needs provide their care."

Bernard clutched his jaw. "And what terms, y'sly fox?"

"Your lovely daughter, Dorothea, entreated our services with an assurance of a fine price."

"You dare bargain with me when I suffer so?" growled Bernard.

Pieter restrained a smile. "Truth be told, I am confounded to know a better time."

Bernard leaned forward and pressed his nose against Pieter's. "You are a shrewd one," he grimaced. "I hope you are as good in medicine as you are in commerce. Name your price."

"As a man of the cloth," Pieter said slowly, "I have no desire to take profit from thy most unfortunate circumstance, so my humble request shall be modest." He motioned to Bernard's secretary who had been huddled at his corner desk, far from harm's way. "Good sir, please note my simple needs on thy parchment."

The secretary pulled his hood tightly over his narrow head, nervously dipped his feather into the ink, and waited.

Pieter raised a brow at Wil and continued. "I should like five pecks of oats, five pecks of millet, ten of rye, fifteen pounds of salted pork, fifteen pounds of salted fish, twenty pounds of sausage—properly spiced. I should like five baskets of fresh apples, several hands of cherries, a half of salted or smoked venison, some tripe, several heads of cabbage, a basket of leeks, one of turnips, and some sweet honey in wax. I should also like ..." Pieter put his bony finger on his bearded chin and thought for a moment.

Wil took the pause to glance at the eye-popping lord whose face was contorting in a most unbecoming manner. Pieter cleared his throat. "I should also like twenty-three woolen capes for the children; twenty-three heavy, woolen blankets; and three good long bows with hunting arrows—or a French crossbow with straight bolts."

The perspiring secretary gawked at the bold priest and cast a tense peek at his dumbfounded master.

"But, while you consider the matter," added Pieter, "allow me to examine this vexing tooth—oh, I do wish Dorothea would hurry so that we can relieve this awful pain." Pieter pried his spindly fingers into the befuddled lord's mouth and pressed onto the molar.

Bernard reared his head back, howling. "You devil of the north! You black-hooded, dung-breathed ... you ... you one-toothed son of a demon! Keep your thieving fingers out of m'mouth. What kind of cursed priest would pilfer a man in pain! Impostor! I'll never grant your terms! I'd rather have that mad Italian shove his iron claw down my throat than be plundered so."

"Ah, yes, well, my son," answered Pieter calmly, "the ransom of a man's life is his riches, but the poor hears no rebuke."

"Eh? You give me riddles when I need help?"

Pieter smiled at the frustrated patient. "A faithful envoy brings healing."

"Begone!" boomed Bernard, clutching his jaw. "*Mein Gott* ... the pain!"

"Very well, then. We'll be on our way. I do so respect a man who is able to make a difficult decision quickly. But I must confess, I oft wonder which to be the more difficult for prosperous men of commerce such as thyself: taking advantage of others or holding fast from being taken advantage of? It seems to a poor pilgrim as myself that the guarding of such plenty is, indeed, a wretched burden. Ah, but what little I must know—blessing to all."

Pieter turned toward the door and whispered to Wil, "To the pure show yourself pure, but to the crooked show yourself shrewd."

The secretary winced as Bernard pounded his fist on a table. "Come hither, y'miserable, doltish thief. Come fix my tooth, y'heartless madman!"

Dorothea now entered the room with the supplies that had been requested and set them on the table by Bernard's couch. "Is all well, Father?"

Bernard fell back and groaned. "Nay, 'tis not all well. This … this … Teuton you've brought me has a cold heart and—"

"Ah, Papa, his old head is white with wisdom and his fingers nimble with the arts of healing. You must rest easy and on the morrow you shall be happy for his coming."

Bernard grunted, too exhausted to argue and always quick to yield to his daughter's gentle lead. "*Ach!*" he groused. "Give me the order to sign."

Pieter checked his herbs carefully while the secretary handed Bernard a parchment with a sly wink. Bernard nodded approvingly and turned it over to Pieter. The world-wise priest was not unaccustomed to the games of commerce and he read the document carefully by the window's better light. He set the parchment down and smiled. "I thank you, my generous and good lord. May God prosper and bless you and thy issue for generation upon generation. But I do see something. I see …"

"Enough. Enough! I know what you are about to say. I cannot spare all that you asked, but I grant you exactly one-half of what you've asked!" Bernard cried. "Now fix m'cursed tooth!"

By now the nobleman was near tears and Dorothea cast a scolding look at Pieter. The old man hesitated for a moment and stroked his beard. "One-half does not take proper care of my children. But I am neither heartless nor unreasonable, so I shall do this for you, my lord: I'll take away half thy pain for what you've offered."

Bernard's twisted face flushed red with rage and he glared at the priest incredulously. "You ask too much. Where is your charity?"

"Ah, that," answered Pieter. "Mine is well placed in favor of my lambs … and might I inquire where I might find yours? I vow to you that your pain shall leave this room afore I do; of that you can be certain. And I pledge your tooth to stay in its place. You shall enjoy relief and shall retain your tooth but, as added blessing, you perchance eternal gain. For there is no doubt in my mind that our Holy Mother sees His lambs huddled in the cold and is moved to reward those who offer them care."

Pieter paused and watched Bernard tap the table with nervous fingers. "Now, here I stand, offering you both earthly relief and eternal wealth, and all the while am slandered as a common thief and demon." He raised his long, bony nose high in the air as if he were the inculpable victim of incredible slander. "I must confess to you, my lord, I find this most difficult to grasp and I do suddenly fear more for your soul than your tooth."

The outmaneuvered Bernard squirmed on his couch and looked for help from his stunned daughter, who fought hard to not smile at the irony of the moment: Her cunning and shrewd father, burgher of the town, a man feared by nobleman and peasant alike for his ruthless wit and savvy, lay cornered and cowered by a beggar priest.

A sudden bolt of pain racked the lord and he clutched his jaw. "Old man," he whined, "listen to me. By all appearance it would seem that we do revel in bounty, but we've had a lesser harvest than in times past. Your terms are much for a single tooth. I ... I will meet your demands by half, plus half again. I beg this to be enough."

Pieter knew he had found the limit. Even Wil's eyes implored him to have mercy. "Blessings on you, sire. I am humbled by your faithfulness to our Lord." The contest won, the priest now silently implored his Maker for help. *Lord, m'memory of these things does fail me. Forgive my insolence and guide my mind and my hands. Restore my thoughts by Your grace, and may Wil and this wretched servant of Yours leave this place alive!*

Pieter smiled cautiously and dabbed the perspiration now beaded on his forehead before reaching tentatively for his herbs. He withdrew root of peony and mixed it slowly with oil of roses and soaked the linen in the mixture. He placed it gently on the submissive man's forehead. "Uh ... this shall help relieve the pain. You must be certain to sleep this afternoon with this linen on your head. Daughter, you must keep the linen soaked with this solution."

Dorothea nodded.

Pieter hesitated for a moment but suddenly began to work with growing confidence. He smiled a little as he watched his hands move deftly, as if directed by another Mind. He quickly took vinegar, oil, and sulphur; mixed it into a thin paste; and promptly placed it atop the sore tooth. He then gently rubbed the paste into the gum for several minutes hoping something would happen, and, to Pieter's delight, Bernard mumbled that his pain was easing. Pieter set the mixture aside and instructed Dorothea further. "You needs place this substance on his gums every two hours through this day and night, on the morrow and the morrow next."

Bernard was now lying comfortably with the wet linen on his brow and the concoction kneaded well into his gums. Having eased the pain, Pieter turned his arts to the cause of the trouble. He paused for a moment, then smiled as his memory came alive with the exact remedy. The old priest took a candle of mutton fat and rubbed seed of sea holly at the base of the wick. He lit the candle and sat behind Bernard with a half-filled bowl of water readied on the table. Pieter carefully positioned Bernard's head on his lap and held the candle above the nobleman's jaw. He gently pulled Bernard's lip away from the inflamed molar and skillfully lowered the candle close to the tooth so that the hot wax and melted herb could drip onto the rim of the gum. This was intended to kill the worms that were known to sometimes bore the roots of teeth.

Bernard was then instructed to rinse his mouth with warm water and spit into the clay bowl that Wil was holding. The boy wrinkled his nose as Pieter poked about the murky spittle for evidence of the elusive worms.

Pieter repeated the procedure several times over the next hour and at last pronounced the tooth restored. "*Ja, ja.* 'Tis a proper remedy, I am certain of it. Rest well, sire, your complaint has been resolved."

Bernard sighed and smiled weakly, grateful beyond measure for the relief. He ordered his secretary to direct his overseer to honor the terms of the agreement. "Well done, *Vater*, well done. I feel like a new man." He leaned close to Pieter's ear and whispered, "I do admire your skills ... both of dentistry and of commerce." Bernard winked. "Ah, but now give me leave for I must sleep. May God's mercy follow you."

Pieter bowed respectfully, nudging Wil to do likewise, and the pair followed Dorothea quietly out of the house and to the main gate. The waiting band of dirty-faced children raced toward them and waited expectantly for a full report. Pieter, his own relief equaled only by that of Bernard's, grinned a happy, mischievous grin and picked his favored Maria off her feet. "God has been good to us this day, children," he proclaimed. "We have been blessed by this fair lady's master with provisions enough!"

The children restrained a hearty cheer and circled the smiling Dorothea. Frieda and Gertrude took the graceful woman by the hand and touched her fine garments. "M'dear lady," offered Gertrude, "such a beautiful gown and cape. I've ne'er seen better."

Dorothea stroked the girl's tangled brown hair and thanked her gently. "And you, my little one, have such beautiful eyes."

Gertrude's round face flushed and she turned away. No one had ever told her she was beautiful before, and the thought of it warmed her in a pleasing, though unfamiliar way.

By nones, two soldiers appeared from around a corner escorting a bent old man and his heavy-laden oxcart toward the hopeful children. "*Ja, ja* ... good day to all. I bring the master's order to you." The man stopped and coughed violently. "There is fever about the villages ... be warned." He pointed to the cart and motioned for the children to unload it. "Aye, 'tis yours, children, come."

"All lend a hand ... pack every blanket and satchel ... and be quick to it," ordered Wil.

As the others raced to unburden the cart, Maria approached the perspiring man and offered him a tiny flower. He wiped his face and gave the girl a hug as he wheezed a tender *Danke*.

It took but a little time for the happy crusaders to properly pack their new provisions, kneel with Pieter in a heartfelt prayer, and bid Dorothea farewell. Then, with the wooden walls of Olten behind them, the faithful children set their course toward the wide valley leading to Burgdorf and the Feast of the Assumption.

๛

Jon I and his brother Jon II, Lukas, Otto, Maria, Frieda, Gertrude, Anna, Georg, Karl, Conrad, Manfred, Jost and Albert, little Friederich, Pieter and Solomon, Wil and all his other soldiers had once again been joined by their wandering, but oft returning companion—Hope. The terrors of Basel were fading quickly, as were the images of the battlefield and the heavy sadness of friends lost. It was as if the band was starting its journey afresh, far from fear and free from the sufferings it had so recently endured. It seemed to most that God was with them after all, and they pressed into the late day hours renewed and encouraged.

The crusaders followed the Aare River south from Olten, intending to march along its comfortable banks until a sharp westward bend that Pieter knew. They soon found a small road to follow in the center of a wide plain leading to Burgdorf. The group was merry and glad-hearted, many singing or laughing along a river somewhat swollen with the heavy rains that Lord Bernard said often plagued the region this time of year.

The day was rapidly shortening, especially with the darkness cast by a bank of heavy clouds sagging toward the company from the south. Pieter cast an eye upward, then scanned the flat landscape. "Bernard's secretary cautioned me of harsh storms on this side of the mountains."

About three furlongs upstream, a new mill was standing near the river's edge. It had been built at an inside bend in the river where the bank had been dug away to form a deep pond, dammed on one end to feed the mill's wheel. It was a clever way to control the force of the water. Beneath the wheel the water was immediately returned to the river via a narrow, deep ditch. Wil spotted the mill. "There, Pieter. We can weather the storm there."

The sky suddenly turned angry and the children raced for the cover of the mill, only to find its door locked and its windows shuttered fast. A few heavy drops of cold rain began to drop as Wil and Pieter groused about the secured mill. "There, on the bank." Wil pointed to a sheep shed set at the base of the dam about a stone's throw from the turning wheel. "Would be cover enough. Out of the wind and a good roof."

Pieter nodded and the wind began to howl. "Hurry, then."

The company scampered along the low riverbank and rushed beneath the short roof of the three-sided shed, grateful, to be sure. The shed had a good thatched roof, recently repaired by the look of it, and its planked walls guarded them from the wind suddenly blasting sheets of rain. Karl retrieved a fresh flint granted by Bernard, and pulled some dry thatch from the underside of the shed. Others darted to the river's edge and dashed back with float-wood and sticks. Soon a small campfire was snapping and all were happy again.

Night fell upon them like the dropping of a black curtain and a dreadful stillness abruptly blanketed the plain. For a few precious moments only the nervous whines of Solomon and the lapping of the nearby river could be heard. The group stared into the darkness hoping the storm had only been a passing squall.

Then suddenly, as if the night had simply paused to catch its breath, the wind shifted to the east and a stinging rain began to pour and pound atop the river valley in violent torrents. The air turned icy-cold and the frightened children balled together as thunder cracked and lightning blazed across the sky. In the next moment, a horrible gust roared around the shelter's edge and smothered the pilgrims' fire like a scoffing giant snuffing a choking wick. The band now sat in utter darkness.

Pieter offered what comfort he could, though few could hear his soothing voice above the howling tempest. Maria quickly squeezed herself tightly between Karl and Wil, pulling her feet away from the rivulets of mud beginning to find their way inside. Each flash of lightning drew a whimper from the girl and Karl took her by the hand. "All shall be well ... you've no cause to fear...." At the crack of each peal of thunder, Karl desperately wished to believe his own words.

The storm continued for about an hour before the thunder began to fade into distant rolls. Lightning could be seen spidering the sky like fiery veins over the western valleys, but the rain continued to pour as if by buckets and barrels until nearly midnight. Finally, the wind began to ease and the rain changed to an even patter on the soaked thatch above the travelers' heads and its gentler fall steadied them. Relieved and sleepy, the young soldiers soon fell fast asleep, cold, but feeling quite secure.

Solomon, however, blessed by his Maker with senses not common to his fellows, stirred restlessly. He whined and pawed at his irritated master until ordered sternly to silence. But such cautions ought not have been so rudely dismissed, for the dog's instinct was reliable and peril was indeed imminent. The faithful beast laid his head obediently, though reluctantly, upon Pieter's legs but his ears stayed cocked and pointed, his bright eyes wide.

The heavens opened again and once more heavy rain pounded the plain for the next hours. Solomon shifted uncomfortably, wary and anxious as the roar seemed ever to increase. Suddenly he jerked his nose high in the air and tilted his head to one side. He strained to listen with his jaw locked tightly and his keen eyes sharpened. Then, as if jolted by a hot bolt of lightning he sprang to his feet, barking wildly and pawing furiously at the slumbering Pieter. The old man rolled to his side and stretched a calming hand toward his frantic dog. The yelping awakened Karl.

"Why is he barking?" the boy cried over the crashing rain.

"I don't know!" Pieter answered loudly.

But before another word could be uttered, a sound like none had ever heard before enveloped them all. It was like thunder, though deeper and crueler, and the ground itself shook and trembled as if cowered by the might of a terrible thing. Then, before a single waking crusader could do more than cry out, a river of mud, tumbling rocks, and surging water crashed over and around the edges of the quaking shed, filling the refuge with the floodwaters of a broken dam!

The sturdy little shelter had no chance at all against the deluge. It collapsed into a tumbling heap of splinters and was swept into the raging current with the hapless pilgrims. Away washed the children, the old man, and their poor dog. Churning midst rocking logs and swirling brush they disappeared into the night. Mouths gaping, limbs flailing, the wretches were lost on the back of an angry serpent.

Wil toppled head-for-heels beneath the water. Desperately trying to break the surface with his mouth, he clawed and rolled and vainly lurched where nature bid he try. At last, his head bobbed upward and he gasped and gasped again. He pedaled his feet rapidly along the vanishing riverbed and struggled to keep his head above the water when he caught his ankle in the cleft of a rock. The force of the flood immediately pressed him under again.

The lad frantically clutched at the branches he felt dragging against him and could hear nothing but the muffled sounds of his own panic. He writhed and labored to lift his face for a breath and finally broke himself free to ride the currents toward the bank. There he lunged toward the trunk of a well-rooted tree and wrapped his arms around it tightly.

Relieved, Wil sucked air into his lungs and nearly cried for joy. His relief was short-lived, however, for a heavy limb careened close and snagged one leg. The startled lad held tightly but his burning arms soon gave way to his grasping hands, which, in turn, gave way to clinging fingers. Then, though his fingertips dug desperately into the stubborn tree's rough bark, they soon failed him as well and Wil was gone.

≈

As swiftly as the unexpected had arrived, it passed. No sounds were heard other than the wash of calmer waves streaming timidly around displaced trees and rocks. The rain had slowed to a gentle drip and an eerie hush now ruled the night. A passing breeze stirred a rustle among the willows but no sound of the crusaders could be heard.

In the ghoulish calm the storm clouds soon abandoned the night sky, granting consent for the moon and stars to shadow the river that was now shrouded by a heavy mist. And so the silver-eyed keepers of the night held fast until finally chased away by the merciful sun that arrived like the shining armor of a valiant knight riding hard from the east.

As beams of yellow light pierced the fog, magpies began to play and flutter about, indifferent to the carnage all around them. Thrush began to sing and woodchucks poked their whiskered faces from the valley's edges. Here and there, chamois teetered atop the displaced rocks and snow mice scrambled gingerly from log to log. A soaring eagle rode the cool air on his morning's flight, giving nothing more than passing notice to the rutted valley below. As it were, the only few who seemed mindful of the night's tragedy were the groups of vultures now floating in circles with eyes fixed expectantly on the destruction below.

Suddenly, a snow mouse froze. He pointed his little ears toward some strange new sounds. First here, then there, he jerked his tiny head from side to side. Here he heard a cry, there a sob, a whimper, or a cough—finally a feeble call for help, then another and another. The thrush stopped singing and the magpies stood still.

Wil opened his mud-caked eyes and squinted as a ray of sunshine blinded him for a moment. He was confused but regaining his senses. He slowly lifted his head and found himself tangled among broken branches and bound in thick mud. He wiggled and squirmed and toiled to free himself from the rubble to finally crawl atop the soggy bank, grateful for his life. His tunic and leggings were torn; his hands and feet were bruised and cut; dried blood covered one side of his face. He felt no broken bones and found no deep wounds. Satisfied with his own condition, he promptly began the search for his companions.

Wil needed to look no farther than a few paces upstream where he spotted the mud-caked head of his sister. She had been mercifully carried atop the buoyant timber of a broken river willow and, though frightened and nearly buried alive in bramble and mud, she was spared far worse. Wil charged toward her and threw off the debris that weighed on her. He dug frantically with his bare hands through the mud and, before long, he pulled a most thankful Maria to her feet. The two embraced.

Wil surveyed both sides of the river and saw Karl staggering along the bank about a bowshot downstream. "Karl!" he cried. "Karl!"

The redhead waved weakly and climbed carefully over a pile of logs. Near him was Georg, waist deep in a sucking mud-pit and straining to free himself. Suddenly Friederich appeared beside the two of them, rubbing his bruised legs. And, before long, another stood, and then another, each bleeding, coughing, or crying. It looked to Wil like a tedious, sluggish resurrection of sorts as one crusader after another slowly emerged from the ground shrouded in brown.

Pieter was pinned against the bank by a large, broken tree trunk and was holding his bloody nose with a free hand. His lips were split and bleeding badly. Georg stumbled to his side and cried to the others, "Come here, come here! Help me! I've found Pieter!"

At the sound of the old man's name, the company forgot their own troubles and clambered over all obstacles to his rescue. Many hands dragged Pieter from the quagmire and Maria gently wiped the mud and gravel from his squinting eyes. The priest lay shivering in the cold morning air but raised his hand limply and offered a faint smile. He strained to speak but could only whisper. "The others, the others ..." Pieter laid his quivering head down and closed his eyes.

Maria and Frieda placed some leafy willow wands over Pieter to help warm him as Wil ordered the others to continue the search for more survivors. The children dutifully spread across the terrain and hunted in earnest for any hint of a comrade. Karl forded the lowering river and his eye caught the bottom of a foot protruding from a huge heap of debris. "Here! Come ... A foot, I've found a foot!" The boy yanked and tugged at the stubborn tangle as his fast as his hands could move. In a few moments Wil and Georg joined him and with a grunt and a heave, the unnamed fellow was tumbled out of his muddy prison. Georg hastily wiped the mud off the boy's face.

"'Tis Albert," wheezed Georg.

Wil and Karl stood stone-faced and silent as they stared at the mangled corpse beneath them. Wil lifted Albert and held him compassionately in his arms, but he had only taken a few carefully placed steps when he nearly tread on an arm sticking from the ground. "There. Karl ... dig there," he hoarsed.

Karl and Georg were joined by Jon I and burrowed furiously into the river muck around the limp arm. Wil laid Albert gently aside and joined the others until the lifeless body of poor Jost stared vacantly at them from opened hazel eyes. Were that not horror enough, yet another body lay another few feet downstream.

The three were carried to a large, flat boulder near Pieter and set in a solemn row as others in the company continued their search. A voice was suddenly heard drifting from the valley below and Wil raced upstream to find Frieda struggling out of another clump of broken branches and rubble.

"Wil," she sobbed. Tears ran down her bruised face as she embraced her friend. Trembling, Frieda's brown eyes suddenly widened in fear and she began to scream for her brother and sister. Tearing herself away from Wil, she tripped across the rutted bank sobbing and crying desperately. Wil joined her search and the two clambered along the bank in hopes of finding either.

Slowly, more and more stragglers appeared, crawling up

both banks from either direction. They joined their tearful comrades gathering around Pieter. "Could someone help me to m'feet?" whispered the old man.

Georg steadied the priest as he rose. Pieter surveyed the landscape until his eyes locked onto the casualties lying on the rock. "Have you taken a count yet?" he groaned.

"No," answered Karl. "But we're missing many. I've not seen Manfred, Gertrude, Lukas, Otto, and Jon II."

"Conrad and Jon I are searching over there," pointed Maria. "But ... but where'd be Solomon?"

Pieter collapsed on a rock and began to weep. "Chil ... dren. Chil ... dren," he wailed. "Sol ... o ... monnnn."

Karl ordered all to scour the valley one more time. "Go, go quickly and look carefully. Go farther downstream, and find what you can."

Upstream from Pieter an exhausted Wil sat atop a broken hornbeam. Beside him poor Frieda was wailing hysterically and pulling futilely on the limp arm of her brother, Manfred, buried in the rocks at her feet. "Frieda ... he is gone," Wil spoke gently. But his words fell on mute ears until others came to help Wil dig Manfred's body from the mire. Frieda collapsed on the ground.

In the meantime, Karl and Conrad found Gertrude wedged in the base of an uprooted willow, unconscious but breathing, and they quickly carried her to safety. Otto, however, plodded stiffly across the hillside bearing the broken body of his good friend and fellow traveler, Lukas. He tearfully laid little Lukas alongside Manfred, and Wil sadly recounted his company.

"All are reckoned." The boy fought the swelling in his throat. The faces of the dead had not become so habitual, or so very familiar, that the sight of them open-eyed and white-faced did yet pierce his heart.

"All, save Solomon," blurted Maria.

"Aye, sister, all save poor Solomon." Wil paused and cast a sympathetic eye toward Pieter and continued. "We must bury our friends here, by this rock, which shall mark them. We all know what to do."

The bodies were washed respectfully with the brown

water that had drowned them and were placed in shallow graves scraped into the muddy valley floor. The mounds were set neatly in a row and Pieter offered his prayer slowly. His bones ached and his heart was broken. The children stood respectfully, listening halfheartedly to the words. But even he felt that his prayers were empty, impotent, and pathetically inadequate for the grievous occasion. The ritual was like a dream to him, a blurred, confusing interlude that was over as quickly as it had begun. And, when he said his final "Amen," the children simply wandered away to stumble about in search of lost provisions.

After an hour of meager success, Wil led his wet, shivering crusaders upstream, past the broken dam and to the mill that had remained unscathed. With a loud curse he kicked the door open, snapping its locks, and ordered all inside.

Karl and Georg made a small fire within and the group huddled close by. Maria climbed onto Pieter's lap and nestled into his breast. "All shall be well, Papa Pieter. You shall see ... and we'll find Solomon."

Pieter's beard was matted with dried blood, and mud flattened his fine, white hair against his bony skull. He could say nothing, but tears ran freely down his face and he hugged his little lamb.

By midday, Wil assembled his crusaders and inspected what provisions were reclaimed. Content to have recovered a small supply of blankets, satchels, and sundry foodstuffs, he prepared his soldiers to march on. "Listen well. We'll press our calling." Turning a sad eye on Frieda, he said, "Please have your tears, Frieda, but we needs go on. Friederich, your wrist is broken and Jon II ... you've a broken leg. You needs both return to Olten."

"Nay, Wil!" protested Friederich. "I've come this far and I shan't go back—and what might happen to us in Olten?"

Wil hesitated for a moment as he considered what risk Pieter's dubious dentistry might have created, but he masked his fears and answered sternly, "Dorothea shall see to it you've a good home."

"But ..."

"Enough. I order it."

The eight-year-old stared helplessly at his comrades, his eyes begging for a reprieve.

"Friederich," said Georg kindly, "Wil is right. You must go back. Jon II needs a good fellow to help him, and a broken wrist won't do in the mountains ahead. Methinks 'tis God's will."

Friederich nodded reluctantly and bawled a tearful farewell to his friends. He feared he would never see them again.

Chapter 15
NO GREATER LOVE

By nightfall the band had marched southwest into the wide valley separating them from the awaiting Alps. Wil ordered his faithful to make camp in the cold, open air, and soon all were huddled close to a small, snapping fire. Thoughts of friends so recently lost bred a deep melancholy, leaving many a cheek tear-wet and tight. Pieter reached into his robe and, to his relief, found that his wallet was still there. He opened it and and began to unfold the three pieces of parchment. He set his page of Aristotle carefully on his lap and held the Scriptures in his trembling hands. In the firelight he began to read quietly to himself but as he lost himself in the words his voice grew louder. "These all look to you to give them their food at the proper time. When you give it to them they gather it up; when you open your hand...."'

A sudden blast of wind rushed through the campsite, bending the campfire and whisking Pieter's cherished Aristotle off his lap and into the air like a dry leaf in autumn. It flew high above the startled man and began to flutter downward when another wind carried it a bit further. Pieter frantically sprang to his feet. "Boys, boys, help me!" he cried. The old man leapt in the air to snag the fluttering parchment but the wind twisted and turned it farther and farther away. The priest stumbled and lurched through the darkness. At last he stopped and stood pitiful in the moonlight, stunned and silent.

"Pieter," offered Karl as he came to his side, "'tis but a parchment, only—"

"Silence, boy, you've no thought to your tongue! That was one of the dearest things I had ... that parchment and ... poor Solomon."

Karl looked sadly at the frail man now shivering under the moon and left him to bear his disappointment alone.

In the first light of the new day Georg rose before his exhausted comrades to search for Pieter's lost parchment. His pursuit was in vain, but the goodhearted lad was not inclined to return without some comfort for his friend. He entered the waking campsite with a happy smile, a new staff for Pieter, and new crosses for many of the pilgrims.

"Ah, thanks to you, Georg," praised Karl.

"Aye, aye," muttered Pieter.

"And I've a cross for you as well, Wil."

Wil was in no mood for such a gift. "A cross? A cross? I carry no cross! You'd be as mad as Karl. We've just laid five more under mounds of rocks and we've lost nearly all the stuffs we had."

Georg had no heart for combat and had only wished to offer a simple kindness. He smiled timidly and walked away with Karl close behind. But Wil pursued them. "What? You've no answer? Aye. You've nought to say of this good God. And you, brother, look to your sister. I've given some thought to the sort of God that would attach a withered arm to such a fair *Mädel*. Have y'uncovered the sin that earned such a penalty?"

Karl fumbled and fidgeted, wishing to fill his mouth with the morning's gruel instead of answers to such things. But Wil was angry and he seized his brother hard by the tunic. "Tell me, Karl ... I've need to learn more of a God who allows such things!"

The strain of the day past had worn on Karl and his brother's wrath drove him to tears. "I know not!" he cried as he pushed Wil away. "I've no answer, but ... but methinks if we do the good things, He'll love us—as did Mother. We ... we must be in error, we must—"

"Fool. Dolt. 'Tis no error in our ways!" Wil grabbed Karl

by the throat. "You are blind to the world and y've a fool's sense to put the blame to us. The world about you is an evil place, not made easy by good deeds."

Karl gasped for air and pulled hard away from his brother's grip. "Nay, the world is not evil; it is filled with God's bounty for good people."

"Aye? I've seen nought but a wicked world, double-minded people, and a treacherous God."

Karl was confused and his secret doubts grew loud in his own head. He pushed Wil away. "*I* am good, Wil!" he shouted. "Can y'not see? I've a mind fixed on charity. I cared for Mother when you fought with her. I did all that she ordered. I do what is right and good, and God shall give me proper care. He must! I ... I deserve His love; I have earned it. Perhaps 'tis your black heart that brings us trouble!"

Wil said nothing but smirked, choosing to let the boy slander and slay himself with his own tongue.

"You, Wil, you are proud. You are filled with boast. Y'think to be all-wise but you've an empty head. You never loved Mother and she ne'er loved you. But I served her well and she did love me. 'Tis little wonder you see evil all about, for you are evil, brother; your proud heart is black!"

Wil's silence had proven a worthy tactic and the smile crossing his face evidenced the pleasure won in such utter victory. Karl had been unmasked and stood naked and exposed.

Georg stepped between the two brothers. "Please, we've trouble enough. There is no cause to quarrel." He turned to Karl. "You ought not accuse your brother so."

Karl stiffened.

Georg's face flushed with fear, but a boldness born out of genuine affection loosed his tongue. "Your boast, Karl, is every bit as big as your brother's, only yours is different. You ... hide your pride in things with the look of goodness. You are agreeable and virtuous to be sure. You seek the good in all and for all. You act faithful and pious, but ... but ... I fear you to do so to feel all the better of yourself—and to win the affections of others. I do wonder if these be the marks of a true, good heart."

Karl, indeed, had paid little heed to the beams in his own eyes, and such penetrating observations by his friend both flustered and angered him. His blood rose like fire in his ruddy cheeks and he retorted with fury. "By God, fat boy! You dare call *me* prideful? Trickster. Betrayer. I am the one who's protected you from the others. It'd be me who's watched over you like a good friend ought. I ... I ... found you clothing, I shorn that swollen head of yours ... and you turn against me with such words? I've no need for such a friend. Keep away!"

Such rancor was infectious and the long day that followed was quarrelsome and broody. The wide plain was easy marching but the weight of heavy hearts made it more a struggle than the mountains left behind. There was no more talk of feast, no more riddles, no laughter or singing; only the steady step of tired feet on rain-soaked earth. Karl held fast to the rear of the column, dark-eyed and moody, refusing the slightest of gestures from Pieter and resenting every command of Wil. His sister, sensing his hurt, walked quietly at his side.

Another day wore on as the crusaders marched toward the rising mountains in the south, oblivious to the beautiful landscape changing before them. Then, as if their weary spirits hadn't burdened them enough, a heavy sky brought more rain to soak them and cold winds to chill them. Their pace slowed but they finally arrived at the walled city of Burgdorf, wet, tired, and days early for the feast.

They entered the city gate in hopes of gathering a few scraps from the bounty within, but were summarily escorted out by a troop of surly men-at-arms. The crusaders soon stared at one another outside the gate, blank-faced and defeated, far too weary to plead their case. They acquiesced without a murmur and yielded all resolve to wrangle access to the storehouse of plenty that lay but a few paces behind the looming walls.

Provisions nearly gone, clothing tattered and ragged, and with few blankets to share, the company marched another day until they at last entered the pleasing valley of the Emmental. Here their weary eyes warmed to the sun-dappled yellow-green of sheep-dotted mountainsides and the lush of mixed-leaf forests that funneled toward the valley floor. They stopped to absorb such evidence of the Creator's ultimate benevolence and the sight both comforted them and urged them forward toward their trail's narrowing valley and the craggy peaks rimming the distant horizon.

Relying on the good hearts of a few villagers and shepherds along the way, they found food enough to finally climb above the trees and through a rugged, Alpine pass. Their progress had slowed terribly, some days traveling a mere league, others less, some more. But they soon descended to the blue-green waters of a glorious mountain lake and its splendid, shimmering beauty gave all pause to hope.

After a good day's rest by the clear mountain lake they climbed deep into the spruce-timbered forests of the higher mountains, traveling due south toward the rock-faced peaks rising ahead. Pieter had been silent for days. The ascending trails were exhausting and he plodded up them with a gloomy spirit. He had stopped praying at night and ignored his morning lauds. Some claimed to hear him whisper the names of Lukas or Albert or Solomon in his sleep. He did not engage the children in his usual banter, nor did he bore them with his rambling pontifications. Unsettled by his melancholy, his flock now dearly wished for both.

One morning, near terce, the crusaders descended a steep slope and came upon a small village assembled neatly in a spacious clearing. It was a typical *rundling*—a cluster of timbered hovels circling a common center in which there were gardens of sweet flowers, herbs, and vegetables as well as buzzing apiaries. The weary children stumbled into the village with little heart and few words, and approached a housewife busy churning milk. Before Wil could speak, the woman stopped her piston and smiled. The cheerful reception confused the crusaders.

"Ho, ho there, children, welcome. My name is Frau

Muller and you are all welcome." She blew a wisp of graying hair away from her twinkling black eyes, wiped her
callused hands on her homespun apron, and placed them
securely on her broad hips. "Our children have gone
before you on this brave Crusade, but you'd be the first
we've seen."

Wil eyed the woman carefully. "Aye, and greetings to
you. Have you any food to spare, good woman? Or any
blankets or cloaks?"

Frau Muller threw back her head and laughed. "For you
and yours, good lad, we've plenty enough!"

By now a curious circle of village women had abandoned
their dough-boards and baskets and ringed the crusaders.
With grins stretching their round faces the gracious
women led the dirty column to the center of the common
and were soon fussing over them like mother cats with a
fresh litter. They brushed the girls' hair and washed their
faces. The boys, too, had a good scrubbing. Their filthy
clothes were scoured in barrels of heated water and
mended with good stitching.

The children were wrapped in woolen blankets and
promptly set before a long table cluttered with stewed
apples and honey and breads and cheese. The delighted
crusaders smiled again and before long there was laughter
and singing and light hearts all about the smoky mountain
hamlet. When all had eaten, sheep's milk was brought for
the children and a pitcher of mead for Pieter.

The old man studied each face of his beloved flock, especially happy to see the little ones resting so peacefully on
the soft laps of the nurturing women. *Ah, and dear Maria
… so like a tender bloom*, he thought. *And so oft weak and
feverish.*

Wil interrupted Pieter's thoughts and pointed to the
contented children. "Would seem that a mother on earth
has more value than some mother in heaven."

Pieter shrugged. He hadn't missed the boy's sarcasm.
"Aye, lad. There'd be some truth in what you say. These little ones do need a mother who can touch them—indeed,
we all need more than a touch from the clouds."

A few burly woodsmen suddenly burst out of the forest bearing huge broadaxes on their wide shoulders. They stared warily at the strange children but quickly yielded to the stern commands of their wives. "Mind, Hans, these be welcome and you've no cause to frighten them." Behind them two huntsmen returned with their allotted quarry and, with a few quick strokes of their sharp knives, five rabbits and two wild boar were gutted and stripped.

Evening settled over the mountain and the smells of bubbling stew and roasted pork now wafted through the merry village. A crackling campfire and full bellies warmed the grateful children as the cold night air began to fall. Soon they were presented their clean, dry, and mended clothing and were escorted to the humble hovels of the happy peasants. Each was given a straw bed and comforted with a heavy wool quilt and a kindly kiss. Sleep came easily and dreams were good.

The next morning the rested crusaders gathered on the common by the large garden and offered their heartfelt thanks to their hosts for such unusual hospitality. "God's riches on you all," sighed Pieter peacefully. Tasting of kindness had quenched a parching thirst and the relief of it so relaxed the priest that he yearned to simply lie in the grass and sleep.

"And to you, Godspeed," answered the village reeve. "But here, afore your leave you needs receive our gifts."

Giggling women scurried about the wide-eyed travelers and loaded their arms with new blankets bound full of pork strips and apples, venison, cabbage, and the like. "'Tis though we'd be helping our own little ones," smiled one *hausfrau*. "God and His blessed angels be with you."

After a flurry of hugs and farewells, Wil set the column and with little delay they were off, stubbornly continuing their pilgrimage toward the higher mountains. A few of the brave soldiers cast a longing glance toward the waving villagers, but before long the *rundling* was out of sight and the children were crusaders once again.

&

The trail Wil followed took his company southward

through ever-narrowing valleys. The sun felt pleasant in the cooler air of the high valleys and the fragrance of the towering spruce was refreshing. "It shan't be but a few days, children," announced Pieter, "and we'll be climbing through more passes, the Brunigpass being very difficult but the snow-heavy Grimselpass yet worse. And after that we'll be in highlands for some time." Pieter looked at Wil. "And you, sir, shall need to slow the pace yet further."

"Humph. We've lost much time and I reckon us to be on a different route than any of the others."

"So be it; Jerusalem shall yet be standing where it is."

The band pressed on and wound its way along a valley floor until the trail began a steep ascent and Wil reluctantly agreed to stop for a much-needed midday meal. As all went about their various duties, Pieter took Georg aside. "Dear boy, I beg your forgiveness. I only now realized that I never thanked you properly for this fine, stout staff." He held out his new companion and admired it. Georg smiled. Such affirmation was better than a good suck of honeycomb.

"You are most welcome, Father Pieter."

"This shall serve me well for many years, and it shall be as if you are walking by m'side."

"Together we shall set it on the streets of the Holy City!"

Pieter thought for a moment and answered slowly. "Ah, my son, we've needs to consider that matter. I think my journey to end at the water—like Moses at the Jordan. Methinks it fitting for you younger soldiers to secure the Promised Land as your own."

"We'll see about that indeed," exclaimed Georg. "There ne'er was more fit a man to boldly march through the gates of Jerusalem than you! Ha! It shall be a great day when I stand in Palestine with m'three best friends: you, Wil, and Karl. And I ... I ..." Georg suddenly faltered. "Pieter, I must confess to you something. I believe I hurt Karl with m'words. Perhaps I was hasty...."

Pieter studied the boy and pulled on his beard before answering. "Fair Georg, I surely had an ear for the exchange ... was not likely to avoid it. Aye, your words stung Karl, but they were neither made in haste nor off the mark. Indeed, there is a season to prick a friend and only wisdom can determine the proper time and dose. But I offer this comfort: I do truly believe Karl shall, in due time, be grateful for such a rebuke. Your hard words were a treasure yet to be enjoyed." Pieter rubbed his hand atop the boy's broad head and smiled. "Think of it as casting gems upon a frozen pond."

Georg could not resist the old man's infectious grin and began to giggle at Pieter's lonesome, yellow tooth. "I do beg your pardon, Father, but sometimes you just make me laugh."

Karl approached the two.

"And, my dear Karl," said Pieter, "I trust you have healed from your hurts."

Karl shrugged but flashed a hint of resentment in his answer. "Yes, I suppose, Pieter … most of them."

"Well, 'tis good. And I suppose you are thinking clearly and in the ready for the riddle?"

Karl's mood was not nearly as healed as Pieter had guessed. "M'head's always clear and since you've a mind to talk with me, you needs hear m'thoughts of the flood. I have given that matter some time and am now certain of God's purpose in it. Methinks you to be well served to hear my 'prick.'"

Pieter raised his brows. "Ah, well, then by all means … do so."

Frieda and several others had been listening to the exchange and they drew near.

"Pieter," began Karl. "I heard from Wil of your rather *bold* negotiations with the lord of Olten."

"*Ja*," answered Pieter slowly. "I believed that our situation required some measure of firmness. Go on."

Karl's voice rose. "'Tis plain, Pieter, you cheated this man and God punished all of us for it. And I, for one, am tired of you angering God and putting us all in peril. You and all your questions and your strange ways. You burn Dunkeldorf, then pray with the Holy Scriptures so piously. The word 'hypocrite' comes to m'mind. It wonders me that you've not brought death to all of us by now! Methinks sometimes you ought be cast off like Jonah."

Pieter was stunned. He could not answer for a moment; words would not come to his trembling lips. *Is it so?* he wondered. *My hypocrisy does seem oft boundless ... but does such error bring judgment to these? ... Or could the lad be striking out to guard his own path? After all, if the lad loses his way, he shall indeed lose his way.*

At last he looked at Karl with clear and gentle eyes. "My son," he answered gently, "it may be that I am a Jonah, for I am indeed self-willed and oft disobedient. It does take hard lessons for me to learn, for I am stiff-necked and surely I am a hypocrite. I do thank you, my young friend, for having the courage to remind me of these things.

"As far as the other business goes, it may be that I bargained for too high a payment and perhaps God punished us for my greed. Or it may be that I asked too little and He punished us for that. Or it may be that I asked for a just amount and it simply rained a lot that dreadful night. Perhaps God ought be praised for His mercy on those He spared."

Karl pressed insistently. "When we do good, we get good, Pieter, and when we do evil, we get evil! On this journey we have gotten good and we have gotten evil and we have done good and we have done evil and that, my good sir, is what I see."

By now Wil had moved closer. "It would seem m'brother's got a good hold of God's ways. Well done, Karl, methinks such a task a hard one." He laughed. "You do good, you get good. You do bad, you get bad. Simple, eh?"

"Aye," snapped Karl. " 'Tis how I see it."

"And since you've mostly gotten good, you think yourself to be mostly good?"

Karl hesitated but answered with a defiant, "Aye."

"And what evil has ever befallen you, my very good brother, Karl?"

"So my point. I've not suffered evil. I am strong, I am healthy, I've a good mind and a kind heart. All would so say me to be gentle to others, obedient ..."

Wil sneered, "And humble as well."

A number of the children laughed and Karl's face reddened. Before he could speak Pieter added, "Lad, have you not seen evil happen to good men and good things happen to evil men? And have you so soon forgotten the words of the yeoman?"

Karl licked his dried lips. Jon taunted with an angry tone in his voice. "Eh, Karl? We'd be waiting. I should like you to tell me of m'brother's evil for his broken leg."

"*Ja*, Karl," quipped Frieda. "Can y'tell me m'brother Manfred was evil 'cause he wasn't spared, as you?"

"And what about that swine, Father Pious?" barked Wil. "He's a nice house and a fair portion of shillings, I'd wager. Do you think he to be a good man?"

"He is a man of the Lord," muttered Karl.

"A man of the Lord, you say? Is that what y—"

Pieter interrupted. "Now lads and ladies, I think we all have a fair question here, but no need to be bitter. Perhaps we should think of this as a mighty riddle: Why do good things happen to evil men and evil things to good ones? I am certain it is a riddle, one for which I have no answer— at least not yet. But dear Karl, what I say 'tis true nonetheless; good does not always follow good; nor evil, evil. Or better yet: Who is truly good anyway?"

"Enough of this!" shouted Wil. "I am sickened by your silly ideas, Karl. 'Tis fool's talk and not more. And Pieter, I'm weary of working at sorting through all of life with you. I am content to know that I need none other than m'self and I leave the rest be. I've this fair token of my might," he boasted as he plucked his dagger from his belt. "And I've my mind and two strong arms and that's all I need for this world to be mine. Go, Karl, waste your life at earning favors, and you, Pieter, go live and die with your empty quest. But I'll cross these mountains and plant my feet in Palestine whether good or not. And as for you, Georg, heed this: You'll not see *me* slandering those I call 'friend.' Now, on we march."

Georg slowly gathered his blanket. He was cut deeply by Wil's remark and he walked quietly toward the gathering column. He looked cautiously at Karl. "I ... I meant no harm. I only spoke what I did for hopes of your seeing yourself some better. My father says change begins in the looking glass ..."

"I've not the privilege of a glass and I've no need of change," growled Karl.

Pieter sighed as if all the world were now sitting on his own feeble shoulders. He stepped between the boys and leaned hard on his staff. "Good lads, enough. I think it time to walk and let silence be a healing balm."

࿊

The sun had peaked and began to move toward the horizon. Wil was impatient with his company's slow progress and demanded his fellows shorten the route by venturing off the path. "There," he barked, "we needs climb straight up yon sheep trail. That shall gain us back the time we wasted winding this valley path."

Pieter protested gently. "Good Master," he offered, a hint of sarcasm in his voice, "methinks it a harsh course and one of some peril."

"Nay, old man. You've always the right to take your leave, but *we* climb."

With little more than a few grumbles, the faithful obediently followed their leader up the stony path, clutching and grasping at rocks and roots, pulling themselves higher and higher until they emerged from the pines. Having reached the sparse rock-face of the high ridge, they paused for rest before pressing to the summit. Finally, by mid-evening, they gathered around a modest fire and fell to sleep in the cold mountain air.

The next morning the weary company woke to strong gusts and a hard-driving rain. Wil stared carefully at a treacherous sheep trail descending from the camp and the thin mist snaking through the tight valley waiting below. "Pieter," he shouted over the wind, "methinks it best we follow that valley toward the south and ... there ... to the base of that shrouded peak."

Pieter looked nervously at the rain-soaked, perilous trail dropping dangerously toward the deep valley. He said nothing but raised his eyes to the heavy sky and begged the angels to bear them gently down.

The rain fell in stinging sheets and the howling wind blasted over the razor-edged ridge as the column began their descent toward the valley floor. Each little foot was placed warily on the unforgiving mountain's breast, for every step bore the risk of a punishing slide against sharp stones and jagged rocks. The crusaders picked their way slowly down to the dubious cover of scrubby pines until they finally gathered beneath a dripping, low-hung canopy for a brief first-meal of dried apples and crusts.

It was a hurried respite and the shivering crusaders continued their descent, pitching and lurching from tree to tree, until they emerged onto a rocky cleft where they paused to survey the view. Far below was the cramped valley, green and lush and dotted with heavy-timbered huts clustered in tiny hamlets. In the distance stood a brown, stone castle perched precipitously along the rim of an opposing mountain. Despite its rugged edges, the children thought the valley inviting and strangely comforting; perhaps it was the softness of the mists swirled gently on the treetops or the strength of the angular, gray-white rock-face guarding all sides. For whatever reason, it seemed a fiefdom worthy of a life's stay.

Wil wiped wet hair away from his eyes and stared at the sky. The rain had eased to a soft shower, but the clouds were heavy and sagging as if straining to contain the reservoir of water within. And no sooner had the children stepped back to their trail than the clouds lost their strength and released a deluge atop the mountain. The children bowed and bent under the sheer force of the torrent but dutifully followed Wil, sliding from tree to tree, grasping at bark and branches, roots or rocks, or any other handle the slippery mountainside might offer. At last, Wil ordered his troop to the shelter of a grouping of large boulders and the wet soldiers settled into the rocky enclave.

Karl, however, withdrew from his fellows to the wide

trunk of an ancient spruce. He drew his hood over his dripping, red hair and squatted in the mud. He pulled his treasured necklace from under his tunic and followed its steel links with callused fingertips. His mind drifted to memories of his mother—her warm suppers by the hearth fire and the sounds of her rush-broom sweeping stones and sticks from the doorsill and yard path. He closed his eyes and suddenly saw her lying on her bed ghost-white with blood oozing between her lips. Her gaping eyes stared at him vacantly. He covered his eyes with his fists. "Leave me, visions!"

But such images rarely honor such demands and poor Karl's mind flew him to a scene of his mother's shrouded body being carried stiffly toward a simple earthen grave. He could see the miller and the weaver, the dyer and his wretched Uncle Arnold tilting her corpse awkwardly toward its dark and rooty hole. He shook his head and pressed the tears from his eyes.

The boy thrashed about the wet forest, whimpering and rasping across the pitch, warring valiantly against what sanity demanded. Finally he fell across a log and yielded with a loud cry. "There is no miracle; Mother is dead."

Wil's commanding voice was hard to hear above the din of the rain and wind but he reassembled the crusaders and ordered them forward. Karl stumbled halfheartedly to the rear of the reluctant column and followed his fellows down the mountainside. The pilgrims eventually reached the valley floor and their hearts lifted as they followed their trail over easier terrain.

Feeling safe under the thoughtful faces of the peaks rising sharply on all sides, the pilgrims relaxed into a contented, though spirited gait. But before long their quickened pace brought them to the base of their next ascent and all faces fell as they prepared to climb among the cliffs and clefts of the difficult Brunigpass.

Wil wisely ordered camp to be made and the relieved crusaders scurried to their duties. The children found dry kindling by stripping bark off fallen trees and soon a smoky but adequate fire was burning. Were it not for their inordinate fatigue the soaked travelers would have found it difficult to sleep in the cold rain, but eyes were heavy and quick to close.

For most it seemed that they had barely set their heads to pine-bough pillows when they were awakened to a drizzled dawn. First-meal was a cold, rainwater gruel, but the crusaders ate it without complaint. They then gathered in their customary column and waited for Wil's command. The drizzle gave way to another heavy rain as the boy led his company toward their difficult ascent and a troubled Pieter took Wil by the shoulder. "Take good care, lad, m'spirit chills with a dread. Give thought to each step for the sky has not been kind to our way."

The crusaders struggled upward through the rain toward the high pass for most of the morning. The air was damp and pungent with spruce and pine; the pathway rutted and wet. Just before ordering a midday rest, Wil suddenly slipped on a loose rock. He landed hard on his stomach and began to slide helplessly past his surprised comrades, hurtling toward the edge of an unseen cliff not far below. The boy grasped wildly at the rocks and underbrush passing him by, but the mountain simply yielded him hands full of mud and torn roots. Then, as if the angels heard the cries of poor Pieter, Wil's foot abruptly wedged against the trunk of a stout bush and his fingers grappled through its strong branches. To the relief of his comrades above, Wil held fast and, after composing himself, he struggled to his feet. He looked over the edge of a cliff not more than a few paces beyond him and closed his eyes.

The boy clawed his way back to his cheering friends and collapsed. "Aye," he panted. "'Tis good to be alive." After a brief rest he ordered all forward. "Climb with care," he chuckled. "This mountain has a face I liken to my Uncle Sigmund ... holes, scars, humps, and bulges—a terrible thing to meet!"

The tiring crusaders trudged upward until topping the mountain by late day. And, after a brief rest, they immediately began a hard-pressed descent in the hopes of reaching a reasonable shelter for their night's camp. The grade was steep and the trail dropped fearfully between precipitous cliffs. Such danger kept the children's senses piqued but their weary legs had been pressed beyond all reasonable limits.

Suddenly, Karl lost his footing and tumbled headlong off the narrow trail, screaming down the mountain in a wash of tumbling gravel and stone. His shocked companions stood helpless as the boy cascaded toward the edge of a cliff. He desperately plunged his fingers into the rubble rushing all around him and pressed his thin-soled shoes hard against the mountain's breast—but he found no hold. Then, with a loud shriek, he was gone!

Karl's companions stood paralyzed in disbelief. Unable to move, unable to speak, they simply stared at the silent edge of the precipice. All, that is, save Wil who dashed, wide-eyed and panicked down the mountain, crashing from tree to tree, slipping and reeling, frantically sliding down the mud-washed slope to the rim of the cliff. He grabbed hold of a stout branch and inched his eyes over the edge to gape fearfully into the abyss below.

Above, the crusaders shouted, "Karl! K ... a ... r ... l!" To a soul, each faithful comrade stumbled and lurched their way down toward the cliff-top. Wil suddenly pointed and shouted, "There! There! He's there—in a tree!"

Some three or four man-lengths below, growing from the side of the cliff, a gnarly tree extended over a flat ledge some three lengths further beneath. Karl was miraculously cradled in a cracking tangle of its old limbs and wet leaves, too terrified to make a sound.

No sooner had he been spotted, however, when a few dead boughs gave way with a loud snap and Karl dropped through the branches. As he crashed through the limbs his necklace snagged a stout branch and he was suddenly hanging by his neck, choking and gasping for air. The steel links cut deep into the boy's throat pinching any passage to his lungs. He desperately grabbed at the leafy gallows that suspended him! He kicked and flailed his legs wildly and lurched toward the branch, but the twisting necklace soon squeezed all breath from the boy.

The hysterical crusaders lying prostrate on the cliff's edge above screamed in a frightful chorus. Wil stared helplessly at Pieter in hopes of plucking a quick plan from the man's nimble mind, but the poor priest was stalled and blank-faced. Instinct, however, seized the lad and he bolted to the far edge of the cliff and slipped his way down the bordering slope toward a point in line with the ledge below Karl's legs.

Karl's arms now hung limply at his side and his face was beginning to bloat and grow purple. He twitched and jerked slightly, then hung motionless, swaying a little in the wind.

As the rest of the children howled and groaned to the angels for help, Maria clutched Pieter's robes, begging and pleading for the old man to save her brother. None knew what to do.

Then Georg stood abruptly to his feet and set his toes at the very brink of the cliff. He closed his eyes and muttered a few words, then looked briefly at Pieter who gaped at him speechlessly. The boy smiled a quivering smile, kissed his wooden cross, and leapt off the edge.

His startled fellows gasped as Georg plummeted through the air, tucked tightly in a ball of pink flesh and brown wool as he hurtled toward Karl's tree below. "Nay! Georg, na—!" But it only took a moment—a frightening, horrifying, virtuous instant—for Georg's falling body to crash upon Karl's leafy gallows. The tree dared not resist such valor and yielded with a loud crack, dumping the two lads into a tangle of arms, legs, and broken branches on the unforgiving rock shelf below.

Above, the company stared breathlessly, watching for some movement, some sign of life from either boy. At last Frieda cried out and scrambled down Wil's path. "Hurry Wil! Hurry!"

Indeed, Wil had almost reached the ledge and on his heels were Otto and Conrad. Pieter squinted anxiously at the scene below and whispered a prayer. He held Maria by the hand as they waited for word.

It seemed a lifetime before Wil finally reached the boys and he furiously tore away at the clutter of branches covering them. "Karl! ... Karl!" he cried through tear-blurred eyes. "Georg! ... Karl! ...'tis Wil ... I'm here!"

Wil reached Karl first and lifted him out of the debris. He quickly laid him on his back and yanked at the clasp of the necklace until it finally yielded. He pulled the steel off his brother's bloodied throat and stared helplessly at his placid face. Wil groaned and embraced the boy as Frieda collapsed at his side.

Suddenly Karl began to stir. He gagged and coughed weakly, then wrenched himself from his brother's hold and rolled on his belly, gasping for air and crying. Wil wiped his eyes and laughed for joy.

In the meantime, Conrad and Otto had scrambled past to free Georg whose motionless body was facedown, bent awkwardly under a large limb. The two furiously tugged and jerked the branch away and then nudged Georg gently. He did not move and they prodded him a little harder. "Georg ... Georg ... can y'hear us?"

Otto looked nervously at Conrad. "What ought we do?" he asked.

"P-perhaps we needs roll him over?"

The two grunted and groaned and carefully turned Georg on his back. The boy rolled and as he did, the two cried out. "Oh God! Oh God, no!"

"Wil, come quick!" screamed Otto.

Wil sprang to poor Georg's side and held the boy's wobbly head on his lap. He chilled at the lad's opened eyes for a moment, too shocked to move until, at last, he buried his tears in his comrade's chest. "Georg. Georg. Oh, Georg," he moaned. "I'll ne'er forget."

Georg's neck had been broken in the fall, snapping like the bough of the tree that had yielded to his weight. The young lord lay still and lifeless on the lonely mountainside, soiled with mud and wet leaves. But who would doubt that his spirit now soared, bathed and blessed by the tears of angels sent to so honor him?

A trembling Karl crawled to Georg's side and held him

tightly. "My good friend," the boy sobbed. "Oh ... Georg ... I am so very, very sorry." He closed his eyes and wept.

Wil called to the others above. "Georg ... is gone ... we'll meet you ... there ... on yon clearing some below."

Unable to answer, the company simply nodded obediently and gathered in a solemn column behind Pieter to move silently toward their assigned destination.

Wil, Otto, and Conrad strained as they lifted Georg's body from the ledge. Stumbling and slipping, panting and heaving, they struggled to bear Georg toward the valley floor in a manner worthy of his sacrifice.

Frieda attended Karl, who suffered woefully in both body and spirit. "You needs slow yer pace, Karl. And ... wipe yer eyes so y'can see to step," she said tenderly.

"Poor Georg. I ... I ..."

The girl laid a hand on the boy's heaving shoulders. She was all things feminine: strong, nurturing, wise, and gracious. "Take heart, Karl, your friend loved you and he knew you loved him as well. Here, take his cross."

Karl received Georg's wooden cross with his bleeding hands and kissed it. Then, with no more words he leaned into Frieda's sure arm and followed the others.

For all, the descent to the clearing was but a blur; like a dream at daybreak. But as they fell into the embrace of their weeping fellows they knew it was no dream at all, but rather a moment their memories would grieve for all time. Wil and Otto laid Georg's body in the clearing, and the crusaders circled 'round with hands clasped together. After a brief pause Wil solemnly ordered a grave be dug beneath the wide and welcoming branches of an ancient oak tree just beyond them. "Aye, there ... 'tis a worthy marker." Indeed it was, for this old oak stood a remarkable watch over the valley below. It was deep-rooted and strong, well-shaped and stout-hearted, proudly fixed in the bosom of a splendid land, true to the character of such as Georg.

Pieter, Frieda, Maria, and Gertrude bathed the lad's whitening body with puddle water while others plunged their bare hands into the muddy earth and slowly scooped out a shallow grave. Pieter closed the boy's eyes and folded his arms over his heart. The girls placed his hair neatly across his forehead and shrouded him in his torn tunic and leggings.

When all was ready, Wil, Jon, and Otto carried Georg to his tomb and laid him gently down as if to sleep, his feet toward the east and the Resurrection to come. "Aye, and so, too, his cheeks can feel the rising sun," sobbed Maria.

The children each took a turn setting rocks on the grave until it was nicely mounded. Karl set his own crusader's cross securely above the boy's head and Maria placed a bunch of wildflowers neatly over his heart. Pieter choked and wept his way through an agonizing prayer. His tongue felt thick as he struggled to finish his task. At last, however, with barely enough spirit to coax him to the end, he finished with the familiar words, "*In nomine Patris et Filii et Spiritus Sancti…*"

The priest stopped and lifted his hands to the heavens once more. "God in heaven, surely we do not know Your ways; You are a mystery to us. Receive this good servant of Yours, this fine young lord, into Your embrace. May Your loving angels carry him to Your table where he may feast in the presence of our Savior. May he be draped with the finest of Your robes; may the saints that have gone before honor him as is surely due. May he laugh in the sunshine of Your light, delight in the gardens of glory, and rest forevermore. Amen."

Tears poured down the old man's face as he reached into his robe and carefully opened his wallet. He retrieved one of his beloved parchments and unfolded it slowly. "My children, my children, my precious lambs. We have seen such hardship on this journey as defies m'mind. I've not the grasp to explain one whit of it.

"But methinks Georg's death offers us a look at something far greater than the pain it brings our hearts. The lad offers us in his death what he offered in his life—a treasure—a gift from God Himself; a thing called Love.

"And, in this, we do have hope again; hope that love shall indeed triumph over hardship. Aye, I trust that the memory of our own dear Georg shall remind us always that where love is, hope is, and together they rule the darkest hour.

"I have read this to some of you before and I'll read it again because there is nought else better to be uttered at such a time as this. I trust y'shall see good Georg's heart in these precious words."

Pieter wiped his eyes slowly across his rough sleeve and paused to watch Maria as her dainty fingers dropped wildflowers lightly atop the grave. Then, as if heaven itself prepared to affirm his words, long beams of golden sunlight burst through fleeting clouds and shined brilliantly upon the tattered company bowed below.

Pieter held his parchment with shaking hands, but his voice bore not the slightest hint of reserve or waver of doubt. Instead, he spoke with such conviction that it seemed to all gathered that the valley spread beneath them had suddenly hushed in an act of homage due none other than its Sovereign. "'Love is patient, love is kind. It does not envy, it does not boast, it is not proud. It is not rude, it is not self-seeking, it is not easily angered. It keeps not a record of wrongs. Love does not delight in evil but rejoices with the truth. It always protects, always trusts, always hopes, always perseveres. Love never fails.'" Poor Pieter's voice now failed him and he collapsed to the ground and wept.

The crusaders circled the flowered grave and held hands to sing their song, though few could finish.

"Oh," sobbed Karl. "I ... I am so very sorry. I am worthy of shame." Others nodded, uncomfortably aware of their secret contempt for Georg's gentle heart and their hidden hatred of his higher birth. At long last, the crescent moon arched high overhead as the broken band built a small fire to sleep by Georg for one final night.

Chapter 16
THE LIBERATION OF PIETER

awn was calm and a clear sky coaxed the sleepy pilgrims to a gentle awakening. Karl gingerly touched the cuts on his neck and the bruises on his arms and legs. He sat up, only to face Georg's grave and he groaned. He then reached for his necklace and leapt to his feet frantically. "Wil, Wil, where is my necklace? I must find m'necklace."

Wil plucked it from his belt and held it with a clenched fist. "Here is the hellish thing. I should have heaved it off the mountain yesterday!" Wil spun on his heels and threw the chain over a nearby ledge and watched it disappear in the treetops below.

"What 'ave y'done? That was Mother's gift to me. You've been jealous always!"

"That? That was nothing," answered Wil with a snarl. "That was no gift, y'fool, and it was no love. That was but a wage for services."

Karl stared at him blankly.

"You've been a dimwit always. 'Twas no love in that cursed necklace. It was a trinket you earned with your pitiful scurryin' here and about and your ready smile and quick 'aye' and do." Wil pointed a sharp finger at Georg's grave. "If it's love you seek … you'd find it there. Georg loved you, y'blind dolt, and not because he owed you."

Karl's chin quivered. "I am *not* good … and … I am not worthy of goodness."

჻

After a slow dawn's first-meal Wil finally ordered the column to assemble under Georg's oak, and by late prime he was leading them toward the narrow floor of the Aare valley and the village of Meiringen. Having found no good fortune in these manor lands, he veered from the roadway toward some distant smoke in hopes of finding a friendly village that might spare some food.

Unsuccessful, the tired children made camp and finished the last of their rations, chewing ravenously on pork strips and stale crusts. Once finished they sat close to their fire, and its warmth drew happy thoughts of Georg to their lips. Frieda smiled as she braided her golden hair. "Can y'not see him running from the highwaymen with that blanket barely reaching 'round his bottom!"

"*Ja*," giggled Otto. "And what of the tunic Karl got him by Basel?"

"I was sure it would burst," laughed Conrad.

Karl smiled as his mind's eye carried him to the picture of Georg squeezed in such a silly outfit. "I truly thought it a proper fit. It seemed it might keep *two* peasant boys covered ... but it could barely hold one rich one!"

"And what of that shearing, Karl?" chortled Jon.

Gertrude squealed, "*Ja*! His poor head looked like a gourd with a bit o'winter mold atop."

Pieter laughed with the others until a gentle sadness lulled them each to a restful quiet and soon the crusaders were fast asleep.

The troop returned to their roadway and followed the shimmering Aare for two more days before setting an evening's camp by a deep pool to watch Pieter spear a fish with a wooden spike he had fashioned from a pine. Wil was delighted to imagine fish roasting over the night's fire and soon such wishes were realized as the old man tossed his wiggly prey toward the eager hands of his fellows. "Fishing, my young friends, can be used to catch more than a full belly. Ah, yes ... I am certain of it. It is, by truth, a plain reminder that perseverance and long-suffering most surely lead to success."

Wil rolled his eyes and walked away. "I beg y'leave,

Pieter, but I've little heart for philosophy. Can y'not settle for just the fish?"

Undaunted, Pieter pressed on. "Each time we thrust our spear or cast our net or toss our hook, we are saying that we believe that something good *could* happen. And though we may walk away emptyhanded, we always come back to the water's edge believing *this* to be the day we catch a fish." Pieter laughed and jerked his catch from the clear water. "By truth, though, our hope is another's lost!"

That night the sky looked like a rich, black broadcloth sewn heavy with glittering jewels. The children stared from their beds in awe of the sight. "I'll tell you all someday of the message in the stars," said Pieter. "But this evening I fear m'self too sleepy."

"Good!" came a squeaky voice from the shadows.

"Amen," said another.

"Ah, I see." Pieter smiled and settled for a good night's sleep.

Morning came and the children passed through the village of Handegg in the fiefdom of mad Lord Arnold of Grindelwald. Soon they were straining upward along the steep path into higher mountains. "Children," panted Pieter as he struggled, "'Tis ever more perilous and snow waits above the tree line. Take good care. Wil, might we rest now?" He paused to catch his breath in the thinning air.

"It's too early; we stop when I so say!" snapped Wil. "And I say not."

So the crusaders trudged obediently up the long ascent toward the Grimsel Pass with no sound other than their own heavy breath and the occasional clatter of rocks grinding beneath their thin-soled shoes. By late that afternoon they broke out of the timberline and pushed toward the gray-white rock of the snowy pass ahead.

By evening Wil ordered his company to make camp on a massive, flat boulder at the north side of the narrow pass, and the shivering children scampered in all directions to find bits of kindling from bushes clumped in the crevices of the cliffs. The company had barely set camp when a voice suddenly boomed across the rocks. *"Bonjour."*

Wil spun around and faced two strangers emerging around a boulder just behind him. Wil stared at the man now waving cheerfully at him and leading a weary donkey burdened with stuffed baskets and a large, freshly killed deer. Wil nodded warily.

The man seemed safe enough. He appeared to be friendly and well groomed. Wil thought him to be young, not yet twenty-five, with close-cropped hair and a neatly trimmed black beard. He seemed of modest means, though not without. His colorful cloak of tightly woven wool was well stitched and it covered adequate leather leggings. But Wil's curious eyes dropped quickly to the man's feet which were protected by well-worn, wooden shoes. The boy stepped toward the two. "Aye, and what be y'about?"

"So? A Teuton? From parts north, I'd venture?"

Wil nodded.

"Forgive my poor German tongue but please allow my introduction." By now the other crusaders were cautiously approaching and Pieter was close behind. The man continued with a bright, winsome smile. "I am Philip of Cloyes and am here by leave of my abbot."

His friend roared. "By leave of yer abbot indeed!"

The companion was at least a decade older than Philip, a bit broader and rather unkempt. His thick, wavy hair flipped from under the sides of his brown, leather skullcap and his fuzzy, graying beard danced wildly in the mountain winds. The man was still laughing but paused to introduce himself. "Aye, and I'd be Jean of Rideaux—and, *mon Dieux,* we be no friends of any abbot or shaveling in all Christendom."

"Good sirs, *bienvenues,*" offered Pieter. "I am Pieter and these are my fellow … soldiers."

"Greetings, all. Might you dine with us?" invited Philip.

Before the speechless children could answer, the smiling travelers untied a large chamois and dropped it at their feet. "What's this? Frenchmen poaching game from the emperor?" protested Pieter sternly.

The strangers glanced at each other awkwardly. "Uh ... we've, uh ..."

The priest's eyes twinkled and his face warmed with a full grin. "Fear not, good fellows, and welcome. I've yet to give more than a passing thought to young Friederich II, and it'd be a rare day, indeed, that I pass by such a feast for the likes of this!" He extended his hands and took each stranger by the shoulder. "God's blessings to y'both ... but we've naught to share."

Jean hugged Pieter. "*Bon. Bon.* This night the pleasure to serve is for us and us alone. And we serve with gladness."

So, midst cheerful conversation and well within the comfort of a hot, crackling fire, the pair skinned their gutted quarry and heaved large quarters onto long spits. And, before long, succulent venison was roasting just above the tips of the leaping flames.

The water-mouthed children waited impatiently for their fare to finish cooking, and they sat poised and fixed with their fingers fidgeting to tear away at the sizzling meat hanging just beyond their reach. At last Jean jerked a hot strip off a well-seared rump and chewed it slowly. His eyes rolled in delight and a smile crossed his face. He swallowed, then licked his lips and his fingers. "Ah ... 'tis nearly done ... perhaps just a bit more fire ..." He paused and winked at Philip. The waiting children stirred.

"Methinks it to look just good as it 'tis," squeaked Gertrude politely.

"*Oui?* Do you think so?" asked Jean.

"Uh ... yes, good sir. I do."

"Then so it is!" laughed Jean. "*Oui, oui.* My new young friends, enjoy!"

The two Frenchmen hastily lifted the spit off its supports and set the steaming venison atop the flat rock by the fire. The cheering children lunged toward the helpless carcass, tearing into the tasty meat. And, before a single word of thanks could be uttered, the night's meal was promptly transformed into a pile of gnawed bones and gristle. Having stuffed themselves, the crusaders soon collapsed around the campfire to laugh and sing and wish all troubles away beneath a splendid night's sky.

Thrilled to find himself in the company of educated and well-traveled adults, Pieter seized the occasion to engross his guests in discussions of philosophy, astronomy, modern warfare, and the state of the Holy Church. His children sat respectfully and listened quietly until the warm fire drew all but Karl and Wil to deep sleep. But Pieter would not yield to the temptation dragging others away and became, instead, enlivened and invigorated by the conversation.

"The Roman Church," said Philip with conviction, "is an aberration ... a perversion of the Holy Will of God, for nowhere in Scripture is it appointed that any mere man ought stand between God and His creation. I declare no need of a priest to speak for me. I need no pope to put order to my soul."

Wil and Karl exchanged glances.

"Might I inquire of the source of such a bold ... position?" asked Pieter.

"Ha!" answered Jean defiantly. "The Holy Scripture itself. And we are pleased to join with others to bring this good news of freedom to the folk of Christendom. Hear me. You ... all of you ... are *free* ... free to receive God's love without cost of tribute or without bending knee to a shaveling or black-robed priest. The Christ has paid all that's due!"

Jean's flashing eyes took sudden account of Pieter's garb and he squirmed a little. But before he spoke Pieter asked calmly, "Please, tell us more of this ... freedom."

Jean leaned forward. "The freedom to speak to God directly, my friend. The freedom to read or hear His Word in your own tongue. The freedom to depend on *His* perfection, not our own good deeds. Freedom to depend on His payment for our sins; no more bondage to tithes and indulgences, to fasts, to pilgrimages, to penance. And more: for by His Grace alone, *sola gratia*, freedom to enjoy Him forever!"

"*N'est-ce pas,*" agreed Philip. "And freedom from the

thieving grasp of a Church that would deprive a man of his last *denier*. Ha! I trust their tithes and indulgences earn the devils a particular heat in hell."

Jean cast a stern, scolding eye toward his fellow. "*Non,* Philip, we've needs to love them as well. We've no right to throw stones." He turned toward Pieter. "Friend, by your robe I see you are a man of the Church, and we mean no offense to you personally, but conscience charges us—"

"Humph. We do so very much intend offense to your pope!" blurted Philip.

Pieter said nothing but nodded and glanced at his riveted boys.

"And you, lads," continued Philip, "we wish you grace and peace in the name of our Lord, Jesus Christ, and freedom in His name. Your reliance on the Savior alone sets you free, not your reliance on the Roman Church."

The boys did not answer.

"You mentioned others ... by what name are you called?" asked Pieter.

"We are followers of a Frenchman—"

"*Non!*" interrupted Philip. "My brother is wrong. We are followers of Jesus Christ, but have been schooled by a teacher from France named Peter Waldo."

Pieter smiled and nodded. "*Ja,* I have heard of him. I believe him to be a merchant with an uncommon knowledge of Scripture. And are you not oft called the Poor Men of Lyons?"

"*Oui,*" said Jean.

"Of course. I should have remembered that by those wooden shoes you are known for."

"And in the south the Italians call us the *Sabotati.* There are many of us now, mostly in the mountains of France and Lombardy. We travel as peddlers, using our trade as a way of sharing our good news. But from time to time we hide in these mountains, fleeing the wrath of our king and your pope."

"So, fellows, 'tis good by me that y've come upon us. I wear the robes, true enough, but my heart leaps within to hear your words."

Philip studied the old man. "Indeed you've the robe of a priest but I see a different light in your eye."

Pieter smiled and winked at Karl. "I am, as are you, a priest in the service of our Lord. But my title comes not by m'garments. In a time long past I was a priest serving Rome. Ah, but the Church found little liking to my thoughts on much and cast me aside for those more ... submissive to their mind. So now I wander the Empire within these robes to spite such an arrogance as would deny the priesthood of any who call Him Savior."

Jean's eyes sparkled in the firelight. "Yes, yes, *mon ami.* We are all priests. Each who claims the name of Jesus as his own is a priest ... even these young ones."

Karl's heart chilled and he whispered nervously to Wil, "Do y'think we could be hanged for hearing this?"

"Nay, I've no fear of them."

The discussion persisted deep into the night, well past the setting of the moon. The men discussed the role of the Church, the wisdom of the Celts, the liberties of the English, and the visions for the future. At last, though hungry for more, Pieter yielded to the hour and the pleas of his patient companions and snuggled into the crevice of a lichened boulder. But the old man woke before dawn, hurried through his morning prayers, and stoked the dwindled fire roughly, hoping to disturb the Frenchmen. "Ah, begging pardon," whispered Pieter in Jean's ear. "Have I wakened you?"

The sleeping man groused and grumbled, but the stick strategically dropped atop his legs opened his eyes. "*Eh?*"

"A blessed day to you," smiled Pieter mischievously.

Jean sighed. "*Et tu.*"

And, to Pieter's delight, he and the two Waldensians were soon climbing through the cold mountain air to the snow-covered top of a summit overlooking their camp. From here they could see the earliest hues of a new day building over the mountains in the east. Pieter leaned hard on his staff and turned a sincere eye toward his new friends. "I simply cannot grasp this God of ours. My mind fails me oft, for at one moment I see His love in bounty all about me, and on the next, it is as if He abides neither in this place nor any other. He seems, at times, to be the most intimate presence in all the *kosmos;* at others, the most distant.

"*Ach,* my soul is anguished and aches. It cries out in sunlight and in darkness, for my mind is tangled and woefully weak. I have roamed this troubled world for some seventy-seven years and have seen much. But surely, the more mine eyes do capture, the less I discern. I have labored to comprehend that which I encounter so that I might be more certain of what I do yearn to hold ... but I have failed to understand and my faith does fail me often."

The two men listened carefully, even sympathetically, as Pieter lamented the confusions of his life and the vexation of all efforts to snatch meaning from the chaos all about. Pieter finally quieted and sat with his silent friends to watch the sun crest the craggy summits.

Jean filled his lungs with the mountain air and broke the silence with a calming confidence. "*Mon ami,* Scripture teaches us that when times do well we ought be happy, but when times are not, to consider that God has made the one as well as the other."

"*Ja, ja,*" answered Pieter, a quality of impatience ringing in his tone. "I am not ignorant of such counsel. *Ach.* But why ... *why* does He allow evil to foul us, why such pain and misery? Why does His love fade and wither like a weak bloom in autumn?"

"Ah ...'tis a fair challenge," observed Philip. "Might I ask if strong faith is a good end?"

"*Ja,* so it is. And ...?"

"And has struggle with hardship brought you increase or want in your faith?"

Pieter paused. "Surely both, it would seem."

"Then, good fellow, beg my leave to ask how you are so certain such suffering is by His failure? Could it not be a mysterious blessing from the only One who knows what Pieter ... or Jean ... or m'self ... must needs endure to grow in faith?"

Pieter hesitated.

"Might I pose another question? When have you wrestled most with your Maker? When have y'shook your fist or fell, despairing, to your knees?"

"In times of sorrow and pain," answered Pieter slowly.

"*Oui.* It seems we creatures are always wont to drift from the One who longs to but hear our cries ... or see our face turn even an angry eye toward Him. 'Tis sad, but as we are we've little interest to look to Him for any cause save when we've suffered loss or blundered our way."

Pieter stiffened. "Misery seems an odd way to draw us ... yea, perhaps even a cruel way, methinks. I've yet to understand such as He."

Jean smiled kindly. "It is not the heart of God that lacks, but ours. He is not a hard taskmaster; we are stiff-necked students. And you shall *not* know the mind of this God of ours, brother, *not ever*; 'tis not meant for us to know the why. Such a thing would leave little room for faith. We would soon only trust in our own understanding."

Pieter stood to his feet and protested, "Nay, we ought be able to know His ways so we might know what to expect. I wake by lauds and tremble to imagine which of my children I might lose this day or which might be spared! I know not whether He's a mind to feed us or tear our bellies with hunger again, or whether some mischief shall pounce upon us or whether mercy shall lead us. If I could but see His mind ... have a sound hold of His ways ..."

Jean took the old man by the shoulders and faced him squarely. "Though our faith be reasonable, we are clearly instructed, nonetheless, to 'lean not upon our own understanding,' but rather to allow for the mysteries of a God who owes no debt of explanation to His creatures. You, priest, by your own words do toil to deny such submission. Pity, indeed, to waste a life in such futility of effort."

Jean sighed and narrowed his eyes at Pieter's. He spoke gently, but firmly. "Brother Pieter, hear me say this: 'Tis plain that you are a most arrogant and prideful man."

Pieter was startled by the charge and stood hard-faced and flushed in the early light.

Philip set an affectionate hand on his shoulder. "It is love for you that draws truth to my lips. Jean is right to say he sees a haughty spirit shadowing your mind. I discern you to be beset by a sinister, subtle pride, a wily and elusive pride that keeps you in bondage. Come, let us show you something." The confused old man followed the Frenchmen around a boulder atop the summit to behold a panorama spread before them like none other Pieter had ever seen in all his many years.

Fresh sunbeams had just burst low from the east, driving mighty red-and-yellow rays of light against the azure sky and glinting the snow-topped edges of the hale and ardent landscape. The sprawling mountains' silent mass embraced the power of the rising sun, and though the heights' gray-white cliffs purpled slightly, they did not blush without cause. Indeed not, for such a place was the high chamber of God Himself and hallowed with His presence. Here was the form of unyielding resolution and here shined the reflected glory of God's own splendid visage.

In that silent moment Pieter suddenly felt so very, very, small; obscure, insignificant. His eyes teared as they opened to see himself perched atop the lofty peak a wilted, pitiful, inconsequential bit of unkempt and unnecessary matter; an impotent, pathetic pinch of fouled and foolhardy clay. The divergent magnificence before him bent him to the ground, mocked and humiliated by his own folly.

Pieter cried bitterly and lay prostrate beneath the warming sun as his smashed vanity writhed against the moment. At last the broken man groaned loudly, "'What is man that Thou art mindful of him?'" He then lay in utter silence, facedown atop the summit's snowy boulder until, at long last, he climbed slowly to his knees and faced the sun. He spread his arms to the sky and smiled.

Shaking and drained, he turned to his companions. "My dear, dear brothers, you have brought me to the garret of the earth and the end of myself. I am in your debt. Ah, what a fool I have been to imagine I might seize the mind of the One whose hands have shaped these mountains … whose fingers cut such valleys! I cannot understand such might. I cannot grasp His power, His glory. How dare I even strive to do so! That He allows me breath is gift enough, and for Him to grant my feeble mind sight for but a small portion of His is a miracle indeed. Ah, what grace! How dare I demand to know His purposes! How dare I bind my faith to such a quest! May He forgive my arrogance."

Pieter fell to his knees and raised his hands once again. "I believe You to be there and I believe You to care … and I am content."

In all his prior days, old Pieter the Broken had never been so surely touched by the hand of God's Spirit. In all his journeys and in all his tears, with all his study and in all his hours of prayer, he had never before been turned so completely toward the face of his Maker than as on this blessed morn. He sprung to his feet and embraced Jean and young Philip.

"I am free … free. I have seen the truth and am free indeed. *Credo ut intelligam* … I believe to understand." Pieter bounded back down the trail skipping and tripping, laughing for joy; for he had abandoned his self to dance, and dance he did, like a happy child within the safety of the high chamber of his Father.

æ

First-meal was unlike any other for the transformed priest. His eyes sparkled and he frolicked about the campsite like a young master on a bright summer day. What gladness! What deep, heartfelt delight washed through him! After finishing a ladle of gruel, Pieter called for Jean and Philip. He reached into his robe, removed his leather wallet, and carefully unfolded the passage from the Psalms. "You were led here by the angels, I am certain of it … uh, as certain as I am now able to be! *Mes bons amis*, take this parchment as a gift from my heart. Take this and share it with as many as you can. Share it with your blessed Waldensians. God is truly greater than our minds can know…. Ah, 'tis life to accept such simple truth."

Jean and Philip received the Scripture humbly and embraced the old man. "*Merci, merci!* Ah, and 'tis time now that we depart. Blessings on you, brother, and upon all you, dear children. May each of you enjoy God's Holy Land, whether within or without. May all find the many liberties of His good heart.

"And remember this: We are truly free when He fills us with the faith to do nothing ... and the wisdom to know when!"

Then, as suddenly as they appeared, the Frenchmen descended out of sight and were gone. Ah, but Pieter's joy did not leave with them. Instead, it swelled as he assembled with his beloved children in the cold air of the windy, snowy pass, and his infectious bliss brightened the company as they continued their march.

The girls squealed and the boys howled with delight as they hurled snowballs at each other. It was not a time to notice the cold or lack of provisions or the steep ascent; instead it was a time to celebrate the beauty of the world below and the good fellowship each shared. By vespers the crusaders had crested the summit and were descending again, dropping out of the snowline, past the scrubby pines and into the thicker spruce. Night was quickly gaining on them and Wil soon ordered camp to be set.

"Wil," asked Anna as she rubbed her tired eyes before the fire, "we've nought to eat—what are we to do?"

Wil shrugged and searched the blankets for food. Conrad called out. "Wil, you'd be looking for this, I'd venture." The boy held out a final gift from the Frenchmen. "Look here! They hid a wrap of smoked venison and some red cabbage in m'blanket!"

"Ah!" exclaimed Pieter. "Who would have ever thought to hear m'say 'God bless the French'!" He laughed. "So, God bless the French.... *Oui?* Let us eat."

Soon all had filled themselves with the Waldensians's kind gift and each had nestled into his blanket atop broken tree boughs for another night's sleep. Maria was snuggled against Pieter's back and the old man beckoned Karl to his side with a finger. "I've another clue for my riddle if you've such a mind for it."

Karl winced. "I've some doubt I'll ever guess it!"

"Then you've need of a few extra clues to sleep with. Are you ready?"

Karl shrugged.

"Good: A misty dewdrop sparkles well upon a tender blade, but soon it melts to gleam again in which enchanted glade?"

Karl shrugged again. "I'll never ..."

"Be patient, lad. Here is another: Through what canyon walls resound and to what castle bound the whimpers of a frightened child huddled on the ground?"

Karl strained and groaned, eyes squeezed shut. He mumbled past clues and then shook his head.

Pieter smiled. "I'll ponder your good riddle if you vow to work at mine. But now it's time to sleep. Who knows what waits on the morrow?"

Chapter 17
REFLECTIONS AND THE MINSTREL

What day of the month do you think it to be?" Karl yawned as he prepared for the next morning's march.

Pieter rubbed his red eyes. "I judge by our French friends this to be the first days of September. Why do you ask?"

"Did y'not claim your birthday to be at the end of August?"

"Ah, yes. Yes, indeed, 'twas on the twenty-seventh day of the most pleasant of month of August."

Maria was listening as she gathered wood for the fire. "But Papa Pieter, we failed to wish you blessings on that day."

"*Ach*, give it no thought, my little dear."

"But Father," Otto added, "birthdays are to be special ... most specially when there are as many as you have!"

The company laughed.

"Aye, well said, my son," said Pieter. "That was my seventy-seventh year ... and I expect to add no more."

"And why so?" asked Karl.

"Truth is, I was told once by a Jew in Milan that seven is the number of perfection. And now that my sevens are doubled, why not hold fast?" He threw back his head and chuckled.

Wil ordered his crusaders to hurry their first-meal and begin, at once, to press their journey against the difficult trail ahead. So, after rubbing their hands over the morning fire and swallowing hard on a few stale crusts, the young soldiers dutifully tied fast their blankets, bowed to Pieter's customary prayer, and fell into the familiar rhythm of their determined march.

The troop was now high in the mountains and approaching the bare-faced, snowy Grimsel Pass which would lead them to the Rhône River and closer to the lands called Lombardy. After several hours of hard climbing Wil halted his company and surveyed the landscape ahead. "See there, Pieter, see ... there ... snow is blowing hard against that ridge, and look, look beyond to the heavy gray clouds lowering toward us."

"You've good, strong eyes, lad. We needs find shelter, quickly."

Wil stared anxiously at the threatening clouds and then turned kind eyes toward his shivering crusaders. Maria's lips were blue-white and trembling. She looked so drawn and pale, he thought, but then so did the rest of the band. Setting his fists confidently on his hips, as if to inspire courage, he ordered his troop to follow him as he leaned into the stiffening winds. His faithful obeyed without complaint, shuffling and shivering close behind. They panted puffs of smoke into the thin, icy air while squalls of stinging snow blasted hard against their freezing faces.

The sky thickened and lowered and the snow fell hard through the day. By evening the travelers found themselves in a most difficult predicament. Wil called a halt and stared through the twilight as he strained to find his way.

"If only these c-c-cursed clouds would open," he shivered. "We might yet f-f-follow m-m-moonlight to shelter."

The group silently waited for Wil's orders, huddling tightly to protect themselves against the wind. Pieter whispered to the stubborn lad, "M-my son, we are in grave danger. The snow is lying above our knees. These childrens' feet are freezing and they will soon s-s-suffer blacktoe. We've no wood for a fire—both coal buckets have spilt ... we've little f-f-food ..."

Wil snarled, "I've eyes. Have y'not a better thought in yer old head?"

Pieter wrapped his blanket close about him and pulled his hood hard against his cheeks. The blanket-bound faces gawking at him in the deepening darkness tried to detect some degree of hope. Yet the priest could see little as he looked ahead. Drawing Wil closer he whispered, "I heard once of N-N-Norsemen who'd lost their way and c-c-crashed their V-Viking ships against a snowy island. They were wet and near death with nary s-s-shelter or f-fire. It is t-told they dug a cavern in the s-s-snow itself and pressed their bodies close together. They were sh-sh-shielded from the wind and w-were ... warmer than ... outside. It seems we ought do the same?" His trailing voice exposed his doubts.

Karl had shuffled close by to listen. "But Pieter ..." he began to whine. "We ..."

"Enough!" barked Wil. "There is no other way."

Wil shouted the plan over the wind to the incredulous pilgrims. But they stood motionless as if waiting for a better plan. "Did y'not hear me? Do as I say. B-begin digging here." He pointed to a deep drift on the leeward side of a jagged outcropping and threw Otto toward it. "Dig.... All of you ... dig and dig quickly."

The children reluctantly began to scoop a hollow in the snow with nothing other than the cups of their numbed, bare hands. Fresh snow drove hard against their faces as Wil kicked and fisted his comrades deeper into the icy drift. But it was the fearful roar of the wind that served to be the better whip, and the desperate crusaders, at long last, carved themselves an adequate nook and piled safely inside.

As they awkwardly shifted and settled in their dark cavern, Pieter calmed them. "Ah, my little flock. Be still and quiet. *Alles klar.*" His voice was soothing to the crusaders. Even in the utter blackness of their frozen cave, his soothing voice was reassuring and comforting. "We are all little hearths, you know," Pieter continued. "Truth be told, we are little hearths with large hearts." He chuckled, but the children were not amused. "Ah, no matter. Each of us is like a wineskin filled with hot water. If all snuggle close, I think we'll find the miracle that some are hoping for."

The seventeen children and the old man nestled together like a large, woolen yarn and before very long Pieter's words proved true. The pilgrims became as warm as if they were home in their own beds, covered by their mothers' quilted blankets, safe and secure. Reassured by such warmth and so sheltered from the howling world without, each fell to sleep until dawn's touch filtered through the walls of their worthy nest.

The early sun glistened across the rippled mounds of snow, shimmering red and pink. The mountain peaks looked down on the buried trail and waited silently for the crusaders to emerge from their snowy cocoon. The children had slept peacefully but were beginning to stir in their unfamiliar surroundings. Maria was in the very center of the pile and awakened first. "I'm hot," she complained. "I'm hot and cannot breathe!"

Anna was pressed hard against her and woke with a start. "Let me out of here. Hurry, let me out!"

The others woke in some confusion. They could see a little, but very little, and the entrance had been sealed overnight. "I cannot breathe!" hollered Maria again.

"Me neither!" screamed Otto, who began to wrench and writhe in the tangle of crusaders around him.

"Nor I!" cried another.

Soon the woolen ball began to twist and turn in panic as the children pushed wildly against their frozen tomb. Pieter's face was smashed against an icy wall and he was unable to speak. Wil frantically kicked and thrashed with the other anxious crusaders until he broke through a wall with one foot. Finally, the children burst out of their cave and into the deep snow covering their path.

Pieter came out last, dragging himself on his stomach with shaking arms. He lay still for a moment, then struggled to his feet like a fresh chick from its egg. He stood in the bright sun and squinted at the blue sky. A smile broadened and stretched the icicles hanging from his scraggly beard, bringing squeals of laughter from his relieved fellow travelers.

Wil brushed the snow off his blanket and scraped at the ice hanging on his leggings. "My God, that was something I care not to do again."

Karl laughed. His red curls, weighed down by clinging ice balls, hung heavy by his flushed face. "I hope not, as well, brother, but what a legend we'll become!"

రా

The sun rose high and the frigid air began to yield to its warmth as the children dropped through several short descents, jaunted over a modest ridge, and entered the barren Grimsel Pass. "Now children," announced Pieter as they crested an overlook, "let me show you something. There, a quarter off the horizon."

Maria squinted. "I see only white ... a white river of sorts?"

"That, my precious one, might be called a river by some, but 'tis a river of ice and snow. It is the Rhône *Gletscher*."

"And what might be a *gletscher*?" posed Jon.

"Were we to be a bit closer, we'd see it to be a magnificent moving wall of ice and snow that creeps its way through the valleys like a giant slug. It moves but a little and as it melts it fills the river below with good water. It is a splendid sight indeed, is it not?"

Wil stared for a moment, unimpressed but curious nonetheless. "It is but a long white valley to me, Pieter. Odd, perhaps, but of no consequence to us."

"Nay, lad, nay. You'd be about to enjoy its fruit!"

"How so?" asked Frieda. "What sort of strange fruit might snow bear?"

"Water!"

"Then I've seen enough fruit for a lifetime, Pieter," countered Wil.

"Aye." Pieter's eyes sparkled mischievously. "But this water is the sort that moves quickly and might carry some weary crusaders for a good stretch."

"You mean we can float on it?" exclaimed Otto. His green eyes widened.

"Indeed."

"But does it not move north, like the Rhine?" challenged Karl.

"Would seem y'to not trust me, lad," said Pieter. The crusaders shrugged, uncertain of such a plan, but as they marched on through the difficult pass the thought of it began to cheer them. They soon descended past the scrub pines and watched the snow disappear from beneath their feet. "At last!" rejoiced Frieda. "No more footprints." Before long they arrived at the forest village of Oberwald, whose residents offered hospitality as chilly as the Rhône River rushing near their timber walls.

A party of children entered the village in pairs, hoping to find a willing population. But these woodland folk were wary. Wil and Conrad were greeted with oaths and threats, and Anna was thrashed by the stout broom of an angry *hausfrau*. But Maria, Frieda, and Gertrude found one worthy household who filled a blanket with smoked mutton, three large loaves of fresh bread, and a cheese.

While others were begging, Karl and a few fellows had set camp and flinted a promising fire. They waited expectantly, hoping for charity, and chattering of the proposed ride on the narrow river. Through the towering spruce they could hear the sounds of the water surging over its rocky bed and they squirmed with excitement.

The sun was nearly set and all but Pieter had returned. The crusaders, disappointed but thankful nonetheless for what was received, waited patiently. And, to the relief of all, their priest's voice was soon heard crowing through the dark forest as he made his way toward them. Pieter entered the firelight with a huge smile on his face. "Wil, my lad," he said, "a *few* good folk do walk this earth; y'needs take the time to seek them out. I happened upon four timbermen who have agreed to lash two rafts together for us."

Wil looked at the old man suspiciously. "I fear to ask how y'found them so agreeable."

Pieter chuckled and squatted by the fire to warm his hands.

The next morning the children walked tentatively toward the enticing sound of the nearby river, quite uncertain as to what adventures this particular day might bring and especially wary of Pieter's grand scheme. But before reaching the rocky bank they came upon a small fern-draped clearing set neatly in the needled wood. It was a wondrous place; a magical place, cool and fresh, dappled with tints of brown and soft green. Here shafts of sunlight reached between the timbers with ease as if stretching to touch the earth tenderly and warm it with kindness.

Each widening eye stared into the glade with eager hopes of seeing the flight of a fairy or the dash of a sprite. And some were quite certain to have heard the rustle of a gnome. Such an enchantment none had e'er before encountered, save in the happiest of their dreams. Maria's blue eyes stretched with delight as she stepped softly atop a thick carpet of moss. Then, with a smile that could have lighted all Christendom, she glided into nature's sanctuary. Her golden hair shimmered under the sunbeams' yellow rays and her milky skin pinked and glowed with the joy of all heaven. Pieter watched her in awe, quite certain he had been whisked away to behold an angel strolling through the cool of Eden. She seemed to float atop the supple ferns as she laughed and danced, twirled and spun—carefree and happy at long last.

Prancing to the edge of a glistening, spring-fed pool and bending to cup a tiny handful of its crystal water, Maria was abruptly startled by the perfect reflection suddenly opposing her. For a moment she believed that she had equally surprised a pixie lying beneath the water; after all, the poor creature was staring as open-mouthed and wide-eyed as she! But in the next moment she realized that she was gazing upon her own likeness, one no looking glass could ever have equaled. "Oh, my," she said softly.

Maria's fellows noticed her fixation and soon joined her by the water's edge. They formed a ring around the small pool and, for a time, none spoke. Instead, each looked carefully at the exact double lying at his or her feet. For some, it was the first time they had seen themselves in such a way. This shimmering pool was not like the tarnished alms tins at their churches or the muddy fish ponds of home.

Frieda stared curiously at herself. She fussed with her yellow hair, twirling it around her fingers and laying it across the base of her throat. She slowly shaped her waist and hips with her hands and bent nearly in half to look carefully into her own dark brown eyes. She touched a finger to the delicate dimple in the center of her chin and smiled. She saw the blossom of a beautiful woman and was humbly pleased.

Gertrude, Frieda's sister of five years less, looked with some disappointment at the comparison. She thought her nose a bit too large, her brown eyes too common, and worst of all, she was certain it to be only her long hair which kept her from being mistaken for a boy!

Otto stared rather casually at his badly-cropped sandy hair. He hardly noticed his smudged face or tattered clothes. Instead he was having fun pushing his nose flat, spreading his nostrils, and rolling his lips backward. "Hey, Conrad, look at me." Otto pulled his cheeks out and extended his tongue as far as he could. The two boys laughed.

Wil gazed proudly at the tall, blonde squire staring back at him from the water. *Indeed*, he thought, *that is a fine looking soldier. Look at his shining hair, fierce eyes, and strong nose! I think him to look much like a worthy knight.* He held his palms toward the water and clenched his fists tightly. *Strong hands and forearms, too.* He plucked the dagger from his belt and reflected a sunbeam onto the water. He smiled a most contented smile.

Karl gawked rather sheepishly at his dirty face and the tangle of curls perched atop his broad head. *M'face is too round and my arms too short and I look a bit worn ... but ... I do think me sturdy enough to cross into Jerusalem,* he mused. He pulled apart his lips and looked carefully at his teeth as if he were studying the worth of a good horse. *M'teeth seem big. Especially my fronts ... and perhaps too square ... but at least most are still fastened tight.* He wrinkled his nose and pulled his lips back further when Anna started giggling.

"What are you doing, Karl?"

Karl's face turned red as a ripe tomato and he sped away from the pool midst the jeers and taunts of his friends. Maria, meanwhile, was still staring at her reflection and finally fixed her eyes on her withered arm. Tears puddled her eyes as she touched the arm with her good hand. She stepped away sadly.

Some of the children simply stood quietly, lost in thought, but others teased and tormented their comrades with every imperfection they could expose. "See, Conrad, I told you your lips were too skinny," laughed one.

"Shut your mouth or I'll fatten your lips some, you—"

"What's the matter, Conrad? Y'like not what you see?" mocked another.

"Uh … what about that egg head of yours? It … it looks like a double yoker!"

But Pieter, oblivious to the commotion, inspected himself slowly from head to toe, pausing to smile a little at the famous snaggle-tooth everyone took such delight in. *Indeed, 'tis quite a sight,* he mused.

But then a dark mood crept over him. He did not see the sparkle in his blue eyes that others saw. Instead he felt as if he were peering into the windows of a crumbling temple to see the failing light of a weary and ragged spirit within. He watched the breeze have its way with his snow-white hair; where others saw such as evidence of time's wisdom, he saw only an aging head capped and edged by thinning white patches. His nose seemed far too long and bony and his shoulders so very thin and narrow. He looked at his pointy knees protruding from within his threadbare robe and he remembered the days when they carried a muscular, handsome soldier through the storm of battle. He released a quivering sigh and dropped large tears into the pool below.

Maria was watching him carefully. "Why are you crying, Papa Pieter? Please don't cry."

Pieter put his arm around her shoulders and pulled her

close to his side. "Ah, my dear *Mädel*, I am crying for someone," he said, "someone I miss very much." He ventured a
weak smile.

Maria looked at him tenderly. "And who is he? Was he a
friend of yours? Or was she a lady?"

"Oh, my little dear, he was a friend of mine, someone
who knew my every thought, who shared my dreams and
felt my pain."

"Is he dead?"

"Aye—and nay, sweet Maria. He lives in my mind and is
strangely part of me even now."

Maria persisted. "But who is he? Who do you cry for?"

Pieter laid his hand on her head and whispered sadly, "I
miss the man I used to be."

Maria looked confused.

"He is gone, yet some of him remains. But oh, if only I
might fly away in time to see that man again. Oh, to relive
but one day ... but one afternoon or an hour of a single day
of sixty years ago. Aye, to just breathe air into young lungs
... to laugh and dine with one old friend. And, ah, my sweet
Anna Maria." Pieter stammered and choked. "I believe I
might yield my very soul to just brush her cheek with my
hand one more time."

Pieter looked wistfully at the child by his side. "My dear
one, notice your youth. Taste what of it you can and capture it in your mind ... such memories shall be your most
prized treasure."

The old man sat down slowly as sun and sky peeked
between the pines. "But alas, my little cherub, here is the
rub: The very thing that gives such value to our past is that
which steals it away. For 'tis only when the present fades
to a memory that it becomes so very precious ... yet in such
fading it does leave us. Oh, what a double-edged thing:
this that is both friend and mortal enemy, this thing called
Time. If I could but put value to things present before Time
does it for me, I'd—"

"Ho, ho, old priest." Three timbermen suddenly strode
into the glade. "Might this be the group of soldiers you
spoke of?" They laughed.

"Uh, aye." Pieter wiped his eyes on his sleeve. "Are our crafts ready?"

"Indeed!" the eldest boasted. "Now mind you, this water is swift and cold and uncommonly high. We thought it best to lash one large raft rather than two ... it ought be a better float. Y'must needs keep the weak ones to the middle."

Pieter nodded.

Another continued. "My Frau sent some extra food for the children."

"Well, blessings upon your Frau!" exclaimed Pieter. "Come children. Let us follow these good men."

As Wil assembled his column, Karl leaned close to Pieter. "Dare I ask how you arranged this?"

The old man winked. "Ah, do you see that happy, dark-haired fellow? It seems their bishop has banned weddings by the village folk and insists they are only sacred when administered by a priest. But the local priest demands a high price and the man was unable to marry. I told him I was a priest." Pieter pulled the cross from under his robe. "And I said I should be most pleased to wed him and his woman in exchange for some rafts for us. So, his sturdy brothers saw fit to build one as his wedding gift."

Karl grinned.

The children followed the timbermen to the water's edge and stopped tentatively by the large, square raft they had built. It was made of twenty long, stout logs lashed with heavy rope, but against the surging mountain river it looked slight and unsubstantial. Frieda whispered nervously to Wil, "you don't mean to have us ride on this, do you?"

"Aye. You girls shall sit at the center."

Gertrude and Maria held each other's hands and looked fearfully at the rushing Rhône. The ice melts had been heavy that summer and new rains had filled the river to an uncommon depth. The icy flow now rolled and churned against the white rocks of the bed and the noise was terrifying. Anna hid her face in the small of Jon's back.

"Come, come Anna. We've beaten worse than this. 'Tis but water and it shall surely save some walking."

"But, Jon," she whimpered, "I cannot swim."

The new groom took Pieter aside and cautioned him. "Now be mindful of this water, it *is* treacherous. M'brother thinks it best if you stay to the south bank. We've built a short rudder and it needs strong hands. Use these poles at each corner and put them in smart hands with good eyes ... you needs spot the rocks *afore* you land on them. Put the weaker in the middle and tie them with this rope. You'll take a bend in about a half-day where you ought be able to rest, but I'd press on to the village of Fiesch by dusk."

Wil was uneasy but did well at hiding his concern. He spoke in a bold voice. "And how do we know Fiesch?"

"There'd be an alehouse with a short ferry-dock. And you'll see a green pennant at the end of the dock. Some use the rope ferry instead of the swine-ford farther south. There'd be a low stockade 'round a dozen poorly kept hovels, and you'll surely hear the music of a little minstrel sitting by the water.

"You'll also see ahead a sharper bend southward— unless you're asleep y'cannot miss it. Fiesch might be a good place for you to stop for the night, but take care for the villagers; we hear stories of them sometimes.

"The next day you should float until about mid-evening when you'll come to Brig and there you needs land. If you're clever you'll trade the raft for some provisions ... good goat cheese or mutton ... aye, 'tis what I'd do. From there turn south on the trails leading toward the Simplon Pass which is your final gateway to the sunny south."

Pieter scratched his head. "I believe I've crossed it. It seems that we'll then be close to the area of the Lombardians?"

A different brother answered hastily, also eager to be of service. "*Ja*, close. You'll follow some high-walled valleys past the dark-eyed villagers of Gondo and then under the watch of the castle near Domodossola ... beyond that I've no knowledge."

The groom reached his large, callused hands forward and took Pieter's shoulder with one and Wil's with the other. "God and all good spirits go with you and your brave little soldiers." The brothers nodded, slung their broadaxs over their wide backs, and disappeared into the forest.

Wil looked at his nervous comrades and at the log raft rocking impatiently against the shore. He disguised his fear with a good bark in his voice. "Girls, small boys: to the center. Otto, you take a pole. Karl, you take this pole. Gunter, take this one. Conrad, you'll work the tiller with me. Jon, take that corner, and you there ..."

"Heinz, Master Wil."

"Aye ... Heinz ... I forget your new ones' names ... you're a bit small but take this corner with Jon to help."

Heinz was a quiet fellow traveler who had slipped into the column somewhere in the mountains with Gunter, his strapping cousin. No one exactly remembered when he joined and, as with others, he had simply blended with the rest, saying little and working hard. He was a determined lad, but no more than nine years. He had straight brown hair, shining, squinty brown eyes and an upturned nose between freckled cheeks that gave him the look of a woodland elf. Heinz leapt sprightly onto the wooden raft, excited to be included with the bigger boys.

"Now, Pieter," Wil continued, "you needs stay in the center. Take this rope and wrap each of the pole men around his belt. Then tie the rest 'round some of the others. If any falls over, we can all pull them back."

"Or all join them in the water," groused a voice.

The children crawled tentatively onto the raft and positioned themselves as ordered. Unfortunately, no thought was given to releasing the raft and it now weighed heavy atop the rocks beneath. The children sat staring at each other and their predicament when, all at once, they began to laugh at the ridiculous scene.

"Well done, Wil," teased one. Even Wil roared at his oversight as he and two others rocked the craft carefully into the cold, swirling water. Then, with a few final groans and grunts, the green logs were sucked into the shoreline currents of the river. And, with a little help from the determined hands straining against their stout poles, the crusaders were suddenly swept into the powerful grasp of the swift water.

The first rolling surge of the raft gave all something of a fearful start, but after several tentative minutes the little army shuffled itself into a comfortable position. And, before long, the children were squealing with delight as they pitched and heaved atop the surging whitewater. Down the river valley they flew, rolling and laughing, gasping as icy spray splashed over them and cheering as their sturdy raft ploughed proudly through the watery furrows.

The spruce-covered mountains to the left were but a green haze beneath a magnificent blue sky and the rocky peaks to the right but a brown blur. Ah, and the rush of the river was as fine a sound as the children had ever heard! Pieter laughed and clapped his hands like a small child at a May Day feast. "Oh, 'tis so very good to be alive!" he shouted.

Down the Rhône they sped, rocking and tilting for hour after hour toward the distant snow-capped mountains of the west. The crusaders swept past small villages of heavy-timbered hovels and waved gleefully to the surprised peasants pausing for a look. The mountains to the north fell away as the valley began to widen, and soon the river quieted as they sailed by pastures dotted with sheep and goats. Leafy trees began to crowd the banks and the crusaders found themselves floating beneath the sprawling branches of beech and oak and white birch. Some of the children now bravely hung their bare toes into the water at the raft's edge. It felt cold and tickly and they laughed and giggled all the more.

"If only Georg could take this ride!" cried Karl.

"*Ja*," Conrad answered. "But could the raft hold him?"

"Methinks we'd have need of four more stout logs!" Wil chortled.

By midday the band passed the first bend, just as the timbermen had described, and the children were comfortably sprawled on their backs watching the clouds pass overhead. An occasional hawk or falcon soared high above and, if it noticed, would, no doubt, have found an unusual sight: The brown tunics and dirty faces of crusaders blended quite neatly into the mottled brown bark of the raft's floor. The common color would be broken only by the red crosses stitched on each breast, an occasional mound of golden hair, or a bright smile from a laughing face.

The sun began to set and the air grew cooler. Pieter looked anxiously downstream in hopes of seeing the green pennant of the Fiesch alehouse. Early-evening stars appeared in the eastern sky when suddenly Otto pointed to a crooked, badly weathered dock in the distance and a warped, wood-shingled roof alongside it. The company stood to its feet and watched carefully as they floated in an increasing current toward their destination.

Pieter called to Wil, "Move us to the right, Wil. Quickly to the right!"

Wil grabbed the rudder and pulled hard … in the wrong direction, nearly toppling Karl and Otto off their corners.

"Nay, nay!" exclaimed Pieter, "the other way. Push the other way!"

Wil was suddenly confused and, with little time to waste, Pieter stumbled over several of the girls and grabbed the rudder. "Now, you pole men," he hollered, "make ready." Pieter pushed and pulled the rudder skillfully and began to maneuver the craft toward his right.

In a few moments he faced the raft directly into the rickety dock where a little man with a pointed hat was playing a lute. The man spotted the raft hurtling toward him and jumped to his feet just moments before the stout craft crashed into the pilings. The children tumbled headlong over top of one another as the raft swung about and bounced against the large rocks of the shoreline. Pieter recovered himself quickly and boomed orders to his polemen. "Hold us fast, lads. Lean into your poles … lean, lads … hard!"

The raft quivered against the shore, tempted by the currents to draw away, but the poles held. Pieter called to the minstrel, "Take our rope and bind us to the piling afore we sweep away!"

The minstrel was more than a little familiar with such a

predicament and deftly caught Pieter's rope. With a few swift turns of his hands, the crusaders were secured. Pieter checked his precious cargo and, satisfied that all were yet aboard, climbed onto the dock. "Good evening, my friend. Blessings on you."

The minstrel chuckled. "*Buon giorno,* navigator. Welcome to Fiesch. My name is Benedetto." He removed his hat and bowed.

Pieter introduced himself and those who had climbed to his side. "Well, my dear Benedetto, you come from the south?"

The minstrel nodded.

"Would there be a man of charity about who might spare some shelter for these little lambs?"

Benedetto smiled and stroked his pointy black beard. "I should think not, old man. This town is free but not charitable. I play my music and they leave me be, but that is all I do and that is all I get."

Pieter pressed. "Has the cold water chilled their hearts?"

Benedetto smiled. "Ah, my friend, most here have escaped the wars of the Guelphs and Ghibellines in the south and have come to hide in these mountains. Few speak your tongue and none make time for strangers—other than to take their coins—and none offer charity."

Pieter scratched his head and looked at his children. "I am not certain of which wars you speak, but I know that it makes little difference."

"Aye, 'tis truly said. But know this: Your robe has the look of a priest and so you might wish to seek a friend of the Guelphs, but you needs stay away from the Ghibellines."

"How might I know the difference and why does it matter?"

"The Guelphs are in alliance with the pope and the Ghibellines are an alliance of opposing lords. Of course, all do bend the knee to the Church—'tis most difficult to grasp. No matter, in the cities to the south they are at each other's throats."

"And whose friend are you?"

"I am a friend of music and I sing to this beautiful lover of mine, the river."

"Will you be a friend to my children?"

Benedetto sat down on the dock and nervously pulled at the worn points of his brown leather shoes. He twisted his face a little, then scratched the end of his long, narrow nose. "I think you to mean, might I find you shelter and food, so I must ask what such ... friendship ... is worth?"

"We've no money," said Pieter.

The minstrel stood to his feet, smiled, and bowed. He slung his lute around to his back and tipped his hat. "Then, *signore,* I bid you farewell."

Pieter looked at the disheveled village and felt uneasy. The sun was set and more stars were lighting the sky above him. Darkness would be no friend in this place. "I've no money, Benedetto, but I do have a treasure for you."

The minstrel stopped and turned. "*Sí?*"

"I'll teach you a ballad."

The musician raised his eyebrows. Good ballads were all he owned and the addition of a new one was tempting.

"I'll teach you 'The Song of Roland,' a good alehouse ballad."

Benedetto considered. "'Tis a good offer, but there are more than a dozen of you."

"But they are little, like you," noted Pieter. "It takes very little food to feed them."

"This 'Song of Roland,'" continued Benedetto. "Is it a good ballad or a German ballad?" He saw Wil scowling and quickly added, "I mean no offense ... no, certainly not, but I have heard some of your German ballads. They are about war and the bloody May Fields and your wild Saxon knights and things similar. And please say it was not a *sprüche* of your Wolfram of Eschenbach. My taste is of love and wine and butterflies."

Wil rolled his eyes and Pieter shrugged. "Hmm? Uh, do any of you children know a ballad of such things?"

The crusaders stood silently, straining to imagine a song like that. Wil tried to remember a song from the Butterfly Frau of Weyer. Maria finally broke the silence. "We could teach him our song about Jesus."

Benedetto shook his head. "Nay, I think not, little one. I've no heart for a chant. 'Tis a hard place to survive as is, but I fear the villagers might drown me for sure should I offer them that."

"*Ach!*" growled Pieter. "Our song is no chant—and if your fortunes are so hard in this place, why not travel with us? We'd gladly barter passage for a night's stay and some bread. We are headed out of the mountains and to Genoa by the sea."

Benedetto rocked on his feet and cast glances at both the village and the river. He took a long look at the circle of hopeful faces now silvered by the moonlight and his heart began to soften. After tinkering with his tin belt-buckle and fidgeting with his hat, he finally answered. "Indeed. And why not? I have been here for some ten years and perhaps I should return to my home." He thought for a moment. "*Si. Buono.* We've a contract. Follow me and I'll give you a good place to rest and some food."

The tiny man stepped nimbly through a hole in the town's fence and led the children to an empty swine-shed where they would be able to sleep on clean straw and light a small fire. And, before long, the crusaders were sitting around the flame, hoping for something to eat and drink. The campfire added sparkle to Benedetto's black eyes and when he smiled, the children tittered.

Maria whispered to Wil, "He looks like a little gnome from the forest."

Anna giggled.

Benedetto then slipped away, only to return quickly with some bread crusts and boiled mutton. "Here!" he proclaimed proudly. "Here, my little ones. Supper for us all."

The grateful children's eyes brightened, especially at the sight of mutton. Then the minstrel smiled again and held up a flask of wine and a clay pot of goat's milk.

"Ah, well done, good sir. Well done, indeed!" said Pieter.

Before long, the crusaders and their new friend were fast asleep.

Chapter 18
CASTELLO VERDI

he next morning Wil roused his company and ordered them to gather by the raft for the morning's commands. "Be sure the lashings are still tight. Conrad, check the knots. Karl, make sure the rudder is secure."

Pieter stood by Benedetto and looked at the icy water running past. "A wonderful sight indeed, my little friend. See how that sparkling blue water glides so confidently between the lush green on all sides. Ah, and those splendid mountains rising ever closer to the other shore. Indeed, good fellow, on a crisp morn as this my heart does fly."

Benedetto twisted the point of his beard. "For a Teuton you've a good eye for beauty."

"Humph, indeed. And you shall still go with us?"

Benedetto stood quietly for a moment and picked nervously at the neck of his old, wooden lute. "I have given the matter some thought while you slept," he finally answered. "I have been sitting on this dock for some ten years playing my songs for every sort of passerby. A penny here, a bit of silver there ... sometimes a scoff, others a torn blanket or a threadbare cloak, and sometimes just a smile. I have learned to speak in your tongue and some French and a bit of Latin, and yet I feel empty.

"My heart longs to see the sunny shores of the beautiful *Lago di Varese* and my little village of Brabbia in summer. Ah, Pieter, if you could only see the beautiful gardens and orchards of my people! Flowers that bring the aroma of heaven to one's nose and colors that rival a rainbow. Fruit that is large and juicy, dripping with sweet nectar. And the music. Ah ... the music. And the beautiful maidens. Oh, why do I sit here on the edge of the barbaric northland and sing my silly songs to none who care?"

Pieter interrupted him. "Then why have you stayed?"

Benedetto picked up some stones and tossed them slowly into the river. "My family fell from the favor of our lord and we were driven from our home. We could find no refuge with either the Gilarates or the Borgomnaeros. They warred for control of the free-lands and free-towns and everywhere we fled was bloodshed."

"And that was how long ago?"

"Oh, some score or so, I suppose," answered Benedetto. "I have lost count."

"Perhaps things have changed."

"And that was my thought all the night long, *Padre,* but I've come to fear something far worse than violence." Tears gathered at the bottom of his black eyes. "What ... what if my memories ... disappoint me? What if the flowers are not as delicate as I remember nor the wine as warm?"

"Then, good minstrel," interrupted Pieter, "why not simply die? In death you shall be spared the pain of disappointment—perhaps."

Wil paced the bank impatiently and finally ordered his soldiers to board the raft. "Pieter. And you, minstrel ... we're off. Our thanks for your kindness."

Pieter took Wil aside and whispered in his ear, "Lad, the man may yet join us. You'd be wise to welcome him."

Wil looked warily at Benedetto. "And what good would he be?"

"He speaks the language of the south better than I and he knows their ways. He's a fair eye for the passes and he shall most surely find us provisions among those folk. And ... I do believe he needs us."

Wil turned toward Benedetto and promptly set his fists on his hips. His voice betrayed reluctance but he yielded to Pieter's counsel. "Sir, you may join us if you wish, but you shall obey my commands."

Benedetto looked wistfully at his dock, then removed his hat and bowed slowly. "My son, it has been my lot to yield to others all my days and it would be my particular honor to follow you."

Perhaps it was something in the man's melancholy eyes or something about the placid tone of his voice, but for whatever cause, Wil's heart was suddenly pricked by a twinge of compassion and he extended his hand. "Then ... welcome."

The crusaders cheered and clapped and clambered into their assigned positions, happy to have the company of the musician. And, with a few hearty heaves they launched into the river's current.

By midday the whole company was laughing and teasing as it raced down the Rhône past villages their minstrel knew as Betten and Morel. The bright sun above felt good and it warmed them well. "Tell us, minstrel," begged Gunter. "Tell us of your home in the south."

"Ah, my boy! Such wonder that words can barely contain. You children of the north have no idea of such beauty."

The crusaders gathered close as Benedetto shut his eyes and tilted his face to the sky above. "As a boy I lived in a small stone-and-mud house with a flat, clay-tiled roof on the shores of the mighty *Lago di Varese* ... the most beautiful lake in all the world ... deep blue and home to storks and swans. In the hot summer we swam and laughed and splashed in its wondrous waters. Ah, what delight!

"My papa was a simple fisherman. My mind does yet see him mending his nets with his thick fingers. They spun their way across the knots like the finest lutist fingering a melody for angels. And Mama. Oh, Mama! Each night she would bake the most savory meals while singing like a songbird on a spring's new day. *Si, si* ... fresh fish and olives, fine wheat breads and whole fruits. And Papa would pour red wine from the clay bottles my Uncle Fernando wheeled and baked. At night my sisters and brothers, cousins and aunts, old Grandpapa and my uncle ... we would dance and sing until we fell to the ground too weary to go on. And then we would just lie under the stars. Oh, the stars! So very many of them, bright diamonds everywhere, sparkling and shining."

Benedetto's eyes twinkled. "And the women, my lads. The women were so beautiful. Some were fair and some dark, and all moved with the grace of angels. Their smiles were like the bursting of a new dawn, and their br—"

Pieter cleared his throat loudly and cast a stern look at the newcomer. Such discourse was hardly appropriate for the eager ears of his boys!

"Ah, *si, si* ... of course. So, *bambini*, my home was a place of beauty, to be sure."

Anna pointed a finger at Benedetto's lute. "Might you play for us?"

"Would that please you, my dear?"

"*Ja!*" squealed Frieda and Gertrude. "Please play."

As the others joined in pleading, Pieter raised a hopeful brow. *"Buona medicina, amico, buona medicina."*

Benedetto grinned. "I must sing loudly over the river, but I'll sing."

Jon shouted from his corner, "Sing of the women."

The boy's request prompted a reproving eye from Pieter. The minstrel, however, failed to notice the priest's frown. "Of course, my boy," Benedetto answered. He plucked lightly on the tight strings of his lute and closed his eyes. "I'll sing a song of the women of Brabbia." He hummed a few notes before he began, and it was plain that he'd been blessed with a voice well suited for his calling:

> I met once a maid
> Whose touch stole my soul.
> A beauty indeed,
> An angel aglow.
> Silk hair, golden braids,
> Shaped hips, eyes of blue
> Her smile lit the heavens,

> Her kiss was sweet dew.
> Red lips like spring roses
> And breasts full and firm …

"That song is now ended," interrupted Pieter. "Sing another song, one better suited for your audience." He raised a brow high.

Benedetto yielded. "Yes, of course. My judgment oft fails me, I fear. Forgive me, *Padre*." The minstrel winked at Heinz who stifled a giggle. "So, children, might I sing a more tasteful ballad I wrote for a beautiful maiden that passed by me on my dock?"

"*Ja!*" Heinz clapped. "Please sing!"

The musician's face brightened; that simple petition was the source of his joy and upon hearing it his spirit soared. He opened his heart and sang:

> Oh, rose of Arona
> Bloom only for me.
> I wait by yon garden wall
> On bended knee
> Midst sweet-smelling herbs
> And 'neath sweet-smelling trees.
>
> Yet columbine, nor violet,
> Nor cyprus draw me.
> Soft rose of Arona
> My heart yearns for but thee.
> I beg that thee only
> Would ringdance with me.
>
> Methinks of no other,
> Though fragrant they be,
> Oh, rose of Arona
> Bloom only for me.

The children clapped and clapped as Benedetto sang on and on—first songs of love, then of wine and butterflies, of feast days and dancing, of sunshine and moonlight. His fingers plucked and strummed his faithful lute until, at long last, he reluctantly paused to point toward the familiar walls of the village of Brig emerging from the river-bend on the southern shore. "There, Wil, there is Brig ... our destination."

Wil looked carefully at the timbered town set close to the water's edge. He saw nothing uncommon, only dark wood and steep thatched roofs. Smoke pillared above the stockade as the *volk* inside prepared their evening's meal, and the sounds of cows and goats mingled over the swift water toward the boy's straining ears.

Wil and Pieter skillfully ruddered the company toward a large boulder lying in a quiet eddy. It was a good place to secure their craft and, with a few final pulls on the rudder and a good heft of Jon's pole, the crusaders were safely resting against the rock. Karl and Conrad jumped to the bank with their rope in hand and lashed the raft securely to a stout oak. Once all was in order, Wil ordered his fellows onto dry land.

By now a number of curious villagers had gathered to watch the children disembark. It was not common for travelers to arrive from upstream; the river was rarely deep enough to navigate and when it was, few were willing to risk such an unproven course. But this season the ice melts had offered such adventure as a reasonable alternative to days of walking, and more than a few parties had landed by Brig's rock. So, satisfied that the new arrivals were neither fugitives nor highwaymen, the villagers soon returned to their duties-at-hand.

The crusaders stretched atop the boulder with mixed feelings. It felt good to lie on solid ground, but their voyage was pleasant and it was good to be carried by the currents instead of climbing against the unmerciful breasts of the mountains. Mindful of their lack of provisions, Pieter and Benedetto disappeared into the village where they shrewdly negotiated the sale of the raft to some adventurous peddlers headed toward Montreux. And, before darkness had completely fallen, they returned with a bulging leather wineskin of fine red wine and six pecks of millet and oats.

Wil was not pleased. "You ought trade that wine for some good bread!" he barked. Even in the dim of twilight Pieter could see anger in the lad's eyes.

"Our minstrel's throat is parched and I thought it best to repay his kindness with some of our own."

Wil grumbled but yielded. He turned his anger on the others and herded them gruffly toward a flat clearing outside the village wall. "Jon ... Conrad ... Karl ... Gunter ... Richard—gather wood. There's good hardwood all about. You others ... Frieda ... take the pail and draw water ... Anna, Otto ... take helpers and break some spruce for beds. Now off. All."

The crusaders were accustomed to their tasks, and before long a reasonable supper had been eaten in the warmth of a blazing fire. And, after a few hearty laughs and a quiet song by Benedetto, the children fell fast asleep, contented, rested, and well fed.

☙

The next morning the company awoke shrouded by the river's mists but beneath a promising sky. A few sharp kicks into the embered campfire rekindled a smoky fire so that a quick gruel could be prepared with the ration reserved from the prior night. Then, with neither ceremony nor regret, the crusaders left the shadow of Brig's stockade and the rush of the river to ascend the well-worn trail which would lead them through the Simplon Pass.

The children climbed faithfully up the long, winding trail, refreshed and strengthened by their days on the raft. Benedetto struggled, however, more accustomed to respite than labor. He panted and wheezed his way up the stony mountain track, loitering whenever possible to steal large gulps of air.

For days they strained through the narrow, high mountain valleys, ascending beyond the leafy trees and through the pines until, at long last, they crested the summit of the Simplon Pass and began their slow descent toward the plains of Lombardy. The journey became easier, though not easy, and the band paused occasionally to beg aid from the brown-eyed villagers of places known as Gondo and Preglia. These folk had a different manner and look about them, most being darker and shorter than the children's Teutonic kin. And, with the exception of the odd villagers of Gondo, most were warmhearted and welcoming. The breezes bore a different air as well. It was warm and oft sweet and as pleasing as the people it bathed. It was, most assuredly, relief from the chilly air the crusaders had left behind.

As the landscape changed from stark, rock-faced, and hard-edged summits to rolling, leafy mounts of oak, laurel, and beech, the pilgrims' hopes soared. "Aye, 'tis true, *kinder*," Pieter encouraged, "we've no more climbing through the clouds, though we've a range ahead by Genoa. Nay, we've a good march for quite some time. We'll follow this valley known as '*Di Vedro*' until we land by a good lake."

The company marched past Domodossola along a trail now edging upward slightly and cutting across the breast of the mountains midway above the valley floor. The children flourished in the warmth of the Italian sun; they danced and sang and laughed their way toward the stony shores of the Toce River some half-day's journey ahead. Suddenly, however, they rounded a bend in the widening pathway and spotted a squat, menacing castle just ahead.

The crusaders halted to study the *castello*. Its tawny stone walls were thick and heavy and stood firm against the mountain's breast atop a narrow terrace called a list. Its many bow-slits seemed to stare back at the children as if they were eyes keeping a wary watch. Indeed, this was a worthy sentry of the lord's lands. The company had no option but to pass beneath the fortress ramparts, for the trail they marched was so placed. The pilgrims stirred uneasily. Better, thought some, to face simple village folk than a lord and his men-at-arms. But others, such as Frieda, were accustomed to a castle's refuge and knew well of the safety and security it might offer commoners as themselves.

"Wil, there's naught to fear!" she assured. "And there'd be no better store of food than in a keep such as this!"

Wil was annoyed at the damsel's tone. How dare she accuse his reserve as fear! "Fear? Ha! Y'think me to fear a thing as that? Nay, girl, I've no fear of this place. My destiny is to rule lands as a knight and methinks y'to be a fool to say such a thing."

"I ... I only thought y'to be—"

"Humph. You'd be but a girl and not called to think."

Frieda bristled. Maiden or no she was not one to bind her tongue for the likes of anyone, let alone a cocky lad—handsome or not! Her eyes flashed. "You listen well, young master," she said sarcastically. "I'll use m'head as it suits me ... and it suits me well! I may say little but m'brain's not near as mushy as that soft gruel that fills your head."

Wil clenched his fists. Being challenged by a girl in front of his whole command was a sure humiliation. Few men in his village would have restrained from beating the strident wench where she stood, he thought. Yet he always felt it cruel; he'd not beat a helpless beast, let alone a *Mädchen*. His father, he suddenly recalled, never raised a hand to his mother and had been fined once by the village chief for not doing so. He had oft told him to never harm a woman. No, Frieda would not feel the weight of his fist this day or any other. But she surely needed a bit and bridle! The boy faltered for words.

"There. Y'see ... you may be a knight someday and me but a frau with a litter, but it shan't mean me to be your lesser!" The damsel's cheeks burned red but she was not without wisdom; she had more to say but held her tongue.

Benedetto was eager to bring calm. "Ah, *bambini*, look ... look there." He pointed to the four towered corners and the steep pitched roof of the keep that reached above the walls from the castle's center. "I remember this place as a boy," he said.

Wil shuffled his feet and looked away from Frieda. "*Ja?*" he answered halfheartedly. "Go on, minstrel."

"I rode with our village *padre* to learn to sing as he delivered a parchment from our bishop. It was a great honor for a little peasant boy. And he did teach me of the ways of lords and princes and of this family. He said this castle was built by the Verdi family just prior to their wars with the Visconti two or three generations past.

"The Verdi have been lords of these lands for many years, though the Visconti now control most of the world between Milan and Lago Maggiore. No matter, *Signore* Verdi's grandpapa had sworn fealty to Emperor Barbarossa. The Visconti allied with the Lombard cities and when the league defeated Barbarossa at Legnano, the Verdi were without good alliances and lost much land. Even now I have heard they have sworn to Otto and some lords of the Piedmont. Ah ..." Benedetto sighed, lost in the confusion of the times. "No matter, see how our trail rises to the *castello*? All travelers come under its eyes. And see how it is placed high above the valley and guards the whole of the lands surrounding?

"You see the narrow list, the flats in the front? Less land for an enemy to gather on. And there ... *Signore* Gostanzo has a moat ... that water surrounding the outside ... do you see? He is very proud of that. It is most unusual for a mountainside castle."

Wil pointed to an angled fence of wood spikes set on the mountainside just below the list. "It looks to be well defended. An army must needs get through those stakes, cross the list and then the moat. And all the while dodging the archers from above."

"*Si*, the barbican." Benedetto paused and studied the castle's walls. "And I fear there to be some trouble ... the war balconies are hung outside the ramparts ... a sure sign of danger." The minstrel shook his head and lowered his voice. "And see all the wall-slits ... they are filled with archers. Many a man has died on this side of that wall. But also, many a peasant has been shielded by it and many well fed in times of famine. Perhaps they will be gracious to us all."

Wil ordered his comrades forward and in a short time led them onto the drawbridge under the wary watch of a well-armed troop milling nervously by the open gate. The lad moved cautiously and wondered what sort of greeting to offer, when his thoughts were suddenly interrupted by Karl's voice.

"*Ach.* Such a stink!"

"What?" asked Wil.

"The stink … can y'not smell it?"

The company began to whine in unison and paused to peer into the stagnant water beneath them. Benedetto shrugged. "Where else to put the waste?"

Conrad sat on his haunches and stared at the filthy water. "Look there, Jon," he said. "I see floating cabbage."

"And there," pointed Anna, "a bit of onion. And there, scraps of … of something."

Otto suddenly started laughing and chortled. "And look there!" he shouted. "Against that old log."

His friends followed his pointing finger into the water below. Most of the girls, commoners though they were, nevertheless found the sight objectionable and turned away. But the lads found the sight more than a little amusing and howled and cackled at the flotilla of human waste collecting against the log dam.

"Enough of that," sighed Pieter as he brushed them by. "'Tis time to enter."

The boys got off their hands and knees and scrambled to catch Pieter, now waiting impatiently by the chief porter.

Pieter addressed the guard. "*Gentile signore,* we bid enter in peace and request the charity of your lord."

The man stared back from under his round helmet. Pieter noticed he was young and seemed very tired. Dark circles hung beneath his deep-set brown eyes. He teetered a little, straining to stand under the poundage of the steel mantle of mail that hung to his knees. Even his legs were weighted by mail hose that wrapped his feet. Pieter saw he was readied for battle and he turned to briefly survey the quiet countryside.

The porter, well trained for his youth and educated as well, forced a growl. "*Padre,* take this litter and *vattene*…begone. We are in no mood to host strangers."

Pieter looked beyond the gatekeeper to the bailey within and noticed battle-ready soldiers grouped in small companies. "What sort of troubles have you here?"

The young soldier stepped toward Pieter with a menacing stride. He motioned his men forward. "Just turn and go your way, old man. We have no need of you."

Karl was craning his neck impatiently from the rear of the crusaders' column. "What?"

The words had barely left the boy's lips when a trumpet blast suddenly pierced the air from the tower above. Its shrill timbre was cause enough for the courtyard to come alive in a flurry of noise and motion. A soldier high on the parapet could be heard shouting as he pointed, "There! There he comes!"

Pieter and the startled children followed the man's arm and peered across the valley below to see a lone horseman charging up the long slope toward the castle. Pieter strained but could not distinguish what manner of rider it was. Suddenly, a troop of mounted men-at-arms charged past the children, nearly knocking several off the bridge, and raced toward the oncoming horseman. Pieter could not discern if they intended the rider harm or escort, for they crashed past, fully armed but without the steely flush of bloodlust.

The tower bells now began to toll and the men-at-arms within the castle were quick-stepping to their positions all over the walls above. On the slope below one of the horsemen suddenly reigned his mount, turned in his saddle, and cupped his mouth to shout. "Red flag. He bears the red flag!" The man's voice was strong but clearly betrayed a tone of dread and, upon hearing him, the young guard paled before Pieter's eyes.

The message had barely reached the keep when orders began to fly from tower to tower, and streams of soldier and peasant alike ran to new tasks. The porter's voice cracked as he ordered Pieter and his children into the castle with the point of his lance. *"Sbrigatevi,"* he barked. "Hurry! *Avanti. Avanti!"*

Wil resisted. "Wh-what is happening here?"

"You cursed Teutons are no strangers to warfare. We are about to be attacked ... now inside. Now!"

The chief porter ordered his men to herd the crusaders

into the courtyard where they were abandoned in the midst of the chaos within. For several moments the wide-eyed children stared blankly at the beehive bustling all around them. Every wall was webbed with crowded stair-ways and lofts, lifts and lookouts, and each parapet occu-pied by a bowman at the ready. The peasants' scattered workshops and lean-tos lining the interior of the walls were now shuttered and being doused with water by columns of pail-pitching serfs desperate to prepare for the worst. Columns of light-armed cavalry were assem-bling by the gate while the half-dressed knights of Lord Gostanzo were busy cursing vile oaths at their squires and armor bearers.

A blonde soldier spotted the confused fair-haired com-pany and ran to them.

"You there, *Padre*," he called to Pieter as he approached. "Germans, *ja*?"

Pieter nodded.

He stormed toward Wil and fixed his fiery gaze into the boy.

Wil's heart was pounding. "Put me on the wall, sire. I'll fight for this castle!"

The soldier was not impressed with the lad's zeal. He'd seen others with such fire, only to be extinguished at the first sight of blood. "Bind your tongue, whelp, afore I split it with my blade. You shall go where I put you." He turned toward Karl, Otto, Conrad, and Jon and said nothing. He strutted quickly past the girls and the other boys. "Listen carefully," he commanded. "We'll be attacked ... probably by prime but perhaps yet this late day. I want you older boys ... you there ..."

Wil nodded.

"And you with the red curls, and you there ... what is your name?"

"Conrad, sire."

"And those by you ..."

"I am Jon.

"I am Otto."

"I'd be Gunter."

"And I, Richard ... and m'brother, August."

"And I am Heinz."

"Heinz, you'd be the runt. You stand where you be. You, Conrad and you and you ... yes. Follow this sergeant. You others ... you, Otto, Gunter, and ... Richard, and you others ... go with that one. Now you little ones ... stay by these girls and follow this soldier."

The man turned toward his subordinate. "Take them to the infirmary and make ready."

Pieter cleared his throat.

"You, old man, find the chapel and stay out of harm's way. It seems you think of yourself a *padre*. Ha! You may pray for our souls."

Heinz, Frieda, Maria, Anna, Gertrude, and some others were instantly driven across the busy courtyard and chased up a series of stone steps into the servants' apartments near the top of the wall. There they would be safe enough and would prepare to attend the wounded. Meanwhile, Karl, Wil, Jon, and Conrad were taken to the base of the wall near the gate they had recently entered and were ordered to stand by a tangled heap of ropes, pulleys, and baskets. A new soldier glared at them and began snapping orders.

Wil raised his hand. "We ... we do not speak your language. We do not understand you."

The man grumbled an oath in frustration.

"I speak your tongue, sergeant," interrupted Pieter who had followed close behind. "What are your commands?"

"*Vecchio*, tell these boys to stand here ... at the base of this wall and to load these baskets with darts and arrows from these barrels and those that land within. Then they needs hoist them to the archers. The archers shall kick them down when empty, and when they land, by God, they had better fill them quickly!"

Pieter nodded and translated the soldier's orders. Karl listened but he could not help looking across the busy bailey to marvel at the order he discerned amidst what he had just moments before deemed sheer chaos. Peasant women were dropping bucket after bucket into the castle's deep wells and handing them methodically to their men who raced to and from the hand-brigades still soaking the thatched roofs of the fortress' interior.

The boy's eye then drifted to the steady stream of foot soldiers running stiffly to and from the armory at the far wall, arriving empty-handed but leaving well-armed and girded with heavy leather tunics or mail brigantines. His stomach began to flutter.

Wil nudged Karl. "See, there." He pointed to the intricate timber-and-stone battlement, which was built over the top of the gate tower. "And look at those huge cauldrons. I'm told they're filled with boiling fat and water to be dumped on anyone who would try to breech the gate."

Karl wiped the sweat from his face. "I'd rather not be here."

Wil laughed and jerked his trusted dagger from his belt. "Not be here? Y'dolt. 'Tis my call. You'd be but a boy, but when this is done I'll show my mettle! I'd not be the least bit surprised to be invited as a squire for yon knights. But you no needs to fear ... I'll be standing watch o'er you!"

The peals of the tower bells had echoed through the lord's lands and clusters of delinquent peasants were now hurrying toward the safety of the castle walls, urging their oxen and horses forward with familiar desperation. For them there was no option but to race to safety, for should they linger any longer in their fields they would tempt the bloodlust of the castle's foe, and if they failed to reach the gate before it was locked they would be abandoned to certain death.

The interior of the fortress soon settled into a restless calm. The soldiers on the wall stood at their stations, composed and steady, but worry was written upon their faces. Only the cries of infants, the barks of a few dogs, and the stern commands of officers making final preparations for battle broke the silence.

Pieter ambled toward an older soldier who had taken a guard's position by the open gate. He closed his eyes to recall what Italian he could and then spoke. "*Gentiluomo* ... what is the war about?"

The guard stared back from beneath the curled rim of his helmet and shrugged slightly. "My master's family has been at war with the Visconti family for all of my lifetime and some time before."

"Your master's name?" asked Pieter.

The guard looked surprised. "You stand here in his castle and know not his name? He is *Signore* Gostanzo of the family of Verdi, son of Augustino."

"And, brave soldier, by what are you called?"

"I am Sebastiani of Preglia and am not particularly brave. And who might you be, unfortunate pilgrim?"

"I am Pieter and am not particularly unfortunate. My fellow travelers are crusaders en route to Genoa."

"*Si.* We have seen them pour out of the mountains. My master pities their plight and has sent many away with food and good wishes."

Sebastiani looked at Wil and Karl mischievously. A twinkle in his eyes softened his face. "Perchance you boys might even live to reach your destination." He smiled, twisted the corners of his brown mustache, and adjusted the wide belt that girted his mail hauberk. Observing Wil's fascination with his sword, halberd, and leather-clad wooden shield, the soldier added, "Perhaps someday, lad, you shall be so armed."

Pieter translated for the eager boys. Wil beamed. "Indeed sir, I'll be a knight in the service of our emperor!"

Sebastiani threw his head back and laughed. "*Si.* That is quite a dream!" he roared. "Quite a dream indeed."

Pieter returned to the subject of his own interest. "So, Sebastiani, why are you at war?"

"Ah, we've been at war for decades ... but our present troubles began about a fortnight ago. One of our villages was attacked by the Visconti for no cause. My lord sent a troop of footmen and nearly an entire company of armored cavalry to avenge our honor. Alas, it would seem we are not avenged, but instead are in retreat! Perhaps it was a trap." He shook his head. "This war has not gone well for us for many years."

Pieter looked through the gate into the valley beyond. "I see no sign of anything."

"You soon shall, my friend. As in times past a column of exhausted, frightened footmen will soon be seen stumbling toward us followed by a company of battle-weary knights protecting them from the rear. Close behind will come a huge army of shrieking Visconti and perhaps their devilish mercenaries, slaughtering every poor soul who lags."

Pieter translated to the curious boys.

"Then the castle is attacked?" asked Karl.

"We can never be certain," replied Sebastiani.

"But why are these families at war at all?" Pieter wondered.

The soldier kicked at the dirt. "Now there's the riddle of my life. Few know for sure. I've heard it told that a Visconti was murdered many years ago and a Verdi was blamed for the murder. The Verdi claimed innocence and have defended that claim for two generations. Now in my opinion ..." Suddenly, a trumpeter blew three short blasts from atop the keep. All voices muted and a rush of eyes flew to the walls to see what approached. It was as Sebastiani predicted. A confused mob of footmen were staggering and tripping desperately up the steep slope toward their castle followed by a badly battered company of mounted knights. But worse, the far distance now revealed a surging tide of horse and infantry in pursuit.

Before long, the exhausted footmen of Lord Gostanzo picked their way slowly through the stakes of the barbican and streamed toward the moat bridge. In a few moments they stumbled across the bridge, through the gate, and into the security of their castle where they collapsed in the dusty courtyard, whimpering and moaning and gasping for breath. Close behind them thundered a despairing army of bloodied knights who roared into the castle grounds trampling slow-footed, screaming peasants and tumbling from their panicked, rearing mounts.

Pieter and his boys pressed their backs close against the smooth stone walls to avoid danger. From there, they watched wide-eyed and confused. Once the last of Verdi's soldiers had safely entered the gates, the signal was given by the chief porter to secure the castle. Sebastiani immediately barked orders to his comrades, who then heaved hard on the bridge-wheels at each side of the entrance while he released the stays of the portcullis. As the draw-bridge arced upward, Sebastiani's iron-grilled gate slid downward, its clanging iron links pouring through their channels until the grate landed firmly on the ground below. Then the men pushed the huge oak doors of the interior gate closed and dropped three massive timbers into their locks. The castle was prepared for siege.

Chapter 19
SHAME

ook, there ... look!"

Over the courtyard's clamor could be heard a growing cheer. First a smattering of "hurrahs" and then a
few more until the whole castle joined together in a great
"hooray."

The lord of the castle, *Signore* Gostanzo Verdi, son of
Augustino, master of Domodossola and lands surrounding, had emerged from his quarters in the eastern wall and
stood under the evening sky garbed in full battle attire. He
waved an impatient hand to his cheering vassals and
stormed to the center of the bailey where the captain of his
knights awaited.

Though they could not hear the conversation, the boys
and Pieter clearly understood the *signore's* displeasure as
they watched him pound the disgraced officer across his
chest and knock him to the ground. Defeat was not to the
man's liking, for it cost him both coffers of silver and
immeasurable quantities of pride.

Yet, despite the lord's unmastered rage, the young crusaders thought him to be a most magnificent sight. He wore
a well-crafted mail surcoat that fell to his knees and was
covered by a sleeveless, yellow robe. His waist was girded
with a wide leather belt that held a longsword. His arms
were covered with metal defenses hinged at the elbows, and
his head was capped with a mail hood that draped below
his neck from under a large, round, wide-brimmed helmet.

From his broad shoulders flowed a long, red, green-lined cape with a black crucifix in its center. He tread about the courtyard in knee-high leather boots that bore well the authority confirmed by the passion of his close-set, dark eyes. Indeed, such a confident ardor only a nobleman could muster. His strong, protruding jaw and thick, black mustache gave an extra measure of sway to his snarling mouth as he now issued commands to each company sent to reinforce the walls.

Wil held his ears from the piercing blasts of the trumpets above and felt his heart pound and hot blood surge to his neck. A battle was indeed at hand. Karl, Conrad, and Jon were less enthused than their commander and fidgeted where they stood as they watched the archers above ready their crossbows.

All eyes and ears now strained for the sight and sounds of the enemy. Perhaps, hoped most, the Visconti had turned homeward after all, content for what blood they had already shed. But, alas, hearts sank as the chilling sounds of trumpets and drums heralded the approaching army's intent.

Soldiers shifted uneasily at their stations, their jaws set, their bodies perspiring. The earth itself began to vibrate from the fearsome hooves of the enemy's heavy cavalry. A massed horde rose toward the castle from the mountain's base like the raging floodwaters of an irresistible March thaw.

Unable to simply listen, the boys immediately scampered up the wooden steps alongside the tower and crowded before the thin gap of an archer's loophole. Karl gasped as he surveyed the army surging toward them. In the fore, a mass of mail-heavy knights had just halted and opened ranks for the advancing infantry. The boys' hearts pounded at the sounds of kettledrums, clanging armor, and tramping feet. Then a single trumpet blast halted the leading edge of the Visconti army on the slope of the mountain just beyond the angled points of the barbican and barely shy of the castle's archers.

Karl swallowed hard and rubbed his palms. Row upon

row of foot soldiers now aligned themselves in perfect order, shields in front, spears, axes, maces, and swords at their side. Behind them and farther down the slope pawed eager ranks of snorting stallions proudly bearing their straight-backed knights.

The only sounds within the fortress were the hushed prayers and blessings offered by the priests moving stoically among the warriors. But such murmurings only increased the terror of impending doom and pronounced certainty on the ruin to come. Beads of sweat rolled down Karl's cheeks and Pieter's temples throbbed. But Wil flushed with the exhilaration of a fool's fantasy. Though he had not forgotten the image of the bloody battlefield of not so very long ago, his mind now filled with visions of his own vainglory.

The dreadful still was broken by a thud on a single Visconti drum, followed by another and another. The footmen began banging on their wooden shields louder and louder and then began to chant: "*Morte, morte ... morte, morte!*" Karl covered his ears and squeezed his eyes shut to dam the tears of fear welling within. It seemed to all that the very walls themselves would soon collapse like Jericho of old.

Sebastiani trotted to Pieter and instructed him in a dry tone. "Tell the red-haired one that the battle will happen at dawn. They try to scare us with their big mouths. We've readied ourselves quicker than they imagined and they'll not come at night; we beat them in a night attack some five years past by St. Michael's Day. They'll spend the darkness cutting down the barbican and making ready for a first-light advance. Besides, their priests did not yet bless them. Just find yourselves something to eat and sleep here at your station."

Karl uncovered his ears as the chanting and pounding grew less. He looked out his loophole and watched the enemy turn and march toward the valley below.

Wil sneered. "By truth, y'weak-kneed fool, you'd be hoping they went home. Say 'tis not so, Karl?" He plucked his dagger from his belt and thrust it at the lengthening shadows around him.

Pieter made good use of the delay and sought out the rest of his flock. He checked on the other older boys who had been assigned similar duty at the western wall. The old man was comforted for them since an attack from that side seemed unlikely. He then walked anxiously across the bailey now filling with peasant families stirring gruel and roasting venison and mutton. He climbed a steep set of stone steps rising to the quarters serving as an infirmary and found some of his crusaders huddled in a corner under the watchful eye of a kindly matron. "My name is Pieter," he offered. "I am the caretaker of these children."

The plump woman smiled. "My name is Gabriella. I cannot help but love these *bambini* as my very own." The *matrona* gave Anna a two-armed hug, nearly losing the girl's scrawny body in the cleft of her buxom breast. Anna squirmed free but smiled politely.

Pieter chuckled, content for having such an ally. "And you shall take care of them in the battle?"

"Like they are my own!" With that, she reached for Maria. "And this little dear also," she sighed. "I'll take extra good care of her."

Pieter looked around the torch-lit chamber. "I see you've wounded from the day's skirmish."

Gabriella pointed to the smoky room. "*Si.* We have most of the injured here. The worst are bedded in the priests' library, since it also holds those with fever."

Pieter was startled. "I have heard nothing of fever in this place."

"Ah, *si, si.* We have been smitten with pestilence for much of the summer ... my own dear Rosalba died in that very room at the Feast of Lammas." She wiped tears from her eyes. "And many, many others. In fact, it was said that the *signore* himself was sick, but perhaps that is not so. Some say it comes with you Germans ... but I think it not true."

"Gabriella, perhaps my children ought be of service elsewhere?"

A nearby guard overheard Pieter's comment. "Your children'll stay where we put 'em, or the miserable lot of you go over the wall. Humph. Were it for me to say, you'd all be burned for the scourge you've brought us!"

Gabriella stiffened. "You'd be wrong, Fernando. Fever struck a *padre* a fortnight past Pentecost, months *before* the *bambini.*

Pieter gathered his charges in a corner and spoke in a low voice. "Children, stay near to these wounded and far from the library. And this too," he cautioned. "When the battle begins on the morrow always ... *always* keep a roof over you wherever you are sent. Fail me not."

Frieda looked puzzled. Pieter took her by the shoulders and said sternly, "Do you hear me, *Mädchen?* Do not let the children out from under cover when the battle starts. Do you understand?"

Frieda nodded.

"And have any of you seen Benedetto?"

The children shook their heads.

"I think I saw him running past the well earlier," offered Anna. "But I've not seen him since."

෨

Wil was far too excited to sleep and his restless heart inclined him to abandon his station and explore the castle. He crossed the courtyard and entered the great hall built as part of the master's chambers against the castle wall. He slipped past a distracted guard and stared at the chamber's long wooden tables and huge fireplace lit only by the red light of its neglected hearth and a few failing torches. But the embers cast enough light for the boy to marvel at the rich tapestries and fringed banners hanging all about. He walked by the tables, dragging his fingers across their smooth oak planks, and he admired the armaments displayed on the stone walls. *What power, what wealth*, he thought.

Wil noticed a dark hallway at the end of the room. Tempted by its mystery, he ducked his head slightly and stepped into the black corridor with a pine-torch he snatched from the wall. He stepped quickly through, then up a short flight of steps. He emerged in a large, well-lit residence to face a surprised young lady. Wil froze, fumbling for an apology. "I ... uh, I ... am sorry to ..."

The girl composed herself quickly and scolded the intruder. "*Ma come si puo*? Begone at once or I'll have you half-hung and quartered!"

"I beg your leave. I ... I do not speak your language."

The girl put her hands on her hips and threw her head back in disdain. She paused, then answered Wil in his own tongue. "So what are you doing here, peasant boy?"

"I ... I think me to be lost."

"*Si*, you are. Do you know that you have intruded into the *signore's* personal quarters?"

Wil shook his head.

"That is exactly where you are, boy, and if I scream I'll have ten soldiers at my side before you take a single step. And at my word they'll split you in two where you stand." She folded her arms across her chest and scowled at the taut-faced crusader.

Wil fidgeted with his sleeves and tugged on the edges of his tunic. He took a deep breath but could not speak. *By the saints*, he thought, *she is surely the most beautiful woman I have ever seen.* Confused as he was by his predicament, the lad was equally unsettled by the feelings suddenly washing over him. He forced a sound from his throat. "Uh, m ... m'name is Wilhelm ... of Weyer. I am ... uh ... I am the captain of a company of crusaders traveling to Palestine." Hearing such words suddenly emboldened him and he stood erect and square-shouldered.

The girl stepped toward the lad and lifted a torch closer to his face. *Hmm. He is handsome ... in a way ... actually a beautiful face. And those fiery blue eyes and that golden hair.* But suppressing these feelings, she quickly regained her air of condescension. "I think you to look like no captain at all. I see but a peasant with a dagger in his poorman's belt."

Wil rankled at the barb. He bore a steely gaze into the girl's eyes. "I am Wilhelm of Weyer, captain of ..."

The girl's fists tightened. "*Si*. You needs begone."

Wil puffed his chest; he'd not be ordered about by a

spoiled wench. And besides, he was not so sure he was ready to leave her. "Tell me your name before I leave."

The girl's curiosity was piqued. She smiled faintly and, in so doing, Wil felt his anger give way to an unfamiliar weakness in his legs.

"My name, captain," she said flirtatiously, "is Lucia of the family of Verdi."

Wil was speechless. *Lucia! What a perfect name for such a rare beauty as this.* She was about his age, he imagined, with soft shoulders and shapely hips. He stole a quick glance at her young breasts but quickly raised his eyes to her long, brown hair which flowed gently along her smooth, olive-toned cheeks. His eyes finally rested on hers; large and brown, set evenly under dark, arching eyebrows and shining in the torchlight. Wil had stared longer than he knew and his thoughts were suddenly interrupted by Lucia's voice.

"Might you wish to escort me through the castle?"

Wil's heart fluttered and he nearly blurted out a hasty "Surely!" Instead he cleared his throat and shuffled awkwardly. "I ... I suppose I ought return to my post soon ... but I should be pleased to accept m'lady's offer."

Lucia smiled, but a more discerning lad might have seen the sneer behind the masquerade. "Follow me and let me show you what you wish." She extended her hand to the surprised boy who held it lightly. The touch of her soft skin sent his spirit soaring and he followed her deeper into the *signore's* residence. Lucia pointed indifferently to various rooms and chambers as she led Wil briskly through the apartment. "This is Papa's room." Wil stood in awe as he studied the tapestry-covered walls and finely crafted furniture of the lord's private parlor. "And that door leads to my mother's chamber ... and this to her maid-servant's ... and this to my father's secretary."

Lucia led Wil along another hollow corridor and down a musty stairway. They passed a clerk's office and the modest dormitory of the manor's priests. Lucia grinned. "Have you ever been to the top of a tower?"

"Not ... not in this castle."

"Yes, you've been to the top of many, no doubt, but I'll take you to this one. We can look out over the enemy."

They climbed up the spiraling, stone stairway, squeezing past annoyed guards until they reached the lookout. The tower square was crowded with restless soldiers yearning to sleep and anxious sentries staring at the torchlit Visconti camp below. Wil and Lucia were kept from a curious shape hidden by long bolts of cloth but took no note as they leaned over a parapet to see the shadowy army spread through the distant valley.

"It looks to be many soldiers," Wil commented.

"They have been here before," answered Lucia. "Are you afraid?"

"Me? Afraid? Never. I fear none."

Lucia nodded. "I have heard of the bravery of you men of the north. And when the attack begins, might I know that you will protect me?"

"Aye, my lady." Wil spun on his heels and faced her. "I'll stand and defend you and your family with m'very life!"

Lucia stood up on her toes and pecked Wil lightly on the cheek with wetted lips. The startled boy stepped back as the dark-haired girl spun around and scurried quickly down the steps. Wil followed, dumbfounded and melting. They raced across the bailey and charged up the stairs of another tower, facing the moonlit silhouette of the mountains rising above the western wall. "We keep watch here," Lucia panted. "But we are never attacked from this side. The mountain is too steep for an army, but my family had the moat dug all the way around nonetheless. This is most unusual, you know. My people are very clever."

The two held hands and scampered down the tower steps and across the courtyard once again. They climbed to the roof of the northeast tower, then ran down a flight of steps toward a wide doorway. Wil held his nose and Lucia laughed. "This latrine is an invention of my papa's father. He thought of it when the moat was being dug." The girl pushed open a creaking door. "He made it so everything drops to the moat below and is carried away. Isn't that a marvelous idea? No pots carried through the chambers."

Wil smiled halfheartedly and considered the dubious invention. He tried desperately to think of words to honor Lucia's grandfather. "Uh ... and the ... the ... refuse can sink to the bottom or be left to float about the moat ... but none needs shovel it. I—"

"Are you making mockery of *Nonno's* idea?"

"Nay. By my leave, I so swear it. It ... is ... uh ... an interesting idea to be sure."

"*Buono.* Now follow me."

Lucia led Wil further down the tower stairs and yanked open a heavy door. "And one more invention," giggled Lucia. "This one was my Uncle Lucio's. He said he learned of it from an old hospitaler in Damascus."

"I can only imagine," muttered Wil.

"In here is where we hang our finest clothing."

Wil squinted as a strong odor burned his eyes and nose.

"*Zio* Lucio said that the odors dropping from the latrine above would kill the lice on our clothing and it seems to work."

Wil shook his head. "Your Uncle Lucio ... uh ... surely he is as clever as your grandpapa." The boy imagined life in his hovel somehow less crude than life in a castle. Nevertheless, he gladly followed his hostess as she continued her tour through the intricate stronghold. They strolled past the treasury, the chapel, the smith's shop, and the granary. Wil peeked through the shutters of the busy bakery with particular interest and stared for a lingering moment in amazement before moving to the carpentry shop, the wheelwright's shop, and the infirmary.

"Captain Wil," Lucia offered with deceptive deference, "I am told that some of your ... soldiers are assigned to this dreadful place. Perhaps you might introduce me?"

Wil became suddenly uneasy. "I suppose so," he answered awkwardly. "But y'needs remember these are but my followers. I've little ..."

"By truth!" exclaimed Lucia. "You are the master and these your ... vassals."

The two approached the closed doorway when Lucia stopped and whined, "I do not enter such a place. It is where the servants sleep and the sick die. You must order out some of your ... soldiers ... and I'll have a look at them."

Wil hesitated. But with a little prodding from Lucia, he at last agreed and entered the smoky chamber.

Lucia waited outside, tapping her foot impatiently until a short column of sleepy crusaders obediently tramped through the doorway. Wil lined them up beneath a torch by the infirmary's outer wall and introduced each. "Lucia, these are some of my ... followers. This is Heinz, Anna, Maria, Gertrude ... here'd be Frieda ..."

"*Si, si.* I'll not be remembering names," clipped the girl. She stepped close to Frieda. Lucia's contemptuous gaze clashed immediately with the defiance flashing in the peasant's large, brown eyes. Suddenly, they were rivals. "Now, captain," Lucia said frostily, "this ... this ... wench is an unlikely beauty. She's the look of one who'd follow you most anywhere. Is she ... special to you?"

Frieda flushed but stood proud and tall. She lifted her chin and held it there, though it quivered slightly when she heard Wil murmur, "Nay, she is ... but a peasant girl, Lucia." The boy's eyes fell to the ground.

"Ah, I thought so. I can see you have the taste of more noble blood, is it not so?" Lucia took Wil by the arm and nestled her head into his shoulder as she smiled at Frieda.

Wil bit his lips and fidgeted with the edges of his tunic. He answered quietly, almost in a whisper, "Of course, Lucia, I ... I am of noble birth. My title was lost in a wager but I ... I am not as ... these." His voice trailed away.

"Swear it to me! I thought you not of the same blood as these," blurted Lucia. She walked slyly toward Maria and brushed the golden hair from the child's eyes. She turned and touched Wil's cheek. "I see some resemblance, but surely you'd not be of this sad lineage. Look at this poor thing. Such a pathetic claw where an arm was planned. So typical for a common peasant. But not you, my young lord; you are of different birth, sired by a mighty knight or wealthy lord, *si?*"

Wil quickly looked away from his sister's pained face and did not answer.

"Well, Wilhelm? Captain Wilhelm of … is it Weyer? You do bear some similarity. Please tell me this pitiful mutation shares no relation to you."

Wil stared into Lucia's beautiful face and slowly turned his back on Maria. "Nay, Lucia. She … she is no blood of mine. I am of better blood …"

With the look of a victor, Lucia took Wil by the arm and pulled him close as she led him away. Before they rounded a corner, she cast a final, wicked smile over her shoulder at the hapless group of ragged crusaders.

Frieda stood stunned and speechless and looked helplessly at the others as she laid her hand gently on Maria's shoulder. The little girl stood bravely and tried so very hard to not cry as her faithful friend squeezed courage into her.

Wil was not unaware of his betrayal and he turned his head briefly to capture a glimpse of his sister. And when his eyes fell upon her standing in the comforting touch of fair Frieda he felt suddenly ill. He had never seen such weakness in himself before, nor such cruelty. The girl clinging to his side now repulsed him. The power and temptations of her vanity had exposed his own, and shamed him. She had summoned the demons which had been lurking all this time, unadmitted, deep within his heart … and they sickened him.

The two entered the courtyard and Wil stared at the sleeping peasants strewn in the shadows of the smoky torches. *Look at them. These are what I am … poor, helpless … hopeless*, he thought. *But I wager none so weak-willed, so foul-hearted, so wicked as I.*

Wil followed Lucia to the entrance of her apartment where she stopped and turned. He studied her carefully, scornfully. The shame was now more than he could bear and he turned to fury to ease its pain. His heart grew cold. He reached for the girl and pulled her tight against him as if the power of his embrace might restore his mastery. But she was shrewd and yielded with ease to rob him of what pleasure his vengeful grasp intended.

She hissed in his ear. "Farewell, peasant boy. You think too highly of yourself. Ha! Did you think I'd have some common whelp foul me?" She pushed herself away and cackled, "Beware the morrow, captain."

Then she slammed the door behind her.

ฆ

Pieter, Karl, Conrad, Jon, and Sebastiani squatted against the wall around the small campfire they had built on the ground of the bailey. Pieter had done his best to avoid the castle's clerics and was content to spend what he imagined as his last night with his boys. All were too nervous to sleep and Sebastiani was kind enough to entertain their questions.

"Pieter, ask him how the attack might be," said Karl.

Sebastiani twisted his mustache as Pieter posed the question. He shrugged. "Tell the boy, Pieter, firstly, that they *shall* attack ... there'd be no *if* in it. Secondly, tell him that the manner is never certain. They've come against us in many ways over years past. But I fear the morrow might be far worse than other times. They have hired *routiers*, those mercenary devils from the south." The man's face tightened. "With them, nothing is impossible. Those barbarians do their butchery for the highest bidder and they fight savagely. I swear they have no soul, though their cursed priests do cover them with smoke and water."

The boys looked at each other anxiously as Pieter translated.

"I'd wager them to launch rocks over the wall with their *trebuchets* ... perhaps even skins of flaming oil. But my fear is the Greek Fire that they hurled at us once before."

"Greek Fire?" Conrad blurted. "What ...?"

"Ah," interrupted Sebastiani. "Tell the lad, Pieter, that it is not of this earth. It is a ghoulish, sticky fire from the Pit. It cost us then our balconies and what came over the wall clung to many a good comrade. It sticks like flaming honey and even water struggles to douse it."

"I have heard of it," said Pieter. "An apothecary told me it is an ancient Grecian mix of pitch, sulphur, and quicklime."

"*Si?* No matter … we call it the fire of hell and, if you be the priest you claim, you'd better lift a special prayer."

The boys grew quiet as Pieter conveyed the soldier's words. Then Sebastiani continued. "One time, some by Lammas, they worked to drain the moat. By God they did get to the mud but at such a cost they had too few men to press the gate.

"And on another day, a winter's one if my mind yet works, they crossed the barbican in full light and drug a huge wooden bridge across the list and tilted it over the moat. They gave no heed to our archers and died by scores, but the fiends did well by it. By God I still see them charging across that bridge. But they failed at the portcullis. Ha! My uncle, *Zio* Alberto, was then the chief porter and would simply not allow them through his blessed grate! We showered them with a rain of bolts and shafts through the ironwork and poured boiling oil from the ramparts above their miserable heads. It was a glorious day. Poor *Zio*, however, met his Maker … though not before he'd seen the gate hold."

He laughed and adjusted his helmet. "That was a day to remember. Good Maria, Mother of God. I was sure that was the day of my burial. Oh, what a slaughter." Sebastiani sighed. "I see they have come with long ladders this time. They shall try to bridge the moat with them and then throw them against the walls."

He pointed to a companion's crossbow. "You know, old priest, your pope banished these between Christian warriors nearly a hundred years ago … or so we are told. Perhaps the lords only listen to the Holy *Padre* when it is profitable to do so."

A nearby soldier laughed. "Sebastiani, we'd be the lesser sinners … we use one-footers and they the two." A few of his comrades nodded and grumbled in agreement.

The soldier growled. "Ha. It matters little what the Church says. I'd use a two if I had one, and I surely intend to use this on the morrow."

"*Si*," groused another. "But look at these bolts we are issued. Every one is dulled and crooked. How many launches can they take? These have been fired so often they're bound to fly in a circle, not a line. I shot one on All Hallows and it missed my target and hit some bowman in the ear off to my left."

Sebastiani was accustomed to such complaints and waved them off with a casual pass of his hand. He turned to Pieter. "Tell your *ragazzi* this: If we hold the castle for two days ... or perhaps even one ... our allies, the Battifolle family, shall surely arrive to flank the enemy and they'll fall away. Then, after feasting, the *signore* shall seek vengeance, and when the winter fogs are gone our army shall strike back ... and so it shall always be."

The veteran yawned and repositioned his armor. The spellbound boys begged Pieter to coax more from the man and Sebastiani obliged. "I am certain that the *castellerie*—the fiefs of the knights lying all over these valleys—will be set afire this night. Most of the harvests are in store and the burning barns shall light the sky. No spoiled child you've ever heard could whine more pitifully than these knights by nones." Sebastiani laughed and lay down to rest.

As the soldier nestled his back against the faithful wall, Wil ambled across the courtyard and threw himself on the ground next to his brother. "Where have you been?" Karl asked.

"Just shut yer mouth and leave me sleep."

"I've no wish to shut m'mouth!"

Wil grabbed Karl by the throat and squeezed hard. "You'll do as I say, y—"

"Lads. Enough," ordered Pieter. "Now go to sleep. Tomorrow shall bring fighting enough."

Chapter 20
BATTLE AND BROKEN PRIDE

Just before dawn Pieter and his boys were awakened by a strange and sudden sense of urgency. And they were not alone, for though the new day's sun had not yet edged the eastern mountains, the castle was awake and bracing for what terrors it would most surely suffer.

Priests walked quietly along the rows of fidgeting footmen and climbed slowly up the long ladders to the ramparts, muttering their prayers and comforting the frightened amid the cries of waking infants and crows of roosting fowl.

The spotters in the towers had barely time to warn their comrades when balls of fire suddenly scorched through the pink morning sky and sailed over the walls, splashing onto the helpless courtyard below. Amid screams and oaths, trumpets and bells, the castle became as a living thing. The storm had begun.

"Water pails! More water! Here … form your lines here, you idiots! Move!" Hooded peasant men quickly yielded to the orders of their officers and raced to and fro in a scramble to douse the fires now bursting in all corners of the bailey. They passed one sloshing bucket after the other down long columns of grasping hands and threw them on flaming thatch and timber. Smoke filled the castle grounds.

Pieter and his boys watched open-mouthed as the long, fiery tails of the fireballs streaked overhead. Sebastiani heard his captain's command and wished Pieter a hasty,

"Godspeed." He ran several paces but stopped suddenly and raced back to Pieter. "Here, take this crossbow, *Padre*. The boys may not be yet men enough but I've a sense you've the stomach to pull the trigger. It is loaded with a good bolt but have a care ... I wish you and these boys to be standing when the day is done!" With that, Sebastiani turned and disappeared with a troop of his comrades into the battlements above.

The barrage of fire seemed endless. Ball after ball roared high over the walls like rushing winds, and they fell like large raindrops pelting the dust on a summer's day. The exhausted peasants worked valiantly to extinguish the flames with little regard for the danger plummeting toward them from above. And many fell prey to the fiery assault. One after another was caught by the sticky incendiary and many died screaming as they blackened in the merciless flames consuming them.

Wil tore his eyes away from the hellish scene and hid his face in an archer's peephole. Try as he might, however, he could not escape the terror now pulsing through his veins. At the edge of the fortress' list he saw six large catapults launching their Greek Fire. They seemed like living monsters to the lad, lustily heaving their long arms forward and grunting at each release. But Wil's mouth dried when he took notice of the thick infantry now crowding forward. They assembled in some order, though to Wil's eye they were but a horrible brown horde. Their heads and shoulders were protected by long mail hoods and their bodies covered with thick leather jerkins. They fell into their waving lines impatiently, frustrated by the restraint expected of them. He thought them to be like salivating wolves.

Suddenly, the boys felt the earth shake.

"What is that?" shrieked Jon.

"What do you see?" Karl screamed.

Wil said nothing but fell away from his loophole white-faced and drawn.

Karl flew to the hole. "Oh, dear Mother Maria! We'll all die this day."

Conrad pushed him aside to see for himself. The massed

Visconti footmen had begun their advance toward the castle walls, stamping their feet and beating their wooden shields. Behind them, mail-clad knights followed up the slope, their mounts snorting and straining in hopes of breaching the moat-bridge. To the rear advanced rows and rows of archers ordering themselves in proper position to launch their arrows and bolts against the parapeted defenders and those within.

But inside the castle a steady, calming voice suddenly rose over the din of the attacking host. "*Signore* Gostanzo!" exclaimed Conrad.

High on the southeast corner tower stood the lord of the castle, quieting his soldiers and laughing at his foes. His green-and-red cape fluttered lightly along his broad shoulders and the rising sun gleamed against his silver armor. With a defiant smile on his face, he raised an arm and signaled to a sergeant to remove a large tarp from a weapon mounted high on the tower. His soldiers cheered at the sight. "A *ballista!*" one bellowed.

The advancing infantry slowed slightly and glanced upward at the weapon staring down on them. It was a quick-loading catapult armed with buckets of rocks. In that brief moment of hesitation, *Signore* Gostanzo ordered the *ballista* to be sprung. With a loud snap the weapon released, sending a spreading arsenal of rock and of iron hurtling toward their marks. The center of the Visconti line immediately collapsed and backed away in confusion as dozens of men fell dead or wounded on the list. The castle defenders cheered wildly as the large cranks of the *ballista* reset another launching.

Undaunted, the Visconti commander abruptly regained control of his surprised infantry and ordered his soldiers forward again. And on they came, screaming and shrieking as wild demons about to ravage a dying soul.

"Wil, this just cannot be!" Conrad moaned.

Wil swallowed hard and set his jaw. "Nothing to fear, nothing at all. Now be a man!" he snapped.

Pieter was in the dirt, praying desperately for his flock while terror crept over his cold, sweating skin. He pulled himself to quaking feet and put a gentle hand on Conrad. "Good lad, stand easy."

"They're coming with ladders!" cried Karl. "Ladders! And the archers are loading; catapults, too!"

The second line of charging infantry had picked up long ladders lying at their feet and they now stormed to the edge of the moat under a hail of rock and arrow. Triple rows of Visconti archers in the rear quickly knelt as they readied to release more cover for the ladder companies. The fore row then launched a forest of arrows from their longbows over the ramparts and toward the bailey. The middle and far rows then followed with volleys of bolts from their crossbows aimed at the defenders in the balconies and atop the wall.

But the defenders answered well. Shaft and bolt now flew from the ramparts like the heavy rain of a summer torrent. And all the while the *ballista* sent its deadly deluge as quickly as its handlers could load and release its barrels of rock.

Wil and his comrades waited apprehensively for their baskets to be dropped for filling. "Here! Here's the first basket, Karl! Take it to the supply cart and fill it! Quickly!"

The boys scrambled to the armory's barrels and then all across the courtyard to collect enemy arrows and hoist them to the archers on the wall. "Quickly, Karl!" urged Wil. "Quickly load this basket. Faster, Conrad. Faster! Move!"

Pieter was scampering about helping this one, then that. He yelled to Wil, "Watch and listen for the rhythm of the arrows ... pay attention to the *rhythm*! Keep the boys against the wall until the rhythm is right. Send them after ... just *after* a volley lands." Pieter wrung his hands. "Oh, dear God ... Jon, Jon almost took one in the back. Wil, I said watch the rhythm!"

But as with all plans of men, Wil's would not be executed perfectly. Karl was sent in good time but tripped on his return. All froze as the boy stumbled wide-eyed toward his comrades at the wall's base. Suddenly the sky above filled with a blur of shafts arcing toward the courtyard—and defenseless Karl. Pieter closed his eyes.

Some glorious instinct in the boy quickly felled him to the ground and bundled him in a tight ball. And, though the deadly darts fell near, none as much as brushed the lad's garments! "Praise God!" shouted Pieter. "Praise His blessed name. Now up, boy, up!" The old man ran toward the relieved Karl and the two returned to the safety of the wall and the hearty welcome of the others.

Karl bent over to catch his breath for just a moment and a smile began to cross his face, when suddenly several bodies of soldiers above came crashing down around the group, landing with sickening, heavy thuds. Karl's smile disappeared and the boy's face whitened. He stepped over the crumpled corpse of one young soldier and stared at the bolt-end protruding from the man's helmet.

This was no time for reflection and Wil broke the pause. "Karl ... Conrad ... Jon ... more arrows. They're in need of us."

Conrad was shaking. "I ... I cannot move ... I ..."

Wil slapped him hard across his face as another body, then another, fell from the wall. "Y'must, Conrad!" barked Wil. "You must or more'll be landing." He grabbed the frightened boy by his hair and practically threw him into the courtyard toward a mass of arrows sticking in the dirt.

A foot sergeant raced past Karl and snatched him by the neck. He screamed in the lad's face, "*Bambino!* Stay in the middle and load that cart with incoming bolts ... no more hiding by this wall or I'll cut you myself! And you there," he yelled, pointing to Wil. "You stay in the center as well ... fill these baskets and stop hiding or, by God, I'll strike you down. You, black-haired boy. Stand by there and hoist these ropes."

The boys could not understand the soldier and raced for cover as the next volley was surely due. Pieter fell over a burnt corpse and in the nausea of that horrid moment failed to notice the next barrage of incoming arrows. When he heard their deadly rush it was too late. He rose to his feet and stood in quiet submission to the moment, like the lord's marble statue facing him just ten paces away. He closed his eyes and felt the air of the missiles brush him on all sides. The statue cracked in two but the priest was miraculously unharmed. He looked at the deadly spikes piercing the dirt around his feet and gulped a thank-you heavenward.

Arrows and bolts flew past prime, then past terce, and by sext the sun burned hot above the unyielding waves of infantry stubbornly assaulting the weary citadel. The list was littered with dead and the blood-red moat was now clogged with floating bodies. It seemed to some a bridge of corpses might be the Visconti's ghastly plan.

Inside, the exhausted serfs were doing their best to support the soldiers, but many, many, lay dead in the smoke-filled courtyard, pierced by falling arrows or burnt beyond all recognition by the incendiaries. While the young gathered arrows or hoisted fresh oil to the balconies above, old men carried the wounded to the infirmary where Gabriella and her girls worked feverishly.

"Gertrude!" cried Frieda. "Gertrude, help me hold this man." The two girls dutifully sprawled across a young soldier's heaving chest. The man's left arm had been crushed by a bolt from a Visconti crossbow and he was bleeding badly. The surgeon approached with his razor-edged broadax and severed the arm from the shoulder with one mighty stroke. As the heavy ax landed on the wooden table, Gertrude vomited. Frieda paled but did not retch until the surgeon seared the bloody stump with the flat of a heated sword.

The straw covering the infirmary's stone floor was now red and so sopped in congealing blood that walking was difficult. And with each new casualty blood spewed all the more, making it nearly impossible for Heinz to fetch clean straw quickly enough.

Along the room's dank walls, dozens now lay whimpering and moaning, many writhing in pain from their burns. The stench was often more than the children could bear, but Frieda, Maria, Anna, Gertrude, Heinz, and the rest faced the horror with such stout hearts and selfless compassion as would swell the chests of the angels surely standing near.

On the towers it had become clear that the Visconti strategy was not to penetrate the gate but rather to over-whelm the walls with a horde of infantry. And, once inside, the gates might then be seized and the bridge lowered, undamaged, for the horsemen. And so the enemy's infantry pressed up their ladders on all sides, dying by scores but surging ever closer to the fatigued battlements above them.

Pieter stayed close by Karl and Wil in the dangerous courtyard center, gathering fallen arrows and placing them in baskets which Jon and Conrad hoisted to the archers. Suddenly, shouts of panic from the lesser-manned western wall could be heard above the din. It had been breached!

The sight of brown jerkins leaping through the gapped ramparts seized Pieter's chest. He had seen this before: first one, then another, followed by whole companies rush-ing across the wall-walk massacring the defenders. *The western wall?* thought Pieter. *But how?*

Signore Gostanzo's knights rapidly assembled a formi-dable standing defense in the castle bailey and prepared a counter assault. As they were aligning their heavy-armored rows *Signore* Gostanzo ordered his north-wall archers to turn and fire into the brown mass growing atop the western battlements. It was as Pieter feared. At the same time, Gostanzo sent a company of marksmen to the top of the keep at the castle's center where the courtyard could be defended in all directions.

With neither hesitation nor confusion the veteran bow-men drew their strings and, on command, shot volley after volley into the surging mass of invaders now clambering over the wall. Scores fell, dropping like acorns in October. But on they came, nonetheless, pouring over the walls like a floodtide.

Signore Gostanzo raced to join his knights and led them in a furious charge across the courtyard toward the Vis-conti and their mercenaries now massing at the base of the far wall. He swung his huge mace high over his head and was the first to crash into the Visconti's opposing wave. He bashed and hammered a swath through the invaders, splitting heads with a single blow and pounding screaming men hard to the earth.

Inspired by the courage of their lord, the veteran knights fought ever harder, some bearing mighty broad-axes, others pikes or long swords or broad-billed halberds. They ploughed into their adversaries without mercy.

But above the bailey the enemy continued to press. More parapets were breached, some now on the south wall, providing reinforcements to those warring on the castle grounds. The fighting had so changed that Pieter and his boys were no longer able to retrieve missiles, and they huddled against the safety of a corner wall and simply gaped at the slaughter all around them. Bodies of both armies now rained from above, landing at their feet like large sacks of turnips. The crumpling sound of broken bone and smashed metal sickened Karl. "Pieter," he pleaded, "Pieter, please pray this ends!"

Suddenly, two enemy soldiers spotted the crusaders and charged toward them through a thick cloud of smoke. Pieter's sharp eyes caught them and old instincts surged within him. He snapped his crossbow to his shoulder, took quick aim and, without the slightest hesitation, pulled the trigger. One of the men staggered and clutched the bolt puncturing his throat before dropping dead to the ground. But the other kept coming, eyes fixed on Wil.

The boy stood frozen ... for just an instant; too frightened to think, too surprised to feel fear until terror finally rushed over him like the iced water of the Rhône. His bulging eyes blurred; his belly cramped; his limbs tingled. He watched helplessly as the soldier shrieked toward him until, at last, Wil lurched away as if to run. But his legs felt heavy and try as he might he could barely lift them. He took but a few slow steps before stumbling headlong over a broken wheel.

The attacker cackled a ghoulish laugh as he raised his blood-stained ax over the terrified lad. Piercing the air with a devilish cry, he swung with all his might.

Something within the boy suddenly quickened him,

however, and he deftly dodged the blade as he scrambled upright. His enraged foe pursued him, swinging wildly until Wil was backed against the heat of a burning cart and could move no more. He began to weep and begged for mercy. But this was no ordinary footman, no poor peasant pressed into the service of a greedy lord; this was a *routier* and he was about the business of dispatching souls. There would be no quarter.

Yet all the while Wil was not abandoned to his peril. Pieter, Karl, and the others were frantically trying to reload the old man's crossbow. "Oh, God, hurry! Pieter ... hurry!" Karl shouted.

In his haste Pieter's feeble fingers had dropped his bolt not once, not twice, but three times. A frantic, frustrated Karl plucked it from the dirt and jammed it in its channel again. "Pull the cord, all." Conrad and Karl strained to secure the bow's string into its lock ... a task often difficult for even the large forearms of veteran archers.

Meanwhile, the *routier* was delighting in the pleading eyes of his yellow-haired quarry and feigned a swipe at the trembling boy. Wil shrieked and fell backward, closer to the fire behind him. The man raised his ax once more.

Wil, however, suddenly rallied a bit of mettle from deep within, yanked his dagger from his belt, and pointed it timidly at his foe. And seeing its blade glisten ever so slightly in the afternoon sun, he felt suddenly safer—even a bit bold. His jaw clenched, his eyes cleared, and he managed a defiant glare at his amused foe.

The brutish mercenary curled a lip and squinted his eyes. Then, with the skill of a seasoned warrior, he swung a swift blow against the little blade, breaking it in two like a worthless trinket. Wil stared at the useless deer-haired handle clutched in his stinging hand and the last trace of courage drained away. As he collapsed to his knees, he stared up at the rising edge of the *routier's* axe and begged for his life.

But no sooner had the man's ax reached the top of its arc when he suddenly screamed and fell away, landing hard on the ground like a sack of milled wheat dropped from a wagon. Wil's jaw dropped as he saw Sebastiani pull a bloody halberd from his enemy's ribs.

Wil shuddered and gazed into the lifeless eyes of his would-be executioner as Karl raced toward him. "Wil, Wil, look at me! You'd be safe ... and alive!"

The crusaders retreated to the safety of a shadowy corner where Wil collapsed on the ground. Karl turned toward Pieter. "We've needs to reload this bow."

"Aye, lad. But I've no heart for more ... I was certain Wil was dead ... I was—"

"But 'tis not over yet ... we'd all be in danger. I've seen others of us by that wall ... Richard and—"

Conrad grabbed the bow. "*Ja*. Pull!"

The two boys planted their feet inside the arch of the wide bow and pulled hard, finally fastening the cord in its place. Karl grabbed it and set it against his shoulder. Conrad pointed to Sebastiani. "There he is; protect him."

Karl nodded and took aim at the Visconti charging toward the unsuspecting man.

"Shoot! Shoot!" yelled Conrad.

Karl began to shake. He closed his eyes.

"Shoot!" screamed Conrad.

Karl's eyes opened wide and he grit his teeth. The boy could barely gut a goose, and to kill a man was nearly beyond his heart's limit. But the lad had the pluck to pull the trigger and the spring released. It was a long shot for the best of archers and it veered harmlessly to one side, sticking into a wooden barrel. Karl groaned.

Good fortune was with Sebastiani, nevertheless, and his enemy was slain by another. The anxious boys cheered. Conrad grabbed the bow from Karl and ordered him to gather more bolts. In the meantime Pieter had composed himself and touched Wil's head. "Are you well, my son?"

Wil, white-faced and trembling, could not move.

"Are you injured?"

Wil would not speak. Pieter patted him gently on the shoulder and offered a comforting word. "The angels are near to us, lad, I am certain of it."

The battle raged. The Verdi army had retaken control of

the walls, but enough of the enemy was now within to put the gate at serious risk and the fighting in the bailey was fierce. Pieter looked desperately across the courtyard for any sign of his other crusaders but his eyes stopped upon seeing *Signore* Gostanzo locked in a desperate combat. The lord was straining to swing his heavy mace but was evidencing fatigue and his opponent was pressing the advantage with his pike.

Pieter moved quickly. "Stay close by m'back, boys," he ordered. Pieter felt the blood pulsing through his frail body. His eyes sharpened and his senses piqued to the danger all about him. He flew across the courtyard, deftly dodging combatants from all sides until he and his lads lunged for the cover of a short wall of barrels.

"What's this?" Karl panted.

Pieter pointed to the *signore,* who was now frantically fighting two and sometimes three foes. His cape was torn and his face, shield, and breastplate were splattered with the blood of many.

"He is tiring!" exclaimed Conrad.

"Aye, he needs help. His comrades are failing him."

Suddenly, the lord fell to one knee as the force of a sword against his shield drove him downward. He flung his weary mace toward his foe's knee, shattering it and dropping him instantly to the ground. But the force of the heavy weapon toppled Gostanzo forward, and he fell, facedown, into the bloodied dirt. A quick-eyed Visconti sprang.

Gostanzo was desperately trying to regain his feet, struggling against the weight his own armor. Pieter set his armed crossbow tight to his shoulder. He took sharp aim and pulled the trigger.

The crusaders held their breath as the bow sprang; a miss would surely be the death of all. But Pieter's bolt flew true and straight and drove square into the chest of the *routier,* who staggered and collapsed atop the lord's legs. *Signore* Gostanzo lunged forward with a start, unaware until that very moment of the danger just past. A squire pulled him to his feet. The lord shot a brief glance at his would-be killer and then joined eyes with old Pieter some thirty paces away. He saluted weakly and reentered the fray.

"Good shooting!" exclaimed Karl. "Well done, Pieter! Conrad, did you ever see such a shot?"

"Enough, boys. Off to the wall," Pieter directed. He was relieved to have hit his mark, yet his soul yearned for the peace of a hillside pasture. But duty required yet more of the man and in the widening shadow of the wall Pieter and his lads prepared for more bloodshed.

Pieter's boys set the bow over and over again as he picked away at the Visconti infantry one man at a time. But each time the warrior-priest released the spring he wiped tears from his eyes. "May God have mercy," he whispered.

The tide of battle was held at neap. The parapets were being secured at a terrible price and the castle's gate had yet to be breached, but the defenders were exhausted. For the next moments the fate of many teetered on the will of either side.

There was sudden alarm in the Visconti camp, however, and its trumpets sounded urgent commands. The battered infantry immediately began a hasty retreat away from the walls, across the list, and beyond the broken stakes of the barbican. The *routiers* that had successfully breached the wall were now abandoned and trapped inside. They dropped their weapons and raced for the ramparts in desperate hopes of leaping to safety in the moat below. They knew there would be no mercy—and their fears bore true.

"Look, there!" shouted a joyful Verdi soldier on the wall. "Battifolles! Battifolles!" Soon hoorays spread through the castle and bells pealed. The thundering hooves of the castle's allies were bearing down on the flank of the surprised Visconti army, sending it into a hasty, disorganized rout.

Karl was cheering from his loophole. "Look, Pieter!" he exclaimed. "Look! Look, Wil, Conrad! They're running!"

With a few grunts and heaves, creaks and rattles the castle gates were now flung open, the portcullis hauled up its channels, and the drawbridge lowered into position. *Signore* Gostanzo hastily mounted his white stallion and rallied his readied knights to charge across the moat. "On, my people! On with it!" the lord boomed. "This day is no quarter given—ride them down and send them back to *inferno.*"

Conrad, Jon, and Karl surged across the moat behind the horsemen with scores of sooted and bloodied, cheering peasants. But Wil remained seated in his corner and stared sullenly at his feet while Pieter set out to find the rest of his flock.

Those crusaders working in the infirmary were too busy to join the celebration. The groans and cries of the wounded and dying filled the place and none could walk without stumbling over a man or a part of one. Gabriella now ordered her charges into the bailey to tend the wounded where they lay.

Frieda was covered in layers of blood, some dried black, some jelled, and some freshly splashed in her face and hair. She looked sick and so very tired. Dark circles hung beneath her dull eyes and her cheeks were drawn and sallow.

Maria, Anna, Heinz, and the others fared no better. Each now staggered about the courtyard, exhausted, though relieved for the ending of the terrible day. Pieter found them with ease; their light-haired heads appearing as beacons midst the dark-haired crowd pressed all around them. The old man raced toward them each and embraced them one by one with tears streaming down his face. "*Ah, mein kind.* 'Tis so very, very good to hold you." He paused to swallow the lump filling his throat. "And have you seen the other boys?"

Frieda shook her head, wearily, "Not since early. I'd seen Wil with you and Otto's group went to the west wall."

Pieter hobbled hopefully toward the distant wall in search of his other crusaders. He milled fearfully about the evening's dim light and caught a glimpse of a cluster of his lads huddled along a collapsed, smoking storehouse. "Boys!" shouted Pieter as he ran to them. "You've lived a hard day ... but you have lived!"

"Not all," answered Otto sadly. "Look here."

A pain seized Pieter's heart as he beheld the lifeless bodies of three of his company. He kneeled by them and laid his hands gently on each head. "Good Gunter. You joined us in the mountains and did all that was ever asked of you. May God receive you as His worthy servant.

"And you, Richard and brother August ... the stout hearts of the Emmental. Ah, I did so hope to know you better. Forgive this pathetic old man his distractions and sleep well." Tears dripped from the priest's cheeks and he spread his arms to pray for their departed souls.

The busy serfs and castle soldiers paid little heed to the priest and the small band of foreign children slowly circling their fallen friends. Pieter had barely finished his prayer when the death-carts groaned close and the three were loaded for burial. All bade a pitiful farewell to their friends and then embraced one another. All that is, save Wil, who lingered brooding in the shadows. "There is more work to be done, it seems," moaned Pieter as he surveyed the wounded strewn all around them. The children nodded.

Gabriella approached and smiled as she set a shaking hand on the old man's shoulder. "The *bambini* are strong and good," she sighed. "May God's blessing be on them always."

As nightfall settled over the fortress, a new kind of horror filled the courtyard. The joyful cheers and songs of victory now yielded to the anguished cries of the wounded and dying from within the crowded infirmary and without. Smoking thatch and charred timbers still crackled and glowed red while exhausted peasants dragged more water from the wells.

Some past compline the Verdi soldiers completed their task of killing every enemy soldier found alive. Pitiful pleas for quarter had been dispassionately dispatched with axes and lances. The enemies' bodies were then dumped in carts, hauled across the bridge, and set ablaze to a blasphemous liturgy of oaths and curses.

But the bodies of the *castello's* defenders were solemnly

aligned at the base of the keep and stripped naked in the eerie torchlight. Before being carried to their freshly dug graves beyond the list, they were washed and shrouded in linens. Priests walked quietly among them, blessing each row and performing the rites of burial.

Signore Gostanzo returned late in the evening and led the column of his weary knights and the knights of his good cousin and loyal ally, *Signore* Fernando Batti-folle, over the drawbridge and into the bailey. "Well done, my good people," he cried weakly. The lord trot-ted wearily about the courtyard on his sweated mount, scanning his people in the torchlight. The day's victory was complete. "You have fought well and God shall bless you. *I* shall bless you. Two days off labor, two days of feasting."

"Two whole days?" muttered Pieter. "He gives them two days off and some bits of food ... for this?"

The children by his side smiled faintly, too worn to com-ment. Gabriella beckoned the girls with her finger and they quickly followed like little goslings scurrying to be close to their mother goose. "Here, my *bambini* ... rest here," she coaxed. "You have served so well; may the saints bless you."

The girls did not need to understand her words, for they had little doubt of her love. Maria nestled into some loose straw strewn in a nearby corner and huddled close to Anna. Gabriella covered them with a blanket. "Rest well, *carine mie.* May the angels always be close."

While the boys and Pieter spent the night dragging the dead to their graves, Wil retreated to an inner chamber of the castle and hid. For the first time in his life he found him-self on his knees crying out to God. "I denied my sister and I failed in battle. I have doubted Your presence, but I surely feel Your hatred. Withhold Your fist, I beg ..."

The lad squeezed hard against the flood of tears press-ing against his eyes. "I'd be far from the man I thought me to be. I denied m'own sister and a worthy friend for the want of a spoiled wench. And I fouled m'leggin's in the fight ... I ... I trembled ... I shook like a frightened woman."

His shame and disgrace curdled his retching innards more than the worst of spoiled meat had ever done. He accused himself over and over. *Slight of honor and weakhearted. Ach ... and in need of another to save me ... I am nothing as I thought ... nothing!* Wil fumbled for the dagger now gone from his belt, then clutched his knees and pulled them to his chest. He wept bitterly.

Suddenly the boy noticed a single candle coming toward him and he was still. He groaned as Lucia drew near, not failing to notice that she was clean and rested, not touched in any way by the savagery of the day.

"My little captain?" she sneered. "You are, indeed, of low breeding. In fact, by the look of you, I think you to be a coward as well." She tossed her head into the air as she turned and walked away. "I like strong men," she said, disappearing in the darkness. "But you, Wilhelm of Weyer ... you are a most pathetic thing."

Wil stared into the black corridor, broken and abandoned to his shame.

Chapter 21
A FEAST OF GRATITUDE

It was nearly dawn when Pieter and his beloved began to drift to sleep in the shadowed corners and dark recesses of the battered castle grounds. The old man slept well, saddened by the loss of three good lads but grateful for the safety of the others and content for having found Sebastiani in full health just hours before. He dreamed of gentler days and kinder nights until awakened at midday by the restrained nudge of a large, leather boot.

"You there, *Padre*," said a soldier. "Wake."

Pieter sat up slowly and pulled himself to his feet by his faithful staff. His joints ached and he groaned. "Yes, my son?"

"You, *gentiluomo*, are hereby invited to join our triumphant *Signori* for the first day's victory feast!"

Pieter rubbed his bleary eyes and squinted in the sunlight. "Eh?"

The young soldier became a bit impatient. "I said, sir, that you are invited to join our lord, *Signore* Gostanzo, to feast our victory, you and your ... young companions."

"A feast, you say?"

"*Si.*"

"Ah! Then a feast it shall be!" exclaimed Pieter. "Allow me to rouse my fellows and we'll join you." Pieter happily hobbled through the courtyard and gathered his crusaders one by one. "Hear me all! We're to eat and drink!"

"A feast! A feast!" soon sang a column of tattered pilgrims.

They paraded toward the infirmary to find more fellows, but once inside they winced at the stench. "By the saints!" groused Karl. "It stinks!" He turned to see Frieda and her company sleeping in a corner. "Come, come with us!" he cried.

Wil was found sleeping behind a barrel, and over his loud and bitter protest was finally persuaded into joining his comrades. He reluctantly walked in the rear of the procession and surveyed his friends, all splattered with blood and smudged with soot and grime. *What a filthy lot,* he thought, *but more deserving than I of a feast.*

As they approached the great hall of the lord's quarters, a guard halted them and ordered all to stand by the well. The company thought it a bit odd until a party of laughing peasant women suddenly charged toward them. Before any could run, the women took hold of each of the complaining children and escorted the boys to one side of the well and the girls to another. The *matrone* giggled as they stripped the howling children where they stood. They tossed the clothing to a brigade of fullers who carried off the grimy assortment of tunics and gowns to soapy caldrons. And, now that the naked crusaders were helpless to escape, the women stalked them with rough-spun rags, buckets of icy water, and blocks of lye soap! Then, with a zeal matched only by the Knights Templar at the gates of Jerusalem, the women set about the task of scrubbing their charges clean.

"Not so hard, Frau ... not so hard!" cried one brave crusader.

"Ouch! Easier, easier ... I'd not be your enemy!"

The women laughed over all protests and scrubbed all the harder for their victims' yelps. Pieter was delighted to see his flock so well tended and found a barrel in which he bathed his own crusted body and soiled robes. He had finally peeled and scoured the last of himself when he eyed a familiar face. "Ha, ha! Benedetto!" he cried. "Benedetto, where have you been, you little scoundrel?"

The tiny man was peeking out of a beer cask and, upon being found, reluctantly climbed out. He offered Pieter a timid smile and positioned his lute across his back.

Pieter wagged his finger. "I've wondered about you all these two days."

"I … I decided to fight this battle with my prayers," muttered the minstrel.

Pieter's face darkened. He hastily dressed himself and strode over to the man. "Is that so? Methinks perhaps you hid in *that* sanctuary all this while. Praying indeed!"

Benedetto stared sheepishly at the ground.

"I must confess, *Padre*, I am no warrior and, alas, I believe me to be something of a coward."

"And are you not ashamed?"

Benedetto shrugged indifferently.

Pieter shook his head. "Then I am sorry for you, minstrel. I am among the first to entreat mercy for frailty … God knows me to be oft feeble of heart … but to not ache … to not grieve such things … ah, there'd be a shame worthy of rebuke! I fear you needs take care to see what lies within your own—"

Suddenly the *signore* appeared in the entrance to the great hall and summoned his guests, pointing directly to Pieter. "This man," bellowed Gostanzo with outstretched arms. "This old *padre* … you are a priest, are you not?"

Pieter nodded.

"*Si.* All hear me. This *padre* did save my life!" Gostanzo embraced Pieter like a bear wrapping a fragile sapling. His dark eyes glistened and his face broadened with a huge smile. The lord then set one large arm around the embarrassed old man and escorted him into the waiting hall. "And you, *bambini.* Come as well … you are all welcome at my table!"

Escorted by the hall's ushers, the crusaders entered the cavernous hall and marveled. The floor had been covered with fresh straw sprinkled with summer flowers and sweet rushes. The damp, stone walls were covered with beautiful tapestries of trees and birds, angels and heavenly things. A large fireplace roared at the far end of long oak tables supporting heavy trays of fruits, venison, pork, and mutton. Considering the nature of the day gone before, it seemed nearly beyond belief that all could seem so very well with the world.

The children sat with bulging eyes and waited patiently for permission to eat. But the tables were not yet ready and stewards were rushing more trays from the ante-rooms. These were piled high with cheeses, turnips, onions, leeks, and fruits. Two manservants labored under the weight of one magnificent silver tray heaped to overflowing with red grapes from the fine vineyards of Liguria. Hand-carved tankards of ale and goblets of wine were passed among the knights and squires to raucous cheers and loud applause.

Signore Gostanzo stood to his feet and raised his hands over the audience. "Welcome, all. This is a sad day for those we have lost, but a joyous one as well. We have fought a good fight and saved our lands and our people. And more, more—I lift my cup to our faithful allies and loyal kin, the Battifolles."

The assembly stood to its feet and cheered *Signore* Battifolle and his knights. Then, after a two-handed gulp of his favorite red wine, Gostanzo raised his clay goblet once again. "Silence, all. Silence. You there, *Padre.*"

The hall hushed and all eyes turned toward Pieter. He offered a timid one-toothed grin and squirmed on his bench.

"*Padre,* come sit by my side."

Pieter grimaced but obediently left his children and went to the head table.

"Ha!" roared Gostanzo. "This old one *looks* so feeble and frail! But he cut down my enemy with a keen eye and a steady hand. To him I owe my very life." The lord lifted his cup toward Pieter. "You are welcome here always."

Pieter bowed humbly.

Padre Antonio, the Verdis's favored priest, then approached the center of the hall in his finest vestments and pronounced a prayer of thanksgiving and blessings on all gathered. The feast had begun.

Antonio had barely finished his "Amen" when the famished crusaders lunged at the food before them. They grabbed and tore at slabs of boiled bacon, salted pork, mutton, steaming venison, poultry, and roasted fish. They laughed and giggled amongst themselves, returning for portion upon portion; cherries and pears, apples and honeycomb ... ah, the true treasures of God's earth! What pleasure each enjoyed in the lick of a greasy finger or the gulp of stout beer! All that is, save Wil, who picked at his sparse, tin plate, despondent and wanting of all happiness.

Karl's voice cracked high above the din. "Oh, if only Georg were here!"

Jon laughed and tossed a pork bone to one of the dogs drooling by his side. "Georg would surely have stripped this table of all but the trays themselves."

"Oh, Georg," Karl sighed, "I do miss you so. Perhaps you are watching from above? I hope that would be true."

Gostanzo suddenly leapt from his chair and bellowed, "I am told we've a minstrel here. Mine was burned and I've need of music."

Benedetto froze.

"You there, little one. You've the look of a ballad-maker. Come close."

Benedetto stepped timidly toward the lord's table and bowed deeply.

"*Si, Signore,* I ... I am yours to command."

Gostanzo put his hands on his hips and peered at the musician.

"You are a toy of a man, are you not?"

"*Si,* my lord."

"But it is said you've a voice to stir the angels?"

"Some have so said, my lord."

"Hmm. This day past is filled with both sorrow and joy. I command both a sad song and a glad song."

"I ... I oft fail at remembering sad songs, *Signore.*"

"You would deny me this?" Gostanzo was agitated. "My heart is yet heavy and is need of a song of life's brevity, its vanity or—"

"I ... I have no songs of these, my lord."

Gostanzo frowned.

Benedetto began to perspire but suddenly brightened.

"Ah, *Signore* ... I do recall one little ballad that speaks on these matters."

Gostanzo sat down and closed his eyes, preparing his heart for the melancholy it sought. The great lord looked suddenly worn and troubled. He slouched in his beechwood throne and waved the minstrel to his table. "Here, come stand before us atop this plank ... and sing well, little toy ... sing well."

Benedetto cleared his voice and closed his eyes. He let his mind drift to the beloved dock he now wished he had never left and imagined he was sitting on its edge with his feet dangling over the cold Rhône on a hot summer day. He strummed a few chords and began:

> If I but a vapor be,
> Then let me ride the breeze
> In such a form that could be free
> To coil 'tween the trees.
>
> Or free to choose a better place
> And free to choose a form,
> Which drifts a steady, worthy pace
> And weathers well the storm.
> I would not choose a harbor fog
> Which grips the moaning masts,
> Nor would I hang o'er darkened bogs
> Where shadows seldom pass.
>
> I would not choose to join a cloud
> Though lofty seems its quest,
> For thunderheads are brash and loud
> And fickle are the rest.
>
> A coastal haze hides breaker's death
> And I would not be there,
> Nor would I be but heated breath
> Blown into colder air.
>
> Nor would I choose the moon-time smoke

That lurks about the night,
The hedge and thicket are its cloak
It scurries from the light.

If I but a vapor be
Then what sort ought I choose,
For vapors pass so rapidly
That time I cannot lose?

I think to choose the twilight mist
That drifts the pastureland
To waken with a dewy kiss
The tiny and the grand.

It nudges beaded bud and blade
And rolls in clover white,
It readies colors that are grayed
And waits with them for light.

Though vapors are but here and gone,
Yet something should it mean
To rise and meet the blaze of dawn
And fade in meadow green.

Benedetto opened his eyes and stared at his silent audience. *Signore* Gostanzo paused thoughtfully, opened his eyes, and began to clap. "Well done, little fellow," he said slowly. "Life *is* but a vapor … is it not, *Padre*? Well said, indeed. I wonder if I am the sort of vapor I should really rather be?"

Pieter finished his wine and winked kindly at Benedetto. He leaned over to the *Signore*. "Your wine, sire, is a joy to the palate. A bit of a bite and a most lively nose … methinks of the Refosco vine?"

"*Si, si!* How did you know this?"

"I have traveled some in my many days. But I do confess it a wonder that your cellar is home to a grape from Fruili!"

"Ha, ha! It travels well, but not as well as you!" Gostanzo's eyes danced.

"Nay, 'tis a delight, my lord, far better than the Piedmonts—no offense, of course."

"None taken! And you'd be right. Our Piedmonts are not to my liking. Battifole here swears by his Barbera vines but I say they'd be bitter and smelling of cherries. Nor do I enjoy the Nebbiolo wines of Lombardy; I find them to taste of tar and roses."

A goblet flew across the table and crashed at Gostanzo's plate. Battifolle bellowed. "You've no taste for wine *or* woman, y'old fool!"

Before Gostanzo could respond, Pieter changed the subject. "*Signore*, indulge me if I may: I am told that this war with the Visconti was begun over a false charge against your family many years past."

"*Si, si.*" Gostanzo slammed his fist on the table. "A false charge indeed! They will not listen to reason. For two generations we have pleaded our innocence in the murder of their count. We had nothing to gain from it. We have priests who have sworn before the cardinal that the Verdi family bears no blame, yet still they do not believe us. The bishop of our see went to Rome, and it was in vain. And so for two generations they have waged *vendetta* and have kept our people in poverty and our lands in frequent ruin. Ha! And by God, we have kept them in scarcity as well."

Signore Battifolle cried out from his seat. "And we have helped you!"

"Surely, good cousin; without you we would have been crushed."

Pieter pondered the lord's words for a moment. "Have you considered why they've denied good testimony?"

"No, and it plagues me all my days. I cannot grasp their blindness and have no other course than to war with them."

Pieter picked some pork fat from his beard and looked carefully at the *signore*. Unsolicited counsel was often seen as impertinence and the old man needed to choose his words with great care. "As the wise and discerning sovereign of this realm I am certain you have considered that one must open the heart before one can open the mind."

Gostanzo looked at Pieter with a blank stare. He set his forefinger against his pursed lips and gestured the priest continue. A hush fell over the room.

"There is an ancient saying in the northland that is most likely unfamiliar in these parts, for it is somewhat childlike and simple. We say: 'A man convinced against his will is of the same opinion still.'"

Gostanzo sat for a moment, tapping his fingers impatiently on the wooden table. "Yes, yes ... go on!"

"Ah, *ja* ... so ... I'll speak plainly of what my learned lord must surely already know. Behind every belief is a premise; behind every premise lies a desire. Decisions are more often made by the will than the mind. We choose what to believe from our *heart*, not from reason. If one wants to change a man's mind, one must first change his heart."

Gostanzo shuffled in his seat. Battifolle, ever keen and clever, leaned forward. "Are you suggesting the Visconti *want* to believe my cousins guilty of this murder?"

"We all believe as we want to believe. For the Visconti the alternative is perhaps more ... distasteful?"

Battifolle jumped to his feet and smashed a fist into his palm. "*Sì*. Gostanzo, *sì!* This old sage has it! What is it that you have always claimed to be the alternative; what have you always said is the truth?"

Gostanzo stood to his feet and raised his arms in the air. "This is so. I so swear the real murderers are the Malaspina family from the eastern edges of Liguria. They are strong and wealthy, allied with both Genoa and Milan and in league with the pope. Who would *dare* accuse them but me?

"Yes ... yes! If the Visconti were to believe the Malaspinas are to blame, their honor would demand *vendetta* against them. But they seek the same alliances and do not want to war against them. We are the easier mark—allied outside the cities' league and tied to the Piedmont."

Gostanzo paced behind his chair, running long fingers through his black hair. Battifolle slammed his hands on the table. "Now, old man, I see the game is to remove the Visconti's fear of the Malaspinas so that they might embrace the truth."

Pieter nodded.

Gostanzo beckoned his cousin and his counselors to circle close and gestured his other guests to return to their feasting. He pulled the old man to the center of the group and leaned close to him. "And how would one alter their fears?"

Pieter thought carefully. "Sire, you tell me the power of the Malaspinas lies in their alliance with both Milan and Genoa; a remarkable feat given that these cities are oft at war against each other and their hatred grows."

"Yes, yes, go on," muttered Gostanzo.

"Then what you must do is ally with one ... methinks Milan the better choice since the Malaspinas are Ligurians, as are the Genoese."

The *signore's* face tightened but he did not speak.

"Then you needs force a wedge between the Malaspinas and Milan ... some intrigue to cast a doubt on their loyalty. It strikes me plain that they walk in grave peril, being the friend of the other's enemy. Once—"

"Ha!" blurted Battifolle. "We've just the sly fox for a match as this: a cunning falconer and crafty diplomat from Torino. He is skilled in matters of alliance and has no love for the cursed Malaspinas."

Pieter continued. "A man as he must needs walk with eyes in his back and vinegar in his veins."

Battifolle winked.

"My lord," advised Pieter, "a final word: If you succeed in dividing the Malaspinas from Milan, the pope shall surely cool toward them, for he is in great need of the Milanese—especially as it is a key to the whole of the Lombard League of free cities. As your alliance with Milan tightens, the Church may heed your appeal for justice.

"The Visconti also need Milan and the league, Lombardians that they are. Two things shall happen: Firstly, in order to avoid suspicion, the Visconti will find it profitable to reconsider their accusation against the Verdi family. Secondly, as the Malaspinas are isolated from the Lombards and the Church, they shall be seen as weakened and vulnerable. No longer will the Visconti need you to blame. Instead they shall offer peace and surely appeal for justice from the papal courts against the Malaspinas."

Battifolle roared and smashed his fists on the table. "We'll be vindicated. Ha! Or, *Padre*, we might simply gather our new alliances and attack the Malaspinas. They've earned a good butchering. They have broken our trade routes, violated our lands, and not been tested for many years. The Genoese shall be suspicious of the past alliance with Milan. Without support they shall fall like ripe pears into our hands and then, by God, the Visconti shall fall on their knees and beg our pardon!"

The lord's rising voice hushed the hall and to those eavesdropping it seemed evident that the priest had inspired a new call-to-arms. The knights of both families stood to their feet and pounded their tankards on the tables. "War, war, war!" they chanted. *"Morte, morte, morte!"*

Pieter closed his eyes and sighed. *You fools*, he thought. *Always to the sword. You've learned little....*

Gostanzo stretched his arms wide as if to embrace the whole hall. *"Grazie*, brave knights. No man has led better warriors than I. Our course shall be discussed in council. *Padre*, you are as wise as your white hair would claim. Daughter, Lucia ... sit by my side. And, minstrel, sing for us a happy song and let the wine flow."

Benedetto was relieved for the better mood now charging the hall and he leapt atop the table once again. He tipped his pointed hat toward the *signore*. "Now, my lord, now, we sing!" The minstrel laughed and strummed his lute and pranced along the table singing:

> What heals the brokenhearted,
> What helps the weak and tired,
> What hallows sacred moments,
> And hastens good cheer?
>
> What brings both good and evil,
> What brags and boasts unfounded,

What buries serf and master,
And bolsters our fears?

What stains both frock and doublet,
What starts both smiles and quarrels,
What spills from cask or goblet,
And's better than beer?

He threw his head back and crooned:

'Tis something I must have much of!
'Tis nothing fair maids should run from!
'Tis chosen over treasures ...
'Tis wine ... bring some here!

The crowd cheered and clapped and bade him sing it again ... and again. Happy to please, the minstrel jumped from table to table, dodging good-natured jabs of mutton legs and flying grapes.

The revelers sang and danced late into the night. The rollicking knights chased each other over and under the tables like schoolboys, slipping and tripping their way through the well-picked bones and bread crusts underfoot. But soon their lively play and drunkenness turned more dangerous as they began swinging the flats of their swords at each other and lofting javelins across the chamber into the wooden columns behind the *signore*.

Pieter now wisely chose to escort his spellbound children out of the hall and into the safety of a distant corridor.

"But Pieter," protested Otto, "'tis fun!"

"Pieter, Pieter," begged Heinz, "can't we sta—"

"Just follow me," huffed the old man. "Just follow me."

The disappointed children finally settled against the edges of the shadowed corridor; Wil to the farthest edge. And, after a time of pouting and whining, most were soon laughing and sharing stories, belching and wrestling until sometime between midnight and lauds they began to doze in the torchlight ... safe, well fed, and ready for the morrow.

&

At prime Pieter wakened his groggy children and led them through the disheveled great hall, now filled with sleeping knights. They stepped carefully past growling dogs and then passed through the doors into the morning mists of the courtyard.

The bailey was well raked and swept and fit for a new day, and wagons were already arriving with thatch and lumber for the needed repairs. The spirits of the craftsmen seemed high, though the groans of the infirmed wounded restrained them from singing or whistling very loudly.

"Come, my lambs, 'tis time to march again. Good Wil must be ready to move us south."

The familiar voice of *Signore* Gostanzo suddenly broke through the early morning air. He peered down on them from his apartment balcony and rubbed his baggy eyes. "Farewell, brave pilgrims. God's mercy to you on your Holy Crusade."

The children turned and waved to the smiling lord. To be acknowledged by the simplest gesture of a lord was honor enough, but to be spoken to in that manner was inspiration! A very tired Sebastiani then appeared in the courtyard, pulling hard on a stubborn mule. The mule, in turn, labored under heavy baskets of bread and sacks of meats, fruits, and meals.

"My good friend, Pieter," Sebastiani grunted as he approached, "I bear gifts from my lord in gratitude for your valor and wisdom. And for you, my little minstrel, a gift of his finest wine."

Benedetto grinned from ear to ear as he gratefully received the wineskin. He bowed deeply. "Many thanks to your gracious lord from his most humble servant."

"Humble, indeed!" chuckled Sebastiani. "Children, unload this poor beast and God go with you."

Sebastiani embraced Pieter. "I wish you well, my friend."

"And I you."

"Where is the golden-haired lad? Wil is his name?"

"There. I fear he suffers much pain."

Sebastiani walked to Wil and looked carefully at him.

"Good morrow, lad," he said. "If you pardon my saying, you shall be a fine soldier."

Wil kicked at the ground. He'd be happier to be left alone.

"I have rarely seen such fire in the eyes," Sebastiani continued.

Wil looked up slowly as the Verdi warrior stepped closer.

"I am always fearful in battle, my brave friend. It is fear that has kept breath in me—both fear and my comrades. For I would never survive a single combat if not for the good eyes and quick hands of my fellows. No man fights the battle alone, *ragazzo*, not one."

Wil fidgeted uncomfortably and then looked curiously at Sebastiani. "I thought you to not speak our tongue."

"Oh," said he, "I never tell all. 'Tis another trick of an old soldier."

Wil smiled faintly and nodded as the man rubbed his dusty, blonde head and gave him a rough slap on the back. "Now, join your crusaders and take command. Let none quench the fire in your heart."

Wil seemed to gather spirit and rejoined his comrades, though careful to avoid the cold stares of Frieda and the hurting eyes of his little sister. It was a pain he had never felt before.

In a few brief moments, final farewells were exchanged. The old veteran and the old *padre* embraced. The children waved gratefully to *Signore* Gostanzo and then all stepped briskly through the gate and across the moat bridge toward the valley of the Toce River.

ॐ

The September morning was brisk, even chilly, but the sky was bright blue and the Italian sun felt warm in the cool air. The children enjoyed the beautiful green mountains that rose gently on either side of them as they descended through the river's valley. The crusaders marched quietly, contented for ample provisions and happy for a gracious welcome in the villages of Pieve and Vergonte. The further south they moved the more excited they became, for talk had turned toward the easy walk of the wide plain ahead and the wonder of the sea waiting some mere weeks away.

Karl was staring into the brilliant sky one afternoon when he suddenly remembered the riddle. "Pieter," he grumbled, "I've still no answer to your blasted riddle!"

Benedetto perked his ears. "I love riddles."

"Well, he's given me one I can't figure for the life of me!"

"Eh, Pieter?" coaxed Benedetto.

"Karl, shall we let him try?"

"Why not? I'll never answer it."

"Ha! Then both of you listen carefully," said Pieter as he bounced his staff onto the hard trail. "I'll offer the entire riddle, including the final two parts which you, Karl, have not yet heard. Now listen very carefully and consider the words in light of all that has been learned on this journey."

> To what sun-washed haven
> Must the dying daisy flee,
> And in what Wonderland abides
> The snow-laden holly tree?
> The songs of thrush and nightingale
> Are borne upon the breeze,
> But toward what Country do they drift
> While passing o'er the trees?
>
> To what merry hearthstone
> Speeds the twinkle of an eye,
> And where in solemn duty waits
> The grayness of the sky?
>
> A misty dewdrop sparkles well
> Upon a tender blade,
> But soon it melts to gleam again
> In which enchanted glade?
>
> Through what canyon walls resound
> And to what castle bound
> The whimpers of a frightened child
> Huddled on the ground?

"Now, pay attention, boy. These are the last two clues, and, I might add, my favorites!"

> Where can be the valley
> Where the fragrance of a rose
> Can linger centuries after
> It has bathed a maiden's nose?
>
> What hidden harbor greets the fleet
> Of stars which cross the night,
> And where do shadows gather
> After they have lost their light?

Karl scratched his head. "Now, this is truly the very end of it?"

"I swear."

Karl sighed. "I fear I still know nothing of the answer, but … it … it seems that it tells of a place … a special place. Like a magical place or …"

"A wonderful place!" blurted Benedetto.

"Ah, yes, a wonderful place indeed," said Pieter. "I should like nothing better than to gaze upon an eternal valley of flowers! And can you imagine a harbor with unnumbered moorings tethering the stars? Wonderful! But take heart; I have only recently begun to understand the answer myself! And when you finally discover the place, you shall surely be happy."

Benedetto yielded quickly. "This one is beyond my grasp. But my young friend shall get the better of it—I'd wager it."

ൠ

That night the company camped on the shores of the Toce River. It was a good-flowing river, neither wide nor narrow but strong and deep in parts. But without tools to build a proper raft, the crusaders would need to be content to fish and bathe in its cool water. They settled for the night around a warm fire and there enjoyed the bounty of *Signore* Gostanzo: long strips of salted venison, fresh crusts of wheat bread and honey, roasted mutton, venison, apples, and a hearty vegetable pottage.

After eating they lay upon beds of broken boughs while Benedetto sang them to peaceful sleep. Through the night, however, clouds gathered, and the pilgrims wakened to a light drizzle and a gray morning's sky. Wil yawned and rubbed his eyes as he stood to his feet and he twisted his newly stitched tunic into place. He retied his belt and groused a few commands as he supervised the morning's chores. Wil was still in command, but he led barren of the spirit he once had. No more did he feel the ardor of the self within. It was no longer reliable, and without a foundation of such familiarity he floundered. Instead of self-assured confidence swelling his chest, he writhed in secret anguish, tortured by the shame of his own heart. The lad was now trapped in that very hard place between the agony of repentance and the futility of denial. The truth was more than the boy could bear; yet his reasonable mind could not deny it. So, as is with all disappointment of the prideful, a heated wrath now brewed deep within: a fool's remedy for soul-pain. Wil's well-stoked cauldron rolled and bubbled with each imploring glance from Maria or every clipped word from Frieda. And a few acrid darts from a well-informed Karl simply fanned the blaze.

But the shamefaced lad was not alone in his misery. Though the gentle Maria had no anger in her little heart, she did feel pain. Her pain was not unlike her brother's, for it too was the agony of shame, though it differed in that it was a shame cast upon her by another. Her heart had been broken into a thousand sharpened shards and now lay scattered about, cutting and wounding the deepest places.

Karl, too, was afflicted, though that within him which suffered was not apparent to the boy. While moved, in part, by transgressions warranting just and proper indignation, his heart was puffed, in larger part, by the sinister pleasure of his inner claim to higher honor. His thoughts clung fast to Frieda's tale like a spinster's ear to vulgar gossip, each word confirming him as the better.

Wil's conspicuous weakness had sadly clouded Karl's mind's eye to his own vice and none, save Pieter, had the stuff to shield the lad from such a subtle folly. And so the boy's self-righteous anger grew and a self-assured fury took firm hold. *Oh, if I could but smash his pretty face ... were I bigger I'd break his arms and legs ... I'd pull out his tongue for what was said!* he mused. At last, Karl's festering rage could no longer be contained and he pushed Wil from the rear. "You needs answer for how you spoke of Maria and the others."

Spinning around, Wil barked, "Shut your mouth!"

"Nay! 'Tis bad enough you were a coward in battle, but you were a fool with that ... that wench as well. Maria cries each night and you've not the pluck to even—"

"Put a stopper in y'mouth else I'll smash it!"

The castle's combat had altered Karl's easy ways and he felt a different sort of charge now pulse through his veins. The boy said nothing but his eyes flashed and he lunged toward Wil savagely. He bounced his fist hard into his brother's face, knocking the surprised lad backward. Wil howled as blood poured out of his nostrils and rushed over his lips.

Pieter held Otto and Jon with his staff. "Leave them be," he whispered wisely. "Just leave them be."

Karl stepped toward his brother again. "I say you are a coward, and one who'd betray his own."

Wil seethed under the accusation. He knocked Karl to the ground with a quick punch on the chin. "And I say, shut your mouth or I swear to kill you where y'lay."

Karl dismissed the threat and answered defiantly, "You've not the pluck to kill—or the blade! Ha! I've seen you beg in fear."

Wil stood silently as Karl climbed stubbornly to his feet.

"I never thought you to be a coward," Karl pressed. "But you'd be afraid of more than combat and of more than a wench. You fear to face your own faults!"

Wil took a menacing step toward Karl. He glared impotently, then turned and stormed away. The company stood silently and drifted to the wayside until some order was restored. Various clusters gathered to rest while some lay flat to snatch a moment's sleep. Otto followed Pieter to a seat in thick grass and wiped his hands over his face, unburying a host of crust-caked freckles. He shook his head and whispered, "Oft it seems the whole world to be angry."

"*Ja*, my boy. The whole world *is* angry and 'tis wise to learn something of it." Pieter shook his head. "Lad, hear me. There are two kinds of anger. Learn to discern them and life goes a bit better. The first is the anger of God. We share in it when we are outraged at evildoing—our own or others'. It is ignited to defend the innocent; its target is the Evil One. It is a worthy kind of anger that many claim but few have.

"The second is what is common all around us. It is the rage of arrogance, the fruit of hard hearts defending their vanities in as many deceitful ways as the mind can conjure. That anger, good Otto, is the child of disappointment and the grandchild of pride. It is born of bondage and is the snare of Lucifer."

Chapter 22
THE LAKE OF TEARS

he rest of that gray day and the next, the children descended the valley toward *Lago Maggiore* and by dusk they made camp along the stony shores of the quiet lake near the town of Stresa. At dawn, Pieter, Karl, Otto, and the minstrel left the camp to go begging and returned in the afternoon with a fair grant of fish, local fruits, and an assortment of vegetables, cheeses, and breads. The spirits of their comrades were lifted ... though, to Pieter's skilled eye, numbers of them seemed sickly.

The crusaders ate quietly under a sky growing heavy and damp. The air along the lake smelled of fish and wet gravel. Benedetto pointed to a far shore. "Somewhere over there is a hermitage, I'm told. Seems some years before my birth a local merchant was spared a pestilence and endowed a chapel in a cliffside where he is now buried. Many tell of miracles and such."

The group stared at the far shore with mild interest, seeing little more than blue water against rolling green mountains. "Ah, *sì!*" the minstrel continued. "It is the chapel of Caterina del Sasso. Perhaps a miracle shall find us, too!"

Wil, still lost in his own melancholy, motioned for his pilgrims to form their column. He surveyed them carefully, agreeing with Pieter that several were showing signs of fever—including his little sister. "We'll follow the shore. Should be an easy stretch. Benedetto says the village of

Arona lies about three leagues south, so we'll make for it by nightfall."

The children nodded in obedience, though Pieter had grown evermore uneasy. He, too, was feeling poorly. "Might we find a night's stay in Stresa, lad? The folk seemed warm to us and the churches were charitable. Methinks it might be a help to the sick ones."

Wil hesitated. He looked deeply into a long column of imploring eyes but shook his head. "Three leagues are not so many. We've fallen far behind as it is."

So, with no more discussion, they began a slow march along the stony shores of *Lago Maggiore*. The day passed quickly, though, and to Wil's chagrin the march was rather pitiful. Darkness fell with the torchlights of Arona still a ways in the distance. "We simply cannot go on, lad," moaned Pieter. "See ... Anna and Gertrude are far behind. Frieda has carried Maria for the last hour. We've driftwood aplenty and food enough. 'Tis never good to enter a village at night anyway."

Wil growled and spat, disgusted with himself and those who now crowded around him. "So, have your rest. We camp here."

The sky was heavy and the air damp and misty. The lake lapped quietly along its narrow shore as evening fog crept low atop its dark waters. The weary company settled passively around a struggling campfire that laid curling smoke atop them. Indeed, some had been stricken with fever and now languished about the campsite visibly ill. The others spoke in hushed tones as they ate a stew of boiled fish and vegetables.

Since his return from Stresa, Pieter had kept an odd distance from the others and now sat against the narrow trunk of a leafy tree away from the fire. Frieda noticed the old man's change of habit and sought him out. "Pieter, are y'not feeling well?"

"I fear not, dear *Mädchen*, not well at all." Pieter had sensed a fever rising all through the day. His skin felt sore to the touch, his eyesight was slightly blurred, and a clammy sweat had broken across his brow. He had thought it best to remove himself from the children. "Ah,

but Frieda, I am in need of sleep and would beg your leave."
Frieda hesitated. She reached her hand toward the man's
face but he caught it. "Please, my dear, I would be so very
pleased if you would just leave me to rest."

The young maiden was a nurturer by nature. She
would obey her elder though her concern would hardly
be abandoned. She withdrew to the circle of her comrades but kept a secret watch so, later that evening, she
was quick to respond when the priest began to tremble
and perspire heavily. She called for others, and soon she
and Maria were bathing his brow. Finally, over the man's
feeble protestations, some of the boys carried him carefully to a leafy bed they had quickly made alongside the
campfire.

"Good *kinder* ... please keep away," entreated Pieter.
"Please, stay far away."

Wil and Karl quickly set aside their differences and both
leaned close to their old friend. "Have we no more herbs?"
asked Karl fearfully.

Pieter shook his head weakly. "Nay, lads. All were lost in
the flood; now y'must keep a distance from me."

Maria gave the man's words no heed. She offered him a
tender smile and snuggled against his shivering body.
"You've need of us and we love you."

Pieter struggled to sit and pushed her with what little
strength remained in his weak arms. "Ach, nay! My dear,
dear *Mädel.* Y'*must* stay away!" Exasperated, he began to
weep but his tears only drew his beloved crusaders closer.
"Please, I *beg* you all," he implored, "*please* keep distance.
I brought fever to another in my life; God have mercy on me
should I do the same again."

Benedetto gently lifted Maria away. "*Si, bambini.* Pieter
is right. You must keep far off."

But the children would not listen. They vowed to keep a
vigil through the night and circled close around the
fevered priest as the wet mists settled heavy on them all.

The hours passed slowly and each stout heart did its
very best to keep a faithful watch. But, alas, the flames
soon dwindled to red licks over charcoaled wood, the

clouded moon set behind unseen mountains, and, like the disciples at Gethsemane, the well-intended company fell fast asleep.

Pieter's fever broke into a robust sweat sometime in the night and by lauds he slowly opened his eyes. Dawn had not quite broken, but the dim light of a new day had stripped the blackness from the sky and Pieter whispered a prayer of thanksgiving. He wiped his damp brow and neck with the back of his robe's rough sleeve and looked about to find his young guardians sleeping in a ring around him. All, that is, save Wil, who had roused himself earlier to keep a better watch. Pieter turned a heavy eye toward the faithful lad and whispered weakly, "God bless you, dear boy. God bless you, indeed."

Wil shook his head and muttered, "God shall never bless me; for my deeds and for my heart, God's curse shall follow me forever."

Before Pieter could answer, a child's troublesome cough turned him to his side. The startled priest suddenly found himself staring into the flushed face of his beloved Maria who lay sweating in the early light, stirring uncomfortably and struggling for breath. Pieter's heart seized. Then Jon and Anna coughed and moaned close to Wil's fire. Pieter strained against the brawn of his sturdy staff and pulled himself to trembling legs. "Quickly, Wil, quickly!" he cried frantically. "Stoke the fire again and help me wrap these children in more blankets."

Karl was wakened by Pieter's voice and stumbled to his feet. Wil sent him to gather more wood, while he gently covered the sick with blankets. "Otto, waken!" Wil shouted. "All of you ... Frieda, Gertrude ... all ... now. We needs more blankets, more firewood, water and ... and a good broth—now!"

Pieter fell to his knees and opened his hands to the heavens. His face was pale and drawn from his night's battle, and his ravaged body could barely keep his own soul from flying away. But his consumption would never bar his heart's resolve and he engaged all his faculties in favor of his beloved lambs. He recited the Lord's Prayer with a cracking voice. *"Pater noster qui es in coelis, Sanctificetur nomen tuum, Adveniat regnum tuum...."*

Having begged the attention of the high places, the priest crawled to Anna's side and put his hands on her head. He wept a pleading prayer for God's mercy and His healing touch. He then leaned over Jon and begged again. "Oh Father!" he wailed. "Show us Thy grace!"

And though he loved all his children, Pieter's poor heart burst within him when he came to Maria's side, for she had taken a special place near its very center. He stared speechlessly at her perspiring face, and the sight of her suffering so crushed him that he fell back onto his haunches and sobbed uncontrollably.

Maria suddenly opened her yellowed eyes and whispered an indiscernible word. The sound caught Pieter unawares and he moved close to the girl to listen more carefully. Maria reached her hand into the folds of her gown. She smiled faintly and offered Pieter a crumpled bunch of wildflowers she had picked in the evening past. "I ... I ... found these for you, Papa Pieter," she whispered. "I thought they would help you."

Speechless and chin trembling, Pieter stretched his hand slowly toward Maria and received the flowers from her as if he were being offered a favor from an angel. He fought his tears and offered her a quivering smile as he held the tiny blooms to his heaving breast. "Oh, my precious little one. It was love, indeed, that spared me this very night."

Red-eyed and tear-stained, Karl fell to his knees by Maria. "And love shall spare you, sister. God shall bless you with healing by the morrow, I ... I just know it." His voice trailed away.

Maria smiled weakly. Pieter lifted her sweating head onto a pillow of green leaves and carefully tucked a warm blanket under her chin. She fell to sleep as her faithful Papa Pieter groaned to the gates of Zion.

Pieter then turned to Anna and held her feeble hand in his. He stroked her white hair until she breathed more steadily. He moved to Jon, put his hands atop the boy's tangle of sweat-soaked hair, and prayed desperately for his healing as well.

And so through the day Pieter prayed and prayed, choosing to fast rather than feed his own desperate body. In the meantime, Benedetto scampered to Arona in search of a doctor or a willing monastery while Frieda and her helpers tended the sick with cool rags dipped in the clear waters of the lake. But by the end of the day three more crusaders were stricken and all had grown anxious.

Karl pulled Pieter aside, his voice full of desperation. "Pieter, God healed you. It was a miracle, was it not?"

Pieter collapsed on a rock by the water's edge. "Ah, my boy, 'tis not for me to know what is a miracle or what is a natural course. I only know that I am thankful for whatever our Father so ordained. But, indeed, it surely seems like a miracle."

"*Seems* like a miracle!" scolded Karl. "You'd be old and feeble, yet you passed through a devil's fever. God is able to do *all* things ... you've said. 'Tis *certain* He shall save Maria and others!"

"Dear lad," answered Pieter slowly, "God can do a miracle as and when He wishes; but I fear He does not wish it often. Hear this: Y'needs face this troubled world as it is ... not as you would hope it to be."

"But there *are* miracles," pressed Karl.

"Aye, boy, indeed there are. In some ways I'd say they're all around us. 'Tis a wise and faithful man who seeks them and who asks for them. But our task is to act on what is common and reasonably expected. Faith ought not *presume* on God."

Karl would not yield. "Nay, Pieter, methinks y—"

"Enough!" Pieter's fatigue and anxieties had sapped his patience. "Do not stand here and *demand* a miracle. Miracles are not ours for the taking. Our duty is to keep that fire burning and to keep our fellows comfortable and nourished. The rest we yield to the mysteries of an all-wise God. Now to work!"

While Karl and Pieter were dueling, Wil had moved slowly toward his sister and, as Frieda left Maria's side to check Jon, he slipped close to her. He took her frail hand in his own and squeezed it tenderly; he bathed her brow gently and tucked the blanket around her.

Maria opened her eyes and looked weakly at her brother. She fumbled under her blanket for a moment and retrieved a wilted, but yet beautiful, blue wildflower. "I picked this some days past and I am sorry for not giving it to you afore."

Wil fumbled for words but none would form. His eyes moistened and his throat tightened.

Maria offered her gift to him. "I love you, brother, I love you so much, and I am sorry for not telling you."

Wil took the little flower and stroked his sister's matted hair. "I ... I ...," he hesitated. "Thank you, Maria. I ..." He could not say what his heart yearned to say and he turned his face away. His mouth dried and his hands began to shake. The boy looked once more at the suffering little girl but his tongue failed him yet again. Unable to bear the agony of it, he bolted into the forest where he wept against the smooth bark of a broad-backed tree.

෨

The day passed slowly into night with no sign of Benedetto and the help he had hoped to find. The night then passed under the anxious eyes of a vigilant circle, and a new dawn brought little hope, except for Anna who was showing some signs of improvement. By late in the afternoon of this new day, the first of the fevered six died, and by nightfall two more slipped into their eternal rest. Jon and Maria had survived another day but both seemed doomed to join their hapless fellows now being washed under moonlight and readied for burial.

At dawn, Pieter gazed blankly about the campsite. A cloudless sky welcomed a rising sun that cast a glorious morning light across the shimmering lake. A warm, southerly breeze rustled through the trees and tiny waves lapped lightly along the beach. Pieter called for his flock to gather close and, as he was all too accustomed to doing, he prayed over the dead. As before, the children solemnly laid each of their friends in shallow graves and marked them with their little wooden crosses. Afterward, Wil ordered Otto and Conrad to the village to find either Benedetto or some other help.

Unable to imagine more losses, Pieter fell on his face in front of the two suffering children at terce, then sext, nones, vespers, and then by compline. The bells of nearby Arona marked the passing hours and at each ringing the old man groaned the same petition to the heavens: "*Tu es adjutor in tribulationsibus*, You are our help in trouble; *tu es vita et virtus*, You are life and goodness. Dear God of mercy, I beg of You spare these two."

As darkness fell once again on the shores of Lake Maggiore, Pieter was yet praying … muttering and moaning, wailing and sobbing until he had barely the strength to draw breath. Finally, he collapsed alongside his beloved Maria and fell into a troubled sleep.

Frieda faithfully attended both her restless patients through the terror hours of the night. She had watched the moon arc slowly to the horizon and went, once more, to Jon's side to bathe his brow. She loved the boy as a brother and gave of herself in his service without complaint. She reached toward his face to wipe away his hair when her fingers brushed along cold skin. A chill ran along her spine and she felt suddenly nauseous. Biting her lip she hurried to Pieter and shook him. "Pieter, Pieter!" she whispered frantically. "Methinks Jon to be … dead."

Pieter went straightaway to the lad and laid his ear to the boy's still chest. He groaned, then fell across the dear crusader and wept loudly.

The priest's sobs woke others and soon another circle ringed another stricken comrade. Too weak to help, Pieter watched as Wil and Karl rolled Jon's body into his blanket and carried him to the water's edge. Here, beneath the starry night's sky the young soldiers washed the lad's body. Numbed by their sorrow they found refuge in the memories of their fallen comrade.

Pieter raised his hands. "*Ego te absolvo ab omnibus censuris et peccatis in nomine Patris et Filii et Spiritus Sancti.*"

Wil ordered all hands to scoop another grave, knowing he could not put off what needed to be done any longer. Returning to Maria's side, he grasped her hand in his. He had rarely lifted a thought, let alone a word, to his Father above, but the lad now implored his Maker for mercy and pleaded for a healing touch. His prayers would, no doubt, have been mocked as awkward, unseemly mutterings to those trained in such matters, but they gushed sincerely from a heart softened by failure and loosened by love.

Maria had been well tended by Frieda and Karl, but Pieter now wisely gave Wil her charge and ordered all to sleep. With anxious glances and a few weary sighs the caregivers passed the fever rags once more to Wil and settled, however reluctantly, into their own blankets.

Again and again Wil tenderly bathed his sister's brow. His eyes did not grow heavy nor did the heat of the campfire tempt, for a single moment, the slightest drift toward sleep. While the others slept soundly, the lad sat by Maria's side alert and piqued like a devoted sentry keeping guard of the queen's bed.

At the first light of dawn, Benedetto came charging along the shore with a knot of black-robed monks and Otto and Conrad bearing litters. "Ho!" he cried. "Ho, Pieter!"

The camp roused immediately and stood amazed as the group arrived panting and gasping for breath. Pieter's weary face darkened and he scolded the minstrel. "Where have you been, y'sluggard!"

Benedetto shook his head. "Your pardon! I beg all for pardon! I was imprisoned in Arona. I snatched a honeycomb for our sick ones and was spotted by the provost."

A Benedictine stepped forward and bowed. "Father Pieter, I am Brother Chiovo of the cloister by Arona."

Pieter bowed and the two clasped hands. Something about the short monk's cheerful, round face and large belly put the old priest at ease. Under different conditions he imagined the man might be of the jolly sort.

"And these are Brothers Figlio, Palla, and Gaddo. I am the cloister's infirmer. Your little friend speaks truly. He was arrested the very afternoon he arrived and he has been crowing like a desperate cockbird since. Our monastery is not far from the town prison and we heard his pitiful cries night and day! Seems these two other fellows found your minstrel and managed to get the ear of our prior. Finally, the prior sent our priest to find out what was the cause and Benedetto pleaded his case. With a few assurances and the gift of a ballad, the *capo* released him to our care and here we are!"

The crusaders were spellbound and looked at the sheepish minstrel in astonishment. Pieter shook his head and immediately pointed to Maria. "Brother Chiovo, the little one is near death. We are desperate to save her."

The Benedictines lifted their black robes and scurried to the girl's side. Chiovo bent over and listened to Maria's shallow breathing. With a grave look he laid his hand on her forehead. He lifted her eyelids open with a thick, but gentle finger and probed beneath her jaw lightly. With kindly, but knowing eyes, he said, "Father Pieter, I cannot lie. I fear the little one is past hope."

The words stung Karl's cocked ears and he wept loudly. Wil paled and stepped backwards, only to join Karl by their sister's side. Awakened, Maria lifted herself up on her one good elbow. She wheezed and coughed, then struggled to lay her head against the breast of her oldest brother. Wil pulled her to himself and nestled her softly. He patted her and kissed her beaded brow. She managed a weak smiled. The lad's heart warmed and he stroked her golden hair while they joined eyes and hearts for a few precious moments. Then Maria trembled and fell limp.

"Oh, God above!" cried Wil. "Brother Chiovo ... Pieter! Come quickly!"

The churchmen fell to the girl's side, each bending low to listen. "She's yet breath!" exclaimed Pieter.

"*Sí!* And her heart still beats. We needs get her to the infirmary now!" Chiovo ordered two of his brethren to bring one of the litters. "Lift her gently!"

Wil and Karl pushed past the monks and raised Maria from her bed like they were bearing the most fragile treasure of all the earth. They then set her gingerly on the canvas litter and covered her with two blankets. They reached their hands for the handles.

"Nay, boys. My brothers shall carry her. Pieter, are your crusaders to follow?"

The priest stared at Wil, hope filling his imploring eyes.

Wil's face was fixed on Maria's failing form. He licked his dry lips and nodded.

❧

The crusaders raced behind the sprinting monks as Maria was borne up the sloped street leading to the monastery. Both the cloister and the town had grown over the years and both had prospered. The monastery had become a wealthy abbey, complete with manors scattered across the Piedmont. The abbot was currently in residence elsewhere and his absence proved to be of good fortune, for he had grown impatient with increasing numbers of oblates and dependents crowding his cloister. The more charitable prior, however, was pleased to offer what resources he could.

As the column entered the portal, Benedetto informed all that Maria would be served in the healing presence of relics. "The bones of Felinus and Gratian were brought here centuries ago."

The German children shrugged.

"They were Christian soldiers in the caesar's army and were martyred for their faith."

Pieter nodded hopefully. He turned to Karl who was now beaming with hope. "Perhaps, lad, perhaps."

Maria was taken to the baked-brick infirmary where she was given a comfortable straw bed alongside a number of coughing, wheezing monks. Chiovo immediately summoned the herbalist, and the two conferred with Pieter for nearly an hour while the children were fed a generous meal in the refectory.

At last, Pieter emerged, stone-faced and grim, and called for Wil and Karl. "My boys," he said slowly, "your sister lies near death. The brothers fear it shall be so, though none can know for certain. I believe them to be skilled, but the dear is so very weak and frail. 'Tis a miracle what's needed."

Abandoning all his demands, Karl's face sagged and he leaned into his brother, sobbing. Wil, too, could not hold the tears and he held Karl with arms limp from grief. Unable to bear another moment, Pieter embraced the two broken boys and the three wept together.

∾

Morning came and Maria's condition had worsened yet more. Wil and Karl had sat by her bed all the night with Pieter standing near. Brother Chiovo brought the girl a mild infusion and lifted her head gently from her pillow. "Drink, my dear. Just a little?"

Maria's eyes fluttered open, glancing about the ring of anxious faces. She obediently laid her lips on the thin rim of Chiovo's cup and sipped slowly. "The sea, you must ... go," she whispered faintly.

"Eh?" Wil leaned his ear close to her lips.

"To the sea, y'must go to the sea."

Wil repeated the girl's message to Karl and Pieter, then kissed Maria's brow. "We needs stay by you 'til you can join us."

Maria, nearly asleep again, wakened with a start. With a pleading voice she said again, "You *must* go, you must go to the sea." Her eyes rolled slightly and she settled. The others looked quietly at one another but before one spoke, the girl's eyes opened once more. "Karl, see the angels in the garden?"

Open-mouthed, the lad stared blankly as his sister went limp. Chiovo quickly laid an ear to her heart and sighed. Relieved, he turned to Pieter. "The little maiden sleeps now. I vow to serve her until God's will is made plain."

Pieter's eyes were swollen and he nodded faintly. "Our thanks, brother." He walked over to his precious lamb and knelt by her side. He stroked her hair and mumbled a groaning prayer, then peered into her sleeping face. The old man trembled with sorrow and he kissed the little girl's cheek.

The group removed themselves from the chamber and

joined their company waiting respectfully in the court-yard. All waited silently as Pieter asked Wil the question each dreaded. "So, do we wait and keep a death watch?"

The lad faltered, stunned by the sound of the words. Then, wishing for all the world to be by her side at the moment of her passing, Wil nodded.

But Karl disagreed, gently. "Brother, I would rather stay also. But you heard her tell us we needs go to the sea. I believe she truly wants us to go on. It was as if she had been given a vision.

"Besides, if we stay and keep a watch, she'll surely hurry her own death so we can press on! It is her way." He turned to Pieter. "By faith, what say you?"

The old man nodded, distracted by the girl's baffling message. "Why the sea?" he wondered. "Why not Jerusalem or Palestine ... and what of the garden?"

"But ... but we cannot just leave her here alone," Wil protested.

Karl looked around. The abbey seemed peaceful and filled with sweet smells. Flowers grew in every corner; the monks were caring. "She'd be so very happy here." The boy sighed and looked at the others.

Anna stepped forward bravely. "Wil, I should like to stay. I am her friend and am yet weak m'self."

But Pieter suddenly could not bear the thought of leaving Maria. "Wil," he begged, "can y'not just give up this journey? Can we not all rest in this good place and remain with her until she passes?"

Wil stared at Pieter, then his brother, and finally at Anna. "We will honor Maria's wish; we can do little here but frustrate her by our staying." Then, without saying another word, he walked back into the infirmary and knelt by his sister.

The lad stared at his sister for a long while. Memories of their lives melded into bittersweet until he pictured her face in the Verdi castle on that awful night. He whimpered and laid his cheek close to hers, and when her soft breath passed over his skin, he began to weep. He plunged his face into her body and rocked her tightly as tears poured from his eyes. "I am sorry, Maria," he sobbed. "I am so very, very sorry. Please forgive me! Oh, Maria, Maria, please forgive me. I ... I love you. I love you so very, very much."

The child breathed faintly. She was in a deep, peaceful sleep, her soul preparing for its flight to the angels. Her lips were slightly purpled, her cheeks no longer flushed. Her hair lay beneath her head like a pillow of spun gold.

Karl entered and knelt on her other side. He, too, buried his head against her. His red curls pressed against her, his face burrowed into the straw of her mattress. His mind flew to Weyer and the days by the Laubusbach. *She* must *live!* he thought. The lad prayed to every heavenly thing, to the name of every saint he knew, to the angels, to the Holy Virgin, the Christ, the Holy Spirit, and the Father of all. He raised up and ran his fingers along her withered arm. He took the cross of Georg that he had been carrying and set it by Maria's side. "Love, sister, love will heal you ... either here or in a better place." He then took her cross and lifted his face to his brother's. "Wil, we are right to go on," he stated flatly. "By faith, brother, let us be on our way believing that we shall someday find her happy and dancing under the sun."

It was enough. Wil nodded and the two bade Maria an affectionate farewell, each kissing her forehead. Then they emerged boldly into the sun-washed courtyard.

"We go!" announced Wil.

Pieter said nothing. He knew he could not abandon what was left of his valiant company, even for his most beloved little one. He walked to a quiet place away from all the others. There, in a garden rich with color, he sank to his knees and wailed, his worn heart butchered by a grief he had never known. His shrieks flew across the rooftops to the quiet lake below; they were like the anguished cries of Golgotha. Broken and shattered, Pieter fell facedown and mute upon the earth.

~

At midday the heavyhearted crusaders left Maria and a tearful Anna behind, and descended from Arona. They had traveled only a league southward, however, when they found themselves staring aimlessly across *Lago Maggiore* with little thought to their holy call. Karl looked wistfully at the wooden cross Maria had so faithfully carried and hoped they had made the right decision after all. He walked slowly to the priest, who was tossing pebbles aimlessly into the rippling water. "Pieter?"

The man wouldn't speak.

"I do not demand a miracle for Maria, but I do dare pray for one."

Pieter nodded.

The minstrel joined the pair and slowly gathered words to his lips. "*Padre*, my heart weighs heavy and I cannot bear this pain. These poor children ..." He wiped the tears from his eyes and pulled on his beard. "I think I have never felt such loss; to see their graves along the shore ..."

Pieter had no counsel left and was content to simply nod again. His spirit had been pressed beyond all resource.

Wil wandered far away from his comrades and stared at the green mountains that rose around the lake like well-muscled shoulders. The sky was a brilliant blue, the sun warm and the air sweet, but none were of comfort. *Indeed,* the lad pondered, *there is nary a rogue on this earth as wicked as I. I am not the man I thought m'self to be. I am cowardly, selfish, weak; I've no heart. How could I have hurt her so?* He slid his back against a tree trunk and sat in its cool shade. There his mind flew to images of his sister as an infant in his mother's arms, then playing happily by the bakery ovens, or tending sick geese and picking flowers. Melancholy overtook the lad once more. "Dear, dear Maria," he beseeched aloud. "Please, dear *schwester*, if y'can hear my words I beg y'hear this: I am so very, very sorry. Please forgive me."

Frieda brought Pieter a wedge of cheese and some salted fish, then left him to his thoughts. He sat silently on the lakeshore watching the sun slide ever farther west. At last he walked to the water's edge where he cupped a refreshing splash of water onto his face. Feeling revived, he then turned to survey his flock. *This shall not do*, he thought. *This shall not do at all.*

Pieter's voice turned all heads. "*Komm, meine kinder, komm.*" He extended his arms and waited as his flock drew near. He scanned their faces and smiled tenderly. "Where is Wil?" he asked. The children looked about and shrugged.

Gertrude pointed. "I thought I saw him climbing through those trees."

"Heinz," said Pieter, "fetch good Wil. Tell him we have a need of him."

Heinz sprinted across the beach and disappeared into a wooded hillside.

"And as for you, my beloved," Pieter continued, "we have bidden farewell to dear ones before. Poor Georg and Albert and Jost and Lukas and now all the Jons. Gunter, August, Richard, the others …"

"And my brother, Manfred," blurted Frieda.

"Ah, dear one," said Pieter, "yes, and our Manfred. But we cannot linger by this lake."

"Onward!" said Karl at once. "'Tis time."

"Aye!" echoed Otto. "They cannot have died for naught. They'd want it so."

Pieter sighed. "My lambs, it gets some easier to walk, but I would not have you deceived. Other hardships do remain." He looked at the sky and shook his head. "By m'measurement of the stars some nights past, I reckoned us clearly nearing the equinox. You needs know that the change in season shall bring a time of natural melancholy, especially in souls so hard-pressed as yours. The shortening hours call the humors of the body to produce black bile and our sadness may grow ever heavier.

"As a child I did love the crisp air of coming autumn and the fruits of harvest, but as I aged m'mind changed some. Now it seems ever more sad to me; a time when lightness and hope give way to shadows and thoughts of endings. It is the season when youth dies.…"

Pieter began to tear a little. "Ah, yes, these are but the ramblings of a weary, old man in the winter of his own life. The *Secretum Secretorum* tells us, 'From noonday till vespers, the melancholy humors are at their peak.' And I see by the sun that we are at midday."

Pieter turned to Benedetto, who was plucking aimlessly at his lute. "My good friend, do you know these lake parts very well?"

"I know something of them."

"I believe it fair to say we'd all rather float than march. Might y'know how we might sail or row along this shore?"

Benedetto nodded. "Indeed, and if you could sail to Sesto Calende you could then drift south on the Ticino— all the way to Pavia." He turned toward the water. "But, I ought tell you now, dear friends, I'll not be traveling with you any longer."

Karl was stunned. "You must! You'd be one of us now. And we need your songs."

"Dear lad," answered Benedetto quietly, "happy songs must come from a happy heart. I fear I would only sing what my heart now feels and there is not one happy ballad in it."

Wil emerged from his refuge in time to hear Benedetto's comments. "There is no heart heavier than mine own, minstrel. And I'll press it onward."

As Benedetto turned to face Wil, he saw a brokenness in the lad's eyes, a shattering of the soul that had left its mark plainly. The minstrel hesitated, wrestling within himself. "This much will I do," he offered. "I'll seek out some means to float this lake and then decide." With that, he turned and trotted toward the clay-clad rooftops of a small village in the distance.

Pieter realized the most important thing now was for each to be busy about some task. "Wil," he whispered, "I suggest we make camp for the night. The sky is clear, the air is warm, and I think a good meal and deep sleep will help heal us all."

Wil so directed his company. The *signore's* gifts of pots, knives, flints, and sundry tools had made each evening's camp more agreeable, and soon the children were hurrying about their duties.

Pieter had kept a keen eye on Wil and called him aside. "Might we speak for just a moment, lad?"

Wil shrugged.

"I see the pain in your face, and I feel it as well."

"You do not feel the pain I feel. You did not deny your own sister, nor are you a coward."

Pieter placed his hand on the lad's shoulder. "Wrong on each point, dear friend. I have failed more oft than most know. In my first battle I was so terrified that I hid on the ground as though I was slain! I have served my pride in secret ways ... ways that I dread to be exposed. And while I did not betray a sister's love, it is certain to me that had I a sister, I would not be above such a thing."

Wil did not respond.

"Can y'not recall St. Peter's denial of his Lord? And not only once, but thrice. And he was forgiven even that. The Father above loves you much, my dear son. You must believe that He forgives His children, always, and not because it is deserved. Methinks if forgiveness could be earned it might not be forgiveness at all, but rather a bartered reckoning of some sort.

"You are dearly loved, Wil; ne'er forget that. And you are not perfect; forget that neither. I am an old man and I oft imagine I would rather be right than be forgiven. Ah, but it has been good to see I am never 'right' ... always there is a quality of evil, of error, or pride that stains all I do. And, I deserve nothing! So, I've a need, Wil, a need of free forgiveness ... always."

Wil kept his eyes fastened on the ground. "I'll never understand a God who allows such things as I have seen, and I've little heart to reach a hand toward Him."

"*Ja.* I know that struggle well. I've no answer for you lad, for His ways are His own, and we've not been called to grasp them nor empowered to do so. He asks for our trust, and methinks He ordains some mystery so that we learn to trust Him as He is ... our Sovereign."

"But I don't want to trust Him!" blurted Wil. "I would rather work to trust m'self better."

The old man nodded and leaned hard on his staff. "I tell you this, boy: Self-reliance is a merciless tyrant. It blinds the eyes; its appetite is never quenched and it never rests.

I warn you, son: If you choose to trust yourself and not face your need, you shall surely spend your days in the grip of a dragon."

To Pieter's surprise and great joy, Wil's jaw loosened and his shoulders lowered. The spirit within the boy had been nudged ever so slightly and a change had begun. He nodded humbly as he walked away.

The old man drew a deep breath through pinching nostrils and turned his face to the gentle blue lake that rippled in the light breeze of the late afternoon. His mind drifted to his little Maria and how she used to snuggle against him in the cold mountain air. He squeezed his eyes tightly and imagined her happily snuggled in the lap of her precious Jesus. Pieter turned back toward camp and to the meal now steaming in the pots above crackling flames. It was then that Karl approached him. "I am troubled, Pieter," the boy said sadly.

Pieter beckoned the lad to his side. "Yes, my son?"

"I know of no sin that would have caused Maria's suffering." The boy ran his fingers through his curls and shook his head. "But I now know how I wounded Frieda and the yeoman."

Pieter drew a deep breath. He was weary and hungry and ready to speak of other things. But a shepherd's spirit ruled his heart. "I've a question for you. Could you not imagine sufferings to ever be a blessing for the obedient?"

Karl tossed some pebbles into the water and thought for a moment. "I cannot imagine it."

"Aye, 'tis a hard thing. Karl, consider this: Methinks we needs consider our present sufferings in a different way. You see, because God walked this sad earth, He understands how we feel. But because He is God He knows better what we need ... and what we need is to be drawn closer to Him. To come to that place, I fear, some of us are sometimes allowed to suffer sadness, others sickness, poverty, or pain ... or failings. He can turn all evil into good; He offers our trials as paths to His mercies."

Karl stared at the water. "Why must it be so?"

"Ha! Ha, ha! Good one, lad!" He wrapped an arm lovingly around the boy. "There's the riddle I shall *never* solve. I have no answer, boy, but hear me ... hear me, everyone: I no longer need one!"

Chapter 23
STARS OVER THE TICINO

Evening was falling when a voice echoed from some distance down the shoreline. Karl and Pieter stood to their feet with the others and peered through the twilight's mist. Racing toward them was Benedetto, shouting cheerily, "*Bambini! Bambini!* Pieter! Good news!"

The excited children scrambled toward him, Heinz dashing to the lead. Benedetto embraced his comrades as each met him, panting and laughing and clapping his hands. "God be praised!" He gasped for air. "God be praised."

"What is it?" asked Wil.

"I have found you transport from the village ahead. I've come by two barges that were rowed from Stresa by a crew that has run off. The merchantman's deputy is desperate to find another crew to take them to Pavia!"

Karl stepped forward. "Rowed?"

"*Si, si, ragazzo,*" Benedetto laughed. "Rowed. 'Tis less a task than walking. Each boat holds four oarsmen as well as the cargo of wool bales you must deliver. But there is room aplenty for all."

Karl complained. "Ha, minstrel. The small ones can row no boat, and—"

"Nay, but I surely can," said Pieter. "And we've enough strong arms for other oars. Aye! Benedetto can row with us. We'll make this do."

Benedetto stopped smiling. "I beg your leave, Pieter, but my journey ends here."

A chorus of objections rose from the shocked crusaders. "Nay, nay, you must needs stay ... you'd be one of us ... we want your songs!"

Frieda pleaded, "*Bitte, bitte*! You must come with us. We've come to love you, minstrel ... and you know these lands...."

Wil stepped toward him. "Listen to me. We need you."

Benedetto wrung his hands. "I have learned to love you all more than I can say. But since I have known you, I have lost much: I lost what little respect of myself I had at the siege. I lost my heart here, on these very shores by the graves of those tender ones. And, oh Maria, I feel my faith slipping. *Bambini, amici* ... the cost of this journey is far too great and I am but a poor man. I yearn for my dock where I can simply sing my happy ballads in peace and watch life pass me by."

"'Tis not a good choice at all," said Pieter bluntly. "Any man might hide in fear from time to time, but to choose a life of it—*ach.* What selfish cowardice!"

Benedetto was taken aback by the priest's rebuke. "I only wish to sit by the water and play my songs and give joy to travelers. I do not need all this ... this heartache."

"Then have your simpleton's life, small little man. Go! Hide on your miserable dock and deny the world what you've to offer."

"Why do you charge me like this, Pieter?" pleaded Benedetto. "I have served your cause, and at a cost. Cannot I leave in peace?"

Pieter shook his head but softened his tone. He cared greatly for the minstrel and took no pleasure in rebuking him. The children gathered close and waited quietly for Pieter's answer. "Dear Benedetto, if I prayed God's blessings on your wishes I would be no friend. Your own words accuse you, not mine, for they make it plain that your heart's desire is to hide from all that might give you pain. You are not seeking a time of respite, nor are you seeking a better place to serve others. Nay, you are fleeing."

The priest's frank words now drew anger from

Benedetto, a telling sign of arrows on the mark. "I am not hiding!" he declared. "I only seek a simpler life."

Pieter countered calmly. "I am not your judge, nor do I know the inward chambers of your heart. Forgive me if I am wrong, good friend, but I think it wise for you to consider your way."

Pieter paused and set his hand on the minstrel's shoulder. "Some have said simplicity is a higher way to live. I know, for I once withdrew to an order where I lived by simplicity as well. My life was governed by a simple threefold vow: poverty, chastity, and obedience. But it was for naught. We may seek to live simply but the world we are called to serve is a whirlwind of confusion."

Benedetto pulled away. "I was happy on my dock. I suffered no confusion until you and these entered my life. I wish to stay by my simple ways."

"Truly, truly, simplicity may bring joy. But *two* ways of simplicity exist. The first way understands that simple truths do govern the world—and this I admit readily. But this way leads us through the whirlwind first so that we may drink of the simple things more deeply on the far side of struggle.

"But I fear the simplicity *you* run to, Benedetto, is of the other sort—the simplicity of ignorance. The joy gleaned from this is but fleeting, for the press of life ever squeezes against it. Ignorance lives by blindness and blindness is ne'er a virtue. It shall suck you deeper into itself and, in time, leave you in a different sort of misery."

Benedetto was neither willing nor able to yield to Pieter's instruction, and it made him ill-at-ease and anxious. At last he replied, "I ... I am not able to live in the world as others, Pieter. I cannot bear the shame of myself. Look at me. I am little and foolish. I told you of the day the priest took me to the castle? I did not tell you all: It was not a kindly act—my father was offering me to the Verdi as a jester for their court. A jester!" The minstrel's chin quivered.

"I've no keen mind. I've little arms not suited to throw a fishnet or lift sheaves of wheat. Nay, I can do little else but hide in my music." Benedetto fought back the tears.

Compassion filled the hearts of all listening and many eyes watered. Pieter stood silently and groaned within himself. He did not regret his rebuke but wondered if he had pursued the little man with more earnestness than he ought. Perhaps, had he known of the Benedetto's past, his words might have taken a more kindly tack. He reminded himself that he was called to encourage, not destroy.

Pieter smiled kindly, stepped forward, and embraced the minstrel. "Ah, Benedetto, go as God gives you strength and consider my words as you can. Do whatever you must—we'll always love you."

The children circled about the tearful Benedetto and some held his hands. "At dawn," he choked. "I told the merchants you would meet them at the dock at dawn."

॰ॐ

Well before daybreak, Wil roused his crusaders for their short journey along the lake's western shore to the nearby fishing village. "Up, everyone. Up! We've need to move—quickly, quickly."

Like so many mornings before, the children were soon standing in a quiet column, yawning and rubbing faces, gnawing on a few bread crusts or chewing hard on strips of fish and smoked bacon. Once properly ordered, they slipped silently through the fog of predawn darkness, following the silvery edge of the lake until the first light of day grayed the sun-baked bricks of the unnamed village ahead. Benedetto led the children to the single wharf, where a grumbling clerk surveyed the little band. "What did you bring me, minstrel?" he growled.

"These children are strong and trustworthy."

The clerk pulled on the wide sash that girded his round belly and ran his fingers through his hair. "I am not sure of this. I'm on m'way to my office in Stresa and I think I might find a better crew there."

Benedetto whispered, "As I said, my friend, these children will row your master's transport all the way to Pavia for no payment other than the use of your boats."

The clerk looked at his would-be sailors warily. "I see a few strong lads, but what of the little ones?"

Benedetto pressed. "Ah, *signore*. The lake ... she is quiet and the Ticino is smooth. And I have traveled with these children down the rushing Rhône."

"I have never been on the Rhône."

"Never have you ridden the Rhône?"

"No."

"Ha! The Ticino and this flat lake of yours are like bathwater compared to it."

The clerk hesitated. "My master has a heavy hand. I'd not fare well if this idea goes amiss."

"Come, good fellow," urged the minstrel. "They are on Holy Crusade. They have the hand of God on them. Surely you can see that. They have been sheltered by the angels since they left their villages in the far north. They were protected over the great mountains, and you fear to give them charge of two pathetic barges? The angels are offering to guide your cargo at no charge ... and you hesitate?"

"What assurance do I have that they shall arrive safely? My master is waiting in Pavia to return them with barrels of broadcloth from Rome and ..."

"A fair question, *signore*, and I only offer this: I'll remain here as your guarantee until the safe return of your boats."

"And what would I do with a minstrel as a voucher?"

Benedetto shrugged. "I'll play in the common, and any money I earn is yours if the boats do not return in a fortnight. And, if they do, I keep my money and a humble ... percentage of your profits."

The clerk rocked on his feet and stared hard into Benedetto's twinkling eyes. "You are a cunning little fox," he grunted. "But a shilling is your commission and not a penny more."

The two clasped hands and, with a wave and a smile, Benedetto invited his fellows to board their flat-bottomed barges. In the center were neatly piled bales of fleece that had been carted through France and destined for spinning in Milan. At the bow and stern of each boat were wide, wooden benches stretching the width of the boat and placed just behind long oars waiting in their iron eyelets.

The children were ordered aboard and they clambered over and around the roped bales of English wool to seats assigned by Wil and Pieter. The small ones giggled as they set their hands on the thick, smooth oars. The clerk was impressed by the company's disciplined boarding and gave his final instructions to Pieter. "*Padre*, you shall find my master, Constantino, at his shop past the chandler's and alongside the sailmaker on the waterfront in Pavia. You will give him this sealed letter with the boats."

Pieter shook hands with the clerk and stepped toward Benedetto. "I'll miss you, my friend."

Benedetto nodded sadly.

"As shall I," added Wil.

"Good-bye, Benedetto," said Karl.

"God be with you," said Frieda.

Soon a chorus of farewell blessings resounded from the boats. Benedetto choked and smiled and waved at his young friends. He embraced Pieter and watched him climb to position. Dockmen loosed the heavy ropes which bound the crafts to their moorings and pushed the crusaders slowly into the quiet lake. The minstrel held his lute close to his breast and strummed a little tune as the children began to row.

> Fare thee well, my dearest friends.
>
> Fare thee well.
>
> God's breezes gently drift you toward
>
> > your farther shore.
>
> Fare thee well, my good friends.
>
> Fare thee well.
>
> May God's blessings be upon you evermore.
>
> Fare thee well ...

His voice trailed off across the lapping waves.

෨

Pieter did his best to restrain his tongue but his small-handed crew found pulling the oars a difficult and frustrating task. At first he thought it wise to tie the boats together, but this caused more chaos than the separate difficulties they encountered when untethered. At last, however, by midday the children somehow managed to develop a vague rhythm to their rowing, and each craft was kept close to the other. The boat piloted by Otto had finally ceased its endless circling and its annoyed captain now sighed in relief as his crew pulled in more balanced order. Wil had stopped cursing his anxious crew and now steered a course reasonably parallel to the shores of the lake. Others began to laugh at their frequent errors, particularly when their long oars fell short and splashed all aboard! Nevertheless, the crusaders' navy was surely advancing!

The hours passed and idle chatter dwindled. Finally Conrad grumbled, "I am not so sure that this be any easier than walking!"

Others agreed but Pieter chuckled. "Were we marching through the pines, you each would be complaining how much more pleasant it would be to float."

"Perhaps so," answered Otto, "but we're not just floating. My back is hurting, and m'hands are already bad blistered. I can't wait to sleep in Jerusalem with a handful of grapes!"

The other children began to whine. Pieter pointed to the fleecy cargo. "Rub your hands in the wool. Its oil will soften them."

As the children plunged their hands deep into the bales Wil recalled, "Benedetto said the best medicine for aching bodies is a simple song or a good memory."

The crusaders grew quiet and only the dip of their oars and the groaning of the lurching boats could be heard until Frieda laughed. "Remember how Friederich kept those coins? He was a sly fox, wasn't he?"

"And you, Karl," came a voice across the water. "I'll never forget as long as I live those shearings you gave us all." This time the boats rocked as the children roared at the picture in their minds. Karl felt his face heat but he couldn't help but laugh as well.

Frieda giggled. "And you, Pieter, I remember your spins atop the barrel in Dunkeldorf."

Gertrude squealed. "*Ja* ... and you kept falling down!"

"He looked like a top at the end of its spin or a drunken miller dancing atop a cask!"

"And I remember how you made fools of those men in Latin!" added Karl.

"Aye, Pieter," said Wil. "Remember the 'cabbage in the teeth'? And the—"

"Oh, *ja, ja* ... never y'mind," chortled Pieter. "I know the rest of that story."

Then Otto blurted, "And shall any forget Georg and his new tunic?"

There was a restrained ripple of laughter, but then silence.

"Oh, poor Georg," Gertrude sighed. "He was so very kind. If all the lords of the Empire could be as Georg, all the world would be a better place."

Voices muttered in agreement.

Pieter, sensing the drift of mood, asked Wil to allow a rest. With a mild cheer the oars were raised and the old man stood, arms stretched wide. "Children, we've much to be thankful for. And those we have left behind now rest easily in the arms of our Savior. We've good boats under us, some provisions yet left; fish aplenty swim below. We have come out of the cold mountains and are now in the warmth of the Italian sun."

Pieter's words were a soothing balm and as the mists of twilight began to lie upon the water, it was a more contented band that disembarked for a night's camp. Now well acquainted with their routines, the hand-sore pilgrims gathered firewood, rummaged through satchels, and stripped boughs for beds. A welcoming fire was soon crackling on the gravely shore and a stew was boiling in a tin pot.

"Tomorrow we ought find the river, *kinder*," said Pieter. "We'll pass by Sesto Calende and then we'll be near."

"And the currents will carry us?"

"Aye, sister. Hopefully!"

A circle of happy sighs answered and soon all were taking their turn at the ladles for a good night's meal. Wil finished his portion but began to fidget. He had been quiet for a long while and now drew a deep breath before addressing the company. "Listen … all." The boy was visibly nervous, even in the pale light of the small fire. "I … I've something I needs say." He cleared his throat and set his jaw.

"I must beg pardon from each of you for my words in the castle. Frieda, Gertrude, Heinz … you others. I … I ask your forgiveness for my foolishness. I am ashamed and shall always be." He sat down quickly as his shocked comrades stared, open-mouthed and dumbfounded. Pieter wisely, and for once, kept silent, though his heart swelled with joy.

Frieda stood and walked toward Wil while all watched breathlessly. The company braced itself for the tongue-lashing Wil deserved, but Frieda reached a tender hand toward the young man's shoulder and squeezed it lightly. "Wil," she said softly, "I do forgive you." She bent over and kissed his cheek.

Wil's lips trembled but were without speech. He gazed into Frieda's eyes, suddenly enchanted by a beauty he had never noticed. Her face, her form, the sound of her voice now drew him in new ways and he smiled happily.

❧

By mid-morning of the next day, all hands were weary and looking hopefully for some sign of the lake's end. At last Pieter stood in the bow of his boat and pointed to a spire in the south. He smiled like a child eyeing honey. "There, my lambs!" he pointed ahead. "As I promised—the source of our river!"

The relieved children spun in their seats and gawked over their shoulders. "At last, Pieter," complained one. "M'hands are bleeding and m'back is broke."

Before long the determined crusaders rowed their boats past Sesto Calende and entered the narrowing waters of the Ticino River. Pieter suddenly jumped to his feet. "Stop, children. Stop, I say." The old man teetered on his skinny legs and spread his arms to balance himself. "There—can y'not feel it?"

The children were quiet and looked at each other when

Conrad blurted, "Aye ... aye. I do ... I do! The river is pulling us a little."

Pieter laughed and the crusaders cheered wildly. They slammed their oars onto the floor of their boats and plunged their bleeding, swollen, blistered hands into the warm river. Pieter called to Wil, "I think it best we drift through the night and keep away from the shores. Benedetto told me of highwaymen."

Wil nodded and the two boats floated slowly southward in the river's subtle current. The day passed slowly and from time to time the children needed to row through deep waters. Eventually it was decided to tie the barges together so that both would drift the same currents. It proved to be a good idea and soon Pieter was busy navigating his crews into fast-flowing shallows.

Provisions were passed to and from the crafts as the current pulled the company through the night. As they drifted serenely beneath the stars Pieter recalled his years devoted to the study of astronomy. He strained to remember what he could and then announced, "Perhaps on the morrow I'll share of the story of the stars."

The mists carried a few grumbles to the old man's ears. "Nay, enough, Pieter. Can y'not bind yer tongue for once?"

"Or," he continued, "it might be prudent to simply enjoy the sight of them."

The children drifted all that night and into the next day before Wil ordered a brief disembarking and a midday pottage. Karl was sent with Heinz and Otto to trap some eel with a small net Otto had found and, before long, the children were enjoying a satisfying meal alongside a crackling fire.

Frieda noticed the changing landscape. "Look, all, 'tis different."

Indeed, the pilgrims had passed from mountains to plain and were surrounded on all sides by rich flatland and leafy forests of smaller trees. The river had become dotted with islands and its banks and bed covered with clean, white rock and gravel. Above them soared a hawk, and on the opposite bank, a fawn timidly drew a cool drink from the blue-green water. "This is a beautiful land," Frieda said. "It feels warm and easy."

"Aye, it does," agreed Gertrude. "Methinks the air to smell sweet; I like it here."

Pieter nodded. "The land is most certainly beautiful and so are many of its people, but some are not as gentle as the land they dwell upon. I recall a village some day's journey west of here called Novara. As a youth I passed through it in my soldiering and mine eyes do still see a beautiful, young wife of an ugly, terrible old man. I believe her name was Serena, though I am not certain of it. She was a rare beauty with long, braided hair and olive skin."

"What makes you think of her now?" asked Wil.

"Perhaps a return to these parts nudges m'mind some. But methinks it more the boats."

"The boats?"

"*Ja*, the boats. We had come upon the town's fish pond which had but two purposes: the holding of the lord's fish and a place for trials. I remember seeing poor Serena bound by the hands and loaded into a small boat with a priest and the bailiff. She begged loudly for mercy as a rope was wound around her waist—twice if I recall. She was then tossed into the pond to see if she might float or drown. She drowned, eventually, and the townsfolk said it was for the best; she was no witch after all."

The crusaders were quiet for a moment, then Heinz chimed, "M'village had no fishpond, but m'papa held *Mutti's* head in a rain barrel for scolding him in front of a squire."

Some snickered but Pieter shook his head sadly. "Nay, little fellow, women must needs know their proper place, but their place is a high place."

Frieda smiled.

After pausing to nap under the Italian sun, Wil ordered all back to the boats. With few grumbles, the pilgrims clambered aboard and shoved off to the safety of the river, where they floated and lightly rowed themselves south-ward as the moon arched over the Ticino.

Late in the night, Pieter lifted his eyes to the heavens

and smiled. The moon had nearly set and above him was a black canopy sprinkled with countless gemstones twinkling white and blue.

Karl saw him. "You once said, Pieter, that you would teach us of the stars."

"*Ja*, and what a fine night to do so."

"M'*Vati* taught me some of the stars," Otto said. "Methinks that one to be the brightest of all." He pointed a stubby finger carefully.

"Aye, lad, it seems to be. And what would be its name?"

"Uh ... ah ... *S* something?"

Frieda answered quickly. "Sirius. Sirius is the name!"

"Ha! Well done," praised Pieter. "Sirius indeed. The *signore* of the stars. I studied once the works of a man named Claudius Ptolemy who lived about a hundred years or so after our Lord's death. He lived in Egypt in the great city of Alexandria and he wrote some books called *The Twelve Books of Ptolemy* ... and others. My memory fails, I fear, but methinks one of the twelve to be called ... *The Almagest?*"

Pieter paused and scratched his head. "Well, no matter. The point is that the man charted the stars in his books. Of course, men had studied the stars for generations before old Claudius."

"Aye, to be sure!" remarked Karl. "I remember studying some of them at the abbey school." He grimaced as he strained to recall something worthy of a good impression. "Ah, yes; there is a story in the stars of a bowl and a virgin and—"

"And some tell stories of the ancient gods," added Wil knowingly. He cast a proud eye at Frieda.

"Well, yes, that would be true," answered Pieter. "But we have a greater understanding than the poor pagans. The Hebrews, God's people of the past, were told things by God Himself about the stars."

Gertrude yawned. "They're but so many shiny things to me."

Pieter smiled. "Well, did you know that the Holy Word says that God named the stars? It tells us that He 'calls them all by name.'"

His children grew quiet. Pieter continued, addressing both crews. "King David, the great psalmist, wrote that the 'heavens declare the glory of God.' Can you imagine keeping a candle burning as long as He keeps the fire in but one of those stars?"

"He must use a lot of fat," Gertrude said with a laugh.

"Aye! More fat than I can imagine," said Pieter. "Forgive mine eyes, they are poor and ever failing but I'll show you what I am able to see. Ah, but first a little trick for you: 'Tis easier to see a star if you look to its side. When I point, focus your eye next to the mark and you shall be able to see it better.

"Now as with all of creation, the stars are given for our use. They help us measure the seasons and chart our courses, and the like. For example, if you can see m'finger, follow it to Polaris ... there, the North Star. Can y'not see it, Conrad?"

"Nay."

"Then find the shape that most of you may know as—"

"Charlemagne's Wain!" exclaimed Otto. "My grandpapa taught me of it."

"Aye, well said, lad. To some it is the wagon ... do all see it? Those four stars that form something of a box—with a handle. Can y'see it now?"

"*Ja, ja,* I see it now."

"Good ... your first constellation, your first picture in the sky."

The old man raised his brows. "Now! Now you are ready to learn the true wonder of the night's sky! Did you know that God has written a message to us and it is shining down on us now?"

The crusaders stared upward, slack-jawed and waiting.

"For thousands of years the astronomers have drawn pictures in the sky using stars as points to draw between. Pretend there to be lines in the sky and methinks you'll see the wagon more clearly now."

"Aye!"

"Good.

"Now, across the sky travels a group of constellations

called the Zodiac. For most the word is a meaningless thing, but it means 'The Way.'"

Karl scratched his head. "The Way? That is also the meaning of Weyer, our village."

"Aye, good. But listen, some think that 'Zodiac' simply means *the way* the sun travels through the heavens. Ah, 'tis not so. It means the way of redemption.

"Let me demonstrate. If you look to the west and very low you ought see two bright stars that are the elbow and hand of the Virgin."

"It looks like no woman to me."

Pieter chuckled. "I understand. It takes much training—and a strong wine! But it has been such for all people since the days of the ancient Hebrews.

"And there are other symbols in the sky that tell us of our Lord. Look there, high in the northern sky, and you ought see a bright cluster of stars. Just above is something called Pisces, or the Fish. It speaks of the coming Redeemer who will save His people. The Bible says, 'Behold I'll send for many fishers and they shall fish them.'"

The children laughed. Pieter squinted in the darkness and his displeasure could be felt like a chill in the night air. "Nay, children, 'tis so. Now to the east, below the red Betelgeuse, look for another reddish star—that is the eye of Taurus the Bull."

"Yes, I know of it," said Wil.

"Now, see the beautiful cluster of stars, the Pleiades? They'd be part of the bull, and if you look close you ought see a double star. That was found but two centuries past and it was called the Crab Star. No matter, the Hebrews said the bull was the sign of the coming Judge of all the earth at the end of time."

Heinz said, "I remember m'father showing me a hunter in the sky."

"Ah, yes, Heinz, that would be Orion, the hunter. I fear he is at rest, though readying to rise. He is seen better in the later months. M'poor memory fails me to find all the others of God's story, but I know of one called Gemini which means 'Christ the King.' Now look straight to the north and low in the sky and you'll find some bright stars that are part of the famous Leo which is—"

"I know of it!" exclaimed Frieda. "'Tis the lion."

"Good! Regulus marks its heart; that sickle shape marks its head. Leo brings us all the way around to the beginning, and the tail of the lion touches Virgo. Leo, of course, is the Lion of Judah."

The children looked puzzled.

"The Lion of Judah is the Christ!"

They smiled and clapped.

"And more. The star named Regulus means 'treading under foot.' And so shall the Lion of Judah someday tread His enemies underfoot. Oh, I wish mine eyes stronger and m'memory clearer, my children, for there is much more to teach you, but that is all I can do for now."

Karl gazed speechlessly at the silent sky above, intrigued by Pieter's lesson. "I never knew the stars were speaking to me, Pieter. I never knew what a treasure has been over my head each night I sleep!"

"Indeed, my son," Pieter answered. "It is important that we look up sometimes; that we look beyond the steps of our own little journey."

Chapter 24
BOOTY AND A GOOD BATH

he floating crusaders took turns to sleep, as they passed the night with dreams sprinkled with starlight charms. And, at daybreak, when the shoreline seemed safer, they rowed to land for a hasty first-meal and a stretch. Wil granted a few hours sleep and then they were off again. The journey to Pavia was more than twenty leagues and it would be several days before they'd arrive. Indeed, the kindly river had hurried them a bit, but its purpose was more than efficient transport, for it had granted them a merciful rest on its own journey to the virile Po.

On an early morning of a sunny mid-September day the pilgrims skillfully ruddered their crafts around a number of tiny islands and came within sight of the wharves of Pavia. Wil ordered his sailors to prepare for landing and, like seasoned seamen, they sat steady at their stations. Before sext they rowed rather deftly to the moorings and tossed their ropes to a pair of dockmen.

Wil directed his fellows to keep a close watch of their cargo while he, Karl, and Pieter searched for the sailmaker's shop as instructed by the clerk at Stresa. The three walked confidently along the wharf's cobbled road-way and their eyes, ears, and nostrils filled with the sights, sounds, and peculiar smells crowding the busy docks.

The wharf was busy and chaotic as workers grunted and strained at barrels of fish and crates of all sorts destined for parts all over Lombardy and beyond. Kegs of ale, wooden boxes of smoked meats and cheeses, flasks of red wine, and bales of carded wool were heaved from rocking boats and loaded on carts yoked to weary horses and a few oxen.

Karl stopped and peered into the dark, mysterious eyes of a small group of Syrian merchants who smiled at him from under silk turbans. Their robes were brightly colored, ample and soft. Each of them bowed at the two boys who bowed awkwardly in return. But Wil could not but stare at the curved knives that were secured under the foreigners' sashes. He had heard of these weapons from the old men of Weyer. He whispered to Karl, "These are infidels! These are the enemies of all Christendom. What business do they bring here?"

One of the merchants heard the boy and laughed. "We are not infidels, my son. We bring fine spices and silken wares to your lords and masters. They think us their friends."

Wil was confused. "You ... you speak our tongue?"

"A thousand pardons, young master. *Ja*, I can speak as you. I judged by your fair hair you come from the far north, and, if I may presume to question you, I wonder what brings you to this place?"

Wil's face belied his sudden predicament. "I ... I am travelling on Crusade to ... to rescue Palestine from your people."

Karl gulped.

The merchants bowed again. "Again, a thousand pardons. May your God smile graciously upon you and may His angels bear you safely ... home."

Wil was not certain, but a quality in their tone seemed to betray some insincerity in their words! Yet the words themselves seemed right enough. The lad had a keen ear for a bold-faced barb but delicate insult was beyond his grasp. Unsure of himself, he simply gaped at the wry grins of the men who now bowed a final time and faded into the crowd.

Pieter caught up to the two boys and nudged them

affectionately with his staff. "Come, lads, we've business to attend."

"Did you not see those infidels, Pieter?" asked Karl.

Pieter paused and surveyed the throng of unkempt hair and woolen hats until he found several turbans grouped by a merchant's table. "Ah, those, those … uh … infidels, aye. They have been bringing their wares from Palestine and beyond for hundreds of years. They mean you no harm."

"But they are infidels, Pieter!" protested Karl. "Our enemy."

Pieter sighed, wishing for a moment that all the world could be governed by such simplicity, foolish as it was. He answered, "I fear ideas as that are oft more the enemy. Perhaps their armies do us harm, but these men are simply feeding their families as do we."

Karl and Wil shook their heads. "Nay," Karl mused to his brother, "the old man's off the mark. They'd be devils in sandals." The two gaped at the olive-skinned travelers with contempt. "Their skin is nearly black and their noses are long and hooked and I saw fire in their eyes—the look of Lucifer, methinks." Karl folded his arms.

Wil nodded. "*Ja.* They needs be driven off the Holy Land. Our warriors are right to kill them."

Pieter grunted his disapproval but yielded the conversation. Some battles are best engaged another day. "Come, boys, follow me."

The priest led his two charges through Pavia's busy wharf. They squeezed past the dyemaker's shop and the silversmith, stumbled between tables of spices and barrels of wine until at last they found the chandler's shop and the sailmaker's. Pieter stopped and looked carefully past both buildings that the boats' clerk had described and then pointed. "There, lads, there it is."

The three approached a modest, one-story wooden wharf office next to the sailmaker's shop. A short-legged table sat in its doorway and several traders were arguing as the old man addressed them. "*Gentiluomo, scusi.*"

The men stopped and stared at the tattered old man and

his single-toothed grin. A beak-nosed man set his quill hard on the table and rose to his feet. Clearly annoyed, the man whined, "What business do you have?"

"We seek Constantino, a trader in wool, whose clerk hails from Stresa by *Lago Maggiore.*"

A large-bellied man with curly brown hair stepped forward. "I am Constantino. What of it, beggar?" he growled.

"I bear thee good news, *gentile signore.* I have two barges waiting by the dock that are for you."

"Two boats?"

"By faith. Thy clerk sent us with two boats and a shipment of your fine wool. I believe he is expecting you to return them with a cargo of your own?"

Constantino was wary. His shipments had always been announced by the oaths of burly oarsmen, not the delicate words of a disheveled priest and two boys. "And who brought these boats to me?"

"Ah, *si*, a fair question from a careful man of commerce. Truth be told, *signore*, you are setting your eyes upon three of us. The rest of our humble company are guarding your worthy crafts."

"My clerk trusted my boats to you! Now I know he is mad!" The merchant stormed past the three and hurried toward the dock. Pieter and the boys trotted behind the cursing merchant until he abruptly stopped and stomped his feet hard on the wooden planks. "What in God's name?" He slammed his fist into his hand. "What sort of dim-witted, dung-brained, s—"

Pieter cautioned him gently. "My lord, if you will, please regard the tender ears of those … *bambini* smiling at you."

"Humph," fumbled the flustered merchant. "I cannot believe my clerk would have risked these barges with the likes of these. He shall surely hear of this. You could have sunk them; you could have lost them; you could have been robbed; you could have tipped these boats and lost the cargo. Aaahh! I cannot believe he has done this!"

Wil could not understand the man's words, but was annoyed at his rantings. "He ought fast his tongue and be grateful," he grumbled.

"Eh? What did you say, whelp?" bellowed Constantino.

Pieter bowed. "The lad thinks you ought be rejoicing in gratitude, my lord."

"What sort of impudent brat is this?"

"*Signore*, the lad is a bit weary and injured by your apparent displeasure. After all, he was the pilot who delivered your cargo safely from a great distance. And, my friend, he did not lose a single bale of wool."

"Be sure to tell him we now want our payment," added Wil.

"What was that?"

Pieter paused. He wanted to win the man's charity another way, and the boy's impetuous manner was not helping in the least.

"Go on, tell him, Pieter."

The old man smiled sheepishly at Constantino before taking Wil firmly by the arm. "But we were promised no payment," he whispered.

"What is being said here?" barked Constantino. "I've no time for secrets and have had enough of this whelp's disrespect. I see it in his face and hear it in his tone." With that the merchant landed a heavy slap on the side of Wil's head. "I take no more disrespect from the likes of you!"

Surprised, Pieter reddened with rage. He kept Wil at bay with one hand and with the other jabbed the end of his staff squarely into the chest of the merchant. He delivered his words with measured deliberation. "Thy behavior is not warranted. The lad simply reminded me that we were to receive our payment. He'd be right to ask it, so reach for thy purse and we'd be about our business." The priest's conciliatory tone had vanished.

Constantino pushed Pieter's staff away. "Payment? I pay nothing to you! We had no contract."

"I see. So, you claim to be worthy of our respect?" Pieter began loudly. "Ha! Thy very own deputy promised us payment and bound your word to it. He boasted thy family to be shrewd, but honorable. He wisely did not pay us then as a guarantee of delivery—shrewd indeed. Now I would expect you, sir, to be as honorable as he claimed."

Constantino turned a quick eye toward the crowd now gathering. He felt a sudden unease begin to creep over him. "*Si*, my family is honorable. All here would so agree."

"Ah, then, my honorable, respected friend, what sort of fools would bring thy cargo without promise of payment?"

Constantino shifted on his feet. Certainly none would perform such a service without payment, and perhaps his clerk had been wise to hold wages from this lot until delivery was assured. "And how do I know what was negotiated?"

Pieter felt the sealed letter in his pocket and pushed it in deeper. He fidgeted for a moment, cast an uncomfortable look at Wil, and continued. "You must needs ... trust the word of this priest, my son. The payment was a modest shilling."

The merchant sighed. A shilling was not terribly unreasonable and its payment would protect his reputation—a meager price for a treasure as that. "Priest? Ha! Well, I suppose you've the words and robe of a churchman so I'd not be one to judge." He smiled and spoke loudly for all to hear. "Of course I'll pay the fee! Constantino is fair-minded and Christian. Here, *Padre*." The man bounced a small coin-bag in his hand and pried his thick fingers inside. "Here'd be your shilling." He began to count pennies into the hand of a secretary.

"Ah, *si* ... that was one shilling ... per boat," corrected Pieter.

"A shilling per boat!" huffed Constantino. "I'll not be scrumped for a shilling per boat. I'll pay no more than a half-shilling!"

"Ah, but thy honorable clerk promised us a full shilling," insisted Pieter. "And I believe that's what it ought be."

"But we never pay that!"

"Ah, *si*. But thy clerk knew he was helping these *bambini* in their Holy Crusade. He claimed thy family to be shrewd, honorable ... *and* charitable."

Constantino growled, stifling a string of oaths as he ordered his secretary to fetch his strongbox. The iron-strapped box soon was set at the man's feet and he jammed his key into the padlock. In just a few moments he filled a pouch with a dubious count of pennies and slammed it hard atop a beer keg. "There, y'swindler, here'd be payment in full and charity besides!" he roared. "Constantino cheats none and helps the poor." He lowered his voice and snarled at Pieter. "Now take your cheat's money and get those whelps off my boats."

He ordered his secretary to check the cargo as Pieter bowed gratefully. "My good man, I must indeed thank thee and I wish God's blessings ..."

"Oh, enough of God's blessings, priest! I cannot afford any more of them. Now begone with you all."

Pieter's eyes darted about the crowd. "Constantino, my son?"

"Eh?"

"It is good, at times, to hold to thrift, even in charity, for we must be prudent stewards of our plenty. And we are most humbly grateful for thy gift, frugal as it may be. I expect thee to be blessed in like manner. But ..."

"*Si, si* ... go on!"

"Ah ... I scarce know how to put it." Pieter grimaced and shook his head dramatically. "I wish not to embarrass thee before this host of thy friends, but if you could but add a few *deniers* more for the work of the Church, ..."

The red-faced merchant spun around and snapped, "You ... you ..." He could not help but notice the expectant crowd now leaning forward in eager anticipation of his answer. He then plunged his fingers again into his strongbox and threw a handful of coins at Pieter. "That is plenty enough for the Holy Church this day." The man attempted a hasty retreat.

Pieter watched the pennies spin at his feet and winked at his spellbound crusaders. He called after Constantino, "Oh, kind and honorable man?"

The merchant froze in his steps. He feared to face the priest and answered where he stood. "*Si?*" he boomed.

"When thy boats are unloaded would you offer one last charity to these faithful servants? Could you find in thine gracious heart enough kindness to have some oarsmen row us over the river so we might continue our journey?"

Constantino punched his fist into his hand and looked once again at the expectant crowd. Utterly vanquished, the man closed his eyes in defeat and nodded.

Pieter thanked him again and turned to the audience. "If ever a Pavian could earn a blessing, it would be the honorable Constantino, I am certain of it."

The crowd melted away and the crusaders waited by the dock for their transport, each begging Pieter to tell the story of what had just happened. The old man sighed, not eager to share such a tale, and not particularly proud of his accomplishment. But theirs was not a companionship of secrets, and he told all.

When he finished, Karl narrowed a hard look toward Pieter and scolded him. "I confess, Pieter, I sometimes think you to be the most godly man ever, and at other times I think y'to be but a wicked, black heart! We had no promise of payment—I believe y'to have lied. Is it not so?"

Pieter was well aware of his occasional excesses in judgment, but the arrogant piety in the boy's rebuke did not draw him to repentance. "'Do not be over-righteous, why destroy thyself?'"

"Ha! You give me words of Scripture to defend your evil? By truth, Pieter, you do confound me so. I ..."

Wil had enough. "Still the little saint ... is it to be St. Karl of Weyer?"

The others laughed.

"Wrong is wrong and I know I'm on the mark to—"

Pieter interrupted. "Perhaps you are right to rebuke me, Karl, right indeed." The old man sighed. "Methinks you needs now take these coins and cast them into the river— that ought be proper penance."

Karl looked at the pennies and hesitated. "That isn't the point. I just don't know why y'made a fool of the man and used your wits as a weapon against him, all the while claiming the Church and things holy."

"When I was young, Karl, I would have beaten that arrogant belly-hog for striking your brother without cause," Pieter replied. "But I am not young and so, instead of violence, I am left only with treachery; a wicked choice to be sure." He extended his hand toward Karl. "Good lad, I meant not to steal from him, nor did my lies bring me joy. I was angered by his ways and thought him deserving of some justice. Perhaps I ought not be so inclined; perhaps 'tis never a time for treachery."

Pieter paused and then smiled. "Ah, but cunning has its place."

≈

Over the next days the crusaders marched south and slightly westward across the plain of Lombardy, passing by the stone-walled village of Sommo and crossing the wide Po River at a shallow ford. Their provisions were holding fairly well, as each day they successfully gleaned grains from the ample fields stretching in all directions. Though hand-threshing with heavy, flat rocks made for a husk-laden gruel, the crusaders were grateful for full bellies.

The march was easy and took them to the narrow Scrivia River, which they followed southward toward Tortona. The sandy soil of the plain was kind to the crusaders' worn feet and they arrived in good spirits at the ancient town. Though they were not discontented with their present lot, they nevertheless looked forward to what bounty might be waiting for them behind the walls just ahead.

Wil led his company past an agreeable porter and into the town's marketplace on the day before Sabbath. The folk were busy with preparations for St. Michael's Day less than a week ahead. "I had been so certain," said Wil, "that we would be at the sea long before St. Michael's. I am beginning to wonder if there'd be a sea at all!"

The old man chuckled. "Ah, my son, there surely is a sea and I count us perhaps a week away. We needs pass over the edges of Piedmont into the mountains of Liguria and then you shall smell the sea in the air."

"Can't we linger for one day of feast somewhere?" pleaded Frieda.

A chorus of others agreed. "Just one day?" begged one. "Aye, Wil, we can surely spare a single day!"

Wil hesitated. "I think we needs press on. I'd not be pleased to miss Nicholas and the others for one day of feasting. But this day is already by nones and the town seems friendly enough. We can stay here until the morrow."

Happy for any rest, the children followed him into the market square where they were immediately struck by the town's bright hues. Gardens of flowers, fine tapestries, and snapping pennants adorned the otherwise drab, gray-stone buildings. The sky above was a brilliant blue and the sun sparkled overhead. Feast or not, it was a good day.

"The free towns in these parts are wealthy," instructed Pieter. "Here the clever and the shrewd find much opportunity to prosper, and a person willing to work hard might build a good life."

As they rounded a corner Pieter's eyes widened. He grinned mischievously and pointed to a large bathhouse. "Ha! Look in there, *kinder.* You shall see tiled pools of water where, for a few pennies, one can soak in the comfort of a warm bath until he wrinkles like a shriveled grape."

Frieda's cheeks pinked.

"Oh, don't blush, my dear," said Pieter. "The gentlemen bathe separate from the ladies, of course."

The pilgrims tittered and whispered among themselves. Otto winked at Heinz and approached Pieter with a sly grin. "You've some shillings in your pouch. Some here think we ought spare a few pennies to bathe with the rich."

Pieter hesitated for a moment. He took a long look at his dirty-faced flock. "Hmm ... you did already bathe in the Ticino ... but ... you'd still be a filthy litter. Your skin, Conrad, is almost as dark as your hair. And you, Karl, and you, Wil, and Heinz ... *Ach.* You do Christendom some shame. *Mein Gott,* Otto, your freckles are hidden 'neath the filth!"

The children laughed. Gertrude held out her smudged arms and compared them to her sister's. "Wouldn't *Mutti* like to see this, Frieda? She'd take the bristles to us for sure."

The company began to plead for a swim in the baths. "Wil, we needs smell some better or the beggin's in peril," pleaded Heinz. "And what of the other crusaders ahead? What'll they think of us?"

Wil seemed unsure. "I ... I ... there may be better uses for our money and ..."

The crusaders would not yield and they raised a chorus loud enough to waken the Roman spirits that once dipped in these same baths! Wil finally conceded. "*Ach.* Go then. Frieda, take the girls where y'must, and the rest follow me."

The delighted pilgrims cheered and patted Wil on his back as giddy Pieter danced in the dusty roadway. At last, a bit of frolic for the weary band; a proper remedy dispensed in proper time!

The excited children raced toward the bathhouse, cheering and screaming like playmates racing toward the Maypole. Wil counted out the payment to a reluctant keeper and led his boys to a slippery, tile-floored chamber where they ripped away their soiled tunics and leggings. Then, to the utter dismay of the lords and noblemen relaxing in their docile waters, the grimy, wiggling, raucous crowd of little Germans crashed into the quiet water, splashing like schools of famished carp in a spring rain!

The frustrated lords growled and barked at the howling boys. "*Fermatevi ... Andate via!*" But suddenly they fell silent, dumbstruck as if gazing upon some horrid, ancient ghost just risen from a moldy tomb. If the pesky boys were not penalty enough for the indignant bathers, Pieter surely was; a frightful vision not soon to be forgotten in the baths of Tortona!

As naked as the day of his long-ago birth, the old man defied the most artful words of the most learned scribe. He stood at the poolside, blind to his own appearance, though, judging by the grimaces of all who dared gaze his way, he ventured a guess that he must look worse than he imagined. Nevertheless, his vanities were placed elsewhere and he stood there content and grinning, his lone tooth hanging ever proudly from his smooth gums. His blue eyes twinkled, his wispy beard fluttered and frolicked in a light draft; but, oh, the bleached, white skin draped on such old bones. And the ribs, oh, the ribs!

Suddenly a voice boomed from the water, "Have mercy on us, *nonno*, and hide yourself in the water … quickly!"

The whole pool burst into laughter. "No, no!" cried another. "If he gets in, I want out!"

So, midst the roars and laughs, heckles and jeers of friends and strangers alike, Pieter gingerly walked across the slippery tile and down the marble steps into the warm waters of the ancient bath.

In the other courtyard the girls timidly stepped into their own bath, giggling at the sight of the wealthy *matrone* soaking their ample bodies in the healing waters. Despite the unwelcome grunts of the bath's patrons, the girls were soon scrubbing their filthy skin with scented French soaps and tittering at the sight of themselves. The gentle bath was good medicine for their aching bodies and soothing to their heavy hearts.

But, alas, the pleasures were as short-lived as the bathmaster's patience, and the company was soon commanded to leave. After a few complaints and a brief exchange of angry words, the crusaders found themselves clothed again in their leggings and tunics, gowns and robes and marching behind Wil toward the town's center.

"I overheard two remarkable things in that bath," said a most relaxed Pieter to any who would listen. "Two remarkable things, indeed. First, I learned that the astronomers of Cathay believe that a metal needle can be made to always point north. This would mean a new way to navigate. *Ach*, this is beyond my ability to believe."

A metal needle?" quizzed Karl. "What would a metal needle know?"

Pieter shrugged. "I am simply telling you what I heard; and those who spoke it were well traveled and seemed truthful enough. But, it seems unlikely God would be pleased with such a thing. Methinks it good to look upward for direction," mused Pieter, winking.

"And what is this second thing?" asked Karl.

"Ah, yes. This amazes me as well. The mathematicians have proposed a new idea. You understand how we use shapes for numbers? Good. You needs listen: They intend to use a small circle on parchment to mean … nothing."

"What?" blurted Wil. "Nay. How can something mean nothing? Is this another of your riddles?"

"*Ach*, nay. No riddle, boy. They've named it 'zero.'"

"We've no need of such a stupid thing," grumbled Karl. "Why would we want to add a shape that adds naught?"

"Indeed." Pieter scratched his head. "Hmm, a symbol that means nothing. 'Tis most peculiar."

Conrad overheard part of the conversation. "What means nothing?"

"A circle means nothing."

"Nay, a circle means a circle, Karl. Are you mad?"

"Nay. A circle means zero."

"What is zero?"

"Nothing!" snapped Wil.

"Ha! Methinks you all to be mad."

Pieter laughed. "'Tis a strange world we travel, m'lads. I only wish I might see what things shall confuse and confound *you* in your old age.

"Oh, and more, children, m'old brain's failed me again. I had forgotten to tell you of something in Pavia."

The children slowed their pace again. "It was the place where the great Carthaginian general, Hannibal, won a battle over the Roman general Publius Cornelius ... something."

"And why do we needs know that?" asked Wil.

"Ah. Because Hannibal did what we have done. He crossed the Alps with an army, though he first crossed the ocean and his company rode on animals—animals that you have never seen, called elephants."

"Eh?"

"Elephants."

Otto's ears cocked. "And what does an elephant look like?"

"I saw but one in my youth at a fair in Paris," said Pieter. "But I fear you already think me mad."

"No, Pieter, you needs tell us!"

"Hmmm. 'Tis is a most difficult creature to describe. But I'll try. Close your eyes and see a pig in your mind. Now make it as big as a plough-horse ... and then make it twice again as big."

"What?" groused Wil. "Fool's talk."

"I speak the truth and shall utter not another single word if you choose to not believe me."

"Please say on, Pieter," begged Karl. "Tell us more."

"*Ja* ... now take this pig, which would be as high as a timberman's hovel, Karl, and saw its legs so that they are short and fat with round pads for feet."

The girls began to giggle.

"Nay. Listen carefully. I speak truly, I swear it. Now take your pig's snout and pull it out like warm honeycomb ... until it nearly hangs on the ground."

"You've made dolts of us all!" complained Wil. "First circles that mean nothing and now giant pigs. By truth, Pieter ..."

Gertrude eyed the old man suspiciously. "Tell us you'd not be lying to us, Pieter."

"*Ach*, my little dear." He bent down and held her close. "I would never lie to you."

"Is that all of it? Would there be more to this *dream*?" laughed a voice.

"By truth, y'faithless litter, you'll be laying eyes on these in Palestine! Then you'll wish to repent such ridicule. But aye, there'd be a bit more. You needs fix huge ears on its head, larger than shutters."

"And ... and what about the tail?"

"The tail is much like a pig's curl, only longer."

"So you are saying," said Karl carefully, "we needs take a pig and make its body as big as a house and make its legs short and fat, and pull its nose out so it hangs on the ground, and hang giant ears on it that are like flapping shutters—and that is an elephant?"

"Indeed, 'tis true. I swear it."

Karl shook his head. "Meaning no disrespect, Pieter, but methinks the waters of the bath to have soaked your head some!" He and his friends snickered.

Pieter continued. "Well, my point was that General Hannibal rode his elephants across the Alps and defeated the Roman legions by Pavia."

Disgusted, Wil interrupted the old man with orders to

beg at the marketplace. With feast day on the morrow the town was bountiful and filled with plenty, but, despite their friendly manner, the townsfolk were sparing. Gertrude returned with a handful of crust and Frieda with two onions. The boys fared worse and by vespers had no more than three apples, a half-string of garlic, and a pear.

æ

The journey continued and the children soon found themselves marching tight to the sandy shores of the narrow Scrivia River within view of the Apennines rising in the distance. Knowing that the mountains ahead were the last wall between them and Genoa, the crusaders trod with new energy, now emboldened by past sufferings and resolved to reach the mysterious sea.

"What does it look like, Pieter?" asked Frieda.

"What does what look like, child?"

"The sea—what does the sea look like?"

"Oh yes, none of you have ever seen it. My, my, what a sight you have waiting for you."

Wil ordered a brief rest and the crusaders sat around Pieter.

"Can you picture your fishponds?"

"*Ja*, of course."

"Ha! The sea looks nothing like them." Pieter guffawed, though his perturbed audience stared back indignantly.

"Ah, my apologies. The sea ... so much to say about it ... so many moods, so many different ways it has—like a woman."

Frieda and her clique scowled.

"Begging your pardon. So, then ... once again close your eyes and imagine when we looked over the wide valleys from the tops of the high mountains. Do you remember? Do you remember how green it was? Good. Now, in your mind's eye, turn the green to blue and stretch it flat as far as you can see. Of course, when it churns and rolls in the wind 'tis different and when the sky is gray ... and at night ... oh my!"

"And you said it smells good as well?" exclaimed Karl.

"Indeed, and the sounds of it! The waves and the sea birds ... and the ..."

Wil climbed to his feet, unimpressed. "Aye, Pieter, more stories like elephants and zeroes? Methinks 'tis time to press on."

Chapter 25
THE DARK LORD AND THE
HAVEN FOUND

The crusaders marched across the plain toward the foothills of the Apennines, passing through the villages of Villalvernia and Stazzano. The journey was easy and spirits were high, and before long they found themselves climbing through the foothills of the Apennines and taking respite in a small Ligurian village.

The children received a reasonable welcome from the warmhearted folk and were invited to make camp just beyond the walls. Pieter extended a hearty *"grazie"* on behalf of his flock, and the company encircled a good fire heating a bubbling pottage.

The next morning the crusaders roused themselves under a gentle sun and surveyed the landscape before them. "It seems we might follow the Scrivia?" asked Wil.

"Nay … methinks only at parts. Mountain riverbeds tend to be rough and we'd be better staying to the peddlers' trails. I'd wager them to take us to a wider road into Genoa."

Wil agreed.

The company lingered for a few moments facing the scene before them and feeling greater anticipation as they were finally about to ascend their final obstacle. The mountains standing in wait were sharp-edged, but considerably shorter than the Alps. They rose steeply and were divided by tight valleys covered with a stale-green carpet of round-topped trees. Wil thought the trees to be mostly softwood and noticed the silvery undersides of their leaves flashing in the sunny breeze. He missed the tall spruce and heavy oak of his home.

The company left the village camp and climbed a full day into the mountains, following, as Pieter had advised, a well-worn peddler's trail. The following morning Wil woke with a strange odor in his nose. He drew a deep breath through his nostrils. "Ah? Awaken, everyone. What'd be the smell?"

His fellows opened their eyes and obediently sucked in the cool morning air. Uncertain as to the odor, they stood to their feet and held their noses high. "Aye ... something's odd here," said one.

Pieter stretched his arms and inhaled a refreshing, pleasing breath. He smiled. "Ah, *kinder*. 'Tis a blessed day ... a blessed, holy day. This, my lambs ... this is the air of the sea. Feel the breeze—it blows from the south. It is coming over the mountains from the sea."

The children cheered and danced around their campsite. "The sea, the sea, we've come to the sea!" The jubilant children stormed the steep trail with a lighter step. Higher and higher they marched, whistling and singing and hardly noticing the thick forest closing in around them. They strained, grunted, and stretched their way up the paths without regard for the sharp rocks and gnarly roots wearing at their thin, tattered leather shoes and bindings.

Eventually their trail delivered them beneath the watch of two Ligurian castles perched atop opposing ridges but, to the relief of all, they passed between their wary ramparts unchallenged. But by that evening they arrived at the village of Brusalla where men-at-arms waited to seize them. It seems that some bands of children were thought to have pilfered the manor lands of late and Wil's company of strange-looking *bambini* warranted suspicion. However, the ever wise and wily Father Pieter urged a judgment of divine wrath from the sky and a fortuitous cloudburst won the band's freedom.

On the fourth evening in the mountains, Wil ordered his relieved company to set camp in a grassy clearing dappled with wildflowers. Wood was gathered quickly and by nightfall the children were huddled 'round a roaring fire. Pieter sat comfortably in the soft grass and caressed his trusted crook. He thought of Georg and sighed. "My children ... ah ... perhaps I ought say 'my ladies and young masters.' Methinks on the morrow or, at worst, the morrow next, we ought descend to the port of Genoa and you shall behold that which you cannot now imagine. You shall see water that goes beyond sight itself."

A crusader cried from the edges of the campsite, "And then to Jerusalem!" The circle hurrahed!

Pieter sighed. "I know not how our Lord wills for you to cross into Palestine, but I needs say again, that I, like Moses, shall not follow you into the Promised Land."

A loud chorus of complaints arose. Gertrude stood up and pleaded, "Please, Pieter, please, you must come with us! We've come so far together!"

Now all the crusaders rose and circled close to the weary old man. Many clutched at his robe and begged him to remain with them. "Nay, my precious lambs, I have said before that my body is too frail. 'Tis a proper time to release you. I have served you as best I have known and have failed you some, but now is the season for other wings to carry you from my arms."

Large, salty droplets fell down Karl's ruddy cheeks and Wil's face was stained with tears he no longer chose to hide. Both recalled that day in Mainz, so very long ago. "Is there no word we can offer?" Wil choked, "Some vow, or pledge that might change your mind?"

Pieter shook his head. "Nay, good friend, I must remain here and pray for the souls of our dear departed. And, methinks I might do my praying by Brother Chiovo's side."

The man paused and looked over the anxious faces peering at him. He considered his next words carefully and delivered them with deliberation. "*Meine kinder*, I've need to say something to you all. It was, by truth, the hope and solemn pledge of each to set himself upon the Holy Land."

The children nodded.

"Our journey has been both tragic and joyful, both terrible and wonderful—has it not? And each of us has both suffered and been blessed. Methinks such things as we've endured have borne good fruit.

"It would seem our miseries were but the heavy labors of a worthy Gardener, working and kneading God's soil into our hard, barren hearts. It would seem as if He has planted vineyards of sweet grapes within us each. Y'needs not press o'er the sea for what God has already set your feet upon."

Karl stood to his feet. "Pieter? We have come so far … we'd not be going back now."

"Ah, you've made m'point, my son. You have come far, indeed. It was the *journey* that has served the Savior's purpose. The Land has been secured."

"I understand your words," said Wil, "but I should like to see if He would have us put our feet in Palestine as well. I wish to raise a fistful of soil from that glorious shore and lift it to heaven."

The others clapped.

Pieter had done what he could do and it was clear he'd not be altering their course. He yielded them to the mysterious providence of his unseen God. "I cannot command you, beloved. But know this: You are in my prayers always."

৵

The chirps of wakening birds gently stirred the sleeping crusaders. Pieter rolled and snorted under his blanket. He cleared his throat, rubbed his eyes, and relieved his customary gas. It was not unlike other mornings. The others stretched some, unconsciously aware that another day would soon begin. The camp's fire had collapsed into a glowing heap of white ash and red embers. An occasional spark escaped from its snapping coals and floated gracefully away, dancing on the thick, gray mist and disappearing in the forest.

Suddenly, hushed laughter rippled across the tree-walled clearing and nearby birds rushed from their leafy roosts. The sudden flutter of their wings startled Wil and he sat up with a start. The lad's ears cocked and he now thought he'd heard muffled tittering from the clearing's edges. The boy climbed out of his blanket. He stood in the dewy wildflowers and peered intently into the dim-lit shadows of the new day. He nudged Karl and Pieter when a loud, mocking voice rolled over the fog.

"Ho there, valiant crusaders of Jesus!" It was a deep and strong voice, rich and mellow, yet Wil felt a sensation of dread creep over him. The company awakened and climbed to their feet.

"What is it, Wil?" whispered Frieda.

Wil held up his finger. "Shhhh."

A group of murky silhouettes emerged from the wood and swooped toward the camp, ghostlike and ghoulish. The crusaders quickly gathered together and huddled helpless and confused behind the glowing coals of their night's fire. The strange shadows drew ever closer until they broke upon the hearth with eerie laughs and wicked jeers.

A sudden flurry of fiery embers flew from the campfire as the intruders dumped armloads of branches upon it. In the burst of light the crusaders stared across the fire and beheld the terror before them, and they gasped.

Pieter, though startled, leaned on his staff and railed at the strangers. "Who comes here?" he challenged.

A large figure loomed from the mist and placed himself at the fore of his fellows. He stood square-legged in the red light of the campfire. "Who asks?" he hissed.

Karl cast a nervous glance at Wil and then fixed a mesmerized eye on the apparent leader of the trespassers. *He's young*, thought Karl, *but not so young.* Indeed, the man was in his prime, both of body and mind. His face was strong and sculpted like the statues Karl had seen in the courtyards at Tortona. A sharp nose divided his square face evenly; thick, black eyebrows arched perfectly over his bright, dark eyes, and a trim, black beard outlined a strong chin and firm jaw.

The captivating man stood there smiling haughtily, his straight, white teeth gleaming in the light of the snapping kindling. A black-hooded cape was draped along his broad shoulders and cascaded over his arms to the rim of his knee-high, black boots. He heaved his chest and planted his fists on his narrow hips.

Frieda pulled her sister close to her side and glanced about her friends' faces for reassurance. She stared at the sneering man and trembled. He was so very tall, she thought; a full head and shoulders above any man she had ever seen.

"Greetings!" boomed the man. "I say greetings to you, you pitiful band of weak-willed crusaders."

Pieter stepped forward, keeping one eye on the leader and the other on the company of his followers gathering behind him. "You are not welcome here."

The man laughed loudly and spun on his heels to address his companions. "Have you heard the news? We are not welcome here." A chorus of guffaws and taunts sounded. The caped man turned again toward Pieter and scowled. He extended a menacing finger over the fire at the priest. "Who are you, beggar, to tell me where I am welcome?"

Pieter squeezed hard on the grip of his staff. "I see by your dress and manner that you come from some breeding and I should have thought some manners might have come with you. You wake us from our slumber without regard and you have not even the courtesy of proper introduction."

The man paused, then smiled broadly. "So? Before me stands something of a cleric, feeble of body but not of spirit. I beg your pardon for my inappropriate and unfortunate behavior." He bowed deeply, winking at his lieutenants on either side. "Permit me, all, to introduce myself. In my past some have called me, 'Squire,' others, 'Count,' later, '*Pater*,' then for a horrid time, 'Brother,' and for another season I was dubbed, 'Master of Divinity' by the Archbishop of Magdeburg himself.

"But now I am better known as 'Dark Lord,' or 'Wizard,' though others say 'Woodland Sorcerer' and others still, 'Lucifer Incarnate.'" He threw his head back-raised his hands to the sky. "'Lucifer Incarnate,' indeed! I think that to be my favorite."

Pieter had rallied his courage but now trembled as the man spoke. He was, indeed, a dark lord. There seemed to be a portion of hellfire flickering in those gleaming eyes and the old priest chilled. Around the man swirled an aura of evil that Pieter sensed; some wicked presence, some dread essence. Pieter had never felt so close to the Pit and he felt all strength drain away.

Wil felt the same fear and his mouth dried. Though he had learned to depend on his white-haired friend, he was not so certain the scales had not been tipped against him. The boy remembered the many times all seemed lost, however, only to have Pieter call upon some inner wit to win the day. So Wil looked toward Pieter hopefully for some sign that the man was yet able to hold fast against the power now opposing them. But as soon as Wil's eyes fell upon their steadfast guide, stooped in his tattered robe and leaning on his staff with quaking arms, the boy grew anxious. *Nay ... poor Pieter is far too feeble against a force as this.*

The intruder continued. "And so as not to offend you any further, ancient man that you are, these are my good companions ... my fellow travelers ... my brothers and sisters."

Pieter surveyed the company now bending halfway around the campfire. They were children much like his own; children of each and every size but dressed well and clean. A few wore peasants' tunics but most were garbed in fine-loomed doublets with wooden buttons and wide leather belts. Their feet were bound with good boots and shoes. Each had thick, woolen, hooded capes and well-stocked satchels slung across their shoulders. He could not count them in the dim light but they seemed to be a host more than five times his own poor band. He cast a glance to the lightening sky and begged silently for the sun to hurry to its place.

The dark lord smiled again. He put his arm around a boy standing beside him and nodded to him. The boy stepped proudly into the firelight and flung the hood off his head. He folded his arms defiantly and flashed a menacing grin at Wil.

"T-Tomas," Pieter stammered. "Tomas, you've come back!"

Tomas laughed at the priest and glared at Wil and Karl. "Come back?" he spat. "Ha! Indeed, old fool, I've come back and I've come back a different man than when I left."

"Now that is quite enough of your poor manners, Tomas," interrupted the sorcerer. He turned to the crusaders. "I am aware of your acquaintance with my lieutenant. This fine lad has just the sort of heart that I need for *my* crusade."

"And what crusade would that be?" asked Pieter.

"It is our privilege, old man—Father Pieter, I believe, is what you are oft called?" He smiled. "It has been my privilege to crusade the valleys of my homeland and these warmer parts in the south to, ah, how to say ... to relieve many of their burdens."

"And what burdens would they be?"

"Ah, yes ... fair question indeed. And the answer is quite familiar to you, for as a priest you helped many in the same manner. In fact, it was the Church who schooled me in such things."

"*Ja, ja,* so what is it?"

"Your pardon. We ... relieve the wealthy from the burden of their riches. And we relieve temptation from the poor by freeing them from their small bits of wealth as well. And I relieve the wise of knowledge and the devout of faith.

"But it has been my greatest privilege to relieve these poor children at my side the burden of their dreams. A dream put upon them by others—a dream that has ended in death for most and despair for all. Aye, old priest, I am in the business of relieving people from such burdens; that is *our* Holy Crusade."

Pieter stepped toward the sorcerer. "You, black-hearted fiend, relieve none of but things earned and things hoped. And you shall not relieve us of either. I perceive you to be a merchant of deceit and a peddler of fraud. By your own tongue you leave people in the bondage of poverty, ignorance, and hopelessness." Pieter's voice emboldened him to continue. "You would do well to leave us with our scanty means, our moderate temptations, our humble thoughts, and our modest dreams. I bid you farewell."

The dark lord came closer, outwardly angered at the old man's impertinence. "Think not, fool, that I am some dung hauler that you can so easily dismiss!"

"Your deceptions leave a stench in the air. You are a conjurer of foolishness and corruption."

"Conjurer? Conjurer, you say? Ha! Indeed, I am a conjurer, and you as well. You priests conjure angels; I conjure demons. They are one and the same. All of them exist in the same place as your God—in the mind.

"I implore you, priest, beckon your angels and I'll summon my demons. But, wait! Perhaps you speak truth, for your angels ought indeed be feared … for they are mere figments! Ah. But my demons—never. The demons I conjure, fool, are ideas, knowledge of the world we see. These be truth-bearers and your wicked Church names them 'demons.'"

The dark lord now stood with his toes at the edge of the fire. "Understand these 'demons,' old man, and you shall understand indeed. It is what is meant by, 'The truth shall set you free.'"

Pieter set his own feet on the fire's edge. He peered across the rising flames. "'The fool has said in his heart there is no God.' Poor sorcerer, 'lean not on thine own understanding.' You are not made of the stuff that can grasp the eternal. You are made of dust and nothing more."

"You wish to exchange Scriptures?" the sorcerer scoffed. "I have no fear of your holy words: 'discretion shall guard me,' 'understanding shall watch over me.'"

Pieter set his jaw and drove his staff securely into the sod at his feet. "'The advice of the wicked is deceitful.'"

"'But by a man of understanding and knowledge endures.'"

Pieter countered, "'An evil man is ensnared by his own lips.'"

"Ah, fool, but 'the lips of the wise shall preserve him. The folly of fools is deceit.'"

"'Answer a fool as his folly deserves.'"

The lord threw his head back and roared in laughter, clasped his hands behind his back, and walked around the fire to circle Pieter. He smiled and winked at the spellbound crusaders. "Father Pieter," he began, "you believe me to be a deceiver. You accuse me of folly and foolishness, even evil and corruption; yet you have not even heard my words.

"Listen well, old man. You use the words of King Solomon. It is he, not I, who said, 'I looked at all the acts of oppression that were being done under the sun and behold, I saw the tears of the oppressed and that no one had come to comfort them.'

"It is he who said, 'For what does a man get in all his labor? All his days are painful and grievous. Even at night his mind does not rest. This is meaningless.'

"It is King Solomon, *Pater*, who said, 'Who knows what is good for a man during his lifetime, during the few years of his futile life. He shall spend them like a shadow ... for all is vanity.' These are not the words of pleasant dreams, are they, dreamer? These are not the words of faith, are they, priest? But they *are* the words of truth. Your suffering and your agonies, the death and despair that follows you and your pathetic children; your hunger and cold are without meaning.

"You herd these little ones toward the sea for naught. You've buried many along the way for no purpose. And you fill their minds with nothingness, empty words, lies."

The sorcerer strode back to Tomas and put his arm around the boy's shoulders. "My lieutenant tells me of your instruction and *you*, old man, are the deceiver. This world is without the hope you conjure. Look, look at yourself and your litter. You are tattered and worn, hungry and weary, empty of body, empty of soul, longing for friends now rotting in their graves. You are without laughter, without peace. You are all driven by madness, led by angels. Or rather, pushed by the shadows in your own tiny minds! Yet you hope in some good God above!

"What sort of a God do you have? Where is He? Where does He hide? Or is it impotence that keeps Him from defending the littlest among you? '*Almighty* God'—ha! You claim Him to have the power to heal, yet pestilence reigns. He has the power to speak, but He remains mute; to forgive, but He demands an indulgence of blood. He has the means to prosper, but the world wallows in poverty.

"You say He tends the world as His garden; the fields bend heavy with His grain, the orchards and vineyards bear His fruit, the seas are His fishpond. If so, with a single word He might keep His garden watered so that the harvest would be bountiful each season. Yet, instead, all Christendom struggles against the land. He has the power to quiet the raging sea, but sailors drown each day...."

Pieter could remain silent no more. "'Why do you boast in evil, oh, mighty man? The lovingkindness of God endures all the day. Your tongue devises destruction like a sharp razor, oh, worker of deceit. You love evil more than good, falsehood more than truth. You love all the words that devour, oh, deceitful tongue.'"

The sorcerer flung his arms in a wild rage. "Silence! Silence! You will let me finish my words or I'll destroy you where you stand!" His face then softened and he laughed loudly. "Can you not see your own folly, priest? You've no answers to my words so you attack me, which of course, makes my point: 'Foolishness lies in the tongue of a man who slanders without answers.'"

Pieter stood quietly.

"What confounds me most about your kind, priest," continued the sorcerer, "is why you pursue this absurdity of yours. Your God *is* foolishness. If there is an evil afoot in this place, it is to be found in *your* black religion.

"Have you given no thought to your persuasions? Have y'not wondered *why* God would allow His first creatures to be tempted, all the while knowing of their certain failure? And, once fallen, have y'not considered *why* your God did not simply forgive?

"And what of those you call 'His Church'? Consider that blessed collection of hypocrites, liars, and thieves! You, priest, and your ilk prey on the ignorance of others. The fear you wield is the bit and bridle in the suffering mouths of all Christendom. What sort of demons barter fantasies of love and forgiveness for a man's last penny?"

He pointed a long forefinger at the huddled crusaders. "And you, little ones, why would you follow a God who would kill His own Son, only to have His priests press His flesh between their teeth and swallow His blood!"

The wild-eyed man returned his focus to Pieter. "What insanity drives you?" he demanded. "Have you ne'er considered what madness it must surely be to call the men of Scripture 'great men' of your contemptible faith? Ha! The 'great men' are those named Abraham and Jacob, Moses and David, and even the woman Rahab. I tell you this: Your God demands perfection, yet you give honor to a strange family of failures. Abraham was a liar and a coward. He gave his wife to Pharaoh's bed not once but twice to save himself. Yet your God calls him 'righteous.'

"Jacob, the deceiver, cheated his brother from his rightful inheritance and laid claim on it for himself. Yet your God made him the namesake of His special people. Moses was a murderer and an angry man all of his days. Yet your God gave him charge of all the Hebrews. And David! Oh, blessed King David, adulterer and murderer; a man who would steal another man's wife and then send him to his death. Your God called him 'beloved'! And even Rahab, the lying harlot, is exalted as one of the great women of your faith. What a pathetic roll of weak-willed, treacherous, and despicable hypocrites."

Pieter begged God for wisdom and strength, for his mind was cloudy and his heart was pressed within him. He looked at the eastern sky and was grateful to see the red edge of the rising sun.

The sorcerer cackled. "Old fool! I perceive you are crying to your Lord for help? 'How long, O Lord? Wilt Thou forget me forever? How long wilt Thou hide Thy face from me? How long shall my enemy be exalted over me'?"

Pieter answered him calmly. "'O Lord, my God, I cried to Thee for help and Thou hast heard me.'"

The lord returned to Tomas's side. "'The anger of the

Lord has burned against His people and He has stretched out His hand against them and struck them down.'"

Pieter kept the shield of Scripture about him. "'I will give thanks to Thee, O Lord, for although Thou wast angry against me Thine anger is turned away and Thou dost comfort me. I will trust and not be afraid. For the Lord God is my strength and song.'"

"Behold, old priest, the 'Lord lays the earth waste, devastates it, distorts its surface, and scatters its inhabitants. The world fades and withers. The exalted of the people of the earth fade away.'"

Pieter now smiled. "'He shall swallow up death for all time. And the Lord God shall wipe tears away from all faces and He shall remove the reproach of His people from all the earth, for the Lord has spoken. The Lord's lovingkindnesses indeed never cease. His compassions never fail.'"

The dark lord's anger was growing. *By now,* he thought, *this man ought be bending a knee, not standing in defiance.* He flung his arms, his black cape snapping in the light of daybreak. "God has failed you, and you, and you," he shouted as he jabbed his finger at Pieter and Karl and Wil. "And you, and you there, and you, little girl—what compassions, what lovingkindnesses?"

Pieter was not finished. "'The lovingkindness of God endures all day long. Thy tongue devises destruction. Beware to those who call evil good and good evil, who substitute darkness for light and light for darkness. Woe to those who are wise in their own eyes and clever in their own sight.'

"You poor, poor deceived man," continued Pieter. "For all of your finery and all of your wit and wealth of knowledge, for all your strength and power you have an empty soul, a hopeless faith."

"I have no faith at all!" boasted the lord.

"Ah, there," answered Pieter, "there is the chink in your false armor. For to believe as you demands greater faith than I would dare claim. But your faith rests on nothingness—a belief with no sound footing. Yet all of your words do suppose *something*—all words must—but your something is *nothing*. That makes thee something of a zero."

Conrad and Karl could not contain a giggle.

"Do not speak to me in riddles, old fool!" retorted the sorcerer. "I will not have it."

"You shall have what I give!" barked Pieter. "I have listened patiently and unless you fear my words, you shall listen to me."

"Fear?" jeered the dark lord. "Fear?" He clenched his fists at his temples. "I fear nothing, least of all the words of a half-dead priest of Rome."

"And to your many errors, you have just added another: I am a priest of Christ, as are my crusaders, and I speak to you as His servant, not the servant of the pope.

"I have listened to your words and weighed them in my mind. I look at you with sadness, sorcerer, for you are blind to the order and beauty and goodness that lies amidst the confusion and terror and evil. For such is evidence enough that there is a hope which waits to vanquish the evil we all see. Love, my friend, abounds and shall conquer in its proper season.

"The earth may groan for a time, waiting for its redemption, but it groans in hope. For wherever there is evil, there is always a reminder of good. I, too, see tears but I see smiles as well. I see clouds *and* sunshine, death *and* birth, sickness *and* healing, hunger *and* plenty. For every night there is a day.

"I can better endure the darkness in this world than you can the light. The sins of God's *volk* are not evidences of a faith gone mad, but rather proof of the very hope of which I speak! Our father Abraham was truly a coward and a liar, and Jacob a deceiver, and David an adulterer and murderer, and Rahab a harlot. You forgot to mention St. Peter, the betrayer of our Lord, or arrogant Joseph, or the 'chief of all sinners,' St. Paul. Nor did you remember to mention mine own name, for I stand before you as weak-minded and sinful, hypocrite of hypocrites.

"Aye, it is in our weaknesses and in our failures we do gratefully stand to claim the name of Jesus. It does not prove the futility of our faith, but rather the immensity of God's love. Can you imagine greater evidence of hope than this?

"As for the rest, I have no answers, no clever philosophy. I simply cannot understand the mysteries of our God, nor must I. I am content to admit that our sufferings seem to be that which do most surely draw us closer to Him. And in that closeness I see love, not madness; hope, not despair.

"We are changed in our sufferings. Like a thirsty tree in drought, our roots grow deeper in the source of our life. Nay, sad fellow, the confusions and miseries in this world are but tools in His workbox; tools to incline us toward Him and the mysterious joy that awaits our meeting. Oh, poor man, perhaps I ought ever suffer more, so that He draws me closer still!"

The sorcerer pursed his lips and shuffled on his feet. The blaze in his eyes had dwindled and he squinted to hide their fade. "Fool's fantasy, falsehood! Such rantings are beyond a sound mind's grasp."

The rising sun now cast thick beams of light into the clearing and the mist began its retreat. Pieter's face softened, his blue eyes twinkled gently. "Truth is not found in understanding but in the living God. For us it begins in the knowledge that we cannot know all. Ah! But in knowing Him we can know some.

"Our God is the known and the unknown, together and the same. He is the source of sunlight and shadows, smiles and tears. It is the heart of God which is the mighty keep of all joy and all pain, all triumphs and all failures.

"Mystery is our destined boundary, my son, and we choose to stand before either the mysteries of fear or the mysteries of hope. The former has been your choice, my friend, a place of superstition and darkness. But the latter is ready to welcome you into the light of faith."

"I am not your friend!" shouted the dark lord. "I look around me and I see no light; I see no hope, no traces of love ... none. Your smiles and sunshine, healings and days of plenty I claim as poor proofs; they are either shams of fate or natural effects. We wander through a world formed by our own intentions and we beget our own fruit, whether sweet or bitter. *Ach,* show me but one thing that bears the seal of a higher will—but one mark that reveals a Creator's good intent, and I'll yield to your call."

Pieter stood silently, wrestling with the man's passionate assertions and uncertain how to respond. He had, indeed, seen love abound midst the terrible of this world, and such love was surely born from beyond the matter and form of the rocks and waters of the earth. Yet he could not put words to it. He gripped his staff tightly and strained to set his thoughts to order, when a vision of good Georg filled his mind's eye. He drifted for just a moment to the boy's selfless act and he marveled in the knowledge that such manifest love might only have been wrought from the image of a good and intentional God.

Before Pieter could speak, Wil bent to his knees and plucked a beautiful wildflower from the dewy grass of the clearing. His heart lifted as he thought of Maria and he boldly stepped toward the sorcerer. He held the tiny flower by its stem and raised it high in the new day's light. "Here, sire, is our evidence—the simple mark of God's good intent."

The dark lord snatched the flower from Wil's fingers and stared at it, his jaw tightening.

Pieter's soul soared. Taking sudden pity on his adversary, he said, "Look carefully, sorcerer. I beg you to observe that gentle flower and tell me about the heart of One who might design such a thing. Why, see ... even the edges are laced with delicate color so that one's eye might look and be glad. Seems hardly the workmanship of a monster. And tell me of the weaver who might loom such a wonder only to scatter it at our feet to be enjoyed or trampled at our pleasure. Oh, my friend, can you not see hope in this? Can you not see that the God of the storm yet tends the beauty of a wildflower?"

The sorcerer scowled at Pieter and crushed the flower between his fingers. He glared at the crusaders but said no word. He hesitated for a moment, as if wanting to speak, and looked at Pieter one last time. Then he quickly turned and vanished into the wood.

At first, Pieter and his crusaders stood dumbfounded at the man's hasty retreat. Then some began to cheer but were abruptly hushed. "My precious little lambs," said the exhausted old man, "'be still; do not gloat when your enemy stumbles.'"

Pieter's heart now ached for the dark lord, for any without hope gave him cause for sorrow. He wondered what miseries in the sorcerer's past might have so cruelly wounded him. Then he watched the man's entourage begin to fade away, following after their leader. Pieter called after them, "*Kinder!* You are welcome to join us. Please join us."

Tomas glanced over his shoulder and cast an eye at his former comrades that revealed a sudden sadness. But the lad abruptly locked his jaw and turned away. The others ignored Pieter's pleas, except for three little ones who hesitated at the far edge of the clearing. They looked forlornly at Pieter and the tattered crusaders standing with him. There was weariness in their expressions, a resignation in their eyes. Pieter slowly opened his arms for them, praying all the while for God's hand to nudge them. Their eyes lingered for a moment, but they turned and melted away in the shadows of the forest.

≈

A weary Pieter napped through the rest of that hard-fought morn until the company prepared the midday's meal. He awakened to the familiar snapping of kindling and the rustling of busy hands around the campsite and gladly received a ladle of the day's fare. The steaming mash of boiled oats and millet seemed particularly tasty this morning, for Otto had found some honey along the trail and stirred it into the pot. But there was another sweetness to the moment, a quiet joy that seemed to waft among the children like the smoke from their crackling fire.

Wil sucked the final dip from his fingers, wiped them on his tunic, and leaned over to Pieter. "You have taught us well."

"Not I, dear boy, but the lessons themselves."

"Aye, but you've pointed us to places in the midst of troubles that others would not have known."

"Ah ... perhaps. But I, as well, have learned from others and you shall teach many of the journey your heart has taken."

Karl was whistling as the crusaders prepared to leave. The sun had brightened the marvelous colors of the wild-flowers dotting the clearing, and the boy took care to receive the moment of beauty as a gift. He ceased his tune when he noticed Pieter staring at the sky. "You are think-ing of Georg, are y'not?"

"Ah, that dear lad."

"And I, too. When that sorcerer claimed our world to be but darkness and despair—that there were no proofs of love anywhere—I thought of Georg ... and of Maria." Karl secured his few remaining provisions and tied his blanket. He looked at Wil. "And your thoughts were with our sister when you picked that flower."

Wil nodded sadly. "I could see her golden hair in the sunlight. I could see her bending and stooping ... picking flowers for us all."

"Do you think she has two good arms now?"

Saying nothing, Wil set his company in their familiar column and began the ascent of the last mountain ridge that separated them from the sea. They trudged up the dusty trail until, just before twilight, Karl got a pleased look on his face and began to hum. Pieter had seen that impish glint in the boy's eyes before.

"Ah, Father Pieter, you could never guess what I have discovered."

"I yield, Karl. I'll never guess."

"Could you try?"

"Fine. Uh ... I believe you have discovered a pouch of *deniers de Provins*?"

"Nay," laughed Karl. "You think too small."

"Ah, *ja, ja,* most surely."

"*Ach.* I am only playing with you. But hear me. I have discovered something more important to me than a mere bag of pennies, even of the best quality."

The other children drew closer.

"What might be better than a bag of good coins?" asked Heinz.

"Many things," answered Karl proudly. "But especially this."

Wil ordered a brief respite and the tired band collapsed by the side of the trail in a curious circle around Karl. The redhead was flushed with excitement and grinned a wide, happy grin.

Otto grew impatient and scolded the boy. "Speak. We've places to go, Karl!"

Wil agreed. "Aye, say what you must."

"*Ja, ja.* Always making haste, aren't we? Ah, no matter. Listen all—I have solved Pieter's master riddle."

"Ah?" exclaimed Pieter. "This *is* a lofty matter. I was not sure you would ever solve it; even *I* lose the answer daily."

"But I have," retorted Karl. "I have. 'Twas a good riddle. A bit difficult at first, I do admit."

"Aye, aye, lad, get on with it then. Though do not be angry should you be off again."

"Nay, not this time, Pieter. You yielded an important clue in your challenge with the sorcerer."

"I did?"

"Indeed you did. I was listening to every word you said. When you held the little flower I suddenly saw a whole valley of them spread before me in m'mind's eye. I then remembered the clue: 'Where can be the valley where the fragrance of a rose, can linger centuries after it has bathed a maiden's nose?'

"I thought and listened, and then you said the words." Karl became suddenly serious. "You said there is something 'that holds both sunlight and shadows' ... and I knew at once that was from your riddle."

"How did you know that?" blurted Otto.

"Remember the one verse, 'Where do shadows gather after they have lost their light'?"

"Not really."

"Nay? If you gave attention you'd have remembered it."

"I gave attention."

"Not as much as I. That is why *I* am solving this riddle."

"Well then, solve the cursed riddle!" yelled Heinz.

Pieter cast a scolding look at the frustrated youngster while Karl cleared his throat in dramatic fashion. "The question of your riddle is, 'What is the Haven'?

"And the answer is: the heart of God."

Pieter stood silently for a moment and clutched his staff to his breast. Tears filled his eyes. He looked at the bright-eyed boy proudly. "And ... and why do you believe it so?"

"Your riddle was about a place. A place where everything goes to and where everything comes from. It is a place that holds all things together and heals and maintains all things that are."

Pieter nodded his old, white head and laid a hand on Karl's red curls. "God has blessed you, my son, with a tender heart for Him. May you delight in Him for all your days. *Ja, ja!*" he cried. "It *is* the heart of God!" Pieter embraced Karl. "I am so very proud," he whispered, "so very proud." Pieter wrapped his spindly arm around the beaming boy and turned to his children. "This child of a baker has grasped more than that learned sorcerer who now hides in the darkness of the forest. The heart of God, children, is our Haven. It is that which holds all things in its loving keep ... our joys and our sufferings, our victories, our failings, our dreams, and our disappointments. It is that sure place that holds us fast."

Pieter bent over and plucked a white wildflower from the ground and he asked for Frieda's applewood cross from her belt. "The flower, my children, is our symbol of the presence of God, and these crosses we carry a symbol of His love. By them, my precious lambs, know these two things: that God is there and that He cares. Know these and you needs know little else."

Chapter 26
THE GARDEN OF WILDFLOWERS

That night the children circled their campfire at peace with themselves and each other and excited to be near the sea. They laughed and sang and shared memories of their journey—some joyful, some heart-wrenching, some yet terrifying. Pieter leaned against the broad trunk of an old tree and looked wistfully at the snapping flames. His solemn face revealed a pain in his heart. Frieda and Gertrude tugged on his sleeve and looked into his sad eyes.

"You are thinking of Solomon, are you not, Pieter?" asked Frieda softly.

"Yes. I do truly miss m'old friend. I miss him so very much. And I miss my other friends as well. 'Tis the way of life."

Frieda smiled. "I remember watching Solomon spin with you in Dunkeldorf."

"The signal that called you to trust me?"

"*Ja*," recalled Wil from across the way. "I remember watching you turn on that old barrel. I'd wager y'd fallen ten times."

Karl laughed. "Can y'not see him flopping in the dust only to get up and spin some more, with Solomon chasing his tail by his side? Methinks the marketplace thought him to be a madman."

"Ja, surely it was so," said Frieda. "But it was a good signal and it rescued us from danger."

"I was so very proud that day," said Pieter. "You believed

me. You obeyed because you trusted my care for you. I think I never thanked you all." He put his whiskered chin on his chest and let his thoughts drift. He wandered to the mountain passes and the snowdrift, the Waldensians, the flood, the field of dead, the bier of children, Domodossola, the baths of Pavia, the death of Georg, Maria and her wild-flowers, and so much more. He grunted and sniffled, leaned over onto his bough bed, and soon fell fast asleep.

At dawn Wil reminded his company that, at the very latest, on the morrow next they ought enter Genoa. The crusaders were so excited by the very thought of it that they could barely assemble in proper order. But, after a few stern commands and a good scolding for Heinz, Wil gained control and the band continued their march toward the elusive city.

By midday they had come upon a roadway which wound its way down the sloping shoulders of the mountains bordering the port. The dusty road was easy to walk and the descent was gentle, though rolling since the ridges were aligned in parallel to the sea. At each rise the eager crusaders strained to claim the first view of the water, and from time to time this pilgrim or that would cry out in joy. But the fanciful hopes of young minds do tricks on the impatient.

So the stubborn band pressed on, each eye peering over every change in the horizon until, at long last, a voice cried out, "There. *Ja.* 'Tis so. The sea, the sea!"

And it was so. A sparkling light from the waters of the sea shimmered through a tiny space framed by two distant slopes and the crusaders wept for joy. Pieter fell to his knees and raised his hands to his triumphant Maker and sang songs of gladness as his children danced.

Jubilance finally gave way to quiet awe and a voice chirped, "Shall the sea truly part for us, Pieter?"

"Eh? Well, by truth I do confess that am not expecting this to happen, but ..."

"But the vision said it surely would," insisted another.

"Aye, but the sea does not obey visions."

"Nay, but it obeys Jesus!" boomed Karl.

"Well said, lad, of course. But it may be that Nicholas's vision has been misunderstood or perhaps it was but a symbol; after all, what about the poor fish?"

"What about poor us?"

Pieter's eyes twinkled. "Hmm. It seems to me it would be more merciful for God to provide you a worthy vessel instead of demanding you march for weeks over a sea bed ... dry or not."

The children looked at their battered feet and yielded to Pieter's wisdom.

❧

As the company moved closer to Genoa, the roadway became more and more crowded with peddlers, pilgrims, men-at-arms, and travelers of every imaginable sort. Heavy-laden carts groaned and creaked behind horses and donkeys straining against their yokes. Wagons heaped high with fresh-picked pears and apples lumbered and lurched their way along—those heading north working the whip and those pointed south leaning hard on creaking brakes.

The sun was bright and the air was warm. The smell of salt air grew stronger and the joyful crusaders nearly ran down each descent. Then, at last ... at long last ... they rounded a curve and beheld the full majesty of the sea. So stunning was the sight that the children could do nothing else than stop and gasp and stare in disbelief.

Heinz broke the silence. "'Tis truly there?"

The others laughed.

Otto's green eyes sparkled. "Aye, Heinz, 'tis truly there."

Wil and Karl stood shoulder to shoulder. "To think we've come so very far!" said Wil. "And look, 'tis as if the sky and water join somewhere out there."

"I cannot see the end," noted Karl. "I cannot see the end at all. Is that the edge of the world?"

"Look there," said Frieda. "Look there!" She pointed to four tiny white dots.

"Ah, you see the sails of ships traveling south," Pieter instructed. "And look over there; you'll see more."

Wil could have spent the whole day just gazing at the

wonder before him. Though he had not yet set foot in
Palestine, reaching the sea was, itself, a feat that swelled
his heart. Ever mindful of his duties, however, he turned
his eyes away and ordered a midday meal at the very spot
where all could enjoy the beautiful sight. He ordered his
soldiers to build their fire on the shoulder of the road. After
all, perhaps passersby might offer a bit of charity from the
plenty of their wagons.

Before long the crusaders were chewing on strips of
salted pork and a few crusts of bread. Otto and Heinz had
found some apples that had fallen from a passing cart, and
a kindly stranger tossed Frieda a cheese and a small slab
of bacon. To these pilgrims it was a meal that surpassed
Gostanzo's feast. They basked in the Italian sunshine and
laughed and drew their nostrils tight on the intoxicating
smell of the salt air.

Karl was radiant. His blue eyes sparkled like the waves
shimmering in the distance and his ruddy face flushed
with excitement. His curly red hair was dancing in the sea
breezes rising from below. He finished his meal and studied the long, sloping mountains dropping gently toward
the spires of the city. His eyes lingered on the castles
perched atop ridges on his left and his right. *At last*, he
thought, *and then to Palestine*. He looked into the faces of
his many companions and felt warm and good as he
thought of each of them.

When he spotted a patch of flowers on the opposite side of
the roadway, he pictured Maria and sighed. He stood and
secured her cross in his belt. *She would have wanted all the
girls to enter the city with flowers in their hair!* he mused.

Dashing across the busy road, he found himself shin-
deep in a wonderful bouquet. There were yellows and reds,
purples and blues, delicate blooms and bold. He reached
down and gently plucked a long-stemmed, white flower
with a beautiful golden center and held it to his nose; he
reached for broad-petaled, orange flowers and red-laced
blue ones, soft pinks and bright lavenders. He hummed
and whistled, certain that the angels themselves had
planted this majestic garden for just this very day.

Pieter, Wil, and the others were resting peacefully in the grass. The sun felt so good to them and there was such comfort in being finally near the sea. But the quiet of the moment was suddenly broken with the sound of hooves thundering down the mountain. With no thought to the helpless travelers at their feet, a troop of light-armored cavalry were crashing their way through the crowded roadway. Behind them charged a team of thick-chested horses hauling a huge wagon loaded with footmen and barrels of supplies. Midst shouts and screams the company rammed their way through the scattering throng, dumping carts and trampling any in their way.

Wil's quick eye fell on Karl, distracted and lost in thought, and picking flowers dangerously near the edge of the bend. His eye flew back to the soldiers whose reckless path now seemed aimed directly at Karl. He jumped to his feet and called frantically, but the roar of the tumult suffocated his cries. He raced toward his brother waving his hands desperately. "Karl, Karl, move! Move!" he screamed. "Move!"

The deafening sounds of hooves roared closer and closer to Karl until, at last, the startled boy jerked upright. Without a thought, he instinctively dashed onto the roadway in a desperate flight toward the far side. He sprinted a few strides with all the speed his panicked legs could gather, but it was not enough; his red head vanished in a blur of horseflesh, wagon wheels, and clouds of dust.

Wil cried out as one horse stumbled, but when he saw the huge wagon bounce, his heart seized. He knew that Karl was lost.

The crusaders dashed onto the roadway as the soldiers disappeared around the bend. Wil led the frantic charge and reached Karl first. He collapsed by his brother's side and cradled the lad's crumpled body in his arms. "Oh God, oh God!" he wailed. "Not you, Karl. Oh God, not you!"

The others fell about the boy weeping and wailing in utter shock. Fingers spread toward the broken body, lightly touching it as if to impart some spark of life. Desperately,

Pieter pushed his way through the circle of his crusaders until his body folded in the dust beside his
beloved Karl. The old man shook violently where he lay,
weeping and groaning and beating the earth with angry
fists.

Suddenly Karl stirred. Wil's eyes widened and all grew
still. "Qu-quickly ... quickly ... help me, Otto!" he cried.
"We needs lift him off the road."

With the help of many anxious hands, the two boys gently moved Karl to the grass where not long ago all had
lounged in the warm sun. They laid his body on the soft
earth and his head on Wil's lap. Pieter tenderly held one of
his crushed hands in his own, and Frieda stroked the
boy's red curls.

Karl's chest heaved as he gasped for air. His eyes fluttered for a moment, then opened bright and blue. He
smiled faintly and wheezed another breath. Blood frothed
from his mouth and now began to ooze from his ears, dripping slowly onto Wil's sleeves. The beloved lad looked at Wil
and then at Pieter. His eyes offered kindness.

"Dear, Karl," whimpered Wil. "I ... I ..." Wil stroked Karl's
cheek as his tears fell onto his dying brother's brow.

Karl tried to speak but failed. His generous heart, however, urged a quivering smile.

Pieter leaned close to the boy and set a soft hand on his
arm. "This day your soul shall find its rest, my dear lad.
You shall set your feet in the Holy Land, indeed." He laid
his trembling hands on the boy's head and prayed, "*Ego te
absolvo ab omnibus censurius et peccatis in nomine Patris
et Filii et Spiritus Sancti.*"

Wil bent close to Karl's ear and whispered, "Forgive me,
Karl, for the ways that I have sinned against you. Know
that I have always loved you.

"And ... and tell Maria," Wil continued, "I ... I do love her
so." His voice faltered.

Karl shook his head and labored desperately to speak.
"Her ... cross," he whispered hoarsely. "Give ... Maria her
cross ..."

Pieter and Wil stared at each other, astonished at the

boy's unfaltering faith. Wil bent to his ear and answered. "I will believe, Karl. I will see that her cross is returned to her own hand."

Karl's eyes began to dim but he stared about the circle of tear-stained faces drawing close to his own. He struggled to draw another breath into his crushed lungs, then released it with a whisper. "God is good ..."

His body shuddered and his eyes rolled white. His face relaxed and he settled quietly against his brother's heaving breast.

There were no words to be spoken for none could have eased, in any part, the agony each crusader now suffered. The dreadful familiarity of such excruciating pain prompted, instead, a silent ritual that offered what little comfort that might be found. Each comrade laid a hand, in turn, upon poor Karl and bade farewell. All the while Wil rocked his brother and wept. When all had passed by, Pieter laid a trembling hand upon Wil's hardened shoulders and knelt by his side.

They washed Karl's body with water offered by sympathetic travelers and wrapped it in a shroud of linen Heinz begged from a passing merchant. By late day he was carried to his "Angel's Garden" and buried beneath the wildflowers. Frieda removed her crusader's cross and set it lovingly above his head and the fellowship joined hands.

Pieter fumbled through a prayer, but, unable to speak any longer, he simply crumbled by his cherished boy's grave. The children huddled quietly and stared mutely at the distant blue water. It did not draw them as it had, nor did it seem as beautiful. And the sun no longer felt warm and healing, nor did the air smell clean and good. None wished to leave Karl's side and so they gathered around his grave for all that dreadful evening. As night fell they simply sprawled in the flowers and stared at the starry heavens above until, at long last, sleep came.

Dawn broke but was not escorted with fresh joy, and the company yet grieved. Some woke hoping Karl's death was but an awful nightmare ... a wicked, starlight tale spun by rotted pork or green apples. But it was not so, and they rose for the day with little vigor, void of all incentive to press the final day's march.

Pieter took Wil aside. "Karl now rests in the 'Haven.' He rests in the bosom of God. Y'might close your eyes and see him now playing with the others, teasing with Georg. Perhaps he is trying his riddles on the angels."

Wil smiled a little.

"My son, we may stay or we may go; we may press to the sea or return to our homes. You, as always, are the commander of this company and we await your orders."

Wil sat alone by the graveside, staring at the sea while his soldiers choked down reluctant mouthfuls of morning gruel. At last he climbed to his feet and faced Pieter and his patient followers. He straightened his tunic and cleared his throat. "Should there be a time to end our crusade, I'll surely know it. I have considered the matter with care and it is my decision to go forward. Karl and Maria, Georg and Manfred, and so many others did not want our pilgrimage to end on their accounts. And this: I ... I believe God has not told me to stop. I'll trust Him to make it plain if I ought end this journey."

Wil stooped to pluck a long-stemmed wildflower and secured it in his belt where his dagger once hung. He turned to Pieter. "You say you'll not follow us beyond the shore. You say you'll return to find our Maria?"

Pieter nodded.

Wil took Maria's cross from his belt and handed it to the old man. "Then I charge you with this final duty: When you bid us farewell, find Maria and kiss her for us all. Then give her this; set it in her hand with Karl's blessing."

Pieter received the cross and held it to his breast. "This I do vow."

Wil then lashed together two wooden crosses from some poplar sticks. One he handed to Frieda, the other he gripped tightly in his shaking hand. He surveyed his remnant and cast a longing, loving eye at Karl's grave before setting order to his troop. His crusaders then raised all of their wooden crosses high and sang their melody as they marched bravely past their fallen comrade toward Genoa and the sea.

☙

A short while later the crusaders rounded a bend where Wil commanded they stop. "There," proclaimed Wil. "There waits Genoa."

The children were not able to fully savor the sight below them, for their hearts were yet heavy. But they nevertheless were pleased to note gray-tiled rooftops sprawling from the mountain slopes to the curved harbor at the sea's blue edge. Beholding Genoa was like having a large burden lifted from their bent backs and they sighed, relieved and satisfied. They stopped in the shade of short, broad-leafed trees and rested briefly.

"Look," pointed Pieter. "You see the tall spire of the Cathedral of San Lorenzo? Ah, 'twas old when I was but a smooth-faced boy. And look there, at the harbor wall. Do you see the tall masts of the galleys? *Ach, kinder*, this place is not as any other y'have ever seen. 'Tis rich with art and blessed with plenty … but it is not a good place. Heed m'words. Genoa is a proud city and a free city. It owes homage to no lord. Keep close and keep watch. These people are shrewd and wily. Treat them with respect and trust none."

"You'll heed Pieter's words," barked Wil. "Now … to Genoa."

The children formed their column and commenced their final march. The city's walls loomed ever closer, and then at last, with neither fanfare nor salutation, they paraded past the gate's stern porters and onto the streets of the busy port.

The sights and wonders of Genoa slowed the crusaders' steps and they walked over the smooth cobblestone streets gaping at the white-and-gray stone buildings towering over them on all sides. But the jeers of the folk made them apprehensive and ill-at-ease, and they quickly felt like unfit callers from another world. The crowded walkways, the busy markets, and the noise were not unfamiliar; nor was the hostile spirit of the population. After all, they had been witness to such things in Basel and Dunkeldorf. Perhaps it was the foreign tongue or the plastered walls or the septic air that added to their estrangement. But, for whatever cause, the company soon lost its joy.

As the cautious band marched deeper toward the city's center, it seemed that the citizens became ever more mean-spirited. Now curses and oaths were hurled from open windows as well as refuse and dung. Finally, an angry *casalinga* charged from behind her brown stuccoed home and swung her broom wildly at them. *"Tornate a casa!"* she shrieked. *"Tornate a casa!"*

Pieter sighed. "She says, 'Go home you brats.'"

Wil encouraged his friends. "We've met worse than an old hag with a broom." His comment earned a few half-hearted smiles but the disillusionment of their reception would not be so easily overcome. Some wondered if Jerusalem would be equally disappointing.

They trudged along the streets and turned a corner only to pass by an old man sitting on a stubby oak stool. By the look of him Conrad knew more unpleasantry was in store. He set his jaw and stared straight ahead. As all expected, the crotchety old man stood up and shook his tankard of wine violently, spilling most of its contents on his sleeve. *"Tornate da dove siete venuti, via, via."*

Heinz tugged on Pieter's tunic as they walked by. "What did he say?"

"Oh, nothing very complimentary."

Otto pressed. "What did he say? Tell us."

"He said, 'Get out of here. Go back where you came from.'"

The crusaders tightened their column only to walk headlong into several men-at-arms. Three soldiers stepped toward them. *"Andate vi!"* boomed one.

Wil put his hands on his hips and was about to speak when Pieter interrupted. *"Signore,* we are about the business of Crusade and need ..."

"Si, si," said another guard. "We know exactly what you be here for. Legions have come before you and none are welcome."

"But, sir, I implore thee ..."

"Begone. You shall not remain in this city."

"Good sir," insisted Pieter, "we are not without means."

The soldiers eyed the priest suspiciously. They looked carefully at the ripped tunics, the tattered blankets, the worn shoes. One bent low to look at Heinz. He took his helmet from his head and held it under his arm as he placed his long nose close to the boy's dirty face. "You, my little master of the northland," he said sarcastically. "You are of some means?"

Heinz could not understand the man but fully grasped his tone. He puffed his chest and glared.

Pieter stepped to the soldier's side. "I said, my son, we are not without means and that is what I meant."

The guard stood upright and replaced his helmet on his head. He measured his words. "You've the look of a *padre* of sorts; perhaps you claim to follow Francis of Assisi?"

"I don't know the man, but I follow none save young Wil here."

"Yet you wear a black robe and have a strange cross about yer neck."

"*Si.* Forgive me, sire, I ought be more plain. As you, I do follow our Savior."

"That's beside the point," growled another guard. "Our city is overrun with these thieving whelps from the north and we've no need of more. But since you claim to be a *padre*, you've the choice to walk away or to meet our dungeon master."

The sudden image of Basel's terror made Pieter cringe. He quickly plucked the pouch of coins from his belt and bounced it in his hand. "I say again, *signore*, we are not thieves—I am a priest. Unlike others we have been blessed with special means." He opened the bag and pinched out a few pennies.

The soldiers whispered amongst themselves, then turned to Pieter. "Are we to believe that is not stolen money?" one quipped. "Or perhaps you were paid for forgiving sins."

Pieter slowly dropped each coin back in his pouch. He held the last few in his fingers and lifted them toward the group. "Our pardon, sirs, for robbing you of your time. Perhaps we ought pay you for it." He tossed the coins into the air and let them bounce about their boots.

As the soldiers scrambled to snatch the scattering pennies from the cobbled street, the children slipped by and lost themselves in an alleyway. Once certain they were free to move along, they followed the downward streets toward the water's edge.

As they passed through the oldest portions of the city, the crusaders took better note of how very different was this place. Here were no steep-pitched thatched roofs or heavy-timbers. Instead were stone or plastered buildings capped with strange, tile shingles. Instead of brown hues and tans were whites and greys and the trees seemed shorter and stout. At long last the column turned a final corner and faced the busy docks. The children's eyes stretched wide and mouths dropped as they beheld the proud bows of huge galleys from the entire known world. The ships seemed to be waiting patiently, resting comfortably on the clean, blue-green water and tethered to their smooth pilings like mighty oxen tied to heavy poles.

Pieter admitted little knowledge of sailing but pointed his curious flock to the masts and spars bearing tightly wrapped sails. "And see the framework of tholes and pins. Do they not seem to be as a carving chiseled by a master? And there, look to that ship's double-rowed sweeps. Ah, she'll cut through still water with speed enough. I'd wager that barking *capitano* can squeeze the best from her sails, as well."

The children turned from the ships and were equally impressed with the sight of the wharves. It was here where the fruits of the sea mingled with those of the land. Alongside baskets of black pepper and barrels of olives were tables piled high with fish. So many fish, the children thought, that all of Christendom might be fed forever! It was here where north and south melded; jars of fragrant oils from Damascus were set by bales of wool from Linz and barrels of grain from Chartres; casks of northern ales sat by barrels of southern wines. Piles of Nordic timber rose next to heaps of smooth Indian silk, spun cotton, and the finest Flemish linen. Beautiful tapestries were mounded on carts pointed north, while other carts hauled amber or furs destined for Constantinople, Palestine, and far-off Cathay.

The children's ears cocked with the sounds of seagulls and snapping sails, boatmen barking orders, bells and horns blaring, merchants hawking their wares; mules braying, and horses clopping on the sturdy planks of the wharf. It was a sea of humanity beside a sea of water.

But amid the grand spectacle, Pieter did not miss the gaunt faces of dozens and dozens of half-starved children wandering aimlessly along the waterfront begging and pleading for a morsel of food or sip of fresh water. His old heart broke and he beckoned several to him. "Little ones," he said softly, "what are you doing?"

A scrawny girl with long red hair tied behind her back looked at him sadly. Her face was sallow and her limbs but skin on bone. Pieter thought her to be about seven years old. *"Ich habe hunger, Vater,"* she said. "And so tired and lost."

Pieter's eyes moistened and he reached to hold her. Fearful of his touch she pulled away.

"Oh, m'precious lamb," he said. "Precious little lamb, do not be afraid."

She looked at him from round, green eyes. "I have walked far but I have no one."

Others began to slowly gather around, wary, but each dirty face belying a yearning for comfort and protection. Pieter smiled at the ring of hopefuls staring at him.

"And you, good lad, and you, *Mädel*, and you ... and you ... I give m'blessings to all."

A brave boy of about fourteen years stepped forward on his swollen bare feet. His sandy hair was long and dirty. His face was smudged with grime and drawn with hunger and his blue eyes were runny and bloodshot. "M'name is Helmut of the lands of Lord Ohrsbach near Bremen ... and ... and I wish to go home."

Pieter sat on the ground and nodded as his crusaders

now encircled the newcomers. To some of his fellows it seemed that their guide had suddenly aged a hundred years. He did not speak at first, but studied the anxious throng of *kinder* leaning toward him. At last he answered the waiting boy. "And so you shall, dear boy, so you shall."

He turned again to the red-headed girl. "And what is your name, my dear?"

She hesitated for a moment, but answered with a sob. "I am Ava and I don't know where I am from."

"Do any of you know Ava?" Pieter asked the others.

None answered.

"Then, my dear Ava," he said, "you shall be my friend and together we'll find your home."

Pieter beckoned Gertrude to his side and introduced Ava to her. Gertrude took the newcomer by both hands and they each smiled. The old man looked around the growing circle. "Listen to m'words, *kinder*. Any wishing to be m'friend is welcome. But first, I must help m'other friends embark on their journey."

Pieter leaned hard on his staff for his heart was heavy and he was so very, very weary. But the faces that suddenly brightened around him lifted his spirits. "Now all of you, save Wil, wait here and do not move. Greet each other and talk to none other than yourselves until our return."

"Wil, methinks the sea did not open. If you must press on, then we needs find a ship for passage."

"Then let us find a ship," answered Wil. A glint of determination flashed in his eye and Pieter suddenly felt uneasy, concerned the young man's self-reliant pride may have been rekindled.

The two left the others behind and began a search along the docks for a ship bound for Palestine. For the better part of the day their search proved fruitless as they suffered the mockery of nearly every ship's crew they engaged. But they had surely endured more outrage than the oaths of mere seamen and their persistent quest finally led them aboard *Madre Maria*.

"Ho there, my good *Capitano*," announced Pieter, "I seek passage for some pilgrims to Palestine."

The captain strode toward Pieter and laughed like the others. "Ha! Is that so? Pity, you are too late," he said. "Seven shiploads of your fair-faced whelps left this very port some time afore St. Michael's Day."

"Ah, I see. And when was St. Michael's?

"Ha! Just two days past. And 'twas quite a feast, indeed!"

Pieter's face tightened and his skin flushed. "Could not this city spare a bit of feast for the poor *bambini* left behind?"

"Humph. Poor children left behind? The little devils never stop pouring from the mountains. We gather them up and ship them away as fast as we can, but still they come. And thousands left here for ports south ... and some for Rome.

"The wretches that infest these docks are fever-bearers and thieves. Soon they shall be rounded up like rats and drowned."

Pieter stamped his staff onto the deck. "These are children!" he roared. "Poor, helpless children!"

"Not so helpless," added a sailor walking by. "Not so helpless that they cannot steal. When I was a boy we'd 'ave been hanged for less. *No*. They are getting just what they deserve."

"And what might that be?" growled Pieter.

"Stay by the docks this night," said the sailor, "and see what happens to those who cannot hide ... especially those little yellow-haired girls."

Pieter's fury rose like a raging Leviathan from deep waters and between his clenched teeth he pronounced a curse on the grinning seaman. "On you I cast damnation. May thy soul howl in torment through all the ages to come, may ..."

Wil took Pieter by the arm and quieted him as the sailor laughed his way into the ship's hold. When the priest's anger quelled he turned a hard eye to the amused captain. "I say again, *Capitano*, what ship might be leaving for Palestine?"

The man stroked his short black beard and answered, "For a price, old man, I will see what I might learn along the wharf. But I suppose your brood has no fare? Nor do they have the strength to pull the sweeps ... nor hang a sail...."

Pieter snapped a quick reply. "Indeed, sir, you are off the mark. I have less than a dozen of children and they've coins to pay."

The captain laughed. "And I'm sure they've shillings enough for a distance as this! Ah, but I'll see what I can find."

Pieter thanked the man and walked with Wil to the edge of the dock. The two sat on the weather-worn planks and stared at the horizon. "I hope to never forget such a sight, Pieter," Wil said. "It seems the sun is going to drown in all that water."

"Watch and remember. Smell the smells, hear the sounds, taste the air; aye, even touch the rough wood under your young fingers. Feel life, lad. Feel it with all you can!"

Suddenly Heinz raced up to the pair. "Father Pieter! We need you soon. The others tell us we needs hide when the torches light."

Pieter returned to the anxious flock and raised his hands over them. "Fear not. You shall be safe this night; you've numbers enough."

Wil called to his crusaders. "We've a matter to settle," he said in hushed tones. "We may have found passage."

The children nodded.

Wil turned to the newcomers. "Do any wish to join us?"

Most shook their heads and a voice muttered timidly, "We … we just want to go home."

But one boy stepped forward. He was a quiet-spoken lad. "M'name is Paul from Cologne and I should want to go."

Conrad clasped his hand. "Then welcome."

Gertrude had been whispering with Frieda and she stepped forward. "Wil?" she asked in a trembling voice, "would you be angry if Paul used m'place? Methinks I'd rather stay with Pieter and these others; I want to go to Maria and Anna."

Wil looked compassionately at the nervous girl. He set his finger under her drooped chin and lifted her face toward his. His throat swelled. "Of course, dear Gertrude, you may stay."

"Do any others of my company wish to stay with Pieter?" asked Wil loudly.

Most shifted on their feet, but none wished to remain. Satisfied that all was properly settled, Wil led the entire company toward the far end of the city docks where Pieter gave them some instructions. "We've business to attend; then we'll return. Gather wood for a large fire and if we are delayed, stay together."

Wil and Pieter hurried back to the *Madre Maria* in hopes of news. "The stars be with you, old man," announced the captain. "I've found your whelps passage with a friend of mine, but the cost is one shilling each and my fee is one as well."

It took a moment for Pieter to translate the words to Wil. The boy stiffened and wagged an angry finger in the man's face. "We are on Holy Crusade. How dare you demand so much?"

The captain folded his arms and shrugged. "The lad's barbaric tongue means nothing to me. Tell him he pays, else he may march back the way he came."

Pieter bowed respectfully. "Good sir, we've not enough but you may have all we have." Pieter tossed him six pennies. "As for you, we have three pennies for your trouble. Now what've ye learned of the ship?"

The man complained. "'Tis not the bargain!"

"The price is reduced ... so which is our ship?"

"There," pointed the man angrily. "Two slips away waits the *San Marco*. May the demons of deep water have your souls."

Pieter and Wil walked across the dock and stood before the ship rocking gently in the fading light. It seemed to be a good ship, stout and high-sided, with a single row of sweeps and two sturdy masts. It had a hardy look about it, a strength wrought by many seasons on the sea. Wil's heart fluttered with excitement.

But Pieter was uneasy. He sensed danger but dismissed his feelings abruptly as he followed Wil up the boarding plank. The two stepped, unchallenged, on to the warped deck of the *San Marco* and stood quietly to study the vessel.

Wil was bursting. He raised his face and strained to see the tops of the masts. He had only ever seen the boats of the river; stout, single-masted cogs, or flat-bottomed barges, or simple ferries. But this was so much more. He ran his hands along the smooth oak railing and admired the shipwright who had so skillfully crafted it.

"I see you like my little boat," boasted a tall, thin man who emerged from a lantern-lit cabin. "My name is *Capitano* Gaetano and I speak your tongue. This big *furfante* is Otavio, my mate. I am told you seek passage to Palestine."

Pieter nodded.

"*Si.* 'Tis plain your stars are in proper place. This ship sets her sails with the morning tide. We've a shipment of medicines and arms for hospitalers in Acre." The man smiled. "It would bring us luck to escort a company of God's chosen."

The captain raised his eyebrows and turned his look to Wil. "*Ragazzo*, you might like to know that the first of your crusaders are safely bound for Jerusalem. We've heard the infidels have begun to faint just at the word of it!"

"You are certain?"

"*Si* .... as certain as I might be of the word of the sea. Perhaps it is true and perhaps it is not, for sailors are a clever lot."

Pieter was not amused at the man's repartee; he'd have been more content were the captain less clever and per- haps, better still, dim-witted. *Let him know the sea and his ship and no more. He's a quick tongue and a cunning look.*

Further, Pieter felt growing apprehension toward Otavio. The priest set a hawk's eye on the burly seaman and chilled. Otavio stood tall and as straight as the mast behind him, a white shirt hanging loosely from his huge shoulders and a silk sash girding his large belly. His broad head was covered with a red scarf knotted on one side. A single, golden earring glowed in the dim light of the ship's torch and his thick hand rested all too comfortably on the hilt of a silver-edged cutlass that was clearly his familiar companion.

Captain Gaetano continued. "I believe my friend has told you our fare?"

Pieter momentarily reconsidered, then yielded. "*Si,*" he said slowly. "Here is all we have." He set a modest pouch of silver in the captain's hand.

Gaetano threw his head back and laughed. "Now I am certain you to be a priest! I have yet to meet one who was not a scoundrel. The agreed amount, my friend, was a shilling for each passenger ... perhaps fifteen I am told?"

"Well, that was the proposed price, but I told your fellow that we'd be happy to offer all we have and there it is."

Gaetano tested the weight in his spread palm and feigned disappointment. "Ah, *Padre!* You wound me. I must feed them and hear their whinings and ... ah, no matter. Perhaps God may bless the voyage all the more for m'loss." Gaetano tossed the bag to Otavio and smiled. "Be here afore first light or we needs set off without you."

Pieter and Wil returned to the waiting children and announced the news. "We've a ship and sail on the morrow's dawn!" proclaimed Wil triumphantly. His fellows cheered and closed around him to hear his tale of the ship and the exciting news of Nicholas and the first wave of crusaders.

"We're told our brothers and sisters are near Jerusalem, that the infidels are in fear! We'll surely rescue Palestine ... just as promised!"

The children were soon caught up in wild chatter of sailing ships and ocean waves and Saracens. Finally, Pieter interrupted the celebration and herded his ever-growing flock to an open field at the edge of the docks. "There is always strength in numbers," he said. "Even if we are but children and an old man."

Wil ordered the fire be built and his followers were directed to share the last of their provisions with the others. Pieter found two drunken soldiers with whom he exchanged prayers for the souls of their departed mothers for their guard over his growing flock. And, after a meager meal, a bit more chatter, and a few quiet prayers, some two-score children fell fast asleep in the warm glow of a bold campfire.

Well before dawn and some before lauds, Pieter awakened and wandered among the slumbering innocents clustered all around. He fell to his knees and prayed God's mercy on each and every one ... those with whom he had traveled so far and those whom he had just met. When he had laid his hands on the last of them he crawled to a distant corner and lay prostrate in the dew. "Dear God," he groaned, "I've neither the strength to bid my beloved farewell, nor to return o'er the mountains with these others." He felt truly weary and overwhelmed.

Chapter 27
FREEDOM FOUND

As the bright stars of dawn faded in a bluing sky, Wil jumped to his feet and hastily roused his comrades. "Come, soldiers, awake! This is the day we sail. Wake! Wake!"

The lad's words had barely left his lips when his excited companions left their backs and rushed to form their familiar column. They giggled and wiggled, chattering and chortling of adventures past and the glory of their coming conquest. With the larger group of newcomers now crowding around them, the crusaders then raised their crosses and marched confidently to the docks.

As the band reached the *San Marco's* pier it was met by a few grumbling hands grousing about their duties. The sailors were not enthused to board a "litter of whelps," and they were quick to show their disapproval with a chorus of foul oaths and blasphemies. But the sight of Frieda, supple and curved, blonde and fair, stayed their tongues and they set aside their chores to leer. Wil bristled but could do little but glare from this one to that and pray the captain would soon appear.

At long last, Gaetano emerged from his cabin. He and his mate, Otavio, stepped to the top of the plank and welcomed all on board. "*Si, si, bambini!* Board my *San Marco*. She is ready."

The time had come; the moment all had dreamt of, struggled for, died for … and the crusaders were suddenly confused. The thought of leaving Pieter gripped them and they turned to face him with tear-filled eyes.

Pieter stood as bravely as his trembling legs would allow, for he was determined to offer a countenance of confidence and strength. But, as each one embraced him, his will gave way to the grief dammed behind his eyes and swelling his throat. He set down his trusted staff and hugged each tightly, leaving his tears on all.

Brave and stout-hearted Conrad clasped his hand securely into Pieter's and fought the river of tears surging behind his own eyes. And, alas, he too lost the fight and collapsed into his old friend's embrace weeping like the child he still was.

Ever sturdy, dirty-faced Otto rubbed his hands through his matted, sandy hair and hugged the old man briefly, then raced away from his grief, charging up the plank with wet-eyed Heinz scampering close behind.

At last most of the group had boarded and all waited patiently on deck as their few remaining comrades bade their farewells. Frieda hugged Pieter tightly as if to never let him go and sobbed like a toddler in his arms. He stroked her golden hair and whispered to her softly, "Please, young woman, take good care of your family," he said. Frieda nodded and turned toward her sister.

Sobbing, Gertrude stared at Frieda from swollen brown eyes. The two embraced, vowing to meet again.

Finally, it was the moment that Pieter had dreaded from so very long ago. His mind took him back to the day on the road by Mainz. His heart tugged as he envisioned Wil with Karl and Maria and Tomas. He smiled as he remembered how determined they were, how very resolute; such courage!

Pieter now faced young Wil. *Not a boy any longer*, he thought. *Nay ... no longer. He's learned much. Ah, so very brave, noble and strong; a fine young man ... broad-shouldered and handsome. Ha! Look at that flowing hair and the set in those steely blue eyes; confident, but now humble; youthful, but wise for his years.* He reached a shaking hand toward his young friend and, when their palms met, Wil plunged into the old man's arms. "I love you, Pieter," he choked. "I'll miss you."

"I ... I ..." Pieter stammered, "I am without words. You are like a son to me. The son I never had. I bid you grace and peace for all years to come." Pieter's eyes so filled with tears the boy became but a golden blur as he turned away. He wiped them on his worn sleeve and watched helplessly as the ship's plank was removed. He then aimed his failing sight on all of his beloved and faded into his own thoughts, paying no heed to the shouts and orders of the seamen scrambling through the rigging and lowering the sweeps. But, when the thick hemp ropes were jerked off their squeaking pilings, his mind returned with a start. His heart sank and he swallowed hard. The creaking ship then eased subtly from its rest and began sliding toward the sea and away from the reach of Pieter's outstretched arms.

The gallant crusaders started waving from the galley's rail and calling his name. The old man bit his lower lip to stop its quivering and closed his eyes. Gertrude stepped beside the priest and laid her head against him. She wrapped her arm around his waist and gently hugged him as she wiped tears from her own eyes.

Pieter patted the girl on her shoulder and turned a loving eye toward the congregation of strange new faces staring hopefully at him. He smiled. As the ship now slipped quickly away he raised his hand limply and whispered, "Farewell, my beloved."

ও

Pieter watched the rising sun cast its beautiful golden light across the tips of the *San Marco's* tall masts. Her sails were dropped into place, snapping and fluttering and filling with fresh morning air. She lurched forward awkwardly, heaving into the blue water with a splash and leaning toward the far edge of the curved harbor.

Seagulls called and shrieked overhead and the sounds of a new day began to fill the wharf behind him, but Pieter thought only of his children, his beloved lambs, disappearing before his eyes. He felt so very much alone.

Suddenly a loud voice interrupted his thoughts. "You can see them again, *Pater*."

Pieter was startled. "Eh? What was that?"

"I say, you can see them again." The voice came from the throng of newcomers gathered behind him. Pieter turned and saw a pleasant-looking, earnest boy, fourteen perhaps, and smiling politely.

"Ah, *ja*, my young friend, I'll see them with the angels someday."

"Nay, 'tis not what I meant to say. If you walk along that line you shall find a jetty. And at its end is a place where the ships pass quite close, close enough to see the sailors' faces."

Pieter's heart jumped for joy and he hugged the surprised lad. "*Ja*? Well then, m'thanks!" he blurted. "May the saints protect you for your kindness."

"And I thank you for your blessing. I—"

"Ah, 'tis good to hear, lad—you say the jetty is by there?" He pointed east.

The boy laughed. "Aye. But you needs not hurry; the wind is failing already and it takes some time for them to row. And you've this good fortune as well: When they near the jetty you'll find this captain getting as close by it as he can."

"And why would that be?"

"I've heard it to be a wager among the sailors. Each ship works to claim the honor of coming closest to the point without grounding or rowing into a rock."

"Such vanity," said the priest. "But such vanity has such profit for us!" He turned and started toward the jetty in great haste. However, his time-taught instinct for better manners nudged him to stop and he did. He spun around and faced the boy again. "Begging your pardon, lad, I failed to ask your name."

"Rudolf," the boy answered. "Rudolf from the mountains near to Liestal."

A sudden chill charged through Pieter and he stared, open-mouthed and astonished. He thought for a moment. *Nay, could never be unless ... a miracle, perhaps?* "Would your papa be Dieder?"

"Aye."

"And your *Mutti*, Gerta?"

"Aye," he murmured. "Aye. Do you know them?"

Pieter cried out and embraced the lad. "*Ja!* They gave us charity in a time of need. God bless them, and I've a message for you! Y'*Mutti* says, 'Tell Rudolf we love him very much and miss him.'"

Rudolf's face twisted with bittersweet joy. "I ... I can barely believe this! Oh, *Pater*, I miss them so ... might ... might I join you if y'return to those parts?"

"Aye. Aye, a thousand ayes, lad! But, *ach*, we must catch our ship!"

Pieter took the boy by the shoulder and led his new friends in a charge across the docks. Down the wharves they raced, Rudolf and the old man in the lead and a long line of vagabonds following close behind. Paying no attention to the scoffs and ridicule of all around, the parade of misfits pressed on until they reached the turn to the peninsula which narrowed to a rocky jetty at its end. They stopped to catch their breath and took an accounting of the *San Marco's* location. It had stalled in mid-harbor and a relieved Pieter sighed.

The band hurried, nonetheless, and Pieter led them with his staff in hand, looking very much like a shepherd leading a ragged herd of grateful sheep! These sheep laughed, however, quite amused with their new friend's amusing gait and they squealed with delight when he smiled at them with his faithful tooth.

The company passed by rows of houses and shops, past the shipwright's building and the caulkers' guild, the sailmaker and a brawling tavern. Finally, all panting, they found themselves clambering on the rocky end of the long jetty.

"By the saints, Papa Pieter," announced a little voice behind him, "we made haste, but see how far away the ship is yet."

Pieter froze. Papa *Pieter?* With visions of his beloved Maria filling his mind's eye, he whirled about to see the tiny face of Ava staring at him happily. For a moment, disappointment washed over him, but he smiled and laid a hand on the dear girl's head. "Ah, blessings on the *San Marco*," he wheezed.

The jetty's rocks were difficult and hazardous to climb across. They were formed in ages past as long layers of black stone turned edge upright so that each step needed great care. But no obstacle in all of creation would obstruct Pieter's determined purpose and, with a minimum of scraped shins and hushed oaths, the old man and his throng finally arrived at the jetty's point.

The rising sun felt warm as did the ocean's waves splashing over the dangling feet of the laughing children. Pieter had the good fortune of finding one flat boulder upon which he was able to sit his weary rump, and from this spot he fixed his eyes on the timid sails of the *San Marco*.

Certain that he had a little time to wait, the old man closed his eyes and breathed deeply of salt air. He smiled as the spray of crashing waves sprinkled his white head. The sound of the sea was calming and the gentle chatter of the children warmed his soul. He could have asked for no sweeter lullaby, other than to hear the soft voice of Maria or the pleasant chuckle of Karl. Pieter's mind began to drift again to old memories when he heard the faint sound of a distant voice calling his name.

The old man turned and saw someone coming toward the jetty. He pulled himself up, trying to focus, but could only see the blurred image of a large, shaggy man. *Perhaps a dog as well?* he thought.

"Oh, please, dear God, no more magistrates—no dogs to chase us!" he muttered, angry and fearful that the simple joy of a last farewell would be spoiled. He cast a wistful glance at the *San Marco* and huddled his children as the stranger came closer. *He seems anxious*, thought Pieter. *Hurried and quite forceful of stride.*

The more he studied the approaching man the more he imagined something strangely familiar in him. Perhaps it was his stride, or something else … he could not quite see.

Unable to contain his consternation and curiosity any

longer, Pieter began crawling over the rocks toward his visitor. Pieter stood erect and confident, as if to bar all danger to his flock. But no sooner had he set his jaw than the man's dog yelped and bolted toward him. The priest swallowed and gripped his staff with both hands, bracing himself against the charging beast. His mouth dried and his heart pounded but he remained steadfast and determined!

The dog ran like the wind, streaking toward the terrified old man like a bolt of gray lightning. But suddenly, Pieter's heart seized within his heaving chest and he dropped his staff. Tears of joy filled his eyes and he threw open his arms. "Oh, dear God in heaven, oh, dear God—Solomon, Solomon!" he cried.

Pieter fell to his knees as his faithful friend bounded into his arms and rolled him to the ground, squirming and lurching, wagging and whining and licking until his master begged for mercy. "Solomon ... Solomon!"

The panting stranger finally reached the happy reunion and cried in a desperate voice, "Hear me, Pieter!

Pieter pulled himself to his feet and dusted off his robe. He squinted at the man standing in the bright light of the morning's sun. Unable to discern the silhouette, Pieter shielded his eyes with his hand and looked again. He gasped. "Friend! Friend! By the saints above ..." He lunged toward the dusty one-armed man and embraced him. "I ... I am speechless."

Friend was in no mood for an embrace. He brushed past Pieter and stumbled into the crowd of strange faces gathering about. "Where are my sons?" he cried.

Pieter was confused. "Who ... who are your sons?" he asked, incredulously.

"Karl and Wil!" Friend answered. "My name is Heinrich, Heinrich of Weyer! Where are they?"

Pieter hesitated. "Heinrich of Weyer? Father of Karl and Wil ... and Maria? How can it be?" The slack-jawed old man pointed a finger at the ship. "Wil is aboard ..."

He did not finish. Heinrich immediately blurted, "Hear me! They needs off the ship—they're to be sold as slaves!"

All eyes widened in shock as they turned toward the *San Marco* whose sails had gone limp. Staring at the wheezing man in horror, Pieter's mind raced. "Are you sure, man?"

"Aye!" cried Heinrich. "I heard it with my own ears in the tavern just beyond." He pointed an impatient finger to the row of buildings not far away. "We needs get them off that ship!"

Pieter nodded, numbly. The *San Marco* was now ploughing hard toward them. Pieter could see sailors climbing up the masts and he knew they were about to trim her to full sail. A stiff breeze gusted into his face and his mind raced. He clutched his temples with his fists and begged God to deliver them all as he rushed toward the water's edge.

ᔕ

On board the ship, Wil and his comrades were leaning against the salt-smoothed wooden rails and bidding farewell to Genoa and to their many friends left behind. They felt good under the warm, new-day's sun and faced contentedly into the fresh sea air. Several of the crusaders laughed at each other as they wobbled about the deck, tripping and pitching with the roll of the waves beneath them.

Wil closed his eyes. He loved the screeches of the gulls following overhead, the splash of the sea against the bow and the snap of the sails. Next to him stood fair Frieda, watching the shoreline pass by with an expression of wonder and joy which graced her pretty face like no adornment of mere gold or silver ever might. Wil opened his eyes and smiled at her.

He looked about the busy galley, ignoring two snickering guards standing close by. The lurching of the ship created a restful rhythm and he thought he had never felt such peace in all his life. He offered a quick prayer of thanks to his Savior as he scanned the mountains rising behind the city. *Karl is looking over us*, he mused. *And perhaps Maria as well....* His mind carried him to the abbey in Arona and he closed his eyes again.

Then, with a start he opened them. *It must have been the*

wind, he chuckled to himself. But a moment later he thought he heard it again. He looked about the ship and then at the masts above. *Karl? Maria? Are you there?* "Ach! I must be mad."

Conrad poked him in the side. "Eh? You've something to say?"

"N-nay ... I thought I ... oh, never y'mind."

The sails then drooped, fluttering feebly in timid air and the captain ordered his crew about sundry duties. For the next hour the ship languished in a gently rolling sea until the oarsmen were finally ordered to their places. And, with a few growls and kicks from the mate, the ship soon lurched forward again finding a new rhythm as it swept through the water.

The children watched with interest as the oars dipped in ordered sequence, pushing the ship through the water like so many arms, first reaching and dropping, then lifting in unison. But, after a time, the jib caught a fresh wind and the mainsail swelled, proud and firm like the breast of a puffed cockbird.

The *San Marco* splashed forward toward a jetty just ahead and the children crowding the port side watched its approach. Suddenly, Frieda pointed to its edge and she squealed. "Look, look, everyone! Look, methinks ... methinks ... I see Pieter's white head and the others ... waving to us."

The eager crusaders crammed against the rail. Wil cried out above the rest, "Aye! *'Tis* Pieter ... hello, Pieter!"

The sailors were not pleased with the unusual display and became suddenly agitated. Captain Gaetano sensed some vague, indiscernible risk to his cargo and whispered close to Otavio's ear. The mate cast a menacing scowl at the crusaders and beckoned a few hands to come close.

As the ship forged ever nearer to the jetty, Wil and his fellows cheered all the more, jubilant and grateful for the surprise greeting. Wil shielded his eyes from the bright sun and leaned his shoulders over the rail. "Hello, Pieter!" he bellowed. "Good Pieter, ever-faithful Pieter. I'll surely miss you."

Otto suddenly fell silent for a moment and peered at the jetty more carefully. He nudged Wil. "Would that be Solomon?"

Wil's mouth dropped and he stretched forward to focus on the gray dog crowing at Pieter's side. "Aye. *Mein Gott*, 'tis Solomon, I am certain of it! Frieda, Conrad ... look! Solomon!"

All nearly wept at the sight of the unkempt dog, nose high in the air and tail wagging. But before another could speak Frieda suddenly exclaimed, "And ... and look, 'tis Friend from Basel!"

"Friend? Aye!" Chills ran up Wil's spine.

Frieda wiped tears of joy from her cheeks and waved again to the jetty when something about Pieter suddenly caught her eye. She whispered to Wil, "Something's amiss ... I can feel it. He is waving, but oddly. It seems they'd all be beckoning us to come ashore."

Wil laughed. "*Ja? Ach*, but y'know Pieter and his odd humor. And he did truly want us to return home with him. He thinks we've not the pluck to get on without him!"

Frieda wasn't so sure.

અ

Plunging into the surf, Pieter, Heinrich, and the children were now screaming frantically and flailing their arms. Oh, could the ship but hear their desperate cries! The *San Marco* was now close enough for them to see the faces of their comrades and close enough for the crusaders to swim safely to shore. But it would be just a few moments before opportunity would pass. Pieter cupped his hands and wailed his warnings but his beloved simply smiled and waved in return. And poor Heinrich's booming voice did little but frighten gulls off the wave-splashed rocks and he cursed in frustration.

Pieter, despairing and failing of hope, fell to his knees on the sharp rocks and begged God for wisdom. He groaned and stretched his opened hands toward heaven. "Oh, dear God, have mercy!" he cried. "Help us, guide us ... carry our words to their ears! Tell me what to do!"

અ

Frieda would not be stilled and she tugged stubbornly on Wil's sleeve. "I beg your leave, Wil, but I do very much believe them to be beckoning us."

Her insistent tone inclined Wil to consider her words more carefully and he strained to hear the calls from shore. The sounds of the ship made it difficult for the boy to discern any single word, but he agreed the calls seemed more like commands than farewells. A cold fear suddenly gripped him, for indeed, something was amiss.

"*Bambini!*" a voice from the deck boomed. "*Avanti* ...'tis time to go below."

Wil turned and looked into the hard eyes of Otavio and the stern faces of a surly group of sailors forming a wall behind him and his crusaders. Wil feigned confusion and shrugged innocently as he cast another look at the jetty. And, when Wil's gaze fixed on Pieter, his legs felt suddenly weak.

The sailors saw the old man as well and one roared, "Look at that beggar, spinning on those rocks like m'child's toy top. Old fool!"

Now squeezing Wil's arm with both her hands Frieda whispered desperately, "The signal, Wil. The signal! Can y'not see? He calls us to come!"

On the sharp-edged rocks Pieter was frantically spinning and spinning, falling and slipping only to climb to his feet to spin again. And Solomon was spinning too ... just like in Dunkeldorf.

But we've come this far, thought Wil. *Nay ... it cannot be. We've come this far.*

Otavio's voice roared at the lad, "Move off! To the hold with the whole litter of y' fevered scum."

Wil hesitated, now caught in a predicament he had never imagined and without the wisdom of another to guide him. He needed more time. "Beggin' your leave, sire, we've paid handsomely for passage and we'd be entitled to bid our friends farewell."

While Otavio raged, Wil turned a quick eye toward the shore once again and now saw Friend spinning by Pieter, his one arm outstretched. Then there and there again, one after another of the children began to open their arms and spin until the whole of the company were turning 'round and 'round.

Wil wrestled within himself and had but seconds to answer either the call to end his crusade, or the one to save it. And, worse yet, he knew not which was which, nor what the better end ought be!

Why ... oh, God, why? Not my crusade! Why the signal? What to do? What to.... The lad was paralyzed, suddenly bound by a dreadful alliance of stubborn ambition and tainted reason. But it was his love that would set the lad free, and nothing else. He had learned to simply trust the old man's love and, in the end, that was suddenly quite enough.

The boy had barely formed the orders in his mouth when the sailors rushed him and his startled crusaders. Wil cried as loud as he could, "Jump! All jump! Over the sides ... now!"

His comrades heard his command plainly though could barely believe it. But they had no time to consider his words, for they now needed to fly and scramble from the many hands grabbing and grasping at them.

"Jump I say!" Wil shrieked. He snatched a confused little boy by the belt and threw him screaming into the water. Then, with a quick heave, he tossed another and then another. But escape would be no easy task. None would claim these seafarers to be less than a nimble and strong-handed lot. These swarthy fellows could grasp wet cord in high winds with the ease of a knight to his reins and scampering children ought to have been easy prey.

Ah, but this brood was of no ordinary stock! These had been tested and tempered by sufferings uncommon to any but the most stouthearted. These were not the issue of genteel manners and dainty fare. Wily, quick-of-feet, daring and determined, these would not yield to any with ease!

Otavio and his crew set upon their quarry with a vengeance. They lunged and cursed, chased and fell, sprawling this way and that, first catching one, then another, only to lose both to a good bite on the hand or kick to the crotch.

Wil and Otto ducked between the grasping arms of two seamen and threw a crate overboard for any who might not swim. "Jump, everyone. Get off!" Wil yelled. The lad was suddenly thrown to the deck by a pair of monstrous arms, but he scrambled under the man's legs and dashed away.

Conrad, Otto, and Wil raced in and out of the rigging, tossing and pushing comrades over the rail and deftly dodging their assailants. Then, with most of the children finally splashing safely in the water below, stout Otto was ordered over the side.

Wil raced past a furious seaman and was grabbed by the hood of his tunic and wrestled, howling, to the floor. The man struck him across the face and raised another fist when Conrad leapt from behind the mizzen and smashed the sailor in the head with a wooden mallet.

Wil sprang to his feet and the two charged for the rail, kicking and biting and clawing their way through the shouts and curses of their confounded foes. Conrad jumped first, but Wil, the fit commander that he was, hesitated for he thought he heard a muffled scream. He turned quickly to his left and saw Frieda being dragged away by a brawny seaman. He eluded the lunging hands of those rushing toward him and charged Frieda's captor, hammering the man's face with a fist of iron. Frieda dropped from the stunned man's arms and, with a grateful look to Wil, bolted across the deck and dove over the rail.

Wil ran aft, scanning every corner of the deck for more of his company. Seeing none he looked desperately for his own route of escape but saw only the encircling faces of the furious crew stalking him. He felt his heart flutter in his chest and he backed slowly toward the port rail. He spotted a mallet on the planks at his feet and he snatched it as he raced the crew to the edge of the deck. A grinning sailor jumped in his path.

The frightened lad then spun and darted to the starboard rail, but two more quickly blocked his way. He crept backward toward the center of the deck, turning his head to his left then his right, before him and to the rear.

The crew now knew the lad was theirs and they toyed with him, drawing their circle ever tighter, ever nearer, blades now drawn and gleaming. He would pay and pay dearly for their loss; vengeance was the custom of the sea.

Having positioned the helpless young man, they halted, mocking him and offering prophetic, harrowing descriptions of the torture and death he was about to endure. An eerie silence followed as the crew paused to savor the bloodlust titillating their wicked souls; only the wind in the sails and the splash of the bow could be heard above poor Wil's pounding heart. Then, one crewman grunted and the rest rushed the boy with a loud cry.

Wil sprang between the legs of one and bounded out of the circle like a rabbit in chase. He crashed and rolled across the deck, dodging the flying boot of one, then ducking below the swinging sabre of another. His eyes fixed on the starboard rail once again and he charged toward it. But a large leg thrust itself across his ankles and he sprawled onto the boards.

Undaunted, Wil jumped to his feet but now faced a fearsome wall of enraged men charging him. He whispered a quick prayer and snatched a deep breath as he spun to port, only to face a charging row of shrieking men from that side as well. *'Tis port I want*, he resolved. He clenched his teeth and fixed a steely gaze at a towering, dark-eyed brute at the rushing line's middle. *I cannot go under or between … but shall go through.*

The man was on him in three long strides, but Wil flung his mallet straightaway, like David heaving at Goliath, striking his foe on the forehead and dropping him backward to the planks. The sailor was yet falling when Wil bounded over his crumpling body in an effort to spring through the punctured line and hurtle over the rail. He lunged into the narrow breech for no lesser cause than the simple embrace of his beloved fellows waiting breathlessly at the water's edge; the very thought of it empowered his legs with the strength of a raging lion. But the thin gap was no more than a hair-breadth slip between quick-footed, brawl-seasoned rogues and its brief space filled before Wil could escape the gleaming forest of razor-edged cutlasses now overwhelming him. The boy bellowed bravely as the black-hearts engulfed him and he disappeared in a shroud of wool-capped seamen and glistening steel.

Yet, at that fearful, shadowy moment, Wil felt suddenly different. It was as if he was now flying through a world of dreams, free from all danger. It was as if he was enveloped by a legion of angels whisking him through the midst of his enemies, lifting his feet lightly to the rail and gently lofting his body over the side.

Wil closed his eyes and smiled as he felt a rush of warm air sweep softly across his face. He stretched his arms wide, as if to embrace heaven itself. All fears removed, all confusion gone, his heart fluttered like the wings of a butterfly on a fresh spring bloom. His tattered tunic flapped like the royal pennant of a castle keep; his stalwart face was calm and sure. His golden hair shined in the brilliant sunlight of a bright new day and he fell to freedom in the clear, blue water of the shimmering sea.

The End

Readers' Guide

*For Personal Reflection
or Group Discussion*

Readers' Guide

A gainst the backdrop of an ancient time and primitive land, this epic tale carries readers along a beautiful and tragic road. Precious children, some barely out of diapers, are sent from their homes with nothing more than the clothes on their backs. At first glance the tragedy of these young lives is overwhelming—how can these beautiful children be expected to sacrifice so much? How much promise of a generation is wasted? How can loving mothers and fathers fail to protect their children? How can priests send mere babes out into the world where stronger, valiant men have failed? How can a loving God allow such deception and needless suffering? Surely, these precious lives are doomed.

But the remarkable truth is soon realized—these children did not leave everything behind. *Life* goes with them. They experience more living in the long, arduous journey than most will ever see in the comfort of what is familiar. And in the midst of every trial and tribulation, God is surely with them.

Crusade of Tears will challenge and inspire you. Through the adventures of Wil, Karl, Maria, Pieter, and others, we are offered the opportunity to consider some of life's most difficult lessons. Their suffering is not limited by time or experience. Their joy is boundless and eternal. Like the minstrel Benedetto, we can choose to remain on the sidelines while life passes us by, or we can choose to join the journey. It is our hope that as you read, you will consider the following questions. We hope they will inspire you to dig deeper for truth, and that truth will set you free.

BOOK 1

Chapter 1

1. The baker's home is a place of misery and despair, abandonment and abuse, and Wil, Karl, and Maria respond very differently to their circumstances. How does each child cope with the situation?

2. When faced with his mother's sickness, Karl tries to wipe away the reality of the horrible situation. He rebukes Wil for not having enough faith and assures Maria that if she "just believes," their mother will recover. Who or what is Karl placing his faith in and can such a blind trust truly be effective?

3. Wil seeks help from the local abbey, already knowing he will be turned away. But Wil still perseveres in hope of reaching the sanctuary within the walls. What modern application can be found in the walled abbey, the surly gatekeeper, and the death of Wil's friend within—a "rebel" monk? How does the church today respond to those who need help most?

Chapter 2

4. The Bible says, "Get rid of all bitterness, rage and anger, brawling and slander, along with every form of malice. Be kind and compassionate to one another, forgiving each other, just as in Christ God forgave you" (Ephesians 4:31–32). How is Marta characterized by her sickness, and what does this convey about the price of bitterness?

5. Webster's defines "pious" as "marked by sham or hypocrisy; deserving commendation: worthy." How does this seemingly contradictory definition reflect on Father Pious? What evidence indicates that perhaps there once was a more sincere and worthy man who might have pursued true and noble things?

Chapter 3

6. Wil dreams of valor and knighthood upon the fields of war, but he is ruled by his emotions and twice chooses violence as a means to solve his problems. What consequences do these choices bring upon him and his family?

7. Father Pious controls, threatens, and abuses those he is supposed to be shepherding. How should spiritual leaders and those in authority serve God? How does He want us to

deal with violence, injustice, and persecution? (Ezekiel 45:9–10; 1 Timothy 3:1-7; Ephesians 6:10-18; John 15:20–21; Isaiah 34:8; Matthew 5:11–12)

Chapter 4

8. The priests proclaim scriptures to convince the villagers to send their children on crusade. Although taken out of context and manipulated to serve the priests' purpose, do these scriptures still hold some truth and assurance for these children? What difference might it have made if the people were able to read and know the Word of God for themselves?

9. Trusting and responsive, Karl is immediately caught up in the excitement and fervor of the moment and is ready to pursue the holy quest for God's glory. Wil, suspicious and logical, doubts the wisdom of the venture. One brother relies on faith, the other logic. Which is the better choice?

Chapter 5

10. Despite a life filled with suffering and the persecution of his peers, Pieter joyfully serves the lowly and the unwanted. How does Pieter differ from the other priests and powerful "holy" men? (Matthew 25:31–46)

11. Pieter does not support the Children's Crusade and attempts to convince the children to reconsider and return home. Why then does he accompany Wil, Karl, Maria, and Tomas?

12. Karl sincerely wonders, "Does God understand German?" Such a question might seem amusing, but in what ways do we also underestimate God's wisdom and personal involvement in our lives?

Chapter 6

13. Like the Israelites wandering in the desert, the hungry children receive manna from heaven just when they need it most. How is Tomas affected by this supernatural provision after his attacks on Karl and Wil? If the bread was left by some well-meaning individual, does that make it any less miraculous?

14. Why, despite his obvious reluctance, does Wil agree to allow several children and Pieter to join his band of crusaders? What leadership qualities does he possess that help him care for the young crusaders?

Chapter 7

15. Pieter values knowledge and reason, declaring that understanding is necessary before one can believe. How is such a philosophy faulty? What priority and value does God place on faith and understanding? (Job 36:22–26; Proverbs 3:5–6; John 20:24–29; Proverbs 23:23; Mark 12:28–34; Hebrews 11:1–39; Isaiah 55:6–9)

16. Why are the children unable to grasp the message of love Pieter reads to them from 1 Corinthians 13? Why is it so important that we live as authentic Christians, honoring Jesus' command to "love one another. As I have loved you, so you must love one another. By this all men will know that you are my disciples, if you love one another" (John 13:34–35)?

Chapter 8

17. Is the loving hand of God evident in providing welcome refuge and provision for the children? Does God really set "divine appointments"? If so, why have so many other crusaders met with hardship and death?

18. Wil and the other children are suspicious of a lord's son who would choose to join with common peasants. Aside from class distinction, what notable differences exist between Georg's family and Wil's? What cause does Wil have for his prejudice and resentment of Georg, and is it justified?

Chapter 9

19. After a cold reception by the church in Dunkeldorf, Pieter tells the children, "God's people are not always people of God." What evidence of this truth have you experienced in your own life?

20. What similarities do the events of Dunkeldorf—and Pieter's response to them—have with the arrest of Jesus in the Garden of Gethsemane? (See Matthew 26:47–54.) What are the consequences for taking justice into our own hands?

21. While Pieter, Wil, and Tomas are raiding the city and stealing food, God miraculously provides provisions for the children back at camp. What painful lesson does Pieter learn from his foolish actions?

Chapter 10

22. Friederich wakes and is convinced he hears a message

in the trees. Is it more likely that God is trying to warn him of the coming danger? How important is it to listen to the "still, small voice" within?

23. When Wil finds his "hero knights" dead on the field of battle, he is confronted with the futility of his aspirations. That which he trusted in and believed to be invincible is proven to be temporal and mortal. How does God work in our lives to bring us to the point we rely only on Him?

Chapter 11

24. When taken hostage by thieves, the children lie and steal in order to win their freedom. Pieter praises God for delivering them from their enemy, but was it really God's deliverance? How is this behavior reconcilable with Christ-like character? Is deceit acceptable when dealing with evil men?

25. Pieter often engages in unseemly behavior—particularly for a priest. But despite his imperfections, Pieter is still used by God to care for his little flock. What does this tell us about God's ability to use even the most flawed individual? Why do we often hold spiritual leaders to a higher standard?

Chapter 12

26. Despite their tragic circumstances and suffering, the children are still able to enjoy themselves and laugh freely. Is this what Jesus was speaking of when he said, "Unless you change and become like little children, you will never enter the kingdom of heaven" (Matthew 18:3)? How important is joy and laughter when facing hardship? What childlike characteristics should we cultivate in our own lives?

27. When Pieter and the children are taken to jail they once again find themselves in serious peril. But this time they choose to praise God rather than rely on their wits, schemes, or deceptions. What miracle does worship accomplish in the darkest hours?

Chapter 13

28. Karl believes that blessings come through obedient service to the Church and that suffering is the evidence of some moral failure. Why is this reasoning faulty? What is the cause of suffering? What good can God work in our lives and character during times of suffering?

29. What role does Karl's confidence in the Church establishment play in his fear of death? Why is death less frightening when considered in the context of a personal relationship with God?

30. Pieter proclaims the virtues and simple joy that can be found in farming. To the peasant-farmer children, his choice was disappointing. But what significant wisdom can be gleaned from Pieter's parable?

BOOK 2

Chapter 14

31. Without Pieter as guardian and champion, the children surely would have suffered greater hardship. Yet Pieter resorts to manipulation when dealing with the ailing lord. Why is he unable to fully trust in God's grace and faithfulness?

32. The storm and flood wreak further destruction on the little band of crusaders and yet another child despairs at being left behind. Why are these young children so determined to continue in spite of the misery and death that follows them?

Chapter 15

33. Wil insists that the world "is an evil place, not made easy by good deeds." Karl argues that "the world is not evil; it is filled with God's bounty for good people." Are both brothers right? How can such a paradox be explained?

34. John 15:13 says, "Greater love has no one than this, that he lay down his life for his friends." In what tangible ways does Georg show God's love to his friend Karl?

Chapter 16

35. After meeting the two French traveling ministers, Pieter has a life-altering encounter with God. How have the experiences of this ill-advised crusade opened his heart to receive freedom from the burdens that have plagued him most of his life? Would he have reached such a place of brokenness without experiencing such tribulation and helplessness?

36. Jean and Philip speak a blessing over the children, saying "may each of you enjoy God's Holy Land, whether within

or without." What is the significance of this blessing and what does it tell us about where the kingdom of God lies?

Chapter 17

37. Despite suffering cruelly for the physical deformity she bears, young Maria has a pure heart and a sensitive, loving spirit. What is readily apparent to those who see her? How does she react to seeing her own reflection in the pool of water? Why do we so frequently focus on small, inconsequential imperfections rather than the wonder and beauty of God's handiwork?

38. The minstrel, Benedetto, has a rather unremarkable existence—he simply plays his music for little or no reward. Why is he content to let life pass him by? Is he an observer or an active participant in life? What does he risk by becoming involved in the journey?

Chapter 18

39. Wil brashly declares that he knows no fear and is destined for great things. Is Wil truly confident or merely unwilling to be honest and vulnerable? What is the likely outcome when foolishness, pride, and arrogance take root?

40. When the travelers leave the relative safety of the river for the unknown perils of the road, they soon find themselves in trouble again. What divine purpose might have led them to become entangled in a feudal war?

Chapter 19

41. How do the children react to the realization of imminent battle? What does this reveal about their desires and motives?

42. Wil is not the first young man to be played for a fool by a woman. What difficult test of character does Wil face in his interaction with Lucia?

Chapter 20

43. Why are the children expected to defend a castle that is not their own? What right do these soldiers have to demand that Wil and the others fight for them? How is this situation similar to the events that sent the crusaders on this journey?

44. How is Wil changed by his failure in battle and his denial of Maria? How does his overwhelming remorse and shame reflect on his true heart?

Chapter 21

45. The Verdi and the Visconti have been waging war against one another for two generations—over nothing more than an unproven accusation. The soldiers are not even sure why they fight! How much destruction can result from an unresolved offense?

46. Proverbs 10:18 says, "Whoever spreads slander is a fool," yet Pieter suggests that Gostanzo spread slander about the Malaspinas in order to end his conflict with the Visconti. Is there not a better path of peace and reason? What better wisdom could be offered?

47. Sebastiani assures Wil that there is no shame in fear and says, "Let none quench the fire in your heart." How does Wil respond to this encouraging word?

Chapter 22

48. When Maria is overcome by fever, Karl insists that God must heal her, because He can do all things. How is Karl able to maintain his faith in miracles after so much suffering? Is faith always reasonable?

49. Pieter tells the children that God can turn all evil to good. What comfort can we draw from the knowledge that Jesus understands exactly how we feel? Does God truly use trials and suffering to reveal His goodness and mercy?

Chapter 23

50. Benedetto soon parts ways with the company, for he can no longer endure the suffering and longs for the simplicity he once knew. What does this say of the strength and unfailing persistence of the children?

51. When Pieter teaches the children about the stars and constellations, Karl says, "I never knew what a treasure has been over my head each night I sleep!" What unseen treasure has God placed around us that we would see if we "only look up"?

Chapter 24

52. The children have been the recipients of much rejection and persecution on their journey, yet when they encounter Arab merchants, they exhibit a similar disapproving prejudice. Are such attitudes ever justified?

53. Once again, Pieter lies and manipulates to try and gain some advantage for the children. Why does Pieter excuse his own failings, even while attempting to mete out justice to others? Is Karl right to confront him for his hypocrisy?

Chapter 25

54. Often we become so wrapped up in a particular goal that we forget that the purpose of life is in the journey. What remarkable changes have been worked in each child?

55. Having almost reached their destination, the crusaders are accosted by a demonic sorcerer and his followers. Is this merely coincidence or yet another ordained test the pilgrims must face? What tools does Satan often use to keep us from reaching the finish line?

56. As Pieter and the sorcerer debate, one declares truth and the other a perversion of that truth. What similar arguments does the world present to attempt to discredit Christianity? Why does the world seem more willing to accept faith in nothing than faith in God?

Chapter 26

57. After so much loss of life, what irony and symbolism exist in Karl's death—to have finally reached the sea only to have his life cut tragically short? What significance can be found in the fact that he had gained the wisdom to solve Pieter's mysterious riddle?

58. Wil has grown dramatically since his foolish acts at the abbey. How has his leadership and character changed? What evidence can be found of a sincere relationship with God? What is his motive for continuing on to Jerusalem?

Chapter 27

59. What is the fulfillment of Maria's vision of the sea? Why was it necessary for the children to press on to this point? Once there, why do some decide to go on to Jerusalem, while others who have come so far are now ready to return home?

60. Once the children find passage on a ship, it seems as though God's hand is at work. But once again their lives are in peril. As Pieter and Friend desperately try to save them, what finally makes the difference between freedom and slavery, life and death?

GLOSSARY

The Medieval Clock

Medieval time was divided into twelve hours of available daylight. Therefore, a summer's hour would have been longer than a winter's. The corresponding times below, typically called the seven canonical hours, are approximate to the modern method:

Matins: midnight
Prime: daybreak (6 AM)
Terce: third hour of light (9 AM)
Sext: sixth hour of light (noon)
Nones: hour of light (3 PM)
Vespers: twelfth hour of light (6 PM)
Compline: twilight darkness

The Medieval Calander

The Seasons:

Winter: Michaelmas to the Epiphany. A time of sowing wheat and rye.

Spring: The Epiphany to Easter. A time of sowing spring crops (Oats, peas, beans, barley, vegetables).

Summer: Easter to Lammas. A time of tending crops.

Autumn: Lammas to Michaelmas. A time of harvest.

Note: The medieval fiscal year began and ended on Michaelmas.

Holy Days and Feast Days:

- The Epiphany, January 6 (The Feast of Three Kings). A celebration of the three wise men's visit of Jesus.
- Lent: begins 40 days before Easter, not counting Sundays. A time to deny oneself in order to meditate upon the sufferings of Christ.
- Holy Thursday, Good Friday, Holy Saturday.
- May Day: May 1. Not a holy day, but celebrated throughout much of Christendom as a time of renewal.
- Pentacost: 50 days after Easter, usually late May or early June. Celebrates the coming of the Holy Spirit.
- Lammas: August 1. Beginning of harvest.
- St. Michael's Day (Michaelmas): September 25. Celebrates the archangel.
- All Saints' Day: (Hallowmas) November 1· The honoring of all saints, known and unknown.
- Martinmas: November 12. Celebrates St. Martin of Tours who spared a freezing beggar by sharing his cloak.
- December 24. It is the anticipation of the birth of Christ.
- Christmas Day: December 25.
- St. John the Evangelist's Day: Day to honor the disciple, December 27.

Miscellaneous Terms

abbess: female superior of a nunnery.

abbey: an autonomous monastery ruled by an abbot.

abbot: the title given to the superior of an autonomous monks' community.

almoner: official appointed to distribute alms to the poor.

arpent: unit of land rougly equivalent to an acre.

assart: the clearing of woodland.

bailey: inner courtyard of castle.

balk: an unploughed strip of land serving as a boundary.

benefice: a grant of land by a lord.

bloody flux: dysentery.

bowshot: unit of measurement equivalent to approximately 150 yards.

castellan: governor of a castle.

cellarer: monk charged with providing food stocks for the kitchener.

cerebritis: inflammation of the brain.

chain mail: body armor made of small, interlocking steel rings.

chalice: the cup holding the wine of the Eucharist.

chapter: the daily convening of a religious order for purposes of discipline and adminstration.

chapter house: the building attached to a monastery facilitating the chapter.

chin cough: whooping cough.

cloister: a place of religious seclusion. Also a protected courtyard within a monastery.

commotion: concussion.

confiteor: the formal expression of repentence.

cottager: a bound person of the poorest station.

crenels: the gaps in the parapetts atop a castle's ramparts.

croft: small yard adjacent to a peasant's cottage normally used to grow vegetables.

congestive chill: accumulation of blood in the vessels.

corruption: infection.

demesne: the land of a manor managed exclusively for the lord

dowry: originally a gift of property granted by a man to his bride as security for her old age or widowhood.

flail: a hinged stick used for threshing wheat. Also a weapon consisting of a long rod with a swinging appendage on a hinge.

forestor: manorial officer managing woodland, usually under the supervision of the Woodward.

frater: Latin for "brother."

furlong: a unit of measurement equivalent to 220 yards.

glaive: a weapon with a blade attached to a shaft.

glebe: parcel of land owned by the Church to benefit of a parish.

grippe: influenza.

halberd: a lance-like weapon.

hauberk: a heavy, sometimes quilted protective garment usually made of leather.

hayward: official charged with

supervising the management of the fields.

hectare: a unit of land measurement roughly equivalent to 2 1/2 acres.

herbarium: the building in a monastery where herbs were stored.

heriot: death tax.

hide: a unit of land equally about 120 acres.

hogshead: a unit of volume equivalent to 2 barrels.

holding: typically, heritable land.

Holy See: the seat of papal authority

ja: German for "yes."

junge: German for "boy."

kind, kinder: German for "child," "children."

king's evil: swelling of neck glands

Kitchener: the monastery's food overseer.

in nomine Patris, et Filii, et Spiritus Sancti: Latin for "in the name of the Father, the Son, and the Holy Spirit."

league: unit of measurement equivalent to 3 miles.

list: area of castle grounds located beyond the walls.

mädel: German for "maiden."

manor: the land of a lord consisting of his demesne and tenant's holdings.

manumission: fee required to buy freedom from the lord. Also, act by which freedom is granted.

merchet: a tax paid for the privilege of marriage.

merlon: the solid segments in the gapped parapets atop a castle's ramparts.

mark: a unit of weight equaling roughly 8 ounces of silver.

milk leg: inflammation of the leg.

mein Gott, mein Gott in himmel: German for "my God," "my God in heaven."

monastery: a religious house organized under the authority of the Holy See.

morbus: disease.

mormal: gangrene.

mutti: German for "mommy," "mama."

novice: a new member of a religious community undergoing an apprenticeship of sorts and not yet fully committed by vows.

nunnery: a religious house for nuns; a convent.

oath-helper: person who pledges their word in support of an accused.

oblate: a child given to a monastery for upbringing.

ordeal: a method of trial by which the accused was given a physical test to determine guilt.

pater: Latin for "father."

portcullis: iron grate dropped along vertical grooves to defend a gate.

prior: the official ranked just below an abbot. Sometimes the superior of a community under the jurisdiction of a distant abbey.

paten: the dish on which the bread of the Eucharist is placed.

plenary indulgence: the remitting

of temporal punishment due for sins already forgiven by God.

pound: an accounting measurement. A unit of measurement equalling 20 shillings, or 240 pennies—a pound of silver.

postulant: a candidate for membership in a religious order.

pottage: a brothy soup, usually of vegetables and grains.

putrid fever: diphtheria.

pyx: the box in which the Eucharist is kept.

quinsey: tonsillitis.

refectory: the dining hall of a monastery.

reeve: village chief, usually elected by village elders.

rod: a measurement equivalent to 6 feet.

scapular: a long smock worn on front and back by monks over their habits.

Scriptorium: the building in a monastery where books were maintained and copied.

scrofulous: skin disease.

scutage: a tax paid by a free man in lieu of military service obligations to his lord.

see: the seat of ecclesiastical authority, i.e., bishop.

serf: a bound person of little means.

shilling: an accounting measurement. A unit of money valued at 12 pennies.

Anthony's fire: skin infection.

Vitus's dance: nervous twitches.

ard: chief overseer of a manor.

g: a unit of ten persons.

tonsure: the shaving of the crown of the head to signify Christ's crown of thorns. Received as part of religious vows.

trebuchet: a catapult.

trencher: flat board used as a plate.

tunic: garment worn as an overshirt, typically hooded, sleeved, and belted outside the leggings.

vassal: a free man who held land from a lord in exchange for his oath of fealty, usually obligated to perform military service.

vati, vater: German for "daddy," "father."

vellein: a bound person of some means owing labor to his lord and subject to certain taxes.

virgate: 1/4 of a hide. Considered the minimum amount of land necessary to support one peasant family for one year.

wattle-and-daub: construction material consisting of woven sticks and clay.

whitlow: boils.

winter fever: pneumonia

wunderbar: German for "wonderful."

woodward: manorial overseer of the lord's woodland.

yeoman: a free farmer of modest means.